Beyond the Gates

Kayla Davenport

Copyright © 2020 Kayla Davenport
All rights reserved.

No part of this publication may be reproduced, distributed, or transmitted in any form or by any means, including photocopying, recording, or other electronic or mechanical methods, without the prior written permission of the publisher, except in the case of brief quotations embodied in critical reviews and certain other noncommercial uses permitted by copyright law.

This is a work of fiction. Any references to historical events, real people, or real places are used fictitiously. Names, characters, places, and events are a product of the author's imagination.

ISBN: 979-8-9886236-0-1 (paperback)
ISBN: 979-8-7168512-6-9 (hardback)
ISBN: 979-8-9886236-1-8 (e-book)

Library of Congress Control Number: 2023911845

Cover art by Natalie Shain

Second edition 2023.

Independently published by Kayla Davenport Books | www.kayladavenportbooks.com

To my mom—
the reason I'm a writer. I love you.

*That is the problem with revenge—you wind up
destroying the innocent as well as the guilty.*
~ Cassandra Clare

THE CONTINENT SYSTEM

Over 100 years ago, the world came together to form The Continent System, where each habitable continent became its own unit. Countries, states, and provinces morphed into regions within their respective continents. The map below outlines the regions for Mid-North America, formerly known as the United States of America.

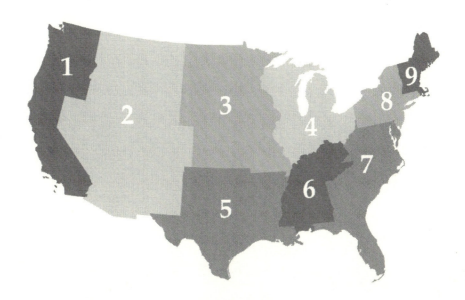

REGIONS
(**1**) Pacific (**2**) Mountain (**3**) Northwestern Central
(**4**) Northeastern Central (**5**) Southwestern Central (**6**) Southeastern Central
(**7**) Southern Atlantic (**8**) Middle Atlantic (**9**) New England

CHAPTER ONE
Emma

I'm going to win. There's no doubt about it. He knows it, too, though that doesn't deter him. He fights back like his life is on the line, like his entire future rests on this one moment.

I take him in as we spar. He's scrawny, as most of the kids his age are. He's also inexperienced compared to the three years of training I have on him. I'm faster and smarter. My limbs thrum with familiar energy; I relish in the power I feel behind every strike.

Sweat pours down his face and dampens his hair. He's flushed a reddish pink and his front teeth dig into his bottom lip, eyes glazed in sharp concentration. His breaths come out labored as he swings at me, rather sloppily, and I block yet again. He's tiring out, which means it's time for me to end this. I bring my leg up and twist around, foot catching the back of his knee, and I apply just enough pressure to knock him to the blue plastic safety mat below. I almost feel bad for the kid. He never stood a chance. Not against me.

"Time!" our instructor calls. Her crisp tone echoes off the concrete walls of the underground training facility. It draws me out of the haze. I was so lost in the fight that it takes me a second to regain composure.

My opponent lies flat on his back, chest rising and falling heavily. I bend down and offer him my hand.

"You did good," I say with a smile. And it's true. Because even though he lost, he'd certainly lasted longer than most who went up against me. *And* he was only in eighth grade. There's no doubt that he has raw talent.

"Thanks," he grins shyly and pulls at a dark curl of hair. He shifts on his feet, staring at the floor, and opens his mouth like he's going to say something.

"What?" I prompt and he flushes. I've never really understood why the younger kids always seem so intimidated by us. I don't remember feeling that way about the high schoolers when I was in middle school.

He hesitates, then looks up and says, "Is it true you're ranked number one in your class?"

I almost laugh. I should've known he wanted to talk about my status at the Academy. It's not exactly a secret, but the look on his face stops me. It's not entirely one of awe and admiration for having the chance to spar and interact with me. No. It's the look of someone who sees beyond that, who sees how much work I must've put in just to make it this far. There's nothing laughable about why he's asking.

"I don't know, kid. They don't really tell us for sure until graduation. I've got another year to go before my class gets Leveled."

"Yeah, but you've gotta be a Level One, even if you aren't actually ranked first, right? I mean, you're *Emmalyn Grant*."

"Emma," I correct out of habit.

He grins sheepishly. "Sorry."

I shrug to assure him it's no big deal. Most know how much I hate my full name, but sometimes the kids outside my grade forget, since they're not around me too often.

Chapter 1: Emma

"So," I say. "You want to go into the Missions program."

Another shy grin. "How did you know?"

"You've got the drive for it," I explain. "I've been there, right where you are now. I've been the kinda clueless kid who gets paired up with someone so much more experienced. But when we were fighting, I saw it on your face. The determination, the need to prove yourself. Yeah, I've had more training than you, but we're not that different. If being a Level One is truly what you want, then don't let anything stand in your way."

He relaxes at my impromptu speech. I glance around the rest of the room. There are twenty of us altogether. Ten eighth graders paired up with ten juniors. I'm not too familiar with the younger kids, but the ones in my grade? I've known them my whole life.

I watch them, talking and laughing with each other in the few moments before we'll be told to quiet down. They're my friends, my peers, the kids I grew up with. We've been through everything together: the boring schoolwork, the rigorous training, the normal drama during our earlier adolescent years.

We were all together on the first day of kindergarten; on the day our instructors finally let us use weapons; when we started high school and everything we did suddenly became so much more serious than before.

How are we already seventeen and almost seniors?

"Okay, listen up!" the instructor shouts. Silence blankets the room. "As I'm sure you all know with today being the first of September, the senior class has their graduation ceremony tonight. Juniors, you know the drill. The rest of you, this is the first year you get to attend. You are all expected to be in the auditorium no later than five this evening. Additionally, as usual, Monday will mark the first day of the new school year. Juniors will become seniors and eighth graders will become freshman. Be sure to check your message boards for your new schedules. If you have any questions, feel free to stay after or ask one of the older students. Class dismissed."

At that, all twenty of us push and shove towards the only door in the room. Bodies and limbs press together in our eagerness to get out. It's cramped and a little claustrophobic as I squeeze my way through, but once we're up the stairs and out into the sunlight, the crowd disperses.

I gulp in a huge lungful of fresh air. The training rooms always have a lingering scent of stale sweat and body spray. As much as I love fighting, it's nice to be out in the open again.

"Ms. Grant," a voice says from behind.

I turn around and come face to face with my instructor. "Yes?"

She smiles. "I overheard you talking to Jamison after that last round of sparring. I just wanted to let you know that I'm sure what you said was immensely encouraging for him. The younger students look up to people like you."

"Um…thanks?"

Where is she going with this?

Her smile widens. "Have you ever considered being a Mentor after you graduate? I know your heart is set on the Missions program, but I personally think you'd made a great Mentor, as well. And you can always do both. Many students are involved in both routes simultaneously."

I already know this. She *knows* that I already know this.

"I'll think about it," is what I say. I won't though. For me, it's one or the other. I can't do both. No way am I going to put a kid through that kind of heartbreak if something happens to me while I'm out on a Mission. I've worked my entire life in hopes of being a Level One. I'm not about to back down now just because my kind words to Jamie were appreciated.

Chapter 1: Emma

She disappears back into the training room, probably to straighten up before Monday's classes. I set off down the walkway that stretches across the grassy lawn towards the dorms.

"Emmalyn!" someone else calls from behind me. Irritation bubbles up. This is the second time I've been stopped in less than five minutes. That's not why I'm upset though. The boy who called out rushes up behind me. I'm more lenient with those who don't know me, but I know that voice, and he knows better.

"Cameron," I turn and fix him with the best scowl I can muster. "How many times do we have to go over this? My name is Emma. Em-ma."

He gives me an offended look. "Your best friend of twelve years returns from a dangerous Mission on the outside, and this is how I'm treated? Unbelievable."

"Dangerous? You were just transporting files from one place to the next. You were gone for like, two days."

"Hey, that can be dangerous. You don't know."

I laugh, roll my eyes, and throw my arm over his shoulders. "Come on."

We walk together. All around us, students traipse across the grass and sidewalks, happily chattering. A breeze blows through the quad, ruffling the leaves that will soon turn colors and float to the ground.

"So are you going to the ceremony tonight?" I ask.

"Of course I'm going! Aiden's graduating tonight. Plus, the Ambassador will be announcing the new Level Ones. I gotta scope out the newbies."

We pass the enormous steel gate, the only entrance and exit in the wall that surrounds the Academy, which has the campus side and the City side. I can't help but glance in the direction of the gate. Four guards flank the entrance, protecting us from every awful thing outside the walls and preventing any of it from getting in. Only those who are selected as Level Ones get to go outside to run Missions for the government and protect the Academy.

The Academy is exactly what it sounds like: a school. Though it's more than that. It's a secret government run program for kids like me. The ones who are…different. Special. Our evolved DNA composition separates us from the humans outside the walls due to a unique genetic strand that only people like us possess. The Academy has raised, trained, and taken care of us even when our own parents didn't want us.

I'm happy here at the Academy. This place has served as my home and school since birth, and after graduation, I'll move out of the campus-side dorms and into an apartment in the City. But sometimes I can't help but want so much more than this. I can survive on the outside. I know I can.

"Stop worrying about it," Cameron says. He nudges me with his elbow, pulling me from my thoughts.

"I'm not worrying about it."

I so am.

"We've been friends our whole lives, Emma. I can tell what you're thinking."

"Really?" I say, sarcasm weaving into my tone. "Sorry, last I checked you were telekinetic, not telepathic."

He puts his hands up in surrender. "Sorry. Jeez, when did this become such a touchy subject with you?"

I stop and face him. "I've got *one* year, Cameron. *One year* to prove to them that I'm good enough. That I deserve a spot in the top five. I've worked my whole life for this. Being in the Missions program is all I've ever wanted. And if they decide I don't rank any higher than number six? Then all that work was for nothing."

Chapter 1: Emma

He stares blankly, deep blue eyes boring into me, mouth hung open just slightly. "You don't know how amazing you actually are, do you?"

I roll my eyes. "Being supportive is kind of in the best friend job description."

"God, Emma, I've *seen* you fight. It's incredible. There's nothing else like it. I've watched you conquer everything you've set your mind to. And you can freaking read the future! That has to be a valuable ability. What can other people do? Run at super speed? Yours is way better. Trust me, they'd be stupid not to pick you."

All of my pent-up energy drains away. Softly, I say, "Thanks, Cam."

"Anytime. Besides, you're better than I am, and they picked me."

I shrug. "Maybe everyone else in your year was just really bad."

He laughs. "No matter what, you'll be okay. I promise."

We reach the high school dorms—two four-story brick buildings. One for the girls, the other for the boys. There's a smaller dining hall building between them. On a normal day, we'd all meet there for dinner. But tonight, dinner will be served in the auditorium after the graduation ceremony.

Cameron and I say our goodbyes for now and part ways.

The lobby of the girls' dorm is warm and cozy, with couches and beanbags scattered around the room. A few freshmen sit around the table in front of the fireplace that blazes in winter. They're working on homework by the looks of it. I've heard that most places outside the Academy's walls have breaks from school. For us, the learning and training never stop.

We exchange quick hello's as I pass by to the staircase in the back. I make my way up to my room on the third floor. Compared to the lobby, the halls are plain. Smooth and cream-colored with no decorations or distinguishing factors. I make up for it in my bedroom, mostly with pictures of my friends and I that are tacked to the walls.

Lacy, my roommate, is sprawled across her pastel pink bedspread when I enter our room. She's tapping away at her phone, no doubt messaging her boyfriend, Aiden.

"Hey," she greets, peering up at me with her deep russet brown eyes.

"You do know we have a ceremony to go to in a few hours, right?" I tease, referring to the tee shirt and cotton shorts she's wearing. I walk over to our closet, tiptoeing across Lacy's side of the room like it's a minefield. My side isn't perfect, but it's extremely organized compared to hers, what with her clothes and school supplies strewn about.

I pull out a knee length dark green dress, knowing it will bring out the color in my pale green eyes. I look at myself in the mirror and contemplate what to do with my hair. Maybe curl it? This is pretty much the only day each year we get to dress up, so I often overthink it.

"I'll change when it gets closer," Lacy says dismissively. "I didn't have any physical classes today, so I'm not all sweaty and gross. All I'll have to do is throw some clothes on."

"Well I did have physical classes, so I'm gonna go shower."

The days where my classes consist of sparring, weapons, and ability training are my favorite. It's the days that are strictly academic subjects like English and math—the kinds of classes the normal humans take, too—that are the bane of my existence.

I grab my shower caddy and a towel and head to the community bathroom at the end of the hall.

Chapter 1: Emma

Steam curls around me when I open the door. It's humid inside and all the mirrors are fogged up. Apparently I'm not the only one who decided to clean up before the ceremony.

"Hey, Em."

I involuntarily tense up at the voice. Laurel, a girl in my grade, stands by the row of sinks. She's already clean and dressed up.

"Hey," I force out.

She smiles. "Are you excited to only have one year left? Sounds like you're pretty much guaranteed a spot in the top five."

"Yeah, so I've heard," I mumble. I wish everyone would just shut up about it. It's going to be a huge, dramatic thing if I don't live up to the hype.

"That's my goal, too," Laurel continues, oblivious to my discomfort. "To be a Level One and get assigned a Mission."

"Cool. Well, good luck," I say and shift on my feet. Out of everyone on this floor to run into, it just had to be Laurel. I don't dislike the girl, but being alone with her doesn't exactly ease my mind either.

It's in that moment my razor that was balanced on the towel in my arms clatters to the floor. The sound echoes off the tile and reverberates in my ears. I bend down to pick it up, but Laurel goes for it too.

Then I make the stupid mistake of flinching when our hands almost touch. It all happens so fast that I don't have time to think it through.

Laurel grabs the razor and stands. "Really? You know our abilities don't work on each other. Touching me won't hurt you."

"No, I know. I um…" I splutter, trying to come up with a convincing excuse.

Laurel just shrugs. "It's fine. Don't worry about it. It's not like you're the first one to ever pull back when I get too close."

Beyond the Gates

She takes a step towards me and I stand my ground this time and don't move. She places the razor on top of the towel and clothes in my arms.

"I'll let you get a shower. See ya."

With that, Laurel leaves the bathroom. I want to smack myself for being so dumb. As uncomfortable as she makes me, she can't help her ability. Most of our powers are useful and relatively harmless. But Laurel's can send a person screaming in agony with a single touch, reduced to nothing but the pain coursing through them until everything snaps to black as they pass out, or die if she holds on long enough.

They would also have to be human, of course. Fully, one hundred percent human. For whatever reason, our abilities don't work on each other. Even though I know this, *know* that she can never actually hurt me, the thought of it prickles my skin.

I continue to the shower side of the room as my thoughts buzz with the interaction.

I do feel bad for Laurel. The only way we can learn how to control our abilities is to use them. For her, that means hurting people. There are a small number of humans who know enough about us and allow us to use their abilities on them for practice, and because our abilities are like muscles that need to be frequently exercised.

It's easy for some people, like Cameron, who's ability doesn't require physical contact. He just imagines moving something with his mind and it happens. But for people like me and Laurel, another person is necessary to the process.

I step into one of the shower stalls and select my preferences on the glass touch screen panel. Scalding water rains down, easing the tension and aches in my muscles from the strenuous school day. I put my hand under the soap sensor and lavender scented shampoo squirts into my palm.

Chapter 1: Emma

Once done, I dry off and slip into my dress.

Lacy is dressed and ready to go by the time I return to the room. I've never understood how she always looks so put together with hardly any effort. Her dark hair falls in soft curls and her brown skin practically glows. We leave together and join the crowd headed for the auditorium.

"You know, this is our last time watching this thing," Lacy comments. "We'll be the ones walking the stage a year from now."

I shake my head. "It's weird to even think about that. We're almost adults. That's insane. What Level do you think you'll be in?"

She emits a short burst of a laugh. "Definitely a Three. Only the very top get anything higher. There's no way I'll be selected for the Missions program or the Elite. But honestly, I don't really care. I'll be perfectly happy working a normal job in the City. I've never wanted the adventurous, dangerous lifestyle. That's all you."

It is all me. Out of our friend group, I'm the only one who's killed myself trying to have that life. Even though Cameron *did* become a Level One, he was still fine with doing whatever. But not me. I've put everything I've got into this.

We get to the auditorium and walk inside. The scene before us takes my breath away, as it does every year. The lights are dimmed except for the few above the stage. Rows of chairs sit in the front for the graduating class. Round tables are set up for the rest of us. The room is fancily decorated and gives off a sophisticated vibe. Soft music plays in the background, just barely heard above the chatter of people. The smell of chicken and spices wafts in from the side room where the food is being prepared for after the ceremony.

I scan the nearby tables until my eyes land on Cameron. In the lighting, his eyes glitter and his dark blonde hair looks almost brown. He beams when we make eye contact and waves us over. Next to Cameron is a tall brown-haired boy with forest green eyes and a smattering of light freckles dotted across his nose. He's wearing a suit with an Academy tie, indication that he's a graduate.

"Aiden!" Lacy exclaims and scampers over to him. I shake my head and suppress a laugh. The tables fit up to six people, so it's perfect for our little group. I walk over and claim the chair between Cameron and Lacy.

Not long after, the room dims further.

"Alright, I gotta get to my seat. I'll see you after." Aiden kisses Lacy's cheek, grins at me and Cameron, then walks off to join the others in front of the stage.

A spotlight appears on stage and the chatter instantly ceases. A tall woman with graying blonde hair that hangs to her shoulders walks out to the podium. She is immaculately dressed in her pressed suit. Power and authority radiate off her. She definitely looks like a leader, *our* leader. The Ambassador.

She helped in creating the program. She organizes and takes care of everything necessary for the Academy to work. She took us all in, despite the abilities we possessed. She never cared that we were different. Instead, she helped us, even though she's been through a lot herself. We've all heard the stories. How she used to have an ability like us, until some humans found out and experimented on her.

I don't know about anyone else, but I definitely admire her. How could I not, when she's given so much of her life to creating a safe and supportive environment for people like me. To make sure none of us ever go through what she did.

"Welcome," she announces with a warm smile. "Before we begin, I want to say a few words." She looks to all the seniors before her. "I remember when we first brought each of you into the program after you had been cast out by the humans for being genetically different than them. You were infants back then, innocent and

Chapter 1: Emma

undeserving of the way they treated you. But I've had the privilege of watching all of you grow into the wonderful adults you are today. You are stronger, smarter, better than anyone outside the Academy could ever hope to be. I am so proud of you for all your accomplishments and I wish you the best of luck as you move forward into the next stage of your life. Remember: The Academy is the future!"

"The Academy is the future!" we chant back.

The room erupts in applause.

"Next," the Ambassador continues. "I'd like to recognize the students who qualified as Level Ones this year."

She pauses, and the room goes dead silent. This is the moment some of them have waited their entire lives for.

"Congratulations to Aimee Bennet and Tyler Henry! The Missions program is excited to have you."

The applause is stifled this time. As to be expected, many of the graduates are disappointed. But that isn't the only shock.

Whispers float through the room like buzzing flies. My heart pounds. Why are there only two names? And is it just for this year, or will there only be two picked next year, too? Will I have to get into the top two instead of five?

Lacy leans over. "Aren't there usually more than that?"

I nod, numb. "It's usually five. Sometimes four. But never *two*."

The Ambassador barrels on as if nothing strange happened. She reads off the list of Level Two students—the Elites—who will work on government affairs from inside the Academy. That list contains ten students, Aiden included.

Anyone not selected for the first two levels is a Three. They hold positions in the City, where we all move to after graduation. It's still inside the walls that surround us, but students live on the campus side until graduation.

The actual ceremony comes next. Each student walks across the stage and receives their Certificate of Completion.

That's going to be me next year.

Dinner is served shortly after, and Aiden returns to our table. The room fills with talk and laughter once again.

"I'm so proud of you!" Lacy squeals and hugs her boyfriend. "When do you start training to become a guard?"

Aiden shrugs. "Sometime within the next few weeks. And my other Elite training starts a couple weeks after that."

We congratulate him and dig into our food.

"Oh, I forgot to tell you earlier, but you're not going to believe what happened today," Cameron says, his face lighting up.

"What?"

"I got selected to be the trainer for the new Level Ones. They'll have training for six months, then another three months of small trial Missions. Which means I'm going to be around for most of your senior year! Plus, it's an amazing opportunity."

I squeeze his arm. "That's great, Cam!"

His smile widens. "It's pretty exciting. And hey, maybe when I get the hang of teaching, I can attempt to teach you how to shoot a gun."

My eyes narrow as I give him my best death glare. "Don't even start."

I can't remember the last time I lost a hand-to-hand fight, but I'm not perfect. I *am* above average at combat, self-defense, and weapons in general. But for some irritating reason, my aim is absolutely atrocious when it comes to guns. Cameron knows that bringing it up is a great way to push my buttons.

He shoots me a mischievous grin.

A supervisor approaches our table before anyone else gets another word in.

Chapter 1: Emma

"Emma Grant?" he says. I look up at him. "I need you to come with me."

"What? Why?"

His gaze shifts to the others at the table before returning to me. "Just come with me. I'll explain on the way."

I stand from the table. My friends give me questioning looks, but I shrug in reply. I have no idea what's going on.

I follow the supervisor into the cool night air. It's dark now, and the stars hang overhead. Cameron's told me that in some cities outside the gates, there's so much light pollution that no one ever sees the stars. It's kind of sad.

Once we're away from the crowd, I ask, "What's going on?"

"The Ambassador has requested a meeting with you," he responds vaguely.

My mind shuts down. Did I hear him right? The Ambassador wants to talk to *me*?

"About what?" I blurt out.

He stays silent.

"I guess you're not authorized to tell me, huh?"

He shakes his head.

"Not even a little bit?" I press. Should I be worried? I've never spoken to the Ambassador one-on-one. Or at all, for that matter. She typically only addresses us in large groups, except for her meetings with the Level Ones and Twos.

"You aren't in trouble, if that's what you're thinking," he assures me. It doesn't help much, because I still don't know what to expect.

Our conversation ends there. He doesn't offer up any more information and I know better than to continue pushing someone who has greater authority than me.

We eventually make it to the building where the Ambassador's office is located. I've never been inside before, but I know all about it. It also contains the conference rooms and offices for the supervisors.

The supervisors are probably the closest to the Ambassador. They assist her with running the program. Most of them stem from the Elites, but a few are humans from the government who have volunteered to help us practice and control our abilities.

I'm led through the building and up to the top floor so quickly that I don't have time to take in my surroundings. My escort knocks when we reach the correct door.

"Come in."

We walk inside and I make sure to survey the place. Electronic file cabinets and bookshelves line the walls. Several glass monitors sit around the room, keeping track of all the progress and security of the Academy, both the campus and the City. The Ambassador sits behind her desk.

"Thank you for joining me, Ms. Grant. Please take a seat." She gestures to the chair in front of her. "Thank you for bringing her here, Samuel. You are dismissed."

Samuel nods, then exits the office, closing the door behind him. It's just me and the Ambassador now. I can't believe I'm this close to her.

She leans back in her seat. "So, Emmalyn. I'm sure you are wondering why I called you in here."

I grit my teeth and resist the urge to correct her on the use of my full name. She probably wouldn't be as receptive as Jamie or Cameron. I nod in response.

"I have a proposition for you."

CHAPTER TWO
Jesse

People are stupid.

They are naïve and so unbearably gullible. Every day, they live their lives as if evil doesn't lurk right outside their doors. They put all their trust into each other, into the media, and worst of all, into the government.

In reality, the government doesn't care about us. They only care about their precious Academy kids—the ones with special abilities that make them superior to the rest of us. The ones us normal, lowly humans aren't supposed to know about. I guess I'm not exactly normal, because I know all about the monsters that live at the Academy.

. . .

Stay calm. Don't move. Don't speak. Don't draw attention.

My heart thuds heavily against my chest as I fight to control myself through the first class period of the day. Fifteen minutes in and I'm already seconds away from losing it.

Ironically, it's a government class.

The teacher drones on about stuff I don't care about. I pretend to read pages from the textbook on my tablet. We have class discussion that I don't participate in. None of it matters. None of them know the truth.

"...which is why we switched to a continent based system over a hundred years ago. Having each continent under one rule instead of separate countries allows us to better work with one another."

I sigh and roll my eyes at the teacher's words. I continue to frown at my tablet, the words bleeding into each other and becoming a jumbled mess.

He pauses, long enough that I look up. He's staring right at me.

"Is there something you'd like to add, Jesse? It seems like you have some thoughts or feelings you want to share."

Snickers spread throughout the classroom.

"No," I mumble and lower my head back to the tablet.

The teacher gets the class back in order, then continues the lecture.

The truth is, I'd share my opinions if I could, but no one would actually listen. They all think the government is so honest, reliable, and trustworthy. They have no *idea* what the government is capable of doing, what they've already done, and what they will do.

The shrill tone of the bell rings through the building, pulling me from my depressing thoughts. One class down, five more to go.

Students flood the school hallways, but I manage to push through the crowd to my locker. I punch the four-digit code into the glass panel and the door swings open. I exchange my materials, then pause.

All around me, students filter past, talking and laughing and being teenagers. None of them care enough about me to wonder where I might be if I were to just disappear for the rest of the day. It would be so easy to just walk right out of here. I knew when I woke up this morning that it was going to be a bad day. Why push it? Why

Chapter 2: Jesse

force myself to be miserable? To endure another pointless six hours of my life?

I glance at the front doors at the end of the hall. Then back at my locker.

With a heavy sigh, I slam the locker shut and head off to second period. As much as I want to, I can't afford to skip class.

So I stick it out, and when the final bell resonates through the halls, I know I made the right decision. What's one more year of hard work in the grand scheme of things if it means a chance at a better life afterwards?

I shove my school supplies in my locker and grab my jacket. The cool air falls over me as I exit the building. Rain mists from the sky, but the clouds above hang dark and gray, threatening a downpour.

The walk home isn't more than ten minutes, but I don't want to go home. Despite the hell I just escaped, home is the last place I want to be. But with a potential storm brewing, I don't have much of a choice. I can't risk getting stranded somewhere and being unable to make it back in time for Charlotte and Oliver.

The rain picks up as I walk down the sidewalk. When I come to an intersection, I have to make a split-second decision. Right or left?

Left is mentally and emotionally easier, but taking a right is half the time. And with the weather, the shortcut is ultimately the smarter option.

With a deep breath, I turn right and head off in the direction of the part of town I usually avoid at all cost. But maybe going past there will help. Maybe it'll ease some of the pain. It's been almost two years since the last time I've walked by.

The stores and shops that line the street quickly give way to houses. I curl my hands into fists, dig my fingers into my palms. My

Beyond the Gates

nails are bitten down to the quick, so the pressure doesn't actually leave any mark. Sometimes I wish it did.

I clench my fists tighter and brace myself for the empty lot at the end of the street.

Rain hurtles from the sky, drips into my eyes, plasters my hair to my face. Almost there. Just a little farther and I'll be able to breathe again.

The empty lot doesn't come.

A new house fills the space. The paneling is a cheerful yellow, the grass lush and green, as if nightmares hadn't come true in that very spot almost ten years ago.

My heart stands still, as do I. The rain pelts my skin, but it doesn't bother me anymore. How is this house here? How could someone build a new structure, a new life, and just erase the past?

I swallow the lump in my throat, press down on the pain, and tear myself away. Lesson learned. No more shortcuts.

My chest doesn't loosen until the tiny house I'm forced to call home comes into view. Greg's truck isn't in the driveway. We're safe for a little while, at least. I type in the house code and press my thumb against the glass scanner to unlock the door.

The inside of the house is cramped, definitely not large enough to properly accommodate four people. I trudge to the bedroom in the back that I share with my foster siblings and throw my weight against the door to force it open.

The room consists of two twin beds that have been pushed together. We have an air mattress that someone could sleep on, but Charlotte and Oliver prefer the three of us sleeping beside each other.

I drop my backpack to the floor and go to the closet. The interior wall is made of paneling. The panel in the back easily pops in

Chapter 2: Jesse

and out of place, which I've used to my advantage. Behind that panel is a corkboard I've hung on the concrete wall.

My obsession began five years ago, just a few weeks before Charlotte showed up. I had just turned twelve. I didn't know back then that my curiosity would turn into the obsession it has become today, but it did.

I remove the panel and take the corkboard down. It's covered in pictures, news clippings, documents, and a map. Color-coded strings and tacks web everything together. Notecards are pinned around the edges, displaying my notes. I write most of them in a shorthand that only I understand, in case anyone ever finds it.

Acquiring the information I need and properly storing it has been a challenge. Using technology would have made organization much easier, but my online activities are no doubt being monitored by the government and Academy. The corkboard itself is untraceable and easily concealed.

I lift one of the floorboards in the closet and extract a stack of folders and papers. Charlotte won't be home from school for another forty-five minutes. I plan to use every second of it.

I'm so close to finding the answer to all my problems. I can feel it. After years of patience, sneaking around, frustrating dead ends, I'm almost there.

I put pencil to paper and get to work.

. . .

The squeak of the front door startles me out of my deep concentration. My heart lurches to my throat as I hastily gather the papers that have spread across the bed and floor. Is my time really up already?

I haphazardly replace the fake panel just as Charlotte enters the room. There's no reason to worry though. She throws her backpack onto the bed and flops face down beside it with a huff.

"What's wrong?" I ask and sit beside her. The bedding muffles her response. I nudge her. "Come on, Char. Talk to me."

"I don't want to," she grumbles and flips onto her back. She stares up at me with her defiant gray eyes. It's a look that challenges me to press on. She doesn't want to discuss what's bothering her, yet she does at the same time. I completely understand. That internal debate is the story of my life.

We stare each other down until she finally gives in and mumbles, "I got a bad grade on a test." She tears her eyes from mine. "And a girl in my class found out and made fun of me for it. I know it's a stupid thing to get upset over, but it made me think how everything I'm doing in school now is going to affect everything later on."

"It's just one grade," I say gently.

"Yeah, one grade that could determine the rest of my life," she exclaims dramatically. "I'm gonna be in the same situation as you. I won't have money to pay for college when the time comes, so I'll have to completely rely on scholarships if I want to be able to get away from here. I can't get those if my grades suck."

Her breath sharpens and tears spring into her eyes.

"Look," I say quickly. "Colleges don't even really care about the grades you get in middle school. It's high school they care about. And even then, it's okay to mess up once in a while."

"Really?" She sniffles and wipes her hand across her eyes.

"Have you met me?" I tease. She cracks a smile. "You know I didn't have the best grades in middle school, but I pulled through and you will, too."

She sits up and leans against me. I wrap her in my arms, as if that will make everything better. It won't, but it's nice to pretend that we live normal lives for a little while.

Chapter 2: Jesse

"So you think you'll be able to get enough scholarship money to pay for college?" she asks.

"I hope so," I sigh. "I doubt it'll be enough, but every little bit will help."

She smiles for a second, but then her face falls.

"Now what's wrong?"

She peers at me with tight, worried eyes. She looks so much younger in this moment. I often forget that she's only twelve.

"What happens?" Her voice is barely audible. "What happens when you turn eighteen and graduate high school? When you go off to college? What'll happen to me and Oli when you leave us behind?"

Her words jolt me. Honestly, I try not to think about it too much. I live my life one day at a time. I don't know what will happen. Technically, they'll still be under Greg's custody and I can't exactly smuggle them into college with me. I do have a plan, but it's not guaranteed. I haven't told her yet, though, and I won't until I know for sure. I don't want to get her hopes up.

"We'll figure something out," I assure her. "But trust me when I say that I'll never leave you behind. No matter what happens or how far apart we end up, I will *always* come back for you."

Her shoulders relax, then she changes the subject. "So how was your day?"

"Fine," I say dismissively. It's hypocritical of me to pressure her about her own problems without sharing mine, but what is there to tell? School was a mix of boredom and downright irritation, and there's no way I'm telling her that I spent almost an hour sifting through stacks of papers only to be no closer to locating the Academy than I had been before.

"How's the search going?" she blurts out. My eyes snap up to meet hers. Her expression is innocent, but her eyes scream the truth. She knows.

"What?" Feigning confusion seems like my best bet. She doesn't buy it for a second.

"You know, the corkboard you keep hidden in the closet."

Yep, I'm screwed. "I have no idea what you're talking about."

It's at that moment there's a thump and a crash from inside the closet. The door swings open as the corkboard falls out. I wince. I guess I really did put it back a little too hastily.

Charlotte gives me a pointed look. "Really?"

I close my eyes and sigh. So much for protecting her from all this. "How long have you known?"

She shrugs. "Not long. You didn't put the panel back all the way one time and I found it. Don't worry, though. Most of it doesn't make any sense, except that you're obviously looking for something and you're completely obsessed with finding it."

She eyes me expectantly.

"I can't tell you about it," I say. She opens her mouth to protest, but I cut her off. "I know you're curious and you want to help, but the less you know, the better. What I'm doing isn't exactly safe."

"I'm not a little kid anymore, Jesse. Whatever it is, I can handle it."

She's so determined; it's in her nature to be. We're the same in that way. And maybe she *can* handle it, but I'm not risking it.

"I know, Char. Honestly, you're a lot more mature than most kids your age, but I can't get you involved in this. It has nothing to do with age. I can't have you getting into trouble or getting hurt because of me."

Chapter 2: Jesse

"I get it," she finally backs down. Her eyes have dimmed. "You don't have to explain it to me, I guess, even though I wish you would. Just promise you'll be careful."

I force a smile. "I promise."

CHAPTER THREE
Emma

I have a proposition for you.

The words tumble around in my mind. "What do you mean?"

"You just finished your junior year," she replies cryptically. I should've known better than to expect an actual answer.

"I'm aware," I say slowly, trying to minimize the sarcastic bite in my tone.

"And as of right now, how do you think you are ranked?"

I blink, taken aback. Is this some kind of test? I resist the urge to roll my bottom lip between my teeth while I figure out how best to respond. I don't want her to know how much self-doubt I have, but it'll also be bad if I come across as overly confident.

"I don't know," I shrug, though that's probably not an appropriate reply either. I add, "Everyone says I'm near the top, but I don't know if they're just trying to reassure me or if they honestly believe that."

"I would say you're definitely near the top. In fact, you have been ranked number one in your class for a while now."

I freeze and become very aware of my heart as it slams against my chest. Number one? That can't possibly be right. "Are you sure?"

Chapter 3: Emma

As if she'd be lying to me.

"Positive. I would even go as far to say that you're one of the best we've ever had." She smiles, but there is an intensity behind it. Whatever comes next is serious. "Which leads me to what I'm about to ask of you. Now before I tell you, I want you to understand that you aren't obligated to do any of this. You don't have to agree to anything I'm about to say. I don't want you to think you're being put in danger or forced to do something against your will."

I sit up straighter.

"As I am sure you noticed, we only had two graduating members qualify as Level Ones this year. While we still have plenty already in the program, there have been several who have recently retired to a normal job within the City. We don't have enough people out in the field as it is, but I didn't want to send anyone out who didn't meet the requirements."

A small hopeful spark works through me. Surely she isn't implying what it sounds like she is. After years of hard work and patience, surely it won't come a year ahead of time.

"I've looked over your records dating all the way back to your first year of school. You've always excelled. After carefully reviewing your progress, as well as consulting with my colleagues, we have come to the same conclusion. Your progress is so far advanced, you are technically eligible for graduation now. Honestly, you've passed up many of the students who graduated this evening. You also fit the profile we need."

I stare at her with bated breath, my muscles taunt. "So you're saying…"

"I'm offering you a Mission."

Five words. That's all it takes to change my life.

She continues before I have the chance to say anything. "Now, you don't have to accept if you aren't comfortable leaving the

Academy as a minor. Though if you do accept, someone will accompany you, as usual, so be thinking about who you might want that to be. And as with all Missions, your housing, transportation, and spending money will be provided." She pauses for a beat. "You can take some time to think about it if you'd like."

Take some time to think about it? I've thought about this moment my entire life.

"I'll do it," I say immediately. "I'd be honored for the position."

The Ambassador's smile widens. "Excellent. I'm pleased to hear that. I'll arrange for another meeting tomorrow so you can receive your assignment."

My assignment. My Mission. This is actually happening.

"You are going to do great, Emmalyn. You've worked so hard for this. I'm proud of you."

My heart liquifies. Those words mean so much coming from her. I have worked hard. I've trained, even on my off days and on the weekends while everyone else was out having fun. I pushed myself, even when all I wanted to do was break. My whole life has led up to this moment, and now it's finally happened.

"Thank you," I manage to say without the words lodging in my throat.

She presses a button on her computer and the door opens as Sam walks back in. I take that as my cue to leave.

"Oh, and Emmalyn?" she says. I glance back at her. "Make sure you don't spread this information around. It would be best if our discussion was kept discreet."

"Of course," I agree. "Thank you again for this opportunity."

We exchange goodbyes and I leave with Sam.

Neither of us speak this time around as he escorts me back. Dinner is still in full swing when I reenter the auditorium. Nothing changed in the twenty minutes I was gone. Not for them, at least.

Chapter 3: Emma

"What was that about?" Aiden asks when I sit back in my seat. I take a bite of food while I rack my brain for something to say. The food has cooled considerably in my absence, but it still tastes all right.

"I'll tell you later," I finally say. After all, the Ambassador told me to keep it contained, not that I couldn't tell anyone at all.

"Aww, why can't you tell us now?" Lacy whines.

I shift in my seat. "Because I'm not supposed to openly talk about it. I'll tell you later when we can't be overheard."

"But—" Lacy protests.

I cut her off. "So, what did you all talk about while I was gone?"

Lacy's face falls and I feel a twinge of regret for maybe being too harsh, but I'll tell her all about it when we get back to our room.

Cameron picks up the silence and I shoot him a grateful look. "After we stopped debating whether or not you were in trouble, Aiden and Lacy started talking about their plans for after Lacy's graduation. Be glad you missed it. They were being all mushy and gross."

Lacy smacks his arm. "We were not. We were just discussing where we want to live when we move to the City. We'll actually be able to live together."

I laugh. "Yeah, then you won't be disappointed every time you get caught trying to sneak him into the dorms."

Aiden's face darkens. "Let's not talk about those days."

Lacy adds, "Remember when the supervisor grabbed you and literally threw you out?"

"Of course! I never tried to get in after that."

Our banter continues through the rest of dinner. The conversation I promised them is not forgotten, but we've moved on for the time being.

The celebration eventually ends when curfew approaches. Cameron and I get separated from Lacy and Aiden on the way back to the dorms, but I doubt that's by accident.

When we reach the dorms, I take Cameron's hand and pull him into the alley between the buildings. He stays silent until we're far enough away from the opening.

"Okay, so what really happened when you left?" he asks, already on the same page as me.

"I had a meeting with the Ambassador," I admit. "And you're not going to believe what she said." I drop my voice to a whisper. "I'm number one, Cameron. Out of my entire class, I'm at the very top."

His jaw falls open. "Emma! That's amazing! I guess that means you're guaranteed a spot in the Missions program next year, huh?" He shakes his head. "All that worrying and you're ranked first."

"I'm not going next year," I say. "I'm going now."

His face pales. "What?"

I explain everything.

He shifts on his feet when I finish. "Are you sure about this? You'll be going outside the gates for the first time without the usual year of training. Do you know who you're going to be paired with yet? The partner can make all the difference. And Missions are so, so dangerous. I know I bring back stories, but I haven't told you everything. I left out the more dangerous stuff because I didn't want you to worry about me. I don't want to lose you like—"

"I promise I'll be really careful," I cut him off. I can't hear the rest of that sentence. I can't. Even if time has passed, it'll always be too soon. "And I don't have to go with some random partner. She said I get to choose…and I want that person to be you. If you want that, of course."

Chapter 3: Emma

There's a beat of silence while he eyes me like I'm crazy, and then, "Are you kidding me? Of course I'll go with you." He closes the small distance between us and folds me into a hug. I wrap my arms around his neck and bury my face in his shoulder. "I'm so proud of you, Emma," he murmurs into my hair.

"Thanks," I whisper. "I'll feel so much better with you there. I can't imagine going with anyone else, especially with someone older that I don't even know."

"Yeah," he agrees. "I'll feel better being the one with you than some random Level One you don't know. And I wouldn't want your partner to treat you any differently just because you're younger than them."

The warning bell rings across the grounds, shattering our moment. Two minutes until curfew. With reluctance, I pull from his embrace. We leave the alley and part ways.

Lacy isn't back yet when I get to our room, so I quickly change into pajamas and flop onto my bed. The door swings open a few seconds later.

"You cut it pretty close," I comment.

"I know," Lacy says. "We didn't hear the alarm at first and then I ran all the way here." Despite that, she isn't out of breath. Her ability allows her to run faster than average for an extended period of time without tiring out.

"Did Aiden make it back okay?"

"Yeah. Not that he had anything to worry about. Graduates are exempt from curfew now." She sits beside me. "So are you going to tell me about what happened earlier?"

I recount the story again, this time hesitantly including that I asked Cameron to go with me.

Her face lights up. "That's awesome, Em. I can't believe they're sending you out a year early. Most don't even go at all."

I chew the inside of my cheek. "And you're okay with Cameron going?"

"Yeah, why wouldn't I be?"

I shrug. "I don't know. We might be gone for a while. That's half the group all at once."

"Emma, this is what you've dreamed of. And it's probably best that Cameron goes with you. They picked him to be a trainer, after all. That means he'll probably do just fine looking out for you and training you while you also actively do the Mission."

I deflate. "Right. The training. If he does go with me, he'll have to sacrifice the opportunity to train the newer Level Ones. With the way the Ambassador talked, it sounds like we might be gone for a while. I can't ask him to give that up for me."

"Seriously?" she exclaims as she slides off my bed and goes to the closet. "He just enthusiastically agreed to go with you. If he really didn't want to, he would've said no. But he said yes. So take him on the Mission, live your dream, and have the best couple of months of your life finally experiencing the outside world. And besides, this is just as much for him as it is for you. I'd kill to live on my own with Aiden."

She has a point, I guess, but, "Cameron and I aren't like you and Aiden, though. We can hang out whenever we want now without getting in trouble. I don't need to live with him to be his best friend."

Lacy raises an eyebrow and purses her lips, pulling her 'you're an idiot' expression as she changes into her pajamas.

"What?" I ask.

"Girl, come on. Don't tell me you seriously don't know."

"Know what? What are you talking about?"

Chapter 3: Emma

"He doesn't want to be your best friend, Emma," Lacy says. When I still don't get whatever she's trying to say, she adds, "He doesn't want to be *just* your best friend."

Then it clicks.

My stomach drops at the weight of the statement, but it's not true. It can't be.

"No," I shake my head. "There's no way. I'd know if he thought of me like that."

"Would you?" she challenges.

"Yes! It's Cameron. We tell each other everything. He would've told me if…if he…"

The words die in my throat. Lacy raises her eyebrows, almost sympathetic in a way.

"Does he?" I mumble. "Did he…say something to you?"

She shakes her head. "But I've noticed the way he acts around you. I don't know, maybe I'm wrong. It just seems like he does."

I rub my hand down my face and sigh. "I hope he doesn't. I can't even imagine thinking of him like that. We've known each other since we were little kids. We're best friends."

"Okay, chill out. Even if he does, maybe he'll just never bring it up and then you won't have to worry about it."

"But now every time I see him, I'm going to wonder if he's hiding how he really feels about me."

After changing, she sinks into her bed. "You think too much. Just forget I said anything. I probably just read the situation wrong."

I know she's lying—she definitely believes what she said—but I let it go. Tomorrow is going to be a big day and I need to be ready for it.

CHAPTER FOUR
Jesse

Greg doesn't come home, which makes tonight one of the good nights. We never know where he goes or what he does all night, but I couldn't care less. Tonight, I don't have to deal with the yelling, the fighting, the fear. I won't have to shield my innocent siblings from harm. They feel it, too. The relief when the digital clock by the beat-up TV indicates that it's well past the time he usually comes home.

Tonight, we're free.

It's not a school night and we have the house to ourselves, so I let them stay up past their usual bedtime. We sit on the ragged couch in the living room and watch TV, an activity we rarely get to do.

I flip through the channels for a while until landing on something we can all watch. I don't actually pay much attention to it, but instead relish in the serenity of relaxing with my siblings.

They get more tired as the night wears on. Oliver is first to go. He's sprawled across the couch with his head in my lap. Charlotte's curled up beside me, still awake, but with heavy eyes.

Chapter 4: Jesse

I reach for the remote and switch the TV off. "Time for bed," I say and sweep Oli into my arms to carry him to the bedroom. He's small for his age, but before long, I won't be able to carry him like this anymore.

"Go change into your pajamas," I tell Charlotte when we enter the bedroom. Oliver's thankfully already in his. "And don't forget to brush your teeth."

"I know, I know," she says dismissively. She grabs her pajamas from her dresser drawer and leaves.

I tuck Oli into bed and throw on a tee shirt and sweatpants while Charlotte is out of the room. She returns in a tank top and shorts. She brushes past me, and I notice something on her upper arm.

I stop her. "What's that?"

"What's what?"

"On your arm?" I clarify.

She turns away, clapping a hand over her arm, and mumbles, "Nothing."

My eyes narrow. "It wasn't nothing, Charlotte. What's on your arm?"

I try to pull her hand away, but she won't budge.

"It doesn't matter," she protests. "Just let it go."

Letting it go isn't an option and I'm done playing around. "Charlotte Marie," I say firmly.

She pauses, then slowly turns back around and removes her hand. Heat flares inside me at the sight. The skin on her upper arm is a nasty blue-purple.

"What did he do?" I seethe. Blood pounds in my ears.

She steps back. "Nothing, Jesse. It was an accident."

The edges of my vision go fuzzy. "Don't lie to me, Charlotte. What happened?"

Don't yell at her. It wasn't her fault. She's not the one you're mad at.

"What happened?" I repeat, much gentler this time.

She draws in a shaky breath and fixes her gaze on a spot above my shoulder. "I was in the kitchen this morning and I guess I didn't get out of the way fast enough. I don't know, it all happened so fast. He grabbed me a little too hard and it left a mark. I didn't even know it was bruised until I saw it in the shower."

I explode. "I can't believe him. I can't believe he hurt you!"

Charlotte hesitantly touches my arm. "Jesse, calm down. It's okay. I'm okay."

"No, you're not!" I shout and she flinches. I sigh, run a hand through my hair, and pace the room. I need to calm down. The last thing I want is to scare her. But the walls spin around me, the temperature rising. My chest constricts. "We're leaving. We can be out of here by tomorrow morning before he comes home. We'll never have to deal with him again and you won't be in danger." She stares at me, eyebrows raised. "I'm serious, Char. We're leaving."

"And where exactly are we gonna go, huh?" she retorts and crosses her arms. "We don't have any money and even if we do somehow steal the small amount Greg has lying around, it won't be enough."

I deflate like a balloon, her rationalism being the pin that pops me. Of course she's right. Of course we have nowhere to go. If we really ran away, we'd need food, money, and a place to actually run to. I can't put them through that.

"Fine," I force out against everything in me that's screaming to go. "But I'm not leaving you alone in the house anymore, especially if he's here."

She nods, her eyes and shoulders drooping, and climbs into bed. I settle between my siblings. Oliver slides closer to me,

Chapter 4: Jesse

somehow still asleep despite the argument. Charlotte snuggles into me as well. Even though I'm their friend and big brother of sorts, I'm also their protector and they know that. I'll always be there to keep them safe.

It's just not enough. Nothing I do for them will ever come close to the life they deserve.

...

I wake the next morning to the clattering of dishes, which can only mean one thing. Greg is home. Charlotte rustles beside me and slowly wakes up. She peers at me blearily for a moment before her eyes widen and her body stiffens.

My eyes flicker to the bruise on her arm. It's worsened overnight, darker and more painful looking than before. Something bubbles deep inside me, pleading to be set free.

I scramble out of bed and storm out of the room. Charlotte follows closely behind.

"Jesse, no. Yelling at him will only make it worse." She grabs at my hand but I shake her off and burst into the kitchen.

"What is *wrong* with you?" I scream at him. He turns to face me, startled. His cold gray eyes burn into mine.

"Excuse me?"

"You hurt her! She did nothing wrong and you hurt her."

I lunge at him. Charlotte cries out. But I never make it. His hand swings out and cracks across my face with enough force to send me staggering back. My cheek stings. It'll definitely welt and bruise, but I'm not fazed. It's not like this is the first time he's hit me.

"Jesse!" Charlotte runs forward and latches onto my arm, trying to pull me back. She's trembling from head to toe. I shake her off again.

"Go to the room, Char," I hiss through clenched teeth. For once, she doesn't argue.

"I swear if you hurt her or Oli again, I—"

"What?" he interrupts and grabs me by the shoulders. His fingers dig into me as he walks me backwards and slams my back into the wall. "What're you gonna do? Call social services? Need I remind you that I let the three of you live here so you don't get split up and sent to three different foster homes. Is that what you want? I could easily toss you out on the streets and be done with this whole thing."

He releases me and pulls himself up to full height. I shake with the effort to not attack him, digging my fingers into my palms. I hold my tongue, too, because he's right. I *despise* him with every fiber of my being, but there's nothing I can do. We need shelter and food and other basic necessities. Greg provides that. And if we do turn him in for being the abusive monster he is, then it's almost guaranteed that Charlotte, Oliver, and I will be split up and sent in three different directions. I can't risk that.

"Just leave them alone," I finish lamely and flee to the bedroom. Charlotte and Oliver huddle together on the bed.

Oliver looks up at me with his emerald green puppy dog eyes. He opens his arms for a hug. I sink into the bed and gently wrap my arms around his small, warm body.

"It's okay," I mumble and run a hand through his dark hair. "Everything's okay."

He only whimpers in response.

In the two years I've known him, he hasn't spoken a single word. I don't know why he doesn't talk, if it's related to how he ended up in foster care to begin with, or if he's literally incapable of speech. Not that it matters, though. He's still my brother either way.

"Come on." I pull away from him and stand up. "Let's get out of the house today. How does that sound?"

Chapter 4: Jesse

Oliver nods, but his expression remains grim.

We get dressed and I pull out the emergency packs that are stashed in the bottom dresser drawer for times like this. It includes toothbrushes and paste, a hairbrush, and granola bars.

After getting ready, I walk over to the single window and undo the latch. It used to screech and stick about halfway up, but now when I lift it, it remains silent from the many times we've left this way.

Charlotte goes first. Then I hoist Oli onto the ledge, and he slides out the other side. I follow closely behind and shut the window behind me.

We go to our favorite place: the park.

It's one of the few places left untouched by the advancements in technology. The playground sits on rotted mulch and the nearby rusted swing set sits on top of the wispy grass.

Most would look at this place in disgust, their noses turned up at the decrepit structure. But this is our safe haven.

I push Oli on one of the swings as a warm breeze filters through the air. Charlotte swings next to him. A few other kids run around the playground, a change to the usual emptiness. Their screams and laughter ring out, so full of joy and life.

Oliver distinctively sighs and gazes longingly at the other kids. It's the kind of sigh that says, *why can't I be like normal kids?*

"It'll get better," I assure him. "I promise. One day you'll be so overwhelmed with happiness, you'll barely even remember what your life used to feel like. Sooner or later, something is going to happen that'll change everything. We just have to wait for it to come."

I'm not sure if I'm trying to convince him or myself.

Beyond the Gates

I continue pushing him on the swing as my thoughts roam. They float for a moment before landing on the Academy. It always comes back to the Academy. The special kids. The government.

My blood sparks at just the thought. They're the reason I'm in this mess. Without them, I'd be at home with my family right now. But no. The government took everything from me. They deserve to get what's coming to them.

I'll make sure of it, regardless of the consequences.

CHAPTER FIVE
Emma

I wake to the chime of my message board. The room is dark, quiet, which means it's way too early to be conscious. The rectangular glass screen on the wall above my bed lights up with a new message. The time in the corner reads 6:00am.

I groan and snuggle deeper into the covers. But the screen keeps flashing, so I sit up and tap the message to open it.

Meeting with Ambassador. 6:15. Supervisor waiting in dorm front lobby.

I blink a few times and rub my eyes to clear the grogginess. I force myself out of bed, throw on some clothes, and run a brush through my hair. I swipe my phone from the nightstand and shove it into the back pocket of my jeans before leaving the room.

As promised, someone stands in the lobby. It's a woman this time, looking like she too has been disturbed from sleep. It's Saturday, after all. People usually sleep in.

A shiver crawls down my spine as I follow her out into the brisk morning air. Bringing a jacket probably would've been a good idea, but it's too late now.

The sky is a dark gray that lightens by the second as sunrise approaches. The grounds are silent and empty. It's not until we're almost to the office building that I see someone else.

"Cameron?" I say in disbelief. He's coming from the direction of the City, so it's safe to say he was probably just asleep, too. "What're you doing?"

"I have a meeting with the Ambassador," he grins slyly.

"*I* have a meeting with the Ambassador."

"Yeah, it's the same meeting, silly," he says and rolls his eyes playfully. The sun's not even up yet. How does he have so much freaking energy? "I told the Ambassador last night how you wanted me on the Mission with you and that I agreed. She approved me to take on the Mission, so we're definitely going together."

Despite my it's-too-early-to-be-conscious state, excitement and relief flood through me with that knowledge. I won't have to do this alone.

The Ambassador is at her desk when we enter her office. *She doesn't look like she's been abruptly pulled from sleep.* She's well put together and already at work. Seriously, how can you not admire this woman? She's constantly working to run the Academy and help all of us.

"Good morning, Emma, Cameron," she says with a warm smile.

"Good morning," Cameron and I say together, though Cameron's greeting is much more chipper. I try to stamp down my exhaustion. She needs to see that I can be alert and ready to go even at this ungodly hour.

"As Cameron has probably already told you, he'll be accompanying you on this Mission and helping you with whatever you need. However, for the time being, most of the Mission will be your responsibility. I want to see how well you do on this first time out.

Chapter 5: Emma

But if it gets to be too much, Cameron will be there to assist and take on more if needed."

She unlocks a drawer in her desk and takes out a manila folder. She thumbs through it, then hands it to me.

"We always give out assignments in physical form rather than electronically," she explains. "Keep it safe and away from the eyes of others. Under no circumstances is anyone allowed to know of its contents except for the two of you. Cameron has access to the conference rooms, so you may use one of those to go over the case together. Emma, you'll have a meeting with my colleagues and I later today so we can go over some basics and prepare you for life outside the gates."

I nod, stomach tightening. I'm beyond ecstatic to have been given this opportunity, but she's right. I *do* need to learn about life outside the gates, about the humans and their world. I know barely anything about it.

"Now," she continues. "We will be sending you to the small town of Willow Creek in the Northeastern Central Region. This is where your target is located. You will live there and attend the local high school under cover. Blending into their society and culture is vital. Usually our potential Mission program students take human culture and behavioral classes senior year to familiarize themselves. Plus a year of training after being selected. You'll only have today. But you are a smart girl and you'll have Cameron, who's already been through it. I'm sure you'll be able to figure it out quickly enough and if you do ever have questions, all you have to do is call."

I nod again. As long as I'm not alone, it shouldn't be too difficult to handle, right?

"You will need to use your ability to obtain a substantial reading on the target's future and report back immediately. He is a serious threat to the Academy as well as the entire government system.

The rest of the information you need is all in the file. Any questions?"

My head spins with the influx of information, but I shake my head.

"Good. I'll contact you when we are ready for our meeting."

With that, we're escorted out of the building. Cameron heads back towards the City, and I'm led back to the dorms.

Lacy is still asleep when I return. I wish I could curl up and doze back off, but there's absolutely no way that's happening now. I climb onto my bed with the file folder in hand.

I want to go through it right here and now, but decide to wait until Cameron can be with me. As miraculous as this whole situation has been, the nerves are still there. The Ambassador seems so confident of my capabilities, but what if I don't live up to her expectations?

I set the folder aside and lay down, trying to fall back asleep, but I'm too wound up. I play around on my phone for a while and try to push the worries out of my mind.

Lacy stirs around 8:00am. "Why are you awake?" she groans and buries her face in her pillow to block the stream of light from the window.

"I had another meeting with the Ambassador this morning," I explain. Lacy opens her mouth, but I cut her off. "And before you ask, I can't tell you anything specific about the case."

"Come on," Lacy whines and props herself up on her elbows. "Not even a little bit?"

"You know it's against the rules. Besides, I haven't actually looked at it yet. I'm waiting to do it with Cameron."

Thankfully she doesn't bring up the conversation from last night. "Promise to keep in touch while you're gone, all right?"

Chapter 5: Emma

"Lace, you know that's against the rules, too. We're not supposed to have contact with anyone inside the Academy when we're outside of it."

Even Cameron never contacted me when he was out on Missions.

Her face falls. "Yeah, I know. I just thought maybe it'd be different."

"I mean, I don't know. But I assume all the rules still apply. We'll probably only be gone a month or two at the most, though."

Lacy quickly gets ready, then we head to breakfast. The hallways are bustling with activity now, compared to their eerie emptiness of earlier. Several girls greet us as we walk by. Most are still in pajamas. It's just a normal Saturday for everyone else.

When we get to the dining hall, Lacy leaves to go find Aiden, who agreed to meet her there. I search for Cameron. He doesn't always eat here anymore now that he has his own place in the City, but I have a feeling he'll be here today.

The food lines run the course of the back wall. Long tables and benches stretch in rows across the rest of the room. Sure enough, I find Cameron at a table with a plate of pancakes and bacon.

"Pancakes? Really?" is the first thing I say to him.

He looks up. "You don't have to sit here. Or you can just pretend they don't exist."

I sit across from him with a sigh and swipe a piece of bacon from his plate.

"Hey!" He reaches across the table, but I pull my hand back and ignore the appalled look he gives me.

"I'm starving and the line is super long. I don't have time for waiting. We have a conference room to get to."

"Yeah, yeah. Let me finish my food and we'll go."

He doesn't protest when I grab another piece of bacon.

Beyond the Gates

...

I already have the file on me, safely concealed in my backpack. So after breakfast, we set off toward the office building. We don't encounter many students along the way. At this time, most are either at breakfast or still asleep. It's good for us, though. It'd be a little difficult to explain why Cameron was letting me into a building that's off-limits to students.

We settle into a conference room on the ground floor and I pull the file from my bag. Cameron sits beside me at the table, and I open the folder. It's filled with papers that have been clipped together. The first page contains basic information on my target, as well as a photo.

It's the picture that catches my attention. In it is a boy with messy, dark brown hair. It's a school photo or something similar. He's posed and smiling, but it doesn't quite reach his golden-brown eyes. Instead, his eyes are haunted, empty.

I stare at the picture, probably longer than necessary. Cameron clears his throat and I move to the rest of the page.

Name:
Jesse Reynolds
Date of Birth:
12/18/2104
History:
Parents and older brother perished in accident when target was age 8. Target transferred to foster care following the event. Currently a senior at Willow Creek High School in small town of Willow Creek, Northeastern Central (NEC) Region.
Purpose:
Target poses a threat to the security of the Academy and government system.

Chapter 5: Emma

> *Task:*
>
> *Obtain a clear reading of target's future and report directly to Ambassador. Will receive further instruction upon this result, including information on elimination process.*

I can't help but scoff. "This is all the information we get? They're practically sending us in blind!"

Cameron just shrugs. "You don't always get a whole lot of background information on a Mission. It depends on how much the government wants to reveal. Sometimes it's detailed, sometimes it's barely anything. A lot of them are on need-to-know bases."

I flip to the second page. This one is all about me. Or the fake me, I guess. The person I'll have to become during my time in the real world.

> *Name:*
>
> *Emma Clarke (do not present yourself as Emmalyn. Emma is a much more common name. You will also be using Cameron's last name to further your disguise)*
>
> *Age:*
>
> *17*
>
> *History:*
>
> *You moved to your current residence from the Mid-Atlantic region. You live with your parents and older brother (Cameron). You have never lived in a small town, so it is expected that you would need an adjustment period. Use this to your advantage when figuring out the human world.*

Cameron's page is similar, though he gets to keep his last name. I guess we need the same last name though if we're pretending to be siblings. I can sort of see it, I guess. We both have blonde hair at the very least. It's passable as long as no one looks too far into it.

However, because he's two years older than me, he won't be going to school with me. I shove that thought out of my mind for now, though. I'll deal with it later.

The rest of the packet contains generic information that's probably sent out in every case. Basic do's and don'ts.

Do:
- *work diligently and stay on task*
- *keep phone on you at all times and answer when contacted*
- *alert Ambassador to any emergencies as soon as possible*

Don't:
- *put yourself in a situation where the target might discover your true identity*
- *tell anyone about yourself or the Academy*
- *contact anyone inside the Academy other than the Ambassador*

Once we both finish combing through it, I shove the file back in my bag and stand up.

"It sounds like a good portion of this Mission is going to fall on you," Cameron says. "I hope you know what you're getting yourself into."

"Yeah, me too."

. . .

The Ambassador scheduled our meeting for that afternoon. We meet in the same conference room Cameron and I had used earlier, except Cameron's not with me this time. The Ambassador and two of her colleagues are already there when I arrive.

Chapter 5: Emma

"Have a seat," the Ambassador says with a smile. I settle in across from the other three and pull out the file in case I need it. "Before we get started, do you have any questions?"

"Yeah. What will Cameron be doing while I go to school every day? His page wasn't clear."

"Oh, yes," the Ambassador says. "I already discussed it with him, so I didn't put it in the file. Basically, he'll work on compiling any information you gather and will aid you in your Mission from more of a behind the scenes approach. He's done this before, so he'll know what to do."

I nod. "And when are we leaving?"

"Tomorrow, 5:00am sharp. Before anyone else is awake."

I freeze. *Tomorrow?* I have less than a day left at the Academy.

"Don't worry, Emma. We'll prepare you as best as we can. But you must also understand the severity of the situation. This is a high-profile case that needs to be addressed soon before matters are made worse."

High-profile case?

"If the Mission is that serious, why are you sending *me*? Surely there's an actual Level One who would be more qualified for the job."

"Like I said, we're running low on numbers recently. As for why I'm sending you, I have my reasons, but most are too confidential to share at this time. However, your ability to read the future is one of the biggest reasons, as it will no doubt be invaluable to us. But if you really feel that unprepared, we can make arrangements to send someone else."

I come to my senses. What am I doing? Why am I questioning the Ambassador's reasoning for sending me on a Mission, the thing I've dreamed of for years?

"No, no. I'll go. I can do it."

She leans back in her chair. "Excellent, now it is of the utmost importance that you do not stray from the task at hand. Being out there on your own for the first time can be overwhelming and there is no time for distractions. Cameron will be helpful to your adjustment, but he can't be with you twenty-four seven."

She gestures to the other two people in the room, who straighten in their chairs. "My colleagues here will discuss some of the key differences between ourselves and the humans. Hopefully this will diminish most of any confusion you may have. But as I said, most students have a year to learn this stuff and we only have a couple hours. Whatever you encounter, your best bet will be to ask Cameron about it, since he's already been on several Missions."

The other two take over after that. They describe how we are physically better than the humans, as if I wasn't already aware. We're faster, stronger, smarter. Even our vision and hearing are enhanced.

They talk about how scatterbrained humans can sometimes be. Their minds aren't sharp and focused like ours. They can't always shed outlying factors and concentrate on one particular task or problem.

I sit and listen for the next couple of hours while they go over everything they deem necessary. By the time I'm dismissed, my head is swimming and a pain has started between my eyes.

I've never felt so overwhelmed in my life.

When I get back to my dorm room to start packing, Lacy isn't there. I'll see her later though. Tonight at the very least.

I drag a duffel bag out from under my bed and start packing everything I'll need for the trip. I don't know how long I'll be gone, so I just pack anything I can think of. When the bag is so filled that it's nearly busting at the seams, I slide the file right on top and zip it up.

Chapter 5: Emma

Packing creates a sense of finality. This is it. Tomorrow, I'm really leaving here. At least for a while. It could be anywhere from days to months.

I meet up with my friends for dinner and we all eat one last meal together. The dining hall buzzes in an unusual fashion this evening, with people talking in clumps or passing words down the table. I don't think much of it, though. I have bigger things to think about. Until that night when I get out of the shower.

The bathroom is empty, except for Laurel who stands by the sinks. She leans against the wall, her arms crossed over her chest. Despite the humidity in the room, her dark hair stays in its perfect ringlets.

"Hey," I say cautiously. I still feel bad about the interaction from yesterday, but the way she's just standing there, staring at me, is unnerving to say the least.

She sneers. "You must think you're so special."

I nearly stumble back a step, shocked by her tone. "Excuse me?"

She pushes off the wall and takes a step towards me. "Bet you think you're so great that you get to go out on a Mission a year early. Perfect little Emmalyn Grant. Always gets whatever she wants. Does everything she's told and never slips up, like a good little Academy kid. All of us work so hard, yet you're the one who gets a free ticket out of here. Congratulations," she spits.

Ice floods my veins as her words sink in. "Wha – how do you know about that?"

"You were at dinner," she scoffs. "Didn't you hear everyone whispering about you? Spreading the news that a non-graduate got a Mission when only two actual spots were filled?"

That's what had been different at dinner. Information must have seared through the hall like wildfire. But how did it not get back to me until now? Why didn't anyone confront me about it then? I was sitting *right there* in the midst of it all.

How did it get out in the first place? I didn't tell anyone but Cameron and Lacy, and they'd never turn on me like that.

Does the Ambassador know? Will she be upset that word's gotten out? Pull me from the Mission due to the backlash it's created?

I push past Laurel, unable to deal with the conversation any longer. Lacy is sitting on her bed when I rush into the room. "Have you heard?" she asks.

"I just found out from Laurel of all people," I explain.

Lacy cringes. "I bet she was thrilled. By the way, you have a message."

Sure enough, my message board flashes with a new notification.

A sense of foreboding hangs in the air as I tap into my messages. It's from the Ambassador.

News of your Mission was somehow leaked, as you may or may not already know. Due to this, we have decided to move your departure up. You will be leaving in the next half hour since no one else is permitted to leave the dorms. A supervisor is waiting for you in the lobby to escort you to the front gates.

"You're leaving tonight, aren't you?" Lacy says, a frown on her face.

I nod. I understand why. If we wait until tomorrow morning, the issue of people knowing about our situation could escalate before we're able to actually leave.

Lacy slips off her bed and throws her arms around me. I return the hug, squeezing tight. We've been roommates most of our lives. It'll be weird to go to sleep and wake up without her across the room from me.

"Be safe," she whispers.

Chapter 5: Emma

"I'll see you soon," I promise.

With a final squeeze, I let go and grab my duffel bag and backpack. I take one last look around the room. My bed is neatly made from this morning. The desk is littered with pencils and homework assignments I won't get the chance to finish. Pictures of my friends and I are pinned along the space above my bed. Lacy stands by her bed, watching me soak it all in.

I thought I'd have one more night here, but I don't have time now to give into that small twinge of sadness. It's finally time to prove myself.

I say goodbye to Lacy, then lug my stuff downstairs, grateful I don't encounter anyone on the way, and follow the supervisor outside. The grounds are dark, chilly. It's too quiet compared to the usual commotion.

I meet up with Cameron along the way and we approach the gates together. The Ambassador waits with another person I don't recognize. A car looms in the darkness, parked right outside the gates.

Two guards relieve us of our luggage and load it into the trunk of the car. The Ambassador turns to me.

"Remember all you have learned today. Remember the rules and abide by them. Always answer your phone when I call you, don't get distracted, and don't reveal yourself to anyone for any reason. Understood?"

"Yes, ma'am," I reply.

A smile breaks through her serious expression. "You are going to do great, Emma. I'm so proud of you. You've excelled in the Academy. This is the next step." To Cameron, she says, "Look after her."

Cameron nods, then walks through the gates. I step forward, until I'm level with the exit. This is it. It's happening. I'm not dreaming.

Beyond the Gates

I look down at the ground, at my feet, as they take that final step...and then I'm on the outside. Cameron's smiling at me when I look back up. I'm glad he's the one going with me. He completely understands how big of a deal all of this is to me.

The car is parked on a dirt path that presumably connects to an actual road once making it out of the forest that surrounds the Academy's walls. The car is sleek black and has special tinted windows designed so no one can see in, but also so we can't see out. None of the students, not even those who have long since graduated, know the location of the Academy. The government keeps it that way for our own safety and protection.

I climb into the back. The leather seat is smooth against my hands. I've never actually been in one of these before. The City is big, but it's not big enough to justify giving everyone a car. Everything can be reached within a ten to twenty-minute walk at most.

A screen separates the front seat from the back. The car is self-driving, of course, but a supervisor will be accompanying us to ensure everything goes smoothly. Plus, they're the ones who know how to work the fancy controls.

The car door closes and tiny lights in the sides of the door and floorboards switch on. I swivel in my seat and squint out the back windshield. Despite the tinting, I can just barely make out the steel gates and the buildings in the distance. The car moves forward and we gain speed.

We turn a corner and the Academy vanishes from sight.

...

"Emma, wake up. We're here," a soft voice whispers in my ear. I shift and peel my eyes open. I'm in a car. It all comes rushing back a second later. I'm in a car, on my first Mission, and we're here. I lift my head from Cameron's shoulder and look around.

"What time is it?"

Chapter 5: Emma

"A little after 8:00am," he replies. It took all night to get here. The car comes to a complete stop and the supervisor opens the doors to let us out.

My heart races as I take that step out of the car and into the human world for the very first time. I'm met with bright, early morning sunshine. There's an apartment complex in front of us. My new home for the duration of this Mission. The supervisor brings our luggage up to the front door of a unit on the second floor.

"The code for the apartment has been sent to your phones and your thumb prints have already been set," she explains. Then she pulls two pocketknives and a gun from her bag. I get one of the pocketknives. Cameron gets the other knife and the gun. "These are for emergencies only. Any questions before I leave?"

We shake our heads. If something comes up later that Cameron can't figure out on his own, I'll call the Ambassador.

"Then good luck and expect your first call from the Ambassador tomorrow afternoon."

She leaves and then we're alone.

I take a deep breath. Cameron places his hand on my shoulder. "Are you ready for this?"

I respond by fishing my phone from my pocket and entering the code to unlock the door. Cameron pushes the door open and we step inside.

Right inside is a small living room, complete with couch, recliner chair, and a flat screen TV that's built into the wall. We have television back home, but the channels are highly restrictive. I doubt there will be any limits on this one though. Unless it's already been programmed by the government. That's possible.

The kitchen-dining room area is connected to the living room. Down the hall are two bedrooms and a bathroom. I drag my luggage to the first room.

It's simple. There's a bed, nightstand, dresser, and small closet. All the usual stuff. I set my bags down on the bed and place the pocketknife on the nightstand. I won't be able to take it to school with me, but it still gives me comfort knowing I have *some* kind of weapon.

It's weird that I'm officially on my own now. All responsibilities fall on me and Cameron. It'll take some adjusting, but I can do this. I have to.

Honestly, my stomach churns at the thought of what tomorrow will bring. I'll be at a public school for the first time in my entire life, surrounded by *humans*. I'll have to blend in and attempt to act like every other teenager there, even though I have no idea how human adolescents act. What could possibly go wrong?

I meet Cameron in the living room after setting up my room. I plop beside him on the couch and get comfortable. We're going to be here a while.

"So," he says and angles himself towards me. "Now that we're all settled in, it's probably time we come up with a plan."

CHAPTER SIX
Jesse

The house is quiet, peaceful, when I wake that Monday morning. But just because Greg isn't here now doesn't mean he won't be back later. I was serious when I told Charlotte and Oliver that I won't leave them home alone again.

Of course, that means they have to wake up the same time I do, which they aren't particularly jumping for joy about.

"It's early," Charlotte complains as I shake her awake. She buries her face in the pillow. Oli climbs out of bed, silent as ever. He has an irritated expression on his face, though, but is compliant, nonetheless. I send him to brush his teeth and get dressed while I continue my attempts to get my sister out of bed.

"Charlotte, I'm serious. You need to get up. I can't be late to school and I've got to drop you and Oli off at the library on my way, which takes extra time."

She groans but finally, thankfully, pulls herself out of bed. I rush around, getting them and myself ready for school. We eat a quick breakfast of cereal and then we're out the door.

We walk in silence on the way there, leaving room for a million things to buzz around my mind. I've hit another dead end with my investigation. I thought I was on to something with a lead in my research, only to realize that I was pretty far off. And that's only the tip of my iceberg of problems and things to worry about. There's Greg, the kids, college, the fact that I'll be eighteen in a few months and released from the system.

"I'm sorry," Charlotte says abruptly.

I look down at her with a frown of confusion. "Sorry for what?"

"For making you mad. I shouldn't have taken so long to get up."

Oh, she thinks I'm quiet because I'm upset with her.

"I'm not mad. I didn't mean to yell at you, okay? I'm just really stressed right now and I want to make sure you stay safe."

"I know." Her voice sounds so small. "I can be a bit…stubborn sometimes."

"Sometimes?" I joke.

"Hey!" She smacks my arm, but a grin spreads over her face. "I got it from you, you know. It's a learned trait."

"Please," I fake a scoff. "When am I ever stubborn?"

Oliver looks up at me, eyebrows raised as if to say *You're kidding, right?*

I laugh and open the library door for them. Once they're situated, I say, "Now don't forget about the bus. The librarian will remind you and make sure you get on, okay? I already talked to transportation and they know to pick you up here, so there shouldn't be any problems."

"Jesse, I'm twelve not two. I got this, don't worry."

I don't know how *not* to worry about them.

"Okay, I'll see you later then."

Once outside, I bolt down the sidewalk, desperate to arrive to school on time. The halls are practically deserted when I enter the building, save for a few stragglers and small clusters who stand

Chapter 6: Jesse

around chatting. They look at me weird when I burst through the doors, but I don't have enough in me to care.

I grab what I need from my locker and pass through the door of my first period class right as the bell rings.

I settle in my seat and prepare to block out this next lesson of how great the government is. The teacher begins class, but that doesn't stop the whispers of the newest piece of gossip from traveling around the room.

"Did you hear?" a girl behind me says to the girl next to her. "We're supposed to get a new student today."

"Really?"

"Yeah," a new voice chimes in, this one male. "She's a senior, I think. Just moved here from the Mid-Atlantic Region."

"Mid-Atlantic? Have you seen her?" the first girl asks.

Of course they're curious. Being a small town, we rarely have newcomers, especially ones from a different region.

"No," the boy replies. "I've just heard things. I don't know if she's even here yet. She might be in the office with the principal or something."

Eavesdropping is a handy advantage when no one cares enough to pay attention to you, but I tune out the rest of the conversation. I don't want to hear about yet another student whose eyes will pass right over me unless I'm doing something laughable. I don't care about another person who won't know my name or bother getting to know me.

I don't need friends, though it'd be nice for someone besides my siblings to acknowledge my existence in a positive way every once in a while. But I know better than to get my hopes up.

CHAPTER SEVEN
Emma

The bedroom door smacks against the wall with a bang. My eyes snap open and I jerk upright in bed, alert and ready to take on any problem. I turn towards the door, only to see that my biggest problem is…Cameron.

"Do you have any idea what time it is?" he demands and barges in. He's fully dressed, his hair damp as if he's just gotten out of the shower. How long has he been up?

"No," I reply. "But if my alarm hasn't gone off yet, then it's too early to be awake." It took me forever to get comfortable and fall asleep last night, so I need every minute I can get.

He huffs and marches over, snatching my phone from the nightstand. "Hey!" I protest, until he shoves it in front of my face and I read the time.

School has already started.

I launch out of bed in a panicked haze. I'm dressed, teeth brushed, and hair fixed in record time. It doesn't matter though. It's the first day and I've already messed up. *Why didn't my alarm go off? Or did I sleep through it? I've never overslept. Stupid new room I'm not used to yet.*

Chapter 7: Emma

I stuff my feet into my shoes, throw my backpack over my shoulders, and hurtle towards the front door.

"Wait," Cameron steps in front of me. "You need to eat breakfast." I narrow my eyes. Is he crazy? "You need to eat, Emma. We didn't even have a proper dinner last night, so don't even try to tell me you aren't hungry."

The kitchen has been stocked enough to get us through the week, but we still only snacked around last night. We were too busy with preparations for the Mission. Dinner hadn't really been a priority at the time.

"Does it look like I have time to sit down and eat a meal? I'm already late and anxious enough as it is."

Cameron runs into the kitchen and returns with a granola bar. "At least eat this on your way."

I take it. "Thanks."

He pulls me in for a hug. "Please be careful," he whispers. "Stay as inconspicuous as possible and try to make contact with your target if you can. Just don't do anything that will put you at risk, okay? And call me, if you need *anything* or if something happens."

"I know, Cameron. I promise I'll be careful." I pull the door open. "I'll call you if there's an emergency. But I'm hoping to survive the first day without anything going terribly wrong. See you later."

Fortunately for me, the school isn't too far from the apartment building and being a small town, it's not too difficult to find. At my sprint down the sidewalk, I'm there in less than ten minutes. I wish I could've taken my time and absorbed everything around me, but that'll have to be postponed until later.

I enter the building just as the bell rings and students flood the hallways. First period has apparently just ended, so at least I won't have to enter in the middle of class.

But now I have to deal with swarms of humans in an unfamiliar place. There are too many people, too many ways to go. I need to find the front office.

I struggle through the crowd until I find it across the hall from the front door. I sign in and retrieve my locker information. The lady at the front desk luckily doesn't seem to mind my tardiness given that it's only my first day.

I slip out of the office and stop right outside the door. There are even more students now than there were before. The Academy houses quite a few, but we're rarely ever all contained to one building.

To avoid drawing attention to myself, I keep my head down and try to look like I'm not utterly lost. I eventually find my locker and punch in the four-digit code. A tablet is inside that I'll need for my classes. I grab it, as well as some of the notebooks I stashed in my backpack.

My schedule is displayed on a glass pane on the inside of the locker door. My stomach churns as I read through my day. All the classes revolve around core subjects. Not a single one deals in combat or weapons. Which is to be expected, of course, but it still blows my mind that people are actually fine with sitting at a desk all day and learning boring material.

Once finished, I turn away and speed down the hallway. The halls have thinned considerably in such a short amount of time. I've already pinpointed my second period class from the map on my tablet. All I have to do now is get there.

Or I can just run into somebody.

He turns away from his locker at the exact moment I pass by and we collide. Notebooks and writing utensils spill everywhere, though I manage to hang onto my tablet.

I drop to the floor. The boy does the same.

Chapter 7: Emma

"I am *so* sorry," I apologize. Why, *why*, did this have to happen today of all days? I help him gather the fallen objects. Why can't anything be simple? "I was running and not paying attention and I—"

I glance up at him and our eyes meet. Familiarity hits me like a train. I've seen those empty, haunted eyes before. Only a couple days ago. The only difference from the picture is the bruise that dusts his cheek.

"No," I whisper out loud before I can stop myself. This isn't supposed to happen. Not here. Not now. This isn't how we were supposed to meet. It was supposed to be on *my* terms, not the by-product of a complete accident.

My eyes are glued to his. He stares back, his brows knit together in confusion. I can't stop reeling from what has happened.

Because it's him. It's Jesse Reynolds.

My target.

I tear my gaze from his and bend my head, continuing to pick up my things. I have to play it off. I can't get caught already. It hasn't even been five freaking minutes since I entered the building.

I draw in a calming breath and rein myself back in. I can do this. Focus on the Mission. He reaches for a notebook and I take my shot. My hand brushes his and that's it.

A tugging sensation bursts through my brain as our minds connect and I fall into his future.

I'm in the front seat of a car, straining myself as I turn around to check on a girl with auburn hair who sleeps in the backseat.

Of course it isn't actually me. The readings are strange that way. I'm not a casual bystander. I view and experience everything through the eyes of my subject. We become one in that moment.

I—he—pulls the panel off the back wall of a closet to reveal a corkboard. Just a few more pieces to the puzzle. So close to revenge.

I can't make out anything on the board before the scene changes again. Unfortunately everything that follows is even more vague: a brown door, walking outside in the dark, looking up at the sky filled with billions of stars.

None of it is relevant to me.

I jerk my hand from his and the connection shatters, images fading from my mind. I hastily stand and avoid his questioning gaze. I mumble, "Sorry again for knocking into you. I've gotta go."

I shoulder past him. What a disaster.

According to the map, my class is on the second floor. The door is already closed when I arrive, even though I'm barely even late.

"Okay, Em," I mutter to myself. "You can do this. He's not in this class. Just act normal. Act human. Everything will be okay."

I just need to get through this, settle down, and then figure out my game plan. I close my eyes, take one last breath, and open the door. Every pair of eyes in the room jumps to me. Previously bored expressions morph into curiosity. Some even sit up straighter. Apparently my arrival to the school is too big to overlook.

Fantastic.

"Are you Emma?" the teacher asks. She has short, curly blonde hair and kind blue eyes. I nod mutely. She offers a warm smile. "Nice to meet you. I'm Mrs. Collins." She extends her hand and I shake it. Intense concentration keeps me from being pulled into her future. "You can take a seat anywhere you'd like."

I cross to the very back row of desks and try to ignore the stares that burn into my back. Once I'm seated, Mrs. Collins continues the class. Throughout the period, glances are cast back to me. Unlike the classes at the Academy, kids here are easily distracted. They whisper to one another and doodle in notebooks. Anyone at the Academy who spoke out of turn or who was not solely focused on the lesson was scolded immediately.

Chapter 7: Emma

The subject is English and it's way below me. What these seniors are learning now, I learned back in middle school. This class will be a breeze. I allow my mind to wander to the Mission and my encounter with the target. I need to get it all straightened out so I'm ready when it happens again.

Even though I only got a few seconds in his mind, it was easy to get a sense of how *intense* he is. He has so much hate towards the Academy and I don't understand why. It was shocking, experiencing all the thoughts in his head. I'm used to reading people, having trained with the human volunteers back at the Academy, but their minds were never this jumbled.

The bell rings before I know it, pulling me out of my thoughts.

Students bombard me as soon as we're dismissed. They hurtle questions at me before I can even get out of the room.

You just moved here, right?

I heard you're from the Mid-Atlantic region.

What's it like living in a big city?

Why did you move here?

My mind spins. How am I supposed to answer everyone at once? How has my cover story already spread around to the students?

"Uh, I have to find my next class," I tell the small group. Their curious expressions deflate. Maybe humans are used to this kind of sporadic interaction? I'm supposed to be blending in as one of them, so I add, "Maybe we can talk later?"

Though I hope it won't actually come to that.

I break away from the group and bring up the map on my tablet. A girl walks up beside me.

"Hi, I'm Aria," she says, her voice soft, gentle. But…different. "Sorry about all of them back there. It's not often we get a new student. They're just excited."

I look up from my tablet at the odd sound of her voice. I can't figure out what it is, but I've never heard anything like it.

She has a kind smile on her face, though. She's a few inches shorter than me with long, straight, raven black hair and striking icy blue eyes that are framed by thick black rectangles.

"I'm from the European continent, Southern region to be exact. If you're wondering about the accent."

That explains it. I've heard of people from the other continents talking differently, but I've never met one before. Still doesn't explain whatever the contraption on her face is, but I don't want to be weird in asking. Maybe it's a human thing.

"I'm Emma," I say, because I'm taking too long to come up with some kind of response.

"I know. Everybody's been talking about your arrival since school started this morning."

"Awesome," I mumble.

She laughs. "Welcome to life in a small town. I moved here two years ago and they did the exact same thing. It'll blow over by next week, trust me.

The thought *how am I supposed to trust you? I don't even know you* flits through my mind first, but I stop myself from saying anything. It's just a human expression. At least I'm smart enough to catch myself.

We're more careful with our choice of words at the Academy. We grew up that way, so it's second nature now, but still. We don't make promises we can't keep. We don't spout information that's not true. We don't tell others to trust us on something if they can't.

Aria seems nice enough, though. Maybe I'll pick up a few things from her about being human. She definitely isn't as annoying as the group from before.

"What's your next class?" she asks as we walk down the hall.

Chapter 7: Emma

"Biology," I reply. "In room 112."

Her face lights up. "Really? That's mine, too. I can show you where it is."

I smile back. "Thanks."

Aria chatters the whole way there, but in a friendly and tolerable way. She mostly tells me about herself – she's also a senior, an only child, likes action movies, plays a lot of video games. I'm grateful she doesn't ask about me. While I've studied my back story, reciting it to others feels like delivering off a script.

When we reach the classroom, the teacher introduces himself and says I'll be Aria's lab partner. I sit beside her at the two-person table in the middle row. It's a perfect situation. I can slide through this class without having to introduce myself to someone new.

We take notes for the first half—or rather I pretend to, since I don't actually need them—and apply that knowledge to a short experiment during the second half. Again, it's information I've already learned. Aria's impressed though with how easy it is for me.

"Man, I guess I'm lucky I spent the first few weeks of school without a partner if it means getting you now. You're really good at this."

We're extracting DNA from strawberries. I did something similar back in fifth grade when we were learning about *our* DNA. We had compared ours to that of humans and other organisms, like fruit and animals, so we could see that special strand we as Academy kids possess. It's not too difficult, extracting a DNA sample. Just meticulous.

The class flies by just as quickly as the previous. Lunch is after. I sit with Aria and a few of her friends. They talk and laugh and don't ask too many questions upon meeting me. When the conversation experiences a lull, I make my move.

"So what's up with that Jesse guy?"

Aria's eyes narrow as she tilts her head and peers at me. "Who?"

"Jesse. Tall kid, brown hair, bruise on his face. I ran into him this morning," I explain. "Do you know anything about him?"

Am I pressing too hard? Will they catch on to my suspicions rather than seeing me as just a curious girl?

Aria exchanges a glance with the boy beside her. One of the other girls whispers to the kid beside her. The boy next to Aria says something I can't hear and then Aria's face clears.

"Oh, you mean the foster kid?" she asks and I nod. "No, sorry. I don't really know him at all. He hardly talks to anyone."

How can they not know him? This is a small town. I thought everybody knew everybody. The number of students in this school is smaller than the number in my grade at the Academy, and I know all of them, their names at the very least.

I give up after seeing the looks they shoot me. They probably think I'm crazy for asking about him. They're the crazy ones if they don't know who Jesse Reynolds really is. How can they be so oblivious to the monster who walks the very same halls as them?

Lunch lasts a billion years, but the rest of the day is smooth. All of my classes are below me and the teachers are nice enough. Aria and her friends are okay, too. There's just only so much I can handle in a day.

Dealing with humans is exhausting, I've realized, and I'm more than ready to get out of here when the final bell rings through the halls. I haven't seen Jesse since this morning, but maybe that's a good thing. I don't need to lose it in front of him again. I'm better than that. Hopefully I'll have it more together tomorrow and I can make real progress.

I push my way out of the building and walk back to the apartment.

Chapter 7: Emma

The living room is empty when I enter, and all is quiet. "Cameron?" I call out.

"Emma?" he pokes his head out of his room. Upon seeing me, he bounds down the hall and crushes me in a hug. "You're back. How was it?"

I pull from his embrace and drop down on the couch with a sigh. "It was…interesting."

He settles beside me. "Interesting how? What happened? Were you able to make contact with the target?"

Oh, I made contact with him all right. Literally.

I explain the situation from this morning, as well as being bombarded with questions and how generally overwhelming the human population is.

"Well, you made some progress today. So that's good."

I huff. "Progress? I didn't even get an accurate reading."

"Hey." He grabs my shoulders and turns me to face him properly. He stays silent until I look up at him. "This assignment is going to take time. Just be patient. They wouldn't have given you the Mission if they didn't think you could handle it."

"I know, you're right," I concede. "It's just a lot, with the humans. There's so much I feel like I don't know."

"Like what?"

I think for a second. "Like there's this girl I met. Her name's Aria and she's from the Southern European region. Which explains her accent, but it really threw me off the first time she spoke. She also has this thing on her face, like sort of covering her eyes, but not really because it kind of looks like glass or something."

Cameron bursts out laughing. "Wow, I'm sorry. I just…forget that you didn't spend a whole year learning about the humans."

I put my hands on my hips. "So are you gonna explain it to me, or what?"

"I'm sorry. Sorry." He pulls himself together, then says, "They're called glasses. Sometimes, as humans age, their vision changes. Wearing glasses helps them see at the level they're supposed to."

That makes sense, I guess. No one at the Academy has to rely on such things, because our eyesight has always been perfect.

"So how was your day?"

"Fine," he shrugs. "A little boring. I mostly worked on prepping for all the information I'll be organizing once you collect it. Plus I got permission to contact the girl that's going to be training the new Level One recruits, so I can help her with lesson plans and all that stuff."

"Yeah, I'm sorry again for making you give that up."

He shakes his head. "I *wanted* this Mission, so stop apologizing."

My phone rings before I can say anything else. The Ambassador. I put the phone on speaker and accept the call. "Hello?"

"Good afternoon, Ms. Grant. How was your first day?"

She's going to want a detailed description of everything, so I recount my day, hitting all the important points and some of the smaller moments.

"I tried to ask people about him, but none of them seemed to know anything," I say after relaying my failed attempt at a reading.

"That may be a good thing," the Ambassador comments. "The fewer people who notice him now, the fewer will notice his absence once you eliminate him."

She has a point.

"Try again tomorrow, Emmalyn. Our main goal for now is to get you situated in a new place and to make sure he doesn't figure out who you are. Enjoy the rest of your day. And Cameron, great work with Hana today. With your help, I think she'll do great in

Chapter 7: Emma

training our newer Level Ones. I will speak to both of you tomorrow."

The call ends.

I close my eyes. Breathe in. Breathe out.

I can do this. It's going to be okay.

CHAPTER EIGHT
Jesse

I can't stop thinking about her. The blonde haired, green eyed girl that ran into me. And she didn't just run into me. She *noticed* me. She didn't look at me like I was crazy or laugh at me. She *talked* to me. We had a conversation.

Well, okay. Maybe conversation isn't the most accurate way to describe it. It was basically just her apologizing for bumping into me, but still. She didn't just grab her stuff, give me a dirty look, and stalk off like anyone else in that school would have done.

Is it pathetic of me to be freaking out over a small blip of human interaction? Probably. But that's not going to stop me from replaying the scene over and over in my mind.

School supplies spill everywhere. The girl who ran into me is already on the floor before I can even process what's happened. I bend down to help her.

"I am so sorry," the girl says, hastily sorting our things. Her long blonde hair falls in waves over her shoulder. Her cheeks are tinted pink and she's clearly frazzled, with the way words are tumbling from her mouth. "I was running and not paying attention and I—"

Chapter 7: Emma

She looks up, and our eyes meet. Something flashes across her face, something like...recognition? But that can't be right. She's obviously the new kid everyone's been rambling on about.

Her face pales like she's seen a ghost. Is it because of me? She tears her eyes from mine and returns to picking up the books. I don't know how it happens, but we reach for the same notebook and her hand brushes mine.

Our hands freeze in their positions; I can't pull away. Our eyes connect once again, but this time she's not looking at me. Yeah, her eyes are locked on mine, but they're glazed over. Whatever she's seeing, it's not me. It's almost as if she's staring through *me.*

Seconds later, she jerks her hand from mine. Confusion sweeps across her face, though I don't know why. What does she have to be confused about? Shouldn't I be the one confused in this situation?

She gathers her things and mumbles, "Sorry again for knocking into you. I've gotta go."

And just like that, she's gone.

I tried to shake it off throughout the day, to just forget about the odd encounter, but I couldn't. I still can't, even as I lie on the bed staring up at the ceiling.

There's something about her, some pull. I don't know her, but I think I might want to. She intrigues me, even though she shouldn't. I mean, I don't even know her name!

But she noticed me. She didn't ignore me or write me off. I can't remember the last time that happened. The small, hopeful piece of my heart that still hangs on against all the destruction I've lived through can't help but wonder if maybe, just maybe, I've finally found a friend.

CHAPTER NINE
Emma

The second morning is much smoother than the first. For one, I got a good night's sleep and actually heard my alarm go off. I wake immediately, fresh and alert. Today will be different than yesterday. Today, I will succeed. I'll obtain an accurate reading from my target while remaining undetected. I have an idea of what to expect now and won't be taken by surprise.

What does surprise me is that I'm up and moving before Cameron. He's usually the early riser, but today he's still in his room with the door closed. After quickly getting ready, I make breakfast with the supplies left to us by the Academy. Cooking is a skill I learned in freshman year, but because of the dining hall, I rarely got to use it. I'm in a good mood, so I search the cabinets and pull out the ingredients and utensils to make pancakes. It's risky, but at some point, I have to move on from associating pancakes with death.

Pancakes used to be one of my favorite foods, especially blueberry pancakes. That's why I choose strawberries for the batch I make today.

Cameron enters the room as I pour the batter onto the griddle. I glance at him, unsurprised to find him staring open-mouthed at

Chapter 9: Emma

the stove. He's well aware of my usual aversion to the food. His eyes meet mine, but I know he won't say anything about it.

Instead, he smiles. "Look at you, up and making breakfast. I didn't even have to drag you out of bed."

The tension in my body uncoils. I'll take his teasing banter over the dark turn this conversation could have taken any day.

"I miss my alarm *one* time," I play along. "One mistake and I'm never going to hear the end of it."

The look on his face tells me I'm right.

I hand him a plate of pancakes and we sit at the table. I stare at the stack on my own plate. The crimson juice from the strawberries oozes down the sides like blood. The thought makes my stomach queasy.

"Are you ready for today?" he asks, oblivious to my internal struggle. I concentrate on his question and take a bite. I force it down. My sudden urge to make pancakes is gone now and replaced with regret.

I nod and try to keep a straight face. "I'm doing it today. I'm going to get a perfect reading and find out exactly what he's up to. I can do it."

I might be trying to reassure myself more than him. Just a little bit.

"I know you can," he says gently. "But it might not happen today, and if it doesn't, that's okay. One of the biggest things I've learned is that these things can take time."

"I know," I agree, but I don't want it to take time. I want to prove myself. I want to show that I'm capable of doing what needs to be done. I don't want the Ambassador to regret sending me into this.

I finish eating, somehow managing to not throw it back up, and make to leave.

"Hey," he says as I open the front door. "You'll do great, okay? You've got this."

"Thanks," I smile. "See you later."

...

The halls overflow with students again, but at least I know where I'm going today. A few people wave to me. I vaguely recognize them from yesterday, but I don't remember their names. I haven't seen Aria yet.

I scan the hall on the way to my locker, on the lookout for my target. I do not need a repeat of yesterday. The screen in my locker lists government as my first period, the only class I didn't attend yesterday. I grab my tablet and notebooks.

My target has to be in this first class, right? He's not in any of my others. I walk into the classroom and there he is. He looks up, as if sensing my presence, and our eyes meet. His are still empty. I avert my gaze and stride up to the teacher.

"Can I help you?" he says.

"I'm new," I inform him. "My name's Emma Clarke."

He checks the roster on his tablet. "Right. Okay, Emma. I'm Mr. Jones. Welcome to Willow Creek. I don't assign seats, so just sit wherever.

There are multiple seats still open since class doesn't start for another five minutes. However, the only one I care about is the vacant spot beside my target.

Okay, kid. Remember when approaching a target, stay calm and act natural.

I freeze up. That voice. *His* voice. Why is it in my head? I've worked so hard to eradicate his random words of advice from my mind. I shouldn't have made pancakes this morning.

I shake it off. Now is not the time.

Chapter 9: Emma

I saunter over and slide into the seat without giving Jesse a glance. Instead, I busy myself with preparing my tablet and notebook. If we're going to talk, it'll be on my terms. I'm in control now.

The bell rings and class begins.

"Today we will be starting the projects that will be due by the midterm," Mr. Jones announces. "You will need to partner up for this assignment. Choose partners wisely. Most of the project will take place as homework outside the classroom. The actual assignment is fairly flexible. I want research papers expressing both facts and opinions on the development of our government system and how it has affected society and technology today. You can take this in whatever direction you desire."

The classroom buzzes with chatter when he finishes. Friends find each other from across the room and pair up. When no one claims my target, I turn to him.

"Do you want to be my partner?"

His eyes widen for a split second like he can't believe I'm asking such a thing. But then he composes himself and nods. "Sure."

I flash a fake smile. "I didn't have time to introduce myself yesterday, with the whole running into each other thing. I'm Emma." I hold out my hand and focus all the energy I have.

He pauses but takes my hand. The real world fades away, replaced by the world to come unless I can stop it.

Vague images spiral across my mind at first, similar to what I saw yesterday. I dig around in his mind and future and then I see it. The Academy.

It's dark, nighttime, but he can still see the Academy buildings looming through the pitch black. The dorms, the offices, the training rooms. Further in the distance is the edge of the City.

This is it. This is the part of his future I want.

Beyond the Gates

He crouches down, hidden by the forest. He's right outside the Academy gates, waiting for something to happen. The tangy scent of something strange meets his nose. Something like…like gasoline?

What is he doing?

A loud pop splits the night air. The ground rumbles beneath his feet. And then comes the deafening roar. The force blasts him backwards, sends him flying through the air. He slams into the ground, head knocking against the cold, hard earth. He looks up in time to witness the Academy burst into colors of orange, red, and gray. A feeling of satisfaction and accomplishment surges through him.

I pull from his mind and jerk my hand out of his grip. The room spins around me and my skin feels like it's on fire. The reality of what I've just seen sinks in and fully hits me.

An explosion. *An explosion!*

That's his big plan? Blow up the entire government program? Is he freaking insane? Who does that?

He looks at me, confused. I can only imagine the horror on my face. The reading only took a few seconds, but it felt like so much longer than that.

"You okay?" he asks.

I nod. "I'm fine, just got a little dizzy for a second."

Just shaken by how you plan to destroy my home!

"I'm Jesse, by the way," he says with a smile.

"It's nice to meet you, Jesse," I play along. He's surprisingly polite, which kind of throws me off. How can someone so nice and civil on the outside have obsessive thoughts of destroying an entire government system?

I don't have time to sort through my thoughts right now, though. I'm his partner for this assignment and I have to play my part. We brainstorm for a bit, and I try to pay attention. But my thoughts keep roaming back to what I saw.

Chapter 9: Emma

Once the bell rings and I'm away from him, I let my mind go wild.

First of all—and I really should have been asking this a while ago—but how does he know about the program to begin with? We're a *secret* government program. No one outside the gates knows about us. Why is he the exception?

That brings me to the next thing: why does he want to blow up the Academy? We're trained to do good in the world. We're sent out on assignments to help people, or in my case, stop a crazy person. Is he jealous of our abilities or is he just plain evil?

At least he doesn't know where the Academy is located. That must be what the corkboard from yesterday's reading is for. He's trying to find the Academy.

Good luck to him considering it's a pretty impossible task. *I don't even know where it is, and I live there.*

Even though I know all of this now, I have to continue to act normal around him. If I do that, maybe he'll start to see me as a friend. Maybe he'll start to trust me with the things in his life. I'll reel him in, get the information I need, and pass it along to the Ambassador.

And then I'll destroy him.

...

Cameron's waiting for me when I get home. As soon as he sees my solemn expression, he rises from the couch. "It's okay. I know you're super determined, but it's going to take time. I—"

"Cameron," I interrupt, because he's got it all wrong. "I did it. I got an actual reading from him."

He blinks. "Oh, that's great, Emma! Sorry, you just seemed upset."

"It's what I saw." I draw in a shaky breath. "He's going to blow up the Academy, Cam. I watched the whole thing go up in flames. He's gonna destroy our home…our family."

"Why didn't you call me?" he demands.

"What?"

"You promised you would call if there was an emergency. That seems like a pretty big emergency to me."

Is he serious right now?

"I couldn't call you about that at school. Someone could've overheard me. And I couldn't just skip the rest of the day. People would notice. Besides, it's not like he was planning to do it during second period. He doesn't even know where the Academy is yet."

"Okay, I get it," Cameron grumbles. "It's just, I'm supposed to be looking out for you."

"And *I* get *that*. But this is *my* Mission, Cameron. You've gotta let me handle some of this stuff on my own and trust that I'm doing what I think is right. And in my mind, waiting until school was over to tell you seemed like the best option."

"Okay, okay," Cameron concedes. We walk over to the couch and sit. "Let's just go over what you saw. What happened exactly? Are you sure what you saw was accurate? Maybe you weren't concentrating hard enough and it got jumbled up with other stuff."

He's grasping at straws. I know what I saw.

"I was prepared this time," I explain. "I knew what I was doing going in. I focused on the government, on the Academy, and that's what had the strongest pull. It's real, Cameron, unless I can stop it."

And suddenly the weight of what I saw in my target's mind crashes into me.

"How am I supposed to do this?" I whisper. My chest tightens. "I don't even know how he's going to do it. I mean, he's seventeen. How is he even going to get the materials he would need to cause

Chapter 9: Emma

an explosion? Is this what the Ambassador wants me to do? Does she want me to stop a psychotic teenage murderer from hurting everyone at the Academy? *Me?* I can barely interact with an average human being. I have no idea what I'm doing!"

"Hey, come here." He opens his arms and I move into him. He hugs me tight. "It'll be okay. You're not alone. That's what I was trying to tell you earlier, but it didn't exactly come out right." I laugh a little. "The point is, you have me. And you have the Ambassador. She isn't going to leave you to fend for yourself. We won't let him hurt anyone."

"Okay," I mumble into his shirt. "Okay."

While we wait for the Ambassador to call, I flip through TV channels, just for something to do. I was right when I suspected that the Academy had programmed our TV. We still only have the few channels we had while inside the gates. It doesn't bother me, though. It's what I'm used to. I can't miss something I've never had, and there must be a good reason why we aren't allowed to view other things.

Cameron slings his arm over my shoulders. I settle in and try to focus on the TV, but my mind is too loud. It's a relief when the phone finally rings.

"Good evening," the Ambassador greets. "How was your second day?"

"I achieved the piece of the target's future you wanted."

"Excellent. Continue."

I recite everything I'd seen in the vision and all I had pieced together afterward. Cameron explains how he'll start compiling the information I'd gotten and start doing as much research as he can on the target.

"You did great today," she compliments. She doesn't seem at all worried about the news I delivered. "Now that that's out of the way, I need you to figure out his specific plan and how he expects to carry it out. You'll need to get close to him, develop a trust. Make him think you are his friend. I'll need updates on his progress in finding our location and the extent of his knowledge on the program."

"Yes, ma'am," I promise and then ask, "What should I do about what I saw? Shouldn't we figure out a way to prevent it from happening? It verifies he's a threat to us, right?"

"We'll handle it, Emma. Your only concern for now is getting more information out of him."

I press on. "But why don't we just kill him now if he's so dangerous? I just want to make sure everyone in the Academy is safe."

"I understand," she says, her voice strained. "There are several reasons as to why we are waiting and why we want additional information. Most are classified, but a big one is security. If you can find out how he plans to attack the Academy, we can strengthen our security accordingly and ensure there will be no attacks in the future."

That makes sense, I guess. But I still hate waiting and taking that risk.

"Keep in mind," she continues, "that while today was a major accomplishment, we still only know his endgame. We need to know how he plans on getting there if you really do want to keep the Academy safe. This is only the beginning of a much longer process."

"Don't worry," I assure her. "I can handle it."

And I can. Gone are my worries from earlier. There's only determination flowing through my veins now. I will finish this assignment. No matter what, I will find a way to save my home.

A plan forms in my mind within minutes of ending the call. The readings supplied me with the basic information. Now I need details and there's only one way to get them.

Chapter 9: Emma

I stand from the couch, startling Cameron with my abrupt action.

"What're you doing?" he asks.

"Come on, we're going on a field trip."

...

"This is insane," Cameron whispers beside me. "You've actually gone insane."

"Please," I scoff. "Like you haven't done crazy things on a Mission."

"Well I usually put more planning into it than this," he hisses.

"Yeah, well we're doing it my way this time. Now shut up before someone hears you."

"Yeah, because just seeing two weirdos trying to hide in a bush isn't enough."

I shush him again as the front door to the house across the street opens. Out comes Jesse and his two foster siblings.

Yes, Cameron and I are hiding in the shrubbery across the street from Jesse's house. Yes, it's uncomfortable. But it'll be worth it if my plan works.

They always leave the house around this time. I saw it in his mind. Who knows where they go every day, but hopefully they'll be gone long enough. They walk down the street and vanish from view.

"Okay, stay here while I go inside. I'll call you when I get in and if you see them coming back, tell me."

Cameron shakes his head. "This is a terrible idea. By the time I see him, you won't have time to get out before he sees *you*."

"Then I'll go out the back door," I say and bolt across the street. After I had devised my plan, I'd called the Ambassador back and she gave me the four-digit code to Jesse's house and disabled the finger scanner for the next hour. I type in the code and push the door open.

The first thing I notice is how small and cramped it is. How do four people comfortably live here?

I explore the whole house. The living room is simple. The kitchen is, too, though a lot messier. Dirty dishes and empty bottles litter the sink and counter. The room that I assume to be their guardian's is also a mess. Bed unmade, rumpled clothes all over the floor. There's one door that won't open. It's locked and requires a physical key, but that's not important right now.

I get to the other bedroom last. It's also small, but definitely more organized than the other rooms.

My phone buzzes in my pocket. I quickly pull it out and answer.

"What happened to calling me as soon as you got inside?" Cameron's irritated voice comes through the speaker.

"Sorry. I'm just trying to take everything in."

"Well hurry up. You've been in there forever."

"Wow, a whole five minutes," I reply jokingly. "Calm down. I doubt he left for just a few minutes. We've got time."

"I don't like this," Cameron mutters. I walk to the closet and pull the back panel off the wall like I'd seen in his mind. And there's the corkboard.

"You just don't like that you have to keep watch. Sorry you don't get to do the more exciting stuff on this Mission."

"Will you quit messing with me and get what you need so we can get out of here."

I force the corkboard off the wall and ease it onto the bed. "Okay, jeez. Just trying to lighten the mood. No need to get all worried."

I focus my attention on the board. It's covered in little notes, strings, and tacks. Most of it doesn't make much sense. The notes are written in a shorthand, something unique to him and

Chapter 9: Emma

indecipherable to others. There's no key for the meaning behind the different colored strings and tacks. The only thing that I slightly understand is the news clippings and their headlines, though I don't know what they have to do with the Academy.

Gas fire kills family of three.
Infant disappears from local hospital.
Research lab shut down by government.

There are several tacked around the board, but none have to do with the Academy, which doesn't make sense if the board is him trying to find it.

All in all, the board I came here for is pretty useless. So maybe it wasn't the best plan, but at least I had *something* more than before I came in. I use my phone to take pictures of the board before returning it to the closet. Maybe I'll be able to make more sense of it later when I'm not so pressed for time.

"Come on, Emma." Cameron's voice is tense, impatient.

"I'm coming."

Since the coast is clear, I exit through the front door and meet back up with Cameron. We slip off down the road without anyone noticing a thing.

CHAPTER TEN
Jesse

Emma sits next to me in first period again, even though we aren't working on our projects today. She doesn't speak to me at first, but rather busies herself with her tablet. Then, she randomly turns to me.

"Good morning," she says with a smile. It's pretty much how she's been interacting with me all week. Maybe she just needs time to settle in each day before speaking to anyone.

"Morning," I reply. She seems less tense today. Relaxed even. Maybe she's getting more acclimated to the new school. At least she still wants to talk to me. She hasn't shut me out yet or started ignoring me like everyone else. Maybe she'll be different after all.

The teacher starts class shortly after our brief exchange. She goes back to her tablet and I focus on mine. We don't speak again after until the bell rings.

I don't know why I do it. I'm not the kind of person to put myself out there, but before she can leave the classroom and disappear into the sea of students, I stop her.

"Do you, maybe…want to, um, sit together at lunch?"

Chapter 10: Jesse

A slight smile plays at the corners of her lips. "I already told Aria and her friends I'd sit with them, but you can join us if you want. I don't think they'll mind."

I haven't been asked to sit with a group of people since I was eight years old, when I was first transferred to Willow Creek and put into the foster care system. I wasn't exactly looking to make friends as a scared and angry kid whose entire family had just been killed. People quickly learned to stay away from me and I liked it better that way.

But now, getting that offer again, I'm tempted to say yes. Instead, I say, "Okay, cool. I might do that then."

And then I leave, knowing full well that I won't be sitting with them. One friend, I think I can handle. A whole table of people, most of which I've gone to school with since I moved, will never work out in my favor.

The rest of the morning passes smoothly, and I put the conversation out of my mind. It's not until I'm walking to the cafeteria for lunch that I notice the change. Whispers float through the hall, furtive glances are cast in my direction. *My* direction. Hardly anyone ever pays attention to me, so what's going on?

Even stranger, I pass two girls at their lockers. They whisper to each other, but abruptly stop as I walk by them. Something is definitely up. But why now? Why is today any different than yesterday? Or the hundreds of days before that?

I shake it off and continue to the cafeteria. Maybe I'm just being paranoid. I get my lunch and sit at my usual table off to the side of the room. I scan the cafeteria and quickly find Emma. Sure enough, she's sitting with Aria and a table full of their friends. They talk and laugh as they eat their lunch. It's a weird experience, watching them from afar.

Beyond the Gates

Sometimes I wish I could be that carefree and easy going. To just laugh with a group of friends and not worry about anything but homework and school drama.

I focus in on Emma. She seems…different from the others. I can't place my finger on it, but it's almost like she's thinking about each move she makes before she makes it. So maybe she's less like them that it would appear. Maybe she feels more like me. An outcast, someone who doesn't quite belong, but she's trying hard to.

I tear my gaze from her and glance around the room. I don't usually pay attention to whatever else is going on. I come in, eat by myself, then go to my next class. But today, I can't help but notice the unusual buzz. The energy. It's like everyone else knows something I don't. I've always blended into the background, which can get lonely sometimes, but I'm fine with that. I don't need anyone else. But today it feels like *everyone* notices me. When people walk past my table to get their food, their eyes don't skip over me. They *see* me.

And I hate it.

While I want to be friends with Emma, I definitely don't want to be the school's center of attention. That's the exact opposite of what I want.

Two girls sit at the table next to mine, though they at least seem to not have noticed me since my back is to them. They whisper to each other and this time I'm close enough to pick it up.

"Do you know what's going on?" one asks. "Everyone's acting weird."

"You haven't heard?" the other says. "It got out that the new girl, Emma, has been asking about Jesse Reynolds."

I freeze. *What?*

Without drawing their attention, I lean closer to hear them better.

Chapter 10: Jesse

"Wait, the foster kid? Why would she be asking about him?"

"I don't know. Maybe she's just curious."

Yeah, I don't believe in 'just curious.' As I listen, I stare at the table across the room where Emma and her friends are sitting. Are they talking about me right now?

"But why would someone like her care to know anything about someone like him? I mean, he barely ever talks to anyone and has kind of isolated himself since he got here back in elementary school."

"How should I know?"

I tune them out after that. I don't need to hear anymore.

Emma is what changed. She's the reason all of this is happening. Why, *why*, is she asking people about me? We sit next to each other in first period. She can just talk to me herself. Unless...

No. Maybe she really is just curious. She did just move here, after all, and we've interacted more in the past few days than I had with everyone else in the last several years. Yet she had to have noticed that I'm always by myself. So it's probably just innocent curiosity.

I'm about to turn my focus back to my lunch and stop worrying about the girl across the room, but something stops me. I'm too far away to hear their conversation, but that's not important. It's the way she sits there and interacts with them that catches my eye. It's not exactly discomfort or fear of rejection like I suspected before. No, there's something else there.

From the angle I'm at, I can see her face as she talks with the group. There's a fake smile plastered on. I know that smile. It's the one I wear when I tell my siblings that everything is okay, that *I'm* okay. Whatever they're talking about, it's not just a casual conversation to her. There's more to it and I can't figure out what.

Beyond the Gates

I'm probably being paranoid again, but I know what I saw. That realization fills me with dread. Something is off and I need to find out what.

CHAPTER ELEVEN
Emma

I don't make much progress over the next couple of days. I try touching my target again, but it never works. I either never make contact, or he moves away before I get the chance to see anything. It's frustrating, failing over and over again, but my spirits haven't been completely shattered. As Cameron said, these things take time. If I can be patient, it'll pay off eventually.

The payoff comes on Monday morning, a week after we moved to Willow Creek. I'm at my locker when Aria walks up to me.

Without so much as a good morning or introduction, she says, "Hey, so I did some research on your boy over the weekend."

My stomach drops. "Excuse me?"

My *what?*

She blinks, her face blank. "Jesse Reynolds. You wanted to know about him, right?"

"Oh, yeah," I say hastily. "Right. So what did you find?"

I shut my locker and we walk down the hall together. Aria spills everything she learned.

"He rarely ever talks to anyone, which is why no one here knows that much about him, but anyway, his parents and older brother died in an accident almost ten years ago. It was some kind of gas fire from a malfunction in their house. I couldn't find anything specific though. All the records on it are super vague. But I did find records for all the foster homes he's been in since then."

I already know about the accident, so that's not much help. But my ears perk up at the mention of his foster care records.

"He bounced around for a while after the accident. He was in and out of different homes every few months. I think the longest he stayed in one place, before being put where he is now, was a little over six months. From the notes I could find, the foster parents often commented that he was emotionally unstable and prone to outbursts. He never stayed long because the parents couldn't handle him. He eventually ended up in his current placement and he's been there for almost six years."

Then she proceeds to reach into her backpack and pull out a folder full of papers, all the records she could find.

Her information is beyond what I could have hoped for. It doesn't necessarily help me figure out how he plans to set a secure government facility on fire, but it'll definitely help me better understand his background and personality.

"Thank you, Aria."

"Why did you want to know about him anyway?" she asks, which I guess is justified. I think fast.

"Um, well we ran into each other on my first day and he just seemed a little odd." It's an awful explanation, but it's not like I can tell her the truth. "I didn't expect you to do all this research though. Seriously, how did you get all that information? Is it public?"

She hesitates. "If you're asking if I looked him up on your everyday search engine…not exactly. The vague story about the accident, yes. The specific stuff and the records…it's sort of my specialty to get around certain…blockers that prevent the average person

Chapter 11: Emma

from viewing private records. So I got around those blockers to get into the foster care system."

Wow. Who *is* this girl? Is it normal for humans to be able to do this kind of stuff? Is it normal for them to go this much out of their way for something as simple as curiosity about another person? Or maybe that's just her. Either way, I'll have to keep it in mind. Her skills may come in handy later if I ever need additional information.

Aria and I part ways when we reach her class. Mine is the next hall over. Other students greet me as I walk by. After being here a while, I'm finally putting names to faces. Simply saying hi or good morning back isn't really that different from the Academy. I'm finally getting the hang of blending in. I'm not perfect at it, but at least no one's called me out for acting differently.

When I get to the room, I sit beside Jesse as usual. We exchange good mornings, I pretend like I'm not scrutinizing his every move, and I try to find a way to touch him, but fail yet again.

The day passes pretty uneventfully, other than Aria's information. I relay that information to Cameron as soon as I get home and we spend the next few hours pouring over Jesse's foster care records. Most of the comments are negative.

He's a good kid, just too closed off and tends to blow up when upset.

Jesse is unpleasant at best, violent at worst. The smallest things will set him off.

Compulsive liar and manipulator. Told CPS that we were abusive, which was untrue.

Prone to outbursts.

Violent.

Manipulative.

The list goes on. Everything past foster families have said about him. Repeated over and over through all the homes he's been through.

"Dang this kid's had it rough," Cameron mutters as he drops another paper into the stack of ones we've read.

I look up from the one I'm currently reading through. "Does it matter? He's not exactly a good person."

"I know," Cameron says. "But just imagine it. Being eight years old and losing your parents. You have nowhere to go and everyone that takes you in ends up sending you away."

I scoff. "Yeah and imagine being five years old and asking where and who your mom is and then being told that she abandoned you at birth because you were different. Oh wait, that's us."

"Point taken," Cameron says. "I'm not saying the bad things that have happened to him excuse what he's planning to do. I'm just saying I get how hard his life must be. Sometimes you have to do that on Missions. Delve deep enough into who they are and how they think and why they think what they think. If you understand your target, you can beat them."

Later, after we finish sifting through the records and talking with the Ambassador, Cameron suggests a round of sparring.

"Come on, we haven't trained at all since we've been here."

"We don't have any training mats, though," I point out.

He pushes his bottom lip into a pout. "Aww, do you need a safety mat so you don't get hurt?"

I smack his arm. "No, but you do unless you're cool with getting knocked out without any protection to break your fall."

He grins and backs into the living room. "Has anyone ever told you you're overly confident when it comes to training?"

I follow him. "Yes. You do. All the time."

He laughs, then lunges at me, as if he can actually take me by surprise. I dodge, catch his arm and twist it behind his back.

Chapter 11: Emma

He yelps, but I know better than to ease up. We haven't fought in a while due to his busy schedule as a Level One, but we used to all the time when we were younger.

Cameron kicks his foot into my shin. I stumble, lose my balance, and release him. He barrels into me, slams me into the wall. I push back and we continue like that for a while. I let my body take over. I stop thinking about the moves I'm making. For me, fighting is as simple as breathing, and it feels good to be doing it again after so long without it.

Eventually, I have enough of playing around with each other. I sweep his feet out from under him and knock him to the floor.

"I win," I say with a smug grin.

He groans in response.

I help him up. "See? I told you we needed a safety mat."

CHAPTER TWELVE
Jesse

I can no longer deny that something is up with Emma. With running into me that first day, noticing me, talking to me, offering to be my project partner, asking other people about me, it doesn't feel right.

I wanted to believe that it had, but when I think about it, when I'm *really* honest with myself, it doesn't. I just can't figure out exactly why and that's more irritating than anything.

So here I am, lying on my bed again, thinking about the same girl as I have so many other times. I replay our interactions and what I've seen of her when she isn't with me.

Sure, she appears nice enough, but out of everyone in that school, why me? Why ask about me? Why pick me to talk to?

And then there are the things that don't quite add up.

For one, she showed up out of the blue. She did just move here, but news of a new student usually circulates the school days in advance, not the morning of.

There's also the way she acts around me. She was flustered when we first met, which is understandable given it was her first day and she'd just crashed into me, but there had also seemed to be some

Chapter 12: Jesse

sort of control behind her actions. I've noticed it more and more over the past week, too. When she talks to me. When she talks to other people.

We've also touched twice, which is a whole issue by itself. After both times we made physical contact, she seemed a little out of it, a little tired, her eyes not as bright as before. And now that I think about it, her eyes glazed over when we touched, too. Kind of like…

"No," I jerk into a sitting position. Blood rushes to my head from the sudden movement, making my vision fuzzy around the edges.

No, no, no, no, no.

No!

She can't be one of them. It's not possible.

But our interactions keep flooding my mind.

Maybe running into me *had* been a mistake, but everything after that wasn't. The recognition in her eyes the first time she saw me. The way our hands met as we reached for the same notebook. The look on her face after we shook hands. The way she acted around other people, like she's not used to interacting that way. How she was asking people about me.

The way her eyes glassed over like Academy kids who are using their mind-abilities.

Emma is from the Academy.

As soon as that thought passes through my mind, it all clicks into place. Of course she is. That's the only reason she noticed me at all, why she seems so curious about me. It's not because someone actually wants to be my friend. No, it's because it's her job to focus in on me.

I should have realized it sooner.

God, I'm so stupid. Blinded by how much I wanted us to be friends.

She isn't even the first one I've seen in person, either. They pass through every now and then. There's a certain way they hold themselves, speak, interact with us lowly humans. They're superior to us and are well aware of it.

But she's different. None of the others had shown up and enrolled in school. So why is she here?

I mean, obviously she's here for me, or she wouldn't have spared me a second glance. And if I'm being completely honest with myself, she's probably here to kill me. I won't be all that shocked to discover that that's her true motive. I've always known in the back of my mind that they'd come for me one day. Just like they came for my family.

Maybe her being here means I'm getting close to pinpointing the Academy's location. With all their fancy technology, I've probably been on their radar for a while, yet they only just now decided to intervene.

But what if I'm wrong?

I shake my head. No, the look in her eyes definitely proves it. She's not human.

Did she use her ability on me the day we met or when we shook hands at the start our first class together? For the few seconds we touched, it was like she wasn't mentally *there*. According to the research I've done, some of their abilities stem from the mind and often require extreme concentration. But what is hers specifically?

Mind control? Is she physically doing something to my internal body structure? Maybe she's slowly killing me from the inside out and each time she touches me, she pulls me closer and closer to death.

Or maybe I'm being too dramatic. But something is definitely going on with her and this is the only conclusion that makes sense.

Chapter 12: Jesse

I'll have to pay extra close attention from here on out. I wonder if I can use her to find out information on the government.

God, this was so not what I needed in my life right now.

I sigh heavily and slide off the bed. I get the corkboard out and sit it on the floor. I grab a stack of notecards from my dresser drawer and hastily scribble out all my thoughts before I forget anything important.

I pin the card to the board just as Charlotte walks in. She stops cold upon the sight before her.

"What happened?" Her voice is unusually tense.

"What do you mean?" I ask without looking up.

She ventures farther into the room and drops her backpack by the foot of the bed. "I mean, you never leave the corkboard out. I've only ever seen it once and that was by accident. Something must have happened for all of *this* to happen."

She's more perceptive than I often give her credit for.

"Yeah, something happened."

Something that could put both her and Oliver in danger if I'm not careful.

Charlotte lowers herself to the floor beside me. "Are you going to share, or do you still not trust me?"

She attempts a teasing tone, but it doesn't completely mask the bitterness underneath.

"I *do* trust you, Char, but I'm also supposed to protect you."

"I don't need protection," she argues. "I'm the same age you were when you started all of this."

I stare at her. "And how do you know how old I was?"

She shrugs. "Almost everything on there is dated. It's one of the only things that actually made sense that one time I saw it. The earliest date I could find was five years ago."

I lean my head back against the dresser and gaze at her. She stares back eagerly, fully aware of the cracks in my defenses. I don't want to drag her into my mess of problems, but she also needs to be prepared, just in case. Especially if the girl really is what I think she is.

I shift into a more comfortable position. "Remember this conversation the next time you try to tell me you aren't as stubborn as me."

She rolls her eyes.

I sigh. "I guess it's time I tell you what all of this means, starting with an evil and corrupt place known as the Academy."

CHAPTER THIRTEEN
Emma

"When do you want to meet to start working on our project?" my target asks the next morning toward the end of first period. His voice is tense, eyes calculating. It's a different expression than the one I've gotten used to. Maybe he ran into a problem with trying to find the Academy, or he's just generally in a bad mood.

"How about tomorrow?" I suggest. "I can't today. I have something after school, but I'm free the rest of the week."

He raises an eyebrow. "What do you have going on?"

Why do you ask so many questions? I want to respond.

I shrug. "Just hanging out with a friend."

Which isn't a lie. Aria can be an extremely persuasive person and she talked me into hanging out after school so she could show me around. I didn't want to decline either, since she helped me out in getting information on Jesse.

"Oh, okay." He looks at me for a few seconds longer. Maybe I'm imagining it, but it seems like his eyes narrow just a fraction, like he knows something's different about me. Is he catching on?

I force that thought out immediately. There's no way he knows who I am.

The bell rings and I hastily stand. "Well, see you tomorrow."

Hopefully working on the project together will allow me to finally make more progress. It's getting increasingly difficult to get any information out of him while we're at school.

Aria finds me in the hall. She runs up and crushes me in a hug. I stiffen at first, but then relax. I've learned to roll with her hyper and excited personality, but it still catches me by surprise sometimes.

"I'm excited for later. Seriously, I don't have many friends that I'm close with, so I'm glad I have you."

Her smile spreads across her whole face. I can't help but smile back. It's infectious. She's not too bad for a human. It's actually kind of nice to have someone I can spend time with that isn't directly involved in my Mission.

"Me, too. Do you mind if my brother comes along? He hasn't seen much of the town yet either."

"Sure." Aria's face lights up even more, if that's even possible. "I didn't know you had a brother."

"Yeah, he's nineteen, so he already graduated high school."

"Cool, well I can't wait to meet him."

We walk to our next class, letting the conversation roam. Now I just have to convince Cameron to come with us.

. . .

"No," he says as soon as the words leave my mouth. "I'm not hanging out with some stranger. Plus, we don't have time for silly human stuff. We're supposed to stay focused, remember?"

We're standing in the living room, staring each other down. I place my hands on my hips. "She's not a stranger. She's my friend. And I am focused on the Mission. Part of that is blending in. Besides, I think it'll really benefit you to get out of the house for a

Chapter 13: Emma

while. You've barely left since we've been here…and I kind of already told her you were coming."

His face pales. "You *what?*"

"Sorry," I say with a shrug. "So will you come?"

He sighs dramatically. "Fine. It's not like you're giving me much of a choice."

"Awesome," I grin. "We're leaving in ten minutes."

"Of course we are," he grumbles. "You so owe me for this."

"Love you, too." I race down the hallway to my bedroom to drop my backpack off.

Aria shows up at the apartment right on time.

"Hi," she beams when I open the door. Cameron's a few steps behind me, lurking like a weirdo.

"Hey, this is my brother Cameron. Cameron, this is my new friend Aria."

"Hey," Cameron says. I peer back at him as we leave. His muscles are taunt, his face blank.

I slow down to put a bit of distance between Aria and us. To Cameron, I whisper, "Calm down. She's not going to attack you. Jeez, it's like you've never been around humans before."

"I am calm," he mumbles back defensively. "They just make me uncomfortable. Yeah, I've dealt with them before, but not in the capacity you have. I didn't go to school with them or anything. But don't worry, I got this."

I roll my eyes. "Mhmm, I'm sure you do."

He playfully shoves me. I laugh and catch back up with Aria.

"What was that all about?" she wonders.

I shrug nonchalantly. "Just a sibling thing."

"Huh. I'm an only kid. Kind of wish I had a sibling, though."

"No you don't," Cameron chimes in. "Siblings, especially younger ones, are the worst."

"Hey, excuse you." I punch him in the shoulder and glare.

"You know I love you," he grins.

Pretending to be his sister really isn't that bad. We just act the way we always do when we're around each other.

Aria shows us around the town: the stores and shops, the movie theater, the library, and everything in between.

Around dinner time, she takes us to a diner. We sit in a booth, Aria and I on one side and Cameron on the other. By this time, Cameron's settled down and gotten a lot more comfortable around her.

We order our food, and then Aria asks, "So how's the thing with Jesse going?"

Cameron's eyes widen and he shoots me a frantic, yet scathing look that clearly says *you told her?!*

I ignore him.

"What thing?"

"Well, you were asking about him and everything. I thought maybe you liked him or something."

She went through all that trouble to dig up information on my target because she thought I *liked* him? I wonder what she would have done if I said it was a much more serious matter than that.

By some miracle, Aria isn't looking at Cameron, whose facial expressions somehow get even more dramatic. His eyes are bulging. His face is flushed.

But then he blurts out, "Wait, you didn't tell me that *she's* the hacker girl."

Smooth, Cameron. Smooth.

I kick him as Aria hisses, "Can you please not shout that out for everyone to hear? Thanks."

"Sorry," he replies sheepishly. It's weird. I've never seen him like this before.

Chapter 13: Emma

Aria sighs. "Look, I know what I did was wrong, especially for something so unimportant, but I'm good at it. It's quick and easy to me now. And...I haven't been able to do it in a while. I kind of...missed it, as crazy as that sounds."

She shifts in her seat, fidgeting with her hands.

"You don't have to explain if you don't want to," I say. It's not like I'm going to tell on her. She keeps talking though. She's so much more direct than the other humans I've interacted with so far.

"You know how I moved here a while back? Well, my dad got into a bit of trouble where we used to live, so we left the European continent and moved here. Dad cleared some stuff off our records and everything, so we couldn't be traced. He taught me everything I know about all this. It's really not that difficult to get access to stuff if you know what you're doing, especially with how virtual everything is."

I resist the urge to ask what kind of trouble her and her dad got into in the past. She's already helped us out a lot and I don't want to upset her by prying into it.

"Anyway, I *don't* like him like that," I clarify. "I was just curious about him, that's all. And no one seemed to know anything, which only intrigued me more."

"Oh, okay."

She doesn't seem convinced. Though I guess it's better for her to assume that I like him rather than knowing the truth.

We finish dinner and walk back to the apartment. Aria apparently doesn't live too far from us. Cameron goes inside while I stay behind to say goodbye to Aria.

"Thanks for this," I say. "It was a lot of fun and it was nice to finally explore a little bit."

"No problem," Aria smiles. "Like I said, it was rough for me when I moved here. I didn't want it to be the same way for you."

It's strange how a human like her can be so kind and thoughtful, while someone like my target is so evil and destructive.

"It was fun hanging out with your brother, too. He's kinda cute," she says with a grin.

"Aria!"

She grins and gives a little shrug. "What?"

I shake my head, failing to suppress a smile. "Well, I'll see you tomorrow."

She leaves and I go inside. Cameron's waiting for me.

"So? Was I convincing enough? What'd she think?"

I bite my lip and try to keep a straight face. "She thinks you're cute."

He blinks, stunned. "Okay, well not exactly what I was going for. But I guess as long as she doesn't think I'm an evolved human from a government program, I'll take it. And I guess you were right. I did need to get out for a little bit, and getting some more experience with humans was good, too. It's been a while since I've had a Mission that dealt with them directly."

"Well, *bro*, as fun as this outing was, we should probably get back to work."

"Yeah," he agrees. "The Ambassador should be calling soon, but we can go over some of these notes I've put together."

He shows me on his tablet.

Even though things aren't moving as fast as I sometimes want them to be, we *are* making progress. I finally feel like I'm getting the hang of this whole Mission thing.

CHAPTER FOURTEEN
Jesse

After my discovery, I watch Emma even closer than before. With the knowledge I now have, it's even more obvious where she comes from. She's a good actor, I'll give her that. If you don't know about the Academy, you won't notice anything different in the way she acts. But now that I do know, it's impossible *not* to pick up on the differences.

How she holds herself, like she's better than us. How she waits just a little longer than normal before speaking, like she's thinking through what she needs to say. How she looks at me from across a room or hall, like she's tracking and analyzing my every move.

I'm clearly in danger with her here, but if I pretend to be friends with her—without her knowing that *I* know what she is—maybe I can get information out of her about the Academy.

I sit at my desk in the only class we share as I think this over. She's not here yet, but she'll sit next to me just like she has since that first day. If she thinks working on a school project together will be enough to hinder my plans and keep me from getting the revenge I deserve, she's sorely mistaken.

When she arrives, she slides into her usual seat and we exchange greetings like always. We don't speak after that. The teacher lectures during the entire period, and I block it all out.

When the bell rings, Emma shoots out of her seat and leaves. I bolt into the hall and catch her before I lose her in the crowd. My hand coils around her wrist as I stop her.

She spins around, ripping her hand from my grasp. She glares for a split second, a wild look in her eyes, but she quickly masks it with soft kindness.

"Hey, Jesse. What's up?" Her tone is so casual. From a distance, it's hard to believe this is the same girl who probably plans on killing me somehow.

I deliver the perfect excuse to spend time with her to see how much she knows. "Are you able to meet after school today so we can get started on the project?"

She smiles. "Sure."

"Great," I say with fake enthusiasm. "I'll meet you on the front steps right after school and we can head to the library. I have to be home by 3:30 though, so we'll have about an hour."

She blinks, as if surprised. "Oh, do you have a job or something?"

Like she doesn't already know. Getting a job would be fantastic. It would mean extra money. But it would also require me to leave Charlotte and Oliver home alone, and that's out of the question.

"No, that's when my younger siblings get home from school."

"Oh, okay. That's fine. See you after school."

We part ways and she's engulfed by her friends. Everyone seems to love her. If only they knew the truth.

I walk to my next class. Our conversation went better than expected. I wasn't sure how she'd react to the library thing, but I'm

Chapter 14: Jesse

definitely not taking her to my house and I'm not stupid enough to go to hers. The library provides a safe, public environment and also keeps her away from Charlotte and Oliver.

The rest of the day passes by in a blur and is blissfully normal. Despite being on her radar and the whole school knowing about it, I've pretty much gone back to being invisible, which is definitely a relief.

Before I know it, the last bell rings and it's time to meet with the monster. I push the front doors open and walk out. She's at the bottom of the steps, leaning against one of the pillars that holds up the awning. Her head is bent over her phone, fingers tapping away and blonde hair shimmering in the bright afternoon sunlight. She glances up and smiles when she sees me.

And it doesn't exactly look fake. I force myself to return it and descend the steps. My smile probably isn't as convincing as hers, but hers isn't genuine either. I have to remind myself of that. She's here to destroy me, not become best friends. Her smile is anything but real.

It's all part of the game.

CHAPTER FIFTEEN
Emma

We walk side by side in silence, the scrape of our shoes against the sidewalk and the rustle of the breeze the only sounds. The lack of talking enables me to survey the town. I recognize most of the places, since Aria so enthusiastically pointed out just about everything.

It's really not all that different from the City within the gates of the Academy. The Academy's City is just more advanced and hi-tech than the town here.

How is it that not even two weeks ago, I was still at the Academy? It feels like another lifetime. It's been so long since I've taken normal classes, hung out with my friends, spoken to Lacy. I miss her like crazy, but the Ambassador would probably know if I tried to call or message her from my phone.

"So you just moved here, right?" Jesse asks, shattering the silence. I internally sigh at the painful idea of small talk, but maybe he'll slip up and reveal something about his plans. It's worth a shot anyway. I nod and he follows up with, "Where did you move from?"

Chapter 15: Emma

I frown. "Mid-Atlantic region. Didn't you already know that? Everybody in the entire school was talking about it when I first got here."

Though they have settled down now that it's been a while, just like Aria had promised.

He shrugs. "I try not to listen to what people in that school say. It's mostly gossip and rumors anyway."

Right. He doesn't have friends.

"So why did you move here? If you don't mind me asking."

He sounds so innocent and polite. It's a little unnerving.

"We moved for my mom's job," I answer, thinking back to some of the more specific pages of my fake background. "She works for this tech company and they transferred her to the branch a town over, but we moved here."

"What's she like?"

Now what am I supposed to say? My file wasn't *that* detailed, and it's not like I have an actual mom to base my answer off of.

An image of the Ambassador pushes to the front of my mind, though. I smile. "She's amazing. She's so supportive. I mean, she can be tough sometimes, but it's only because she wants me to reach my full potential in everything I do. She's my role model."

"That's great that you're so close with her."

My turn. "What about you? What's your family like?"

His step falters. "They used to be great. I'm uh…I live in foster care now, though."

I resist the urge to sigh at the lack of new information.

"I'm sorry," I say, even though I don't mean it. But it seems like the thing to say in this kind of situation.

"It's fine. I've gotten used to it. Do you have any siblings?"

I tell him about Cameron.

"That's cool."

Beyond the Gates

This conversation is turning awkward real fast. Luckily, we arrive at the library before the tension between us fully sets in. I wonder if he feels it, too, or if it's just me since I know the truth.

He holds the door open. I'm barely through when I stop.

Bookshelves. Rows and rows of shelves filled with tons of books. We have books at the Academy, but not like this. We mostly have non-fiction and textbooks used for school and research, and even then, there aren't many. The ones that make the cut have been government approved.

But now there are hundreds of books spread out before us. Not just non-fiction, but fiction of all genres. There are no limits here.

"Do you like books?" he asks from beside me.

It takes me a few seconds to find my voice, and even when I do, I sound breathless. "I don't know."

But I want to find out.

I'm in a trance with the need to explore all these aisles stuffed with endless amounts of words and stories. I want to sort through all of them and discover what I've been missing out on for the past seventeen years.

A tingle shoots through me as my curiosity spikes...then burns out. I snap out of the trance just like that. My head clears of the fog and whatever eagerness I harbored towards exploration has been extinguished.

"Come on. We should get to work," I say, voice hard and firm. I stalk towards one of the tables in the back where it's mostly empty.

"So, I guess we should decide on a specific topic to focus on," he starts.

"Sure," I agree. "I was thinking maybe we could focus more on some of the recent changes in technology, since the way the government functions hasn't really changed all that drastically."

Chapter 15: Emma

"It depends on how recent you're talking," he counters. "We didn't use to be on a continent system."

"Yeah, but the switch from individual countries to continents was before we were even born. Before our parents were even born. It's been over a hundred years since the switch became official. Technology is constantly evolving. It might be easier to discuss the changes we've experienced just within our own lifetime to show how quickly it changes."

He nods. "That could work."

I add, "We can still incorporate background information about how each continent is under its own government system instead of each country having their separate government. We can even talk about how having only six governments makes communication between the continents easier and more organized and how that has affected the expansion of technology."

"Having only six government systems also makes it easier for one government to gain power and take over the rest."

There's force behind his words. He truly believes what he's saying.

I shift the focus back to technology. The last thing I need right now is to get into a fight with him over the government. And trying to change his views would just be a lost cause.

We agree on technology for the most part. The only issue appears to be our views on driver-less cars.

"I don't understand what you have against them," I exclaim. "They get you where you need to go in a safe and punctual manner. Accidents have gone way down since manual cars were made illegal."

"Yes, but it also takes away your freedom," he protests. "You can't drive by yourself. You are completely reliant on the car. Maybe it is technically safer, but people should at least have a choice."

He tries to hide it, but I see his hands curl into fists. Is there any conversation we can have that isn't a touchy subject for him?

"Okay, well maybe we can include information from both sides," I concede. He blinks, as if he didn't expect me to give in so easily.

He calms down and brings the assignment up on his tablet. "The directions say we need both online and print sources, so we should probably go search for a couple books that relate to our topic while we're here."

He stands and I follow. He walks with purpose over to the research section. On the way over, I attempt to brush my hand against his for another glimpse of his future, but it doesn't work. I can't find a way to do it without causing suspicion.

He stops in front of a row of books and reaches for a thick volume with a gray spine. I grab for the same book and knock my hand against his.

I'm instantly pulled into his head.

A brown wooden door opens to reveal the silhouette of a woman. The scene changes before I see her face. The next flash takes us to a small, dark space. Slats of light shine through the dark as if he's hiding in a storage room or closet of sorts.

Next is a scene of the two kids he lives with. They chase each other around a playground. I see through his eyes as he sits on a swing, so when he turns away from the kids, I turn too.

There's a girl on the swing next to him. Her long blonde hair ripples in the slight breeze. The corners of her mouth tug upwards in a smile. Her green eyes sparkle.

Oh, wait.

I was so focused on the tiny details that it took me a second to see the whole picture.

I'm that girl.

Chapter 15: Emma

My stomach drops like I've missed a step running down the stairs. I tumble out of his future, a future that doesn't make sense. I offer a sheepish grin, as though the entire occurrence of our hands bumping had simply been an accident. It only lasted a split second, so he doesn't suspect a thing.

He grabs the book we need and heads back to the table. I trail behind him and try to remain calm while my brain works itself into overdrive.

Why was I at the park with him? Why was I *smiling* at him? It looked so real and genuine, like I wasn't just playing him for information. But that's ridiculous. Of course, it was all fake. I must be a better actor than I thought.

I need to know more, but I'll have to wait to get answers. I hate prolonging things, but I have to be careful. I've waited my whole life for a Mission and there are lives at stake, mine included. Messing up isn't an option.

CHAPTER SIXTEEN
Jesse

I wake that Saturday from a fitful sleep. Charlotte is curled up beside me, dark circles under her eyes. Greg came home crashing around the house a little after 2:00am. It's safe to say none of us got much sleep. Sometimes I wonder how we survive under these conditions.

I want nothing more than to throw the covers over my eyes and get a few more hours of sleep, but I'm running out of time. So I force myself up and get the corkboard out.

I've pretty much ruled out the entire Mid-Atlantic region as a location for the Academy. The region isn't very big to begin with, and I doubt she would say that's where she's from if the Academy was actually there. At this point, I think I've narrowed it down to three possible regions: Mountain, Southwestern Central, and Northwestern Central. It's still a big area to cover, but I'm getting closer.

Charlotte and Oliver slowly wake up over the next hour.

"Greg's still home," I whisper. "We're going to get out of the house for the day, okay?"

Chapter 16: Jesse

They nod and silently slip out of bed. We've been through this countless times. They know the drill by now.

"Are we gonna eat before we leave?" Charlotte asks, her voice so small as her stomach grumbles. Her wide eyes stare into mine and I have another one of those moments where I remember how young she really is. So often, she's my voice of reason. I keep her safe, but she does the same for me. Sometimes I forget she's just a kid.

"We'll try," I say, because I don't want to sugarcoat it. Empty stomachs are better than bruises, and we're out of food in the stash we keep in the room.

They stay in the room while I venture into the rest of the house. It's quiet now, unlike the early hours of the morning. I press up against Greg's bedroom door. His heavy snores come through the door. We're in the clear.

I run to the kitchen on the balls of my feet to lessen the noise. I grab three bowls from the cupboard and a box of cereal from the counter and rush back to the bedroom.

Their faces light up at the confirmation of breakfast. We're out of milk, but that doesn't damper anyone's spirits. We sit on the floor and pass the box around.

Once we're done, I usher them out of the house and lock the door behind me. After being on edge all morning, it's a relief to finally relax the farther away we get.

"Are we going to the park or the library?" Charlotte asks.

"I managed to get a hold of the foster care check before Greg did when it came in the mail the other day, so we're going to the store first, then we'll go wherever you want."

We make it to the store and I select a cart. Once we're inside, the familiarity of the place washes over me. My heartbeat slows and a calm takes hold. It's weird, but the grocery store is one of my favorite places. It hasn't been taken over by the rapid advances in technology. At least not yet.

I can wander up and down the aisles at my own pace. There's something rewarding about putting in the effort to accomplish my goal of getting everything the kids and I need.

"So how has it been going with your search and with the girl?" Charlotte asks as I pick up a loaf of bread.

Oli shoots me a look, eyebrows pulled together. I take that to mean *what search, what girl?*

"It's been fine," I say tersely. "I tried to get information out of her yesterday while we worked on our school project together, but I'm pretty sure everything she said was a lie. She's was acting weird, too. Probably using her ability on me."

Charlotte huffs. "I still don't understand why you won't let me help with this."

"We've been over this. I'm not putting you in danger, end of story. Be happy that I told you about any of this."

Oli tugs on my arm. I look down. His eyes narrow. *What girl?*

Charlotte mutters to him, "I'll tell you later."

"Charlotte!" I splutter.

"What?" she protests. "He deserves to know what's going on."

Oliver nods in agreement, a stern look on his face meant for me.

"Fine," I cave. Telling them no is impossible sometimes, especially when they gang up on me like this. "I'll explain when we get home. Now, what kind of cereal do you want?"

They each pick out a box. I turn the corner, prepared to leave this aisle and enter the next, and have to abruptly stop when my cart bumps into the cart of none other than Emma Clarke.

Why do I always run into her at the most inconvenient time?

CHAPTER SEVENTEEN
Emma

Cameron and I decide this morning that it's finally time for us to go shopping. We made it this far with the food and supplies the government stocked beforehand, but now we're running low. The Academy left us with a credit card of sorts for any expenses like food, clothing, and emergencies.

I'm excited to be out of the apartment for a little while. Cameron and I chat aimlessly on the way there, but when we walk in, I stop dead.

This isn't what I was expecting.

"What kind of grocery store is this?" I exclaim. There are rows upon rows of shelves full of goods. "Where are the kiosks?"

Cameron chuckles. "I've been waiting to come here to see your reaction. So, some of the smaller towns still have traditional grocery stores. Everything is organized by aisle and you physically go get the items you need, then take them up to the registers to check out and pay."

We walk further into the store and Cameron grabs a cart.

"Why would you want that though? The kiosks are so much easier. You just click what you want and then you get it. No hassle and it takes like two minutes."

Cameron shrugs. "Most places have the kiosks. Like I said, it's just some of the smaller towns that still like having traditional stores. I've run across a few during Missions and stuff."

"Huh. Well I guess we better get started then. Lead the way. You know more about this than I do."

I follow him up and down various aisles. We grab things we need off the shelves as we go and put them in the cart. It's actually not too bad once I get over the initial shock. But nothing is ever simple for long.

I have control of the cart now, and as I come out of an aisle, we bump right into *him*. Of course.

Cameron tenses beside me. His eyes go wide in disbelief. I nudge him so he'll calm down and not give us away. This is the first time Cameron's actually seen him in person.

The target stares at me with wide eyes, too, clearly not expecting to see me here. His two foster siblings stand beside him. The younger, dark haired one is half hidden behind his brother. The girl fixes her gaze on me like she's analyzing my every move, which is definitely unsettling.

"Uh, hey Jesse," I say awkwardly. Even after all the time I've spent with him, the use of his actual name still feels weird on my tongue. Cameron shifts uneasily. "This is my brother, Cameron."

"Hi," the target responds, then gestures to the kids. "This is Charlotte and Oliver, my siblings."

In a way, I feel bad for the kids. How do they stand living under the same roof as someone like their foster brother? How are they able to trust him?

Chapter 17: Emma

"Are you Emma?" the girl asks. The target shoots her a stern look, but I nod. He glances at me and I swear for a second, his eyes change. They seem softer somehow, less empty. His eyebrows furrow in concentration, like he's trying to convey some sort of message within a split-second look. His throat bobs and it almost looks like he's going to shed a tear.

But then it passes. I would have missed the whole thing if I blinked. Finally, he says, "Well, we've got to go. See you in school, Emma." With that, he turns the cart around and walks off, the two kids trailing behind him.

Cameron and I continue in the opposite direction.

"So that's Jesse," Cameron comments once we're out of earshot.

"The target," I firmly correct. "Call him the target."

There's no reason to call him by his actual name when he's not here.

We don't talk about the encounter after that. But I'm starting to get frustrated. It's been a few days since I've gotten relevant information from him, especially with that reading that didn't make any sense.

I want concrete answers and I'm not going to wait much longer to get them.

...

"We need to talk," Cameron says that night after I get out of the shower. I pull my damp hair into a ponytail and sink onto the couch beside him.

"About what?"

"Earlier," is all he says, knowing I don't actually need the clarification.

"Cameron," I sigh. "I don't want to—"

"I know you'd rather not talk about it, but I just want to make sure you fully understand the situation."

I frown. "What situation?"

He shifts so that he's angled towards me, his face solemn. "When we were talking to your target in the store...I don't know, it seemed like there was a moment or something."

"A moment?"

"I don't know how to explain it." He drags a hand through his hair. "It was only a couple seconds, when you both just looked at each other. It didn't last long at all, but for that second, it was so intense. Like maybe there was something...more. Like maybe you saw him as more than just your assignment."

A small laugh of relief escapes my lips. That's it? "Cameron, it's just acting. I have to make him think we're friends so he'll trust me. He *is* just my assignment. I know that, and whatever fake friendship occurs between us isn't going to change that."

"Just be careful, okay? Believe me, you wouldn't be the first to get distracted by the human world or to sympathize too much with your target. So stay on your guard and don't let that happen."

"I won't," I assure him. "Jeez, have a little faith in me. I got this."

His blue eyes study me, sweeping over my face, then meet my own. "You do understand how this ends, right?"

I lean back against the couch and break my gaze from his. "I have to kill him," I say. "And if I don't, the Academy will." I turn back to Cameron and muster some confidence. "It's not that big of a deal. I knew that when I was offered the Mission. That's how most of these things end. It's what we're trained to do: neutralize all threats against the Academy and government."

"I know," Cameron agrees. "I just want to make sure you remember that part of the job. Don't get attached to him or anyone else here, like your little hacker friend. We won't get to stick around

Chapter 17: Emma

once this is over and I don't want you getting hurt when it's all said and done."

I shake my head. "It's in our blood, Cameron. Using our abilities, protecting the government, doing what is necessary no matter the cost or risk is *literally* coded in our DNA. If killing him is what it takes in order to carry out my Mission and protect those in danger, then that's what I'll do." I grin and add, "I didn't spend my whole life learning how to fight and use weapons for nothing."

His face hardens. "I'm serious, Emmalyn."

My blood runs cold. I glare at him in warning. "Don't call me that."

"I'm serious, *Emma*."

I lean away from him. "What's your problem?"

He sighs, drops his head in his hands. "Nothing, nothing. I'm just tired." He stands up. "I'm going to bed. See you in the morning."

I watch him retreat to his bedroom and close the door.

What just happened?

CHAPTER EIGHTEEN
Jesse

Another week passes. Emma and I meet up a couple days after school to work on the project, but I still haven't gotten much out of her. I've settled for watching her from a distance throughout the day and listening to what other people say about her.

All the teachers and students love her. She has her small group of friends, but other people talk to her, too. She's hardly ever alone. She tries to keep a low profile, but she's pretty unsuccessful. No one seems to notice how much she actually despises all of us.

I catch it every now and then. A flash of disgust in her eyes. The twitch of her lips when she's talking to someone, like she wants to frown. The cold and calculating way she studies not only me, but everyone else as well. She might want to kill me, but she hates the rest of them, too.

The part that's really frustrating is how meticulous she is in her façade. The only reason I even catch what I do is because I know what to look for. She never slips up or makes a mistake. Every time we meet after school for that stupid project, she's entirely focused on the assignment and refuses to give in to any of my subtle questioning. She has her guard up as much as I do.

Chapter 18: Jesse

The tension between us is building. We both want answers and it's only a matter of time until one of us cracks under the pressure.

I just hope it's not me. As long as everything goes according to plan, it *won't* be me.

But first, I have to actually find what I'm looking for, which means braving Greg's bedroom. I don't even remember the last time I went in there. But when the kids are still at school and I'm almost positive Greg won't be coming home anytime soon, I push his door open and gag at the stench of sweat and stale beer. When was the last time he cleaned in here? The bed is unmade and rumpled. Dirty clothes litter the floor and the dresser in overrun with empty bottles.

None of this is important though. I'm here for one thing and one thing only. I march over to his bedside table and rummage through the drawer until my fingers close around the small medicine bottle. I pull it out and look it over to make sure it's Greg's stash of sleeping pills from claiming he has insomnia. I'm not sure if that's true or not since he's hardly ever here at night, but whatever. It's what I need for this plan to work.

I open the bottle and let one of the oval pills slide into my palm. Then I leave the room as I found it.

...

The next day, I sit alone at my usual table during lunch. Emma's with her group of friends across the room. She smiles and laughs and talks to them. I've never seen anything so fake, but they buy right into it.

How can someone so seemingly normal be so horrendous in reality?

Her smile falters for a second and her head turns in my direction. My heart stutters and I quickly tear my gaze from her. I look down at my food and continue eating, as if I wasn't just intensely staring at her, attempting to unravel the secrets and mysteries that surround her.

I refuse to glance at her again for the rest of the period. Instead, I focus on my plan. All the pieces are in place and ready to be set in motion. With as much work as I've put into it over the past week, it better not turn into a complete disaster.

What I'm about to do is wrong on so many levels. I know that. But it pales in comparison to what she'll do to me if I don't act. I *have* to do this. There's no other choice.

When the bell rings that afternoon, I find her waiting outside at the bottom of the steps. I reach her and say, "Do you want to go somewhere different today? There's a diner not too far away. They have really good ice cream and milkshakes."

She bites her lip as she considers my offer. But ultimately, she agrees. "We can do that. I actually had dinner there last week. It was really good."

I flash a fake smile. "Great, let's go."

And the plan is off.

My hands tremble and my heart races as we walk down the sidewalk. If I fail…well, the results won't be pretty. Time is almost up. If I'm going to back down, it has to be now.

If I get caught, I'm dead. But everything will be okay as long as Charlotte and Oliver go to the library after school instead of going home. I gave Charlotte leftover money from the foster care check for dinner and stressed to her the importance of keeping both of them safe until I pick them up later. As long as they're out of harm's way, I have one less thing to worry about.

We enter the diner and I guide Emma to an empty booth. The place is mostly empty save for a few high schoolers and a family with kids too young to be in school yet.

Chapter 18: Jesse

"What do you want?" I ask. "I can go up to the counter and order while you get our project stuff set up."

She glances at the menu. "Mmm…blueberry milkshake."

"Got it. Be right back," I say with a smile. It's a struggle being this nice to her, but it's the kind of sacrifice I'm willing to make.

I leave her at the table and order her milkshake and an ice cream sundae for me. The lady at the counter makes our desserts and hands them over after I pay for both. I glance back at Emma. She's leaning over the table, looking at one of the books we checked out from the library.

Before heading back and after I ensure no one's looking, I pull a baggie containing the crushed up sleeping pill from my pocket. Deep breath. I can do this. I dump the contents into her drink and use the straw to stir it up.

Another deep breath. I can't believe I just did that.

I walk over and hand it to her.

"Thanks," she says. I sit across from her as she continues reading. I pretend to be reading from my own book, but all of my attention is on her. She hasn't taken a sip yet, but instead is rolling the straw between her fore finger and her thumb.

I want to yell *just take a freaking drink already!* but I have to be patient. I can't mess this up.

Finally, *finally*, she drinks.

"Wow, you weren't kidding. This is amazing!"

"Yeah," I say. It's the only thing I can get out without my wavering voice giving myself away. I'm not in the clear until she drinks the whole thing.

We work on the project for a while, until I've eaten all my ice cream and her milkshake is gone. It's over now. I've officially passed the point of no return.

Beyond the Gates

We clear the table. I stuff my own supplies back into my bag. In the parking lot, she turns to me with another one of those fake smiles. "Well I guess I'll see you Monday. I would say unless we run into each other over the weekend again, but Cameron's actually doing the shopping today."

I force out a laugh. She'll definitely see me before Monday. And the information about her fake brother makes my life even easier. One less person to deal with.

I wait until she turns the corner and then follow after her. I trail her all the way back to her apartment building.

She skips up the stairs while I hide behind one of the cars in the parking lot. She enters the code, presses her finger to the scanner, and disappears inside.

I wait a little longer, just to be sure. If I go in too early, the whole plan will fall apart. I wipe my sweaty palms on my jeans, take a few deep, steadying breaths, and dart out from behind the car.

It's finally time to get some answers.

CHAPTER NINETEEN
Emma

When I get home, I throw my backpack down on the couch with a huff. After an entire week, I haven't acquired any new information from my target. I hate feeling so unaccomplished and even worse, I think the Ambassador is starting to get a little irritated with my lack of helpful insight. Cameron, too. I wish Cameron could help out more, but there's no situation in which he could talk to Jesse without tipping him off that something's up.

Cameron still isn't home when I get here, but hopefully he'll be back soon. Things are still a little off between us after our conversation last weekend, but he's still my best friend and I need him.

My face felt flushed and overheated on the walk home, probably from the frustration. I go to the kitchen and splash cold water on my face, but it doesn't help. Instead, the heat spreads throughout my body. My heart slows. The room spins around me as I stumble back into the living room and collapse on the couch. My stomach churns sickeningly and something heavy presses against my eyelids. It actually hurts to keep them open.

What's happening to me?

Before I can come up with a solution, a knock sounds on the door. Who could possibly be here? I've never spoken to any of our neighbors. The knocking continues, pounding at the pace of the throbbing in my head. Reluctantly, I heave myself off the couch and try not to sway too much on my way to the door.

I shouldn't have opened it. I should have called Cameron. I should have laid down until the sickness stopped.

I don't know who I'm expecting to see when I open the door, but it's certainly not Jesse Reynolds.

Warning bells explode in the back of my mind, but I can't think straight enough to understand it. Everything's fuzzy.

"What're you doin' here?" I ask. My words come out muddied.

He shoves me backwards into the apartment. The room spins faster. Everything doubles. The edges of my vision darken.

His eyes are the last thing I see before everything goes black. For the first time, they aren't dead and empty. Instead, they're filled with unadulterated rage.

And in that moment as the darkness engulfs me, I know I've failed.

. . .

I don't know how much time has passed when I finally regain consciousness. What I do know is that I'm no longer in my apartment.

I blink several times, my mind sluggish. The room spins at an alarming rate and my head pounds ferociously. My left arm screams in agony. From the corner of my eye and in my hazy state, I catch a glimpse of dried blood coating my upper arm. I try to reach up to inspect the apparent wound, but my arms won't budge.

That's when I take in my surroundings. I'm sitting in a chair, my arms behind my back, and thick rope coiled around my wrists to keep me in place.

Chapter 19: Emma

I look around. Where am I?

The room is large, yet empty. Concrete floor. Cinderblock walls. It appears to be some kind of abandoned warehouse. There's a door that presumably leads outside, given the thin strip of light at the bottom. A few bulbs cast the room into an eerie glow.

I jerk against the bindings, but the rope bites into my skin. It's tied too tight for me to get it off on my own.

What happened before I blacked out? I felt dizzy and feverish. Someone knocked on the door. I went and opened it and...

"Look who's finally awake."

I thought I was completely alone wherever I am, but then Jesse steps out of the shadows.

He was on the other side of that door.

I glower at him as best as I can, but in my weakened state, it's probably more of a grimace.

"What happened?" I demand, wincing at the fire that scorches down my sore throat. How long have I been out of it?

He takes a step toward me. "I kidnapped you," he says bluntly. He smirks and stares at me as if I'm stupid for asking a question with such an obvious answer.

"I can see that," I retort against the protest of my vocal cords. "*Why* did you kidnap me?"

"Because you have valuable information that I desperately need." He shrugs. "And I got tired of waiting."

That's when it all clicks into place. He's smart. Way smarter than I gave him credit for. This whole time, I thought I was playing him. I couldn't have been more wrong. He knows exactly who I am and where I come from. How long has he known? This whole time?

Despite my revelations, I maintain my façade. I won't let him win.

"What information?" I ask, my breath heavy and flustered. Maybe I can confuse him, make him think he's made a mistake, that I'm not who he thinks I am.

He scoffs and crosses his arms. "Really, Emma? You can stop pretending. I know you aren't some sweet, innocent girl from a big city who hasn't done a single thing wrong in her life." He pauses and stares right into my eyes. "I know what you are."

My heart lurches. What, not who. *What* I am, as if I'm not even human in his eyes. I mean, technically yeah, I'm not human in the same way he is, but that doesn't give him the right to talk down to me, like he's better than me. He's not.

"And what exactly do you think I am?"

"A monster," he says at a lower volume, his tone cold and menacing. "Something that lacks any humanity. Something evil."

I let out a dry laugh. "Says the guy who abducted a seventeen year old girl and tied her to a chair. Maybe you should reevaluate your definition of evil."

"I am *nothing* like you," he hisses through clenched teeth. I grin, satisfied that I've hit a nerve. "You're here to *murder* me, aren't you? All I did was knock you out with a crushed up pill for insomnia and bring you here."

So that's why I felt sick when I got home. He probably slipped it into my milkshake. No wonder he suggested going there instead of the library like usual. God, I'm stupid. *This* is why I needed to be trained before getting sent out.

"First of all, you didn't just crush up a pill. You *drugged* me," I snarl. "And what? Once I give you what you want, you'll let me go? Just like that?"

He nods.

Yeah, right.

Chapter 19: Emma

He plans on blowing up an entire city of innocent people. Does my singular life really matter to him?

I go along with it anyway. "What do you want to know?"

He blinks, clearly surprised by how easily I give in. "The Academy," he says slowly. "Where is it?"

I sigh. Of course that's what he wants from me.

I shake my head. "I can't tell you that."

I honestly can't. I don't know the Academy's location. But he doesn't need to know that. For one, he probably won't believe me. But there's also the chance that he will. Once he knows I can't provide him the information he seeks, I'm dead.

"Fine," he growls. "Don't tell me. You won't be going anywhere until you do. I've got all the time in the world."

He pulls up a chair from the back of the room and sits across from me.

"You can't keep me here forever," I retort. "I'm not alone, or did you forget?"

Cameron. He'll come for me. He'll tear the world apart to find me if that's what it takes. He'll contact the Academy and get the government involved. I will not die at the hands of Jesse Reynolds. He's *my* target, not the other way around.

That annoying smirk reappears on his face. I really want to punch it right off of him.

"And I ripped out your tracker, or did you forget," he says, mocking my tone.

My heart stops. "What tracker?"

He rolls his eyes. "The tracker in your arm. What did you think the blood was from?"

My mind blanks. What is he talking about? He cut something out of me? That's why my arm is covered in blood. What tracker? Has he finally gone completely insane?

He must sense my bewilderment because his face lights up. "You didn't know, did you?" I stay silent and he laughs. "Wow, well that certainly changes things. I can't believe they didn't tell you."

Is he just messing with me, playing with my head?

"All of you were implanted with micro-sized tracking devices when the Academy took you in as infants. They've been tracking your every movement since the day you were born."

The world slows. The room threatens to start spinning again. I vigorously shake my head. Eyes wide, I whisper, "No, you're lying."

He has to be. There's no way the government would do something so drastic to us without our consent or knowledge.

"I'm not," he promises and stands up. He towers over me. "I knocked you out with the sleeping pill and dug the tracker out of your arm and hid it somewhere in your apartment where it'll never be found. The Academy won't even know you're in danger."

I'm about to retaliate and remind him of Cameron, but he beats me to it. "As for that 'brother' of yours," he uses air quotes and everything. "I sent him a message from your phone saying that you're out following an urgent lead and may be gone for a few days. You even asked him to cover for you when the government calls for updates."

Everything. He's thought of everything.

And I'm completely alone.

"So," he drawls. "Now that you know no one is coming to save you, tell me where the Academy is."

He stares me down, his brown eyes hard and sharp.

"And what if I don't?" I challenge. "Are you going to torture the information out of me you sick, twisted, psychotic—"

"Shut up!" he snaps. I almost miss it, but it looks like he flinches for some reason.

Chapter 19: Emma

He bends down until his face is level with mine. "Tell me what I want to know."

"No."

His hands curl into fists. Is he going to punch me?

Instead, he takes a step back. "I have to go," he says with strained composure. "I'll be back tomorrow morning. Consider my offer. Tell me what I want to know, and I'll let you walk out of here."

Silence ensues after that. He unties me and leads me across the warehouse to what ends up being a bathroom. I struggle against his grip, but I'm too weak. The drugs must still be in my system. He shoves me into the tiny room.

There's only a toilet and a sink enclosed by four dingy brick walls. No window. No means of escape.

I sigh and trudge to the sink. Yellow water splutters from the faucet but soon turns clear. I splash it onto my arm to rinse away the blood. Once clean, it's easy to see the small laceration on my skin. Luckily it's already scabbed over. Judging by its size, if there really was a tracker it would have been tiny enough for none of us to ever notice.

However, even if the government did implant us with trackers, they obviously had a good reason for doing so. Everything they do is to protect us. This isn't any different. He just doesn't understand that.

The target is waiting right outside the door when I'm done. He grabs me and drags me back to the chair. Once I'm tied back up, he turns off the lights and exits through the sliding door that is my only way to freedom. The door slides shut, and I'm drenched in darkness with nothing but my exhaustion and confusing thoughts.

CHAPTER TWENTY
Jesse

Why does she have to be so grating on my nerves? Why can't she just take the stupid deal and tell me where the Academy is? Does she really believe I'll torture her for the information she so carefully guards?

Does she not realize that despite the medicine to knock her out and the wound to her upper arm, hurting her is the last thing I want to do? I've been punched, kicked, and tortured myself. I never want to inflict that same pain on anyone, no matter who—or what—they are.

My plans against the Academy are different. The government has to pay for what they did to me. That's not the same as hurting her for information. She clearly knows nothing about me.

All of these thoughts tumble around in my mind on the walk from the warehouse to the library. A part of me still can't believe I actually managed to pull it off.

I stop walking as it fully hits me.

Oh my god.

I *kidnapped* someone.

There really is no going back now.

Chapter 20: Jesse

Maybe you should reevaluate your definition of evil.

She said a lot of things that really pushed my buttons, but that particular statement strikes home. Does abducting her make me just as bad as the rest of them? Does it make me evil, inhuman, a monster?

I shake the thoughts away. No, no it doesn't. I'm doing the right thing. I am. I didn't kidnap a person. I captured a monster.

The night air chills my skin. The sky darkens the later it gets. I arrive at the library right at closing time. Charlotte and Oliver are both perfectly safe and unharmed. The knot in my chest loosens once I'm sure of that.

Charlotte, on the other hand, looks nothing even remotely close to relieved upon seeing me.

"Where have you been? she demands, hands on her hips as if she's a parent scolding a child for being out after curfew.

"It doesn't matter," I reply and lead them down the sidewalk towards Greg's house.

"It absolutely matters," she hisses. "You tell us to go to the library after school with no explanation whatsoever and then you don't come get us until after dark." She stops walking and stares me down, concern clouding her eyes. "It's about Emma, isn't it?"

I sigh. "You know, sometimes you're too smart for your own good."

She stares at me. Oliver does, too. I can't lie to them or shrug it off, so I nod and confess what I've done.

"You idiot!" Charlotte smacks my arm. "You can't just go around kidnapping people. What's wrong with you?"

Her expression might have been funny if not for the severity of the situation. She's absolutely right. What I did was beyond reckless and wrong on so many levels. I know that. But it's too late to turn back now.

"I have to do this, Char. It's for our own safety. Besides, you're the one who suggested I use her for information."

Charlotte throws her hands up in exasperation. "I meant pretend to be her friend, not engage in illegal activities." She sighs heavily, making my stomach clench. I don't want my actions to burden her. "I'm just worried about you. I don't want you to get hurt or mixed up in the government's mess."

"I got mixed up the minute she walked into my life," I say.

"Yeah, I know. Do what you've got to do, just try not to get killed or arrested in the process, okay?"

I grin. "Deal."

Greg's truck is in the driveway when we reach the house. My heart drops to my stomach. I hesitantly enter the code and scan my finger. I usher the kids inside, hoping to make it to the bedroom in time.

But Greg is in the entryway…and he's livid.

"Do you have any idea what time it is?" he yells, face flushed with rage. If I had a normal life, I might think he's concerned for our safety or upset that we were out after dark.

But I know better. He's just worried we'll leave and never come back. If he loses us, he'll lose the monthly check that comes with us. That money is all we're good for.

I try to ignore him and get Charlotte and Oliver to safety.

"Where were you?" he roars and blocks our path.

Fire licks my veins as I step forward. "Why should we tell you? You never tell us where you go when you're out in the middle of the night. At least we come home at a decent time instead of two o'clock in the morning."

Will I ever learn to keep my mouth shut? Greg is already angry. It doesn't take much more to push him over the edge.

Chapter 20: Jesse

There's no time to react before his fist connects with the side of my face. I stagger back against the force of it but stand my ground. It stings, but at least he's too distracted with me to stop Charlotte and Oliver as they slip past him. I take a swing at him, but he grabs my arm and forces it behind my back.

Searing pain splices through my shoulder when he releases me. He swings again but misses and I duck under his arm. I run after the kids and lock us in the bedroom.

I face the door for a moment, my chest rising and falling heavily. I close my eyes and focus on calming my ragged breathing and racing pulse. When I finally turn around, Charlotte is on the bed with Oliver in her arms. Both are trembling.

"It's okay," I whisper and join them. My cheek aches and my shoulder is probably dislocated, but I need them to believe that everything will be all right.

We sit in silence until Oliver falls asleep. I tuck him into bed and lay down. Charlotte curls up beside me. Tonight, I'm not concerned with whether or not they brushed their teeth or if they're wearing pajamas. It's too much of a risk.

"I'm sorry for yelling at you earlier," Charlotte mumbles through the dark. "I understand that you have to do what you think is right and best for all of us. I just don't want to lose you."

A heavy weight crushes my chest, suffocating me. I hate what she has to go through because of me. Because of the government. Because Emma won't freaking tell me what I need to know.

"You aren't going to lose me," I promise. "You'll never lose me. Everything will be okay. That's why I did this. The Academy kids aren't people. They're evil creatures that lack humanity. But I've got everything under control. It's gonna be okay."

Beyond the Gates

She sighs, nods, and the tension finally leaves her body. It's not long before she drifts off, leaving me alone with my thoughts that crash against my skull like tidal waves.

Tomorrow I'll have to face Emma again. Hopefully I'll get some answers. Hopefully this will all be over soon.

Maybe you should reevaluate your definition of evil.

Her words ping in my mind again. She's still aggravating, even when she isn't here. It doesn't matter, though. She can say whatever she wants to me. I'm not evil.

I'm nothing like her.

CHAPTER TWENTY-ONE
Emma

I never fully fall asleep, but rather doze in and out of consciousness. My limbs ache from being tied up and I feel stiff from barely moving, especially compared to the constant action I'm used to. My stomach grumbles. I haven't eaten since the blueberry milkshake yesterday.

Light eventually filters in through the cracks in the wall and under the door. My target will probably be back soon.

I want out of here. I want to see Cameron and make sure he's okay. I don't trust anything my target says about the situation. For all I know, he has Cameron tied up somewhere, too.

The door slides open and I straighten in my chair. He won't catch me off guard again. No matter what happens, I'm going to stand my ground.

He's a mess. His hair is disheveled and there's dark circles under his eyes, like he didn't get much sleep. Good. He doesn't deserve to sleep if I don't get to either. There's also a fresh bruise on his cheek. The old one just faded not too long ago. None of this is important, though.

I almost lose my concentration when I catch sight of the apple and granola bar in his hands.

Almost.

He sits in the chair across from mine, gaze steadily fixed on me. He remains silent, waiting for me to be the one to break it. We stare each other down. When I refuse to give in, he sighs and says, "Answer a question and you get a bite of food."

It won't take much for him to obliterate my resolve. Because my situation with getting a Mission was so unorthodox, I haven't been trained for these kinds of scenarios. I don't know what I'm supposed to do when an enemy gets you, when they want you to spill information.

I ignore the gnawing pain in the pit of my stomach and say, "And what if I'm not hungry?"

My stomach roars in protest and he chuckles. "I think your stomach says otherwise."

"I'm not telling you anything."

But won't food be important if I'm going to build my strength back up? Without strength, I won't be able to break out of here.

He runs his hands down his face.

"Just…just answer my questions. Just give me what I need so we can both go home. Is keeping their secrets really worth starving to death?"

The Academy probably thinks so.

But my stomach rumbles again and that stupid smug grin reappears on his face.

"I'm going to ask you again. Where is the Academy?"

Does he not have any other questions he deems important? It's a shame he went to all this trouble to retrieve information I don't have.

Chapter 21: Emma

"I don't know," I say and enjoy every second of the annoyance that flickers across his face.

"I'm not messing around, Emma. Tell me where it is, and we can be done with this."

"I'm *not* messing around. *I don't know where it is.*"

He flies out of his chair and turns around, his back to me. He runs a hand through his hair, tugging on the ends. My split second of cooperation got his hopes up, only to be crushed by the cold truth.

"Think about it," I say. "They put a tracker in my arm and didn't bother to let me know. Why would they allow us to know where their entire government program is located?"

He spins back around, his eyes on fire. "How do you *not* know? You *live* there!"

I glare up at him. "It's completely surrounded by a forest, probably miles and miles from anything else. When they brought me here, the windows in the car were tinted on both sides. I couldn't see out. I don't even know how far away it is from here. Does that adequately answer your question? Do I get a piece of food now?"

I hate the desperation in my voice, but I can't help it. Starving and exhausted, my temper is short lived.

He rolls his eyes but breaks the granola bar in half and puts it in front of my mouth. I take a bite. My stomach sighs in relief once I have food in my system again, even if it's not much.

"How do you even know about the Academy anyway?" I ask, then take another bite.

He pulls back. "That's none of your business."

"Oh, and the Academy's location is yours?"

"Okay, next question," he continues. "Why is the government out to destroy the world?"

I blink. Seriously? "How many times do I have to tell you we aren't evil? The Academy, the government…we're doing good in the world. You're just too blind to see it. They send us out on Missions to help people, to help the world, to use our abilities for good."

He scoffs. "Yeah, okay. So, killing me is a good thing?"

"It is when you're a threat to society, to the government, to all the innocent kids in the Academy."

He seems offended by that comment.

"*I'm* the threat? What about—"

"You're planning to blow up the Academy! My friends, my *family*. I'm here to make sure that never happens."

The color drains from his face and he draws in a sharp breath. My eyes widen, too, as I realize what I've just said.

His voice shakes when he asks, "How do you know that?"

"I…I, never mind. It doesn't matter."

The gears turn in his mind. Comprehension dawns on his face. "Your ability. You kept touching my hand and your eyes would glaze over. What, did you read my mind?"

"I don't know, did I?" I fire back.

My target's irritation returns with my vagueness. He holds up the apple. "Tell me what your ability is and you get the whole thing."

My stomach snarls as I peer longingly at the fruit. Would it really hurt to tell him the truth? He's bound to figure it out on his own anyway. He's figured almost everything else out. Besides, what will he even be able to do with the information?

"I knew you were planning to blow up the Academy because I read your future."

His eyebrows knit together. "Explain."

Is he ever satisfied?

Chapter 21: Emma

"When I touch you, I can see pieces of your future if I concentrate hard enough. I saw you outside the Academy's gates right before it exploded."

He stares blankly at me for a moment and I wonder if he doesn't believe me. But a grin slowly emerges on his face, his eyes with a far-away look.

"So I do it," he whispers in awe. "I find the Academy and I really follow through with it."

Pleased, he goes as far as to untie one of my hands so I can eat the apple. I'm not stupid enough to try to escape yet, though. I still need to build up my energy.

I shake my head. "That's the future you had at that moment and probably still have now. But it's not the future you'll get. That's why I'm here. I'm supposed to stop you no matter the cost. I can't let you murder innocent people."

"Innocent people?" he exclaims. "Are you kidding me? None of you are innocent. Maybe you think you're doing good in the world, but you're not. The government is corrupt, which makes the Academy kids corrupt. And in case you hadn't noticed, killing me isn't really proving your point."

"Well *you* drugged me with a sleeping pill in my milkshake and then kidnapped me. That's not really helping your case either."

"I think tying you to a chair is a lot better than brutally torturing someone to death, or however you were planning on killing me," he shoots back.

"But it goes to show you that humans aren't any better than Academy kids. In fact, we're the better ones."

"Of course you think that. It's all you've ever been told. All of you view us that way. But none of you have ever considered the number of lives that have been destroyed by the government."

We argue back and forth. It started with his specific plans for eliminating the government, but has turned into an all-out fight on morals and values.

He thinks I'm a monster. I think the same of him. Around and around we go until we run out of daylight.

As he walks towards the door, I shout, "The Academy is the future!"

He turns to look at me. His voice is empty when he says, "The Academy's gonna be the end of the world. But maybe the future is a world that's ended."

He closes the door and I'm in the dark once more.

CHAPTER TWENTY-TWO
Jesse

I wake the next morning to a peaceful silence. I stealthily slip out of bed, careful not to wake my siblings. I quickly get ready and pack a bag of food and water for Emma.

Today is the third day of interrogation and I sincerely hope it will be the last. I can't keep her locked up forever, especially when tomorrow is a school day. People might not notice my absence, but they'll definitely notice hers.

Before leaving, I gently shake Charlotte awake. "I'm leaving, Char. Greg isn't home, so you should be safe. If he comes back, go to the library. Look after Oli while I'm gone, okay?"

"Sure," she mumbles without opening her eyes.

"I'm serious, Charlotte. You said you wanted to try staying here without me again, but if I feel like you can't be responsible enough—"

She cuts me off. "Okay, okay. I promise we'll be careful and leave if he comes back."

She swats me away with her hand and rolls over. I hate leaving them here, but I'm trying to trust her more. Let her shoulder more responsibility since that's what she wants.

I grab my jacket and bag and walk outside.

I'm grateful for the crisp, early morning air. It clears the fuzziness in my head and allows determination to swell inside me. Today, I'm going to get the answers I need. I'm going to accomplish my goals no matter what it takes. I'm going to get my revenge.

Nothing can stop me.

I reach the abandoned warehouse in no time. I found it last week when I was scouting for places to do this. It's run down and far away from prying eyes. I pull the door open and step inside.

Emma's head hangs low but whips up upon my arrival. Her limp, tangled hair frames her tired face. Her eyes connect with mine and that's it. That's the moment everything stops for me. My mind stops. My heart stops. The entire world stops.

It stops. Ends. And then begins.

I can't explain it, but I know. Something is different. Something has changed. I see it in her eyes. *She* is different.

And I know that from this point on, nothing will ever be the same.

CHAPTER TWENTY-THREE
Emma

Something is wrong with me.

I actually slept last night. I was fine then, but now I'm not. My hands shake uncontrollably and not from hunger. My heart pounds in a way it never has before, threatening to escape right out of my chest. Something fierce, electric, courses through my veins and prevents me from thinking straight.

My mind is a blur of all the things I haven't given much thought to the last couple days. Is Cameron okay? Where is he and is he safe? Where does he think I've been all this time?

And then there's the concern for my own well-being. I gave Jesse a lot of information yesterday. He still wants more, but eventually my usefulness will expire. What happens when he doesn't need me anymore? I doubt he'll really let me go, so will he kill me? I don't want to die.

I haven't thought about it too much, but now it consumes me. He can't keep me here forever. Eventually the scale has to tip one way or the other.

The door opens. My blood freezes beneath my skin as Jesse enters the building. My eyes meet his and I know. There's determination written all over his face. Today, one way or another, he's going to get everything he's been searching for.

I shiver as sweat breaks out over my skin. A chill oozes and trickles down my spine. I'm lightheaded, disoriented. I want out of this situation. I want this feeling to stop.

Jesse comes closer and my body reacts on its own accord. I thrash around in the chair, twisting and pulling in a fruitless attempt to break free. I have to get out, have to get away from him and away from whatever is happening to me. He places his hands on my shoulders to restrain me.

It occurs to me then that this could very well be his doing. He's already slipped something into my drink once. Maybe he poisoned the food or water he gave me yesterday, along with another pill to make me sleep while the chemicals worked their way into my system and made me into this uncontrollable thing. I'm going insane.

"What did you do to me?" I scream. He jerks back, eyes wide in alarm.

"What're you talking about?"

The ropes slice into my wrists as I struggle against them. It stings, but I don't care, not even when my wrists have been rubbed raw. I need to get free of the bindings and get out. I also need to complete my Mission, but right now, all I want is to get as far away from him as possible.

"You...you poisoned me or something. I don't know, but you did something to cause this...this *reaction*. I can't think straight. I can't breathe. And it won't...it won't *stop*."

He looks at me like I'm crazy and maybe I am, but he already knows that. He's the reason for it.

There's something *inside* of me, trying to claw its way out, ripping and tearing away at my chest in the process. Shredding me to pieces.

Chapter 23: Emma

And while I'm having a breakdown over here, Jesse staggers back a few steps and claps his hand over his mouth. His eyes widen and he looks like he's going to throw up.

"Oh my god," he whispers. "*Oh my god.*"

He starts pacing, muttering to himself. From what I catch over the blood pounding in my ears, it's complete nonsense.

"I didn't think it was true." He shakes his head. "The research. The papers. They said it failed."

"What're you—" I begin, but he barrels on like he didn't hear me. He's too busy working through whatever puzzle he's rambling on about.

"But if they perfected it…if they found a way afterwards, then *of course* they'd use it. What better way to control everyone than to take away the one thing that gives them free-will," he hisses in frustration and drags a hand through his hair. "I can't believe I didn't think of it until now. I'm so stupid."

He kicks his chair and sends it tumbling backwards to the ground.

His words spike the ferocity that bubbles up within me. I struggle and thrash against the restraints. I close my eyes and try to calm down, but I can't. My heart's beating too fast, my breath coming out in sharp puffs.

Something warm touches my cheeks and my eyes fly open. Jesse is kneeling in front of me. He grasps my face between his hands.

"Emma…Emma look at me," he pleads. I've never heard him sound so desperate. I jerk away and try to break free, but I'm tiring out. It doesn't matter that my years of training allows me to take down anyone I go up against. None of it matters if I'm not strong enough. I've barely eaten or slept and whatever Jesse did has greatly weakened me.

I surrender and go still. His hands gently lift my head to meet his. His golden-brown eyes are wild, frantic. I've never seen him so out of control before.

"Emma, you have to listen to me," he says in a rush. "Just listen to me and I promise I'll untie you."

I stare at him, bewildered. I hear his words, but they don't make any sense.

I blink and something runs down my face. I try to breathe, but the air won't enter my lungs properly. Jesse skims his thumb across my cheek.

"Don't cry," he whispers. I blink again. It's tears that are running down my face, tears that he's brushing away. Why am I crying? I've never shed a single tear in my entire life. "I'm not gonna hurt you."

The panic that surged through my body slowly dissipates. I hold his gaze through tired eyes. "Not going to hurt me?" I whisper. "You've already hurt me."

He releases my face and rocks back on the heels of his feet. He sighs, "I didn't poison you, Emma. They did."

"What're you talking about? Who did?"

This has to be some nightmare. A really bizarre nightmare and I'm going to wake up in my bed back at the apartment and Cameron is going to yell at me for oversleeping again.

"The Academy," Jesse says bitterly. "You know, those people you love so much."

I tense at his harsh words and look away from him. Something different than before curls in my stomach, making me sick.

"You're saying the *government* drugged me?" I try to sound strong, but I'm so utterly drained. "They aren't the ones who slipped me a sleeping pill, tied me up, and interrogated me for three days straight."

Chapter 23: Emma

"They didn't do it today," he says impatiently. "They did it after you were born, when they put the tracker in you."

"Jesse stop," I beg. He's not making any sense. What I *feel* doesn't make any sense. I want to understand what's going on and he's making it more confusing. "I swear if this is some kind of trick to get me to answer more of your stupid questions—"

"Listen to me. Please listen to me. I'm trying to explain what's going on."

"Well, you're doing a great job of it."

He sighs, his expression unreadable. He stares at me for a moment and finally says, "I'm sorry."

Not what I was expecting.

"Sorry for what?"

He shakes his head and squeezes his eyes shut for a second, like he's the one trying not to cry.

"Sorry for all of this. I didn't know. Emma, you have to believe that I didn't realize it was all real."

"What's real?" I exclaim. "Jesse, what are you talking about?"

I'll never admit it, but he's kind of starting to scare me.

He looks at me and our eyes lock. Then, he explains.

"There was this chemical formula that I found. Its purpose was to regulate and suppress emotions. If manipulated in the right way, it could even *create* artificial emotions. The government had scientists experiment with the formula. I've read documents about how it failed time and time again. But that was years ago, before the Academy was officially created."

He pauses and takes a breath. This thing he's telling me, it's hard for him.

"I always thought that was the end of it, but I realize now that I was wrong. I don't know how or when they did it, but the government must have found a way to make it work. Those formulas, according to the research, were to be coded into the trackers, and the trackers were to be updated and replaced once a year. Not only do the trackers pinpoint your exact location, but they're wired to your brain. They mess with the chemicals in your body to prevent you from feeling real, undiluted emotions."

Too much. This is all too much.

"And then I cut your tracker out," he continues with a sigh. "It must have taken a few days for your body to return to its natural state, because what you were feeling when I first walked in here? That was fear."

He really has gone crazy. *Fear?* That's what he's going with? The scorching fire that burned through my veins was the result of being *scared?*

As if he knows what I'm thinking, he adds, "Well, fear combined with a panic attack. But still. The formulas wouldn't have let you experience anxiety or panic attacks either, in addition to emotions."

"You are unbelievable," I retaliate. "Do you really think I'm going to trust anything that comes out of your mouth? You *kidnapped* me and—"

He throws his hands in the air. "Are you really going to hold that against me? I'm trying to explain that I did it because I wasn't aware of the formulas."

"That's not a good enough reason." I jerk in my chair. "And in case you hadn't noticed, I'm still tied up."

"Yes, and I said I'd untie you. And in case *you* hadn't noticed, I had to kidnap you before your psycho government organization murdered me."

I ignore that comment and press on.

"The government took me in when my own parents didn't want me. They *hated* me just because I was different, because of my

Chapter 23: Emma

ability. The Academy took care of me, trained me, gave me a family! Why would they be controlling us?"

His eyes bore into mine. He searches for something, some kind of answer. The fire in him dies down when he finds it. "You really don't know, do you?"

"Know what?" It's such a dangerous thing to ask. I'm not sure if I want the answer. The things he's said today are ludicrous. The Academy wouldn't control us like that. The trackers I can understand. They're obviously using them as a means of protection. If they know where we are, they can always find us if we are ever in danger. But controlling our emotions? Impossible.

"God, Emma. You're so naïve. Your parents didn't give you up because of your ability. The government is the reason you have an ability in the first place."

My reply catches in the back of my throat. I stare him down, trying to find a lie that's not there. I shake my head as tears cloud my vision.

No. He's wrong. He has to be wrong. My parents didn't want me. I'm a monster to them, just like I am to Jesse. The Academy accepts me for who I really am.

"They're just using you. They're using all of you. Don't you see that? Don't you *feel* different? I knew as soon as I walked in here that you weren't the same girl I left behind yesterday. Something in you changed." His voice is soft, begging me to believe him. "I know it's a lot to take in. It's a lot for me, too. I didn't realize they were manipulating your emotions to control you. I always thought those experiments with the formulas died out a long time ago. I'm sorry."

What am I supposed to say to that? What am I supposed to *believe*? But none of that matters right now. This is still just a game – a dangerous, fatal game – but a game, at that. All I have to do is win.

"How do you know all this?" I ask, doing my best to make my voice sound defeated, weak.

"Let's just say I have…research and documents on the Academy, plus what I've picked up on over the years. *How* I know what I know isn't what's important. Look, I'll tell you anything and everything you want to know about the Academy if you promise to at least hear me out."

I nod immediately. Hearing him out doesn't equal believing or trusting him. I can get around it. I just need *him* to trust *me*.

Without another word, he moves behind me and unties the ropes around my hands and feet. I rub my sore wrists. The skin is pink and irritated where the ropes dug in too tight.

Other than that, and the exhaustion, I'm perfectly fine. And now I'm free.

I spring from the chair and my eyes dart towards the door. I have enough strength now that I can get away if I want to.

But do I want to?

Jesse watches me carefully. Despite freeing me, he seems completely calm and steady as he waits for me to make a decision.

"You can bolt if you want," he says. "I won't stop you. But Emma…you can't run from the truth forever."

I stand there, torn. Torn between what I want and what I'm supposed to want. I should want to escape and reunite with Cameron, come up with an alternative plan to completing the Mission.

But I want to know the truth. I don't know if Jesse's information is completely accurate, but he at least believes it to be true. And I have a feeling deep down that, if I listen to him, all the pieces will come together and start to make sense.

Both halves of my mind struggle for dominance. Part of me tries to leave while the other insists on staying. In result, I stumble toward Jesse and away from the door.

Chapter 23: Emma

I guess I'm staying.

He tries to suppress a grin, like he's silently laughing at me for tripping over my own two feet. It's not my fault my mind demands one thing while my heart wants the other.

I steady myself and look him straight in the eyes. "This doesn't mean I trust you."

"I know," he grins. "You'd be stupid to trust the guy who abducted you, right?"

Is he trying to make a joke?

I eye him warily as he walks to the back of the warehouse and slides to the floor against the wall. He pats the spot next to him. I cautiously walk over.

I don't trust him. He doesn't trust me.

Things are different now. Everything has changed. But that doesn't mean I'm not waiting for something to go wrong, waiting for the moment when I'll have to run.

But as I sit down beside him, I wonder if maybe I was wrong. Maybe he's not the evil monster the Academy made him out to be. Maybe that was a lie, too. Just like the trackers and the emotions. Or maybe Jesse is the one lying about everything.

All I know for sure is that my life just got a lot more complicated.

CHAPTER TWENTY-FOUR
Jesse

We sit against the back wall of the warehouse for a while. True to my word, I tell her everything I know about the Academy.

Well, almost everything.

I tell her about the research I collected, though not where it came from or that I keep it under my floorboards. I tell her more about the trackers and the failed experiments.

She stays quiet most of the time, only speaking to ask questions. Surprisingly, she seems to actually believe me. Or at least she acts like she does. I still withhold some information, though, in case I need leverage later on.

I do decide to go ahead and tell her about the object that's been burning a hole in my jacket pocket though.

"I have something for you," I say and pull the threaded arm band out and drop it in her hand. "You should probably wear this at all times."

"What is it?"

"Your tracker," I explain. "I had my sister make the bracelet and I put the tracker inside. As long as you wear it, the government shouldn't know it's not in you anymore."

Chapter 24: Jesse

Her eyes snap to mine. "It's been here this whole time? I thought you hid it in the apartment."

I give her a guilty smile. "If you knew I had it with me, you might have put up a bigger fight. You would have believed someone was coming to save you."

Her face pales. "So...so they knew where I was all this time and they still didn't come for me?"

"I'm sorry," I say softly. "I'm sure this is all a lot to process."

"I just don't know what to think anymore." She stares blankly at the rest of the room. "But I really need food and sleep, so can I go home now?"

"We can't leave until it gets dark."

"Why not?" she demands and the tension floods back. Emma apparently doesn't like being told what to do, at least by me. She doesn't seem to have a problem following everything the government lays out for her. Though that might all be different now that her tracker is out. I'm not sure yet.

I backtrack. She's almost a completely different person from yesterday, now that she has real emotions. How did I not notice until now? On the downside, she's more likely to get angry if I say the wrong thing.

"You can leave any time you want," I amend. "But we're not exactly within walking distance of your apartment, and in your weakened state, you might want to reconsider that method of getting home."

Her eyebrows pull together. "Then how did you get me here? I highly doubt you carried me the whole way if we really are that far."

"I drove you," I say against the voice in the back of my mind that tells me to shut up. I'm headed down a dangerous road by sharing this with her, but she's bound to find out eventually. And if we don't learn to trust each other, we're never going to get anywhere.

"Okay, so what's the problem? Cars work in the daytime, too."

"It's an old car," I explain, much to her confusion. I can't tell her outright. What if this *is* all a lie and she's using this conversation to get information from me? I have to be able to deny everything. "A *really* old car," I add. It takes her a few seconds, but then it clicks.

"Oh." She glances up at me. "So it's...it's a manual." It's not a question, so I remain silent. "But it's illegal to use anything but a driver-less car. Too dangerous."

"Yes, they're illegal and yes, it's because manual cars are considered too dangerous. But we've talked about this before. I still think everyone should be given the choice." I eye her with caution. "I never actually said I have a manual car, though."

Her eyes flash with some emotion I've never seen her possess before. I can't place what it is.

"I won't say anything if that's what you're worried about," she assures me. Her eyes hold mine and for a moment, it feels like I can trust her. This would all be so much easier if only I could ensure she won't turn on me.

But that's not something I can ever be sure of.

"How do I know I can trust you not to? You practically bit my head off when we argued about it in the library."

Emma shrugs. "Things are different now. I'm still here, aren't I?"

She has a point, but that doesn't change anything. I can't start trusting her just because she's displayed a little emotion all of a sudden. But then again, what do I have to lose? She was already sent here to kill me. It can't get much worse than that, as long as she leaves the kids out of it.

"Yes, it's a manual," I confirm. "That's why we have to wait until tonight. The windows are tinted so people can't tell there's

Chapter 24: Jesse

someone in the driver seat, but driving after dark is an extra precaution I like to take."

"That makes sense," she says and then mumbles, more to herself than to me, "Though I guess it really doesn't make sense why they would be illegal in the first place." She looks up at me. "I mean, I get the whole safety thing, but it's like you said. People should have a choice."

She's actually agreeing with me. It's a miracle.

I chuckle. "You really don't know much about the outside world, do you?"

"Of course I do," she scoffs, but then gives me a sheepish grin. She bites her lip like she's trying to decide if she should confess something. "The day we ran into each other in the hallway? That was my first full day outside the Academy gates."

Wow. That means she's only been out for about a month.

"But didn't they teach you about the human world in school? You know, like Human 101 or something."

She laughs and shakes her head. "They don't waste time teaching everyone things that only a few people who get Missions need to know. Most of us never leave the gates, so why learn about the human world at all? Those selected for Missions usually get trained. I didn't."

"Why did they send you here?" I wonder and she raises her eyebrows. "No, I know you're here to stop me from destroying the government or whatever, but how do they decide who gets to go? Why you?"

I'm not even trying to get information for the corkboard. I'm genuinely curious. But she shakes her head.

"I might still be here and maybe part of me trusts you, but not enough to tell you that. Not yet."

"Fair enough," I concede. Of course she doesn't want me prying into her personal life or the inner workings of the Academy. I don't exactly want her asking questions about my life either. "Do you still want me to tell you about the car?"

She hesitates, but then slowly nods.

"Well, it all comes back to the government. Yes, you can argue that driver-less cars are safer and that the accident rate has nearly been extinguished, other than the occasional malfunctioning vehicle. But those cars and the people who drive them...they're like you, Emma. Each of those cars has a tracking device built into the system. The government keeps track of everyone, all the time. There is no sense of privacy whatsoever. Why do you think I have to hide everything I do? I don't have a cell phone. I keep a corkboard stashed in the freaking wall. I have an illegal vehicle because I can't stand the thought of giving the government another way to control me. And it doesn't even matter, because after all of that, you are still here. They are still ruining my life."

My chest heaves when I finish. Emma's eyes are wide, taken aback. I didn't mean to yell or get so angry, but the stress from the past few weeks is crushing me.

I can't seem to shut up.

"And I know it isn't your fault. I know now that they were controlling you and you still might not believe it because they were—are—your family, but you don't know what it's like living the way I do. Even though they're using you, the Academy does take care of you. They've completely *destroyed* my life." I take a deep breath and slowly release it. "I just need you to understand that my reasons for going after the Academy aren't random. To me, it's completely justified."

Silence spreads between us. She looks away and tilts her head towards the door. "It's dark now."

Chapter 24: Jesse

I guess our heart-to-heart is over. I stand and offer her my hand. She ignores me and stands on her own. The tension between us is suddenly a lot tighter. It's been a long day and both of our emotions have been all over the place. One second, we're almost getting along and the next we're back to hating each other and being sworn enemies.

I'm not entirely sure what we are at this particular second, but with her cool attitude, it seems like the latter.

I follow her outside into the breezy night air. She gazes around and takes everything in. She's definitely an observant person.

She stills when she spots the red minivan hidden among the trees. "Is…is that yours?"

"Yeah," I admit. She glances back at me with a grin. The atmosphere shifts like the flip of a switch. Maybe it's because she doesn't understand her emotions yet or how to control them, but the unpredictable changes are messing me up.

"It doesn't really seem like your type of car."

I walk over to the driver side and dig the keys out of my bag. "Really? I take offense to that. I love this car."

"Oh," Emma stammers and her face reddens. "I'm sorry, I just…I-I didn't—"

"Relax," I laugh. "I'm just messing with you. Honestly, I would've preferred anything else, but this was the only thing I could find that was still functional. I've grown to love it."

I get in and start it up. She makes no move to get into the passenger seat. She looks…nervous.

I roll the window down and lean across the seat. "Are you gonna get in or what?"

Emma's wide eyes meet mine. Her voice is tight when she says, "I'm assuming you know *how* to drive this, right?"

"Yeah, don't worry," I assure her and she climbs in. "I taught myself to drive a few years ago and I drive all the time. Usually at night, but sometimes during the day if I stay on the back roads no one uses anymore."

Why am I so calmly conversing with her? Words flow from my mouth as if we're normal teenagers having a completely normal conversation. As if she's not supposed to kill me and I'm not supposed to eradicate her kind's entire existence.

Neither of us say anything as I drive, though. I peer at her from the corner of my eye. She stares out into the night, her head pressed against the passenger window.

"Are you okay?"

She looks at me and blinks, as if just remembering that I'm here. She must have been lost in her own little world.

"I don't know," she whispers. "Apparently everything I thought I knew about myself and about the Academy and life in general is a lie. The person who is supposed to be horrible and evil and a threat to humanity isn't actually that bad. And I'm feeling all these things I've never felt before. I understand that it's real emotions, but I don't know how to deal with it or what any of it means. This whole day has just been so confusing."

It's strange to see her so unsure of herself, as opposed to her usual streak of confidence in everything she does.

"I'm sorry," I blurt out before I can stop myself. "I'm sorry for drugging you, for kidnapping you, and for turning your life upside down. I'm so sorry for hurting you and starving you. I know you see me as a bad person and I know that what I did definitely didn't help my image in any way, but I really am sorry. Ever since I found out who you were, I didn't see you as a person. I think that made it easier for me to justify what I did to you in my mind. But that doesn't make what I did okay, and I'm really, really sorry."

Chapter 24: Jesse

It takes everything I have to blink back tears.

She shrugs with feigned indifference, but her shoulders sag. The weight of today still crushes her. I know we still don't fully trust each other, but that's all right. Because we made progress today.

I pull into the parking lot of her building. I expect her to jump out of the car right away, but she hesitates.

She takes a deep breath. "I'll have to figure out how to control my emotions. I can't have Cameron or anyone else at the Academy thinking something is wrong." She turns to me. "I guess I'll see you tomorrow?"

It's such an ordinary question, but underneath it, she wants to know if we'll still be on the same side come tomorrow.

I nod. "We have government class together, remember?"

The corner of her mouth flicks up into the tiniest of smiles.

"Yeah," she says, then gets out. I wait until she's safely inside the building before driving off. Hopefully the other kid won't ask too many questions about where she's been.

Everything between them will be okay, right? The last thing I want is for her to get in trouble for something that's not her fault.

I run a hand over my face and through my hair. When did I start wanting her to be safe and okay?

It's been a long day and I'm utterly drained. I still have to return the car to its hiding spot and walk home, hopefully to a house that doesn't include Greg. I really don't want to deal with him tonight. I want to go home and sleep because tomorrow is a new beginning.

For the first time in a long time, I feel like I have something to hope for.

CHAPTER TWENTY-FIVE
Emma

The apartment is dark when I tip toe in. Cameron is surely asleep, and I want to keep it that way. Things will go so much smoother between us after I've had a full night's rest and food in my belly.

I slink across the living room, wincing every time the floor creaks. My hand brushes the doorknob of my room just as the hall light flicks on.

Busted.

"Emma?" comes Cameron's groggy voice. I squeeze my eyes shut, take a deep breath, shove the arm band Jesse gave me into my pocket, and slowly turn to face him. He's standing outside his bedroom, wearing a thin gray tee shirt and sweatpants.

My voice shakes as I say, "Hey."

He raises his eyebrows. "Hey? You've been missing for three days and all you have to say to me is 'hey?' Where have you *been*?"

My heart aches. It takes everything I have to stay together, to not give myself away. He can't find out what I've been through and all I've discovered. I have no way of knowing how he'll react to that

Chapter 25: Emma

kind of information. I need to figure myself out before I tell him anything.

He stares at me, waiting for an answer. I can tell he's angry, but it's not the same as I've seen with Jesse. Cameron displays a watered down version of the real thing. It's so obvious now. Why haven't any of us ever figured it out? Though I guess a lack of emotion is all we've ever known.

I think I get it now. The Academy controls our emotions in a way where we'd never question it because it seems normal to us. We still feel things, but it's nothing compared to the real thing.

"I was following a lead," I say, choosing my words carefully. I recall the cover story Jesse invented. "Didn't you get my text?"

He crosses his arms. "Of course I saw your text, but you were gone for three *days*, Emmalyn. And Aria was here, too, asking about you. Apparently you two exchanged numbers and she couldn't get a hold of you."

I cringe at the sound of my full name, but I sort of deserve it. Cameron doesn't know what I've truly been through these past few days and hopefully he never will. However, that also means he'll never know the truth about what we're really up against. But it's a sacrifice I'm willing to make. That, and getting yelled at.

"Wait, so Aria was here? With you? You spent time with her?"

"That is so not the point to any of this," Cameron says, though his face flushes just the slightest bit pink.

I shrug.

"Look," he says with a strained voice. "I know how important this Mission is to you, but you can't just run off for days at a time without any explanation. I had no idea where you were or if you were even alive."

A weird sensation travels down my spine and settles into the pit of my stomach. I felt it earlier with Jesse and now that I understand a little better what's happening to me, I recognize it as guilt. Or at least I think so, given the context of the situation.

Emotions rush through me. My eyes sting and a lump forms at the back of my throat.

Don't cry. Don't cry.

If I cry, he'll definitely know something's wrong. When I think about it, I've never once seen an Academy kid shed a tear. Just another thing to add to the warning signs I should have noticed but didn't.

"Cameron, I'm sorry," I whisper and take a step towards him. His face softens and he brings his arms around me.

"I'm glad you're okay," he says. "And I'm sorry for yelling at you. Just don't do anything like that again. I was really worried."

But not worried enough. That's another difference. He claims he was concerned for me and my whereabouts, but even that small amount must be artificial. If what he felt was truly real, he would have searched for me instead of waiting for me to come back.

He releases me and asks, "So what did you discover while you were gone?"

Oh, nothing much. Just that it's possible the government program who raised us since birth is actually comprised of a bunch of controlling psychos who are brainwashing us.

I wish I could tell him that. I wish I had someone to talk to who I actually trust to keep all the secrets I acquired today.

I wish I could talk to Jesse. He's knows what I've been through, even if I still don't fully trust him.

I push that last thought out of my mind and instead say, "I'll tell you tomorrow."

"Promise?" His tone is neutral, but there's a hint of suspicion underneath. Luckily, it seems more directed at whether I'll actually tell him, rather than whether *what* I tell him will be the truth.

Chapter 25: Emma

"Of course. I'll tell you everything as soon as I get home from school. I just need to sleep."

I guess he decides to believe me, because he waves his hand at the light switch and it turns off.

We say goodnight and go our separate ways. I grab clean pajamas from my room and go to take a shower. I've been in the same clothes for three days, so it's definitely needed despite how much I just want to curl up under the covers of my bed.

My conversation with Cameron went well for the most part. Now I just have to concoct a brilliant lie before tomorrow afternoon to feed to both Cameron and the Ambassador. Then I'll have to deal with the consequences.

I broke two of the Ambassador's rules by not answering my phone and by divulging information to an outsider. Not only an outsider, but the enemy himself. Not that they know that part. But I'll endure the yelling, the reprimands, and whatever punishment is involved as long as she doesn't revoke my Mission.

And then, once everything is straightened out, I'll have to figure out where *I* stand with all of this. I can't ignore what I learned from Jesse, but I also can't just turn my back on my family.

I step into the shower and turn the water on.

My family.

Despite everything, that's still what they are. The Academy is my home...and I betrayed them.

I've done so well since getting back to the apartment. I kept my emotions down long enough to deal with Cameron. But now that I'm alone, everything comes crashing down.

I gasp as a sharp sensation rips through me.

I'm hyper aware of everything. The shower water rains down on me, hitting my back and face. It's too hot and too cold at the same time. I tap my name on the glass pane where my preferences are saved. The dispenser squirts lavender shampoo into my palm. I feel every movement as I scrub my hair. The shampoo is soft and bubbly against my scalp.

I bite down on my bottom lip to control myself, but I dig too hard and draw blood. I yelp and lose control just like that. Racking sobs that have built since Jesse dropped me off shake through my body. I can't stop the tears as they slide down my face, mingling with the shower water.

I can't stop the pain or the confusion or the fear that races through me.

I don't want this. I never asked to feel this, to feel anything. What am I even doing listening to and trusting the enemy like I did today? What if he's lying, manipulating me? Why should I believe *him*, who I've known for a few weeks, versus the government who I've known my whole life?

I was perfectly fine before this happened. Yeah, maybe I didn't know every detail about the Academy, but everything they do is to protect us and take care of us.

I'm a traitor.

That thought only makes me cry harder.

I lean against the shower wall, hands braced, and forehead pressed to the tile. Eventually, my eyes dry out and the water runs cold. I step out, dry off, and put my pajamas on. My stomach hurts from barely eating, but it'll have to wait. I'm too worn out. I trudge to my bedroom and collapse onto the bed. I stare at the wall for a while until my mind goes blank.

But as I fall asleep, one last thought crosses my mind.

What if he was telling the truth?

CHAPTER TWENTY-SIX
Jesse

I'm on edge the next morning as I stand at my locker. The main hall is crowded, but no sign of her. After the weekend, I don't know what to expect anymore. Have I really brought her around to my side or is she still planning to kill me? I probably should have asked myself these questions *before* I turned her loose, but too late now.

When I can't find her through my subtle attempts of searching the hall, I shut my locker and head to first period. I'll see her during class anyway.

I pass through the doorway and stop. There she is, already in her usual seat. I cautiously approach and sit beside her. She doesn't acknowledge me and instead stares straight ahead, her face blank.

"Hi," I say hesitantly.

"Don't talk to me," she growls under her breath.

"What?" I know she's upset over everything that happened yesterday, but I didn't expect her to be this closed off today. Unless she really does plan to kill me.

The teacher speaks before I get the chance to press any further. "We will be working on our projects for the entire class period today. You are allowed to leave the classroom if you wish, to go to the library or computer lab for research. But do not leave campus or disturb the other classes. You must check back in with me at the end of the period."

With that, we are dismissed.

I glance at Emma. Her eyes are out of focus, her breath heavy and ragged. Her entire body trembles.

"Are you okay?" I reach out to touch her shoulder.

She flinches and springs from her seat. "Don't touch me."

I hop up and follow her from the room. Something isn't right.

"Emma, wait!" I call after her, but she keeps running.

"Leave me alone."

I almost catch up to her when she pushes her way into the bathroom. I abruptly stop outside the door, glance around to make sure no one is in the hallway, and go in after her. It's empty except for Emma, who's slumped against the wall, arms around her knees. Her breath escapes in quick, sharp gasps. Tears slide down her face. I close and lock the door behind me, so no one barges in, then kneel in front of her.

"It...it w-won't stop. The emotions. I had trouble last night, but I was doing okay this morning. Until I walked into school and everything felt too loud, too crowded, too bright, too *much*. I can't handle it."

"Yes, you can, Emma." I reach out and she shrinks back. I curl my fingers into my palms to stop myself from reaching again. She's falling apart, but she doesn't want me anywhere near her. I don't blame her, after what I did to her. "I know it's a lot, but you'll get the hang of it. You just have to adjust."

She finally looks up at me, her green eyes rimmed red. "That's the thing. I don't want to adjust."

Her eyes blaze and she shoves me away from her. She jumps to her feet and I stand, too, which ends up being a mistake.

Chapter 26: Jesse

"I don't want this. I didn't ask for this." She pounds her fists against my chest, forcing me backwards. She doesn't punch hard enough to actually hurt, but it's definitely alarming.

Tears stream down her face. She trembles, either from rage or despair. Maybe both. I'm not sure.

"Emma," I say in what I hope is a soothing voice. She ignores me.

"This is your fault." Punch. "*Your* fault." Punch. "*You* did this to me."

My back hits the wall by the sinks. She continues to pummel me, releasing all her pent-up frustration.

And I let her.

Maybe I *am* to blame for her current state, but there's no undoing it now. So, I let her rant and hit me and get it all out. Better out than bottled up inside.

"I was happy before this. Maybe I didn't feel emotions and maybe the government hasn't told me the whole truth, but at least I didn't feel like *this*. And it's not just the emotions for right now. I'm feeling things I should've felt years ago, but I didn't feel them like this."

She gasps and steps back, clutching her stomach as the tears stream harder.

"I-I *hate* you." She lunges at me again, pushing me back up against the wall and pounding her fists against me. "I hate you. I hate you. *I. Hate. You.*"

Without thinking, I wrap my arms around her. She struggles against me, trying to get more hits in, but I hold her tight. I thread my fingers into her hair and hold her head against my shoulder.

"Shh. Shh," I whisper. She finally stills. "It's okay. You're okay."

She grabs the back of my shirt, her hands fisting in the material.

"Breathe. Just breathe."

I'm not entirely sure why I'm helping my enemy, but there's something about seeing her so broken. So weak and fragile.

"It hurts," she whimpers. "It didn't feel like this then. It *hurts*. Make it stop. Please make it stop."

What am I supposed to say to that? This girl who was supposed to kill me is now crying in my arms.

"I'm sorry," she cries. "I'm so sorry, Ian. I didn't mean to. I didn't know you wouldn't come home. I'm sorry."

Ian? I wonder who that is. She continues to mumble sorrys and other words I can't understand. Eventually her tears dry up, her words fade, and her sobs subside. All that's left is her red, puffy eyes. When her breathing regulates, I know it's over.

She untangles her fingers from my shirt and pushes away from me. She walks back across the bathroom to the other wall and slides to the floor. I hesitantly sit beside her.

"I'm really am sorry for everything that happened and everything I did to you," I say softly.

Emma stays silent for a while longer, and I don't push her. If she isn't ready to talk, I'm not going to make her.

"I know," she eventually whispers, her voice dry and scratchy. "I know you were doing what you thought you had to, because you were in danger from me and neither of us knew what was actually going on." She pauses, sniffles. "And I want to trust you. A lot of what you said about the…the government and the Academy adds up, but I can't just flip a switch and not be on their side anymore. I don't think I *want* to be if they really did all the things you claim, but it's not that simple. And there's this whole thing with the emotions. I don't know the first thing about what real emotions are, let alone how to control them. I can't do this on my own."

My brain is apparently done consulting with my mouth, because words come out before I have the chance to think them over.

Chapter 26: Jesse

"No one said you have to. I'll help you…but I can't exactly trust you either. How do I know this isn't just some trick to get me to spill information that you'll feed straight back to the Academy?"

She looks appalled. "Of course it isn't." She contemplates for a second. "But that's the thing. You *don't* know. I guess we're going to have to learn to trust each other."

"Fair enough," I agree with a nod.

Just when I think she's beginning to relax, her body tenses. "That's not all. I also have to come up with false information for the Academy and Cameron. They all think I have some huge lead and they're anxiously waiting for details."

"Why didn't you tell him?" I ask out of sheer curiosity. She gives me a blank look. "Cameron," I clarify. "Why didn't you tell him the truth about what happened?"

She shrugs. "I guess, because…because I couldn't risk your life like that. I had no way of knowing what his reaction would be. He's been my best friend my whole life, but if our feelings were never really our own, then what's to stop him from turning on me? And if the government ever finds out, they'll kill you. I mean, they want you dead anyway, but they won't wait for the Mission to be complete. They'll just kill you on the spot."

I tilt my head to look at her. "Isn't that what you want? To risk my life and watch them kill me?"

She swallows and bites her lip. Slowly, she shakes her head. "I don't think so. Not anymore. I just…I want to be on the right side, and I'm not sure the government is it. And I want the truth. I want to understand what's really going on, even if it hurts me. Even if it destroys everything I thought I knew. I want the truth…and I think you're the only way I'm going to get it."

Maybe I *can* trust her. She sounds so sincere. Hesitantly, I say, "If you want, I can meet you during lunch. We can try to come up with a cover story for the three days you were gone."

She stares at me, considering my offer. "Okay."

"The period's almost over. We should probably go check back in before the bell rings," I suggest. We both stand up.

"We didn't work on our project," she suddenly says.

A short laugh bubbles out of me. "I think we'll be okay."

She smiles ever so slightly.

Emma checks herself in the mirror. We've been sitting here for a while, so her face isn't blotchy anymore. Her eyes are still a little puffy, but other than that, I can't even tell she was crying.

We leave the bathroom, check in with the teacher, and go our separate ways.

. . .

I'm already at my usual table in the cafeteria when Emma arrives. Her eyes dart around the room until she finds me. I watch her as she walks over.

"Hi," she says and sits across from me.

"Hey."

She shifts uncomfortably. Wow, we're awkward.

Before we actually get around to saying anything, however, a dark-haired girl approaches us.

"Hey, Em." The girl glances at me. "What? Are you ditching us for Jesse, now?"

There's a hint of teasing in her tone.

"No, Aria." Emma replies. "We're working on our project for the class we have together."

"Mhmm, well you have fun with that." Aria gives Emma a knowing smile and walks away with a wink.

Chapter 26: Jesse

Emma turns back to me, her face slightly more flushed than before.

"What was that all about?" I wonder.

She shakes her head. "Nothing. Aria's just being Aria."

That's clearly a lie if I've ever heard one, but I don't push.

"Okay, so about the cover story," Emma begins. "I was thinking it might be best if I mixed a little truth in with a lie, with your approval. I won't tell them anything you aren't okay with."

My skin crawls with the thought of her telling the government anything about me, but she has a point. The lie has to be believable.

"You could just say that you were following a lead, and then I kidnapped you and that's why you couldn't contact them for so long. That's not a lie."

"Yeah, but then they'll know that you know about me. And then they'll want to know how I escaped, what I told you, how much you know. That'll just make it worse and they'd probably pull me from the Mission."

"Okay, then what do you have in mind?"

She seems surprised that I gave in so easily. "Well I was thinking of…the corkboard."

My stomach drops. I can try to deny it, but that didn't work out so well the first time. "I wasn't aware you knew about that. I'm assuming you saw it when you were in my head?"

She fidgets in her seat, obviously nervous. She really needs to learn how to mask her emotions.

"Um, yeah." She ducks her head, refusing to meet my eyes. "I saw it in your head, but I haven't told the Ambassador much about it, except for the fact that it exists. I wanted more concrete information before I really said anything. So, since she already knows about it, I was thinking I could make something up to go along with it. You also mentioned it over the weekend, but…we're supposed to be completely honest with each other, right?"

"Right," I agree. "It's the only way we'll learn to trust each other."

"Okay, but don't get mad." She takes a deep breath. "I couldn't get a clear look at the board while I was in your head, so I sort of…broke into your house to get a better look."

"You *what?*" I shriek. A few heads in the vicinity turn towards us in curiosity.

"Hey, you said you wouldn't get mad!" she hisses under her breath.

"I never actually said that," I counter. And I am mad. I'm *outraged*. Not because she broke into my house—or not entirely—but more at myself for underestimating her as much as I did. What if Charlotte and Oliver were home? Would she have hurt them to get what she wanted? I can't believe I'm sitting here with her, helping her. What is wrong with me?

"I needed to find out how much you knew," she says, as if that's grounds for justification. "That's my job. Find out what you know, what your plans are, and report back to the Academy."

"And what would you have done if someone had been home?" I ask. I have to know.

"No one *was* home, Jesse. I made sure the house was empty before I went in. I'm not stupid."

"But what *would* you have done?"

She frowns as the true question sinks in. "I wouldn't have hurt them, if that's what you're getting at."

We stare each other down until I give in with a sigh. "Okay, tell them about the corkboard. Say that I'm using a map to narrow down locations of where the Academy might be."

Chapter 26: Jesse

She relaxes. "Most of the stuff on that board didn't actually make sense though."

"Well, yeah. I have to make sure random people who decide to break into my house can't decipher what any of it means."

The corner of her mouth tilts up, though she tries to hide it. "So, what should I say in addition to that? Like where I was?"

I shrug. "Tell them you followed me to the warehouse and waited until I left. Say you didn't find anything, but maybe you stayed overnight and hid. I came back the next day, but you couldn't really tell what I was doing. I don't know, just make something up. Something that explains why you were gone for so long."

"All right," she agrees. "I just don't want to get caught."

"What happens if you do?"

Emma shakes her head. "I don't know, but if you are right about them, then it won't be good. They'll probably see me as a traitor and either kill me or brainwash me by putting in a new tracker. I'd like to think they wouldn't be that harsh, but the more I think about it, the more I understand where you're coming from. Knowing what I know now...I don't think I can trust them like I did before."

It's weird to hear her use that word. *Traitor*. But I guess it's true, if we're really going to work together. I still can't trust her—at least not yet—but if I ever can, she'll be a lot of help in my quest to locate the Academy.

I could tell her what the notes on my corkboard mean, and maybe she'll pick up on something I completely missed. The possibilities are endless, but of course sharing that piece of information, that piece of *me*, could turn disastrous. At the very least, it's too soon.

The lunch period ends and we split off. For now, it appears that we're on the same team. However, I'm not stupid enough to believe

Beyond the Gates

that all my problems are solved now that she isn't going to kill me. She's still one of them. The things that happened over the past few days don't change that. I know it hasn't changed for her either.

Maybe someday, but today is not that day.

CHAPTER TWENTY-SEVEN
Emma

The sun beats down as I trudge home that afternoon. It's an unusually warm day for mid-September, but maybe I'm just used to the Academy's milder weather.

It takes almost double the normal time to get from school to my apartment, but I arrive when I can't put off the inevitable any longer. It's time to face Cameron and even worse, the Ambassador.

Cameron is on the couch when I walk in. I sit beside him and try to keep my expression neutral. What do I normally look like when I'm not flooding with emotions? Can he tell something's different?

"So, are you going to tell me what happened?"

Here we go. I thought a lot about it on my walk home. I let my fabricated story spill out of me.

"Je—the target was acting weird while we were working on our project for school last Friday. When we left, he went a different way than usual. I just had a funny feeling that he was up to something, so I followed him. That's when I texted you and my phone battery died, which is why I told you to cover for me. He went to this warehouse. I got inside without him seeing me and I hid."

I glance at Cameron to gage his reaction. So far, he doesn't seem suspicious. I continue. "He looked through these old books and wrote stuff down. He was there for so long and I couldn't leave while he was in there. When he finally did leave, I looked through everything he left behind, but most of it didn't make much sense. Since he left it all, I thought maybe he'd be back the next day. I was right. I observed him and tried to figure out what he was doing. He packed everything up and left on the day I came back here."

Despite my internal panic, lying is easier than I expected. No one ever lies at the Academy. At least not about anything important. Maybe about why you're late to class or denying that you broke curfew and stayed out in the City all night. Minor stuff. Nothing like this.

The government has us wrapped around their fingers, and we believe everything they tell us. And now Cameron believes everything I tell him. It's almost too easy considering I haven't actually told him anything specific. He seems to buy my story, about still not being sure what Jesse has been up to, though.

Cameron seems to calm down once I've said my piece. Now I just have to wait to hear what the Ambassador has to say about all of this.

"While we wait, do you think you could help me with something?" I ask.

"Sure, like what?"

"Well I didn't get official Mission program training, so I was wondering if maybe you could teach me how to break out of bindings if an enemy has you tied up."

"Um, okay. I mean, there's several ways depending on what you're tied up with. Duct tape, rope, zip ties, handcuffs, and so on."

"Specifically rope, at least for now," I say.

Chapter 27: Emma

He nods. "Okay, well when you're first being tied up, you want to submit to the enemy, unless you're one hundred percent sure you can fight your way out. They'll see you as passive and not as big of a threat as you actually are. So when they tie you, put your wrists close together, but your elbows out from your sides. *Never* put your arms all the way in front of you."

He retreats to his bedroom and comes back with a bundle of rope.

"And you just happen to have that because…"

He shrugs. "In case we ever need to use it on the target."

He shows me how to place my wrists in front of myself and keep my elbows out, then wraps the rope around me.

"Okay, now relax your elbows."

I do so and immediately understand. Whereas the rope had been tight around my wrists a second ago, relaxing my elbows created a pocket of space between my wrists.

"Now, just wriggle out of it. If you're tied to something, you can also slide up and down to cause friction, which will help soften up the rope and make it easier to break."

I shift my wrists around until I loosen the rope enough to slip out.

"Wow, that was a lot easier than I expected."

"Yeah, as long as you set it up correctly, it's pretty simple."

"What about if my hands are tied behind my back…and I'm unconscious at the time so I can't prepare myself?"

He gives me an odd look. "Why are you unconscious?"

Well, you see. I've already been kidnapped once and I was unconscious then, so…

"I don't know. I'm just trying to cover my bases."

"Okay, well it'll definitely be more difficult, but don't forget we're a whole lot stronger than the humans. As long as you have enough strength and something to loosen or soften the rope up with, then you should be fine. Honestly, we don't tend to have a ton of issues with our kind getting kidnapped or anything."

I want to argue, to tell him that I wasn't able to break free. But that would require telling him the truth about everything, and that's not an option. So I let it go. Hopefully if anything happens again, I'll be ready.

The Ambassador calls a few minutes later.

My nerves come flooding back. I take a deep breath and brace myself. "Hello?"

"Welcome back, Ms. Grant. It's so nice of you to finally pick up the phone when called."

I cringe at the ice in her voice. She doesn't shout, but her calm tone laced with disappointment is almost worse in a way.

"I'm sorry I was gone for three days. I was following—"

"A lead," she finishes for me. "Yes, Mr. Clarke told me all about it. You have important information to share from this lead of yours, I presume."

Wow, she's clearly impatient and irritated already. She's really going to be upset after finding out I didn't actually discover much. Not that any of it's true in the first place.

I recite what I told Cameron, down to the smallest detail. Keeping the story straight is important. I can't risk being caught in a lie.

"So you don't have anything specific."

"No," I admit. My heart thuds heavily against my chest. "But I'm getting closer. I know I am. Oh, and the corkboard. I have an update on it."

I explain the map and how he's using it to narrow down the Academy's location. The Ambassador sighs. "Look, Emmalyn. I know how much this assignment means to you, but if we don't get actual results soon, I'll have no choice but to pull you from the

Chapter 27: Emma

Mission. You're a couple years younger, so maybe you do need that extra training."

My heart stops, then picks up double time.

"I'll get results," I blurt out in a rush. "I promise I can do this."

"Then you have one more week to do so. Goodbye, Ms. Grant."

The phone clicks.

One week. I have one more week to present the government with information they actually find useful, or I'll be sent back to the Academy.

"Hey," Cameron wraps his arms around my shoulders. "It's okay. You're not the only one who got yelled at today. She called me earlier and chewed me out for not having better control over you and knowing your plan and whereabouts. But at least she's giving you another week. Just no more running off without me. Keep me in the loop, okay?"

"Okay."

"And don't stress too much. You've got this. It'll work out."

No, it won't.

Even if I am pulled from the Mission, they'll just send someone else to finish the job. I'll never see Jesse again. We still don't really trust each other, and maybe we never will, but I don't want anyone else assigned to him. Without him, I can't find out the truth. And without me, he has no shot at survival. The next person won't be like me. He won't be able to pull them to his side or win them over so easily.

But Jesse isn't my only concern now. The Ambassador's passive aggressive threat was a wakeup call. So much has happened over the past few days. I've learned a lot and experienced emotions for the first time. So many things have changed. Somewhere along the way, my loyalty started transferring from the people who are supposed to be my family, to the person who is supposed to be my enemy. My life has become so messed up and confusing.

What if I do fail? What if I get sent back to the Academy? My heart lurches at the thought. I realize in that moment that I don't want to go back to the Academy. I don't want to go back to the place that lied, injected me with chemicals, and controlled my emotions.

I don't want to go home. Because after everything I've learned, everything that's happened, maybe the Academy isn't home anymore.

CHAPTER TWENTY-EIGHT
Jesse

I know something is wrong with Emma the moment I walk into first period. She's already in her usual seat, but she's not the calm, collected Emma I'm used to. Though honestly, will she ever be the same after what happened? Will either of us?

She bounces in her seat as her eyes dart around the room, almost frantic. I practically see the gears whirling in her mind as she tries to find a solution to whatever problem plagues her thoughts.

"Are you okay?" I ask, fully prepared to have my head bit off again like yesterday. But yesterday, she seemed overwhelmed. Today, she's scared.

"It wasn't enough," she whispers and looks at me, her eyes pricked with unshed tears. Another reminder that I need to teach her how to control her emotions, or at least how to mask them. "The whole lie I fed the government…it wasn't enough. Even with the corkboard. She said I need to provide actual information and proof that I'm making real progress within the next week, or they'll take me back."

"To the Academy?"

She nods and her lip trembles. "I can't go back there, Jesse. I know it sounds crazy since I wanted to kill you only a few days ago, and maybe I *am* crazy. But I feel sick every time I think of going back. I shouldn't feel this way. They raised me. They're my family. Maybe it's the emotions. I don't know, but I don't want to be under their control again. I just got free."

She stares at me, eyes wide with fear and desperation. Our rushed conversation is cut short when the teacher enters the room.

"Listen," I say hurriedly. "We'll figure something out. It'll be okay."

"You don't know that." She shakes her head. Her breath sharpens into quick gasps. I recognize the signs instantly. Another panic attack is coming on.

"Deep breaths," I say softly. "Just breathe."

She does as I say, in through her nose and out through her mouth as the teacher calls the class to order. I lower my voice, stare at the front of the room, and speak from the corner of my mouth.

"Lesson one on controlling your emotions: if you feel like you are about to cry, swallow and blink rapidly. Fight back and whatever you do, don't let the tears fall."

I don't know if she takes my advice or if she even heard me, but a moment later, I hear a soft, "Thank you."

I monitor her from the corner of my eye. After getting herself somewhat under control, she pretends to focus on the lecture, though her mind is clearly elsewhere. Being so used to that similar behavior in myself, it's easy to spot in her.

I mull over everything she told me in the past few minutes. Emma is apparently more on my side than I thought. Part of her will always be attached to the Academy, but for now it seems she's turned against them.

. . .

Chapter 28: Jesse

Emma beats me to the cafeteria. She's already sitting in the same place as yesterday. I have a feeling it's going to become our usual table.

I sit across from her and jump straight into the conversation. "You said they want information and signs of progress, right? Then show them progress. It doesn't have to be something you found out. *Prove* to them that pulling you out of the equation will only hurt them."

"And how do I do that?"

"Maybe you finally got me to trust you. Maybe I finally believed you to be my friend. Maybe I even start telling you all about the situation and everything I know, without realizing I'm talking to one of them, obviously. If they pull you out after all that, anyone new will have to start over in gaining my trust. Plus, your sudden disappearance would make me suspicious."

A hint of a smile playing across her face. "You've really thought this through, haven't you."

I grin. "What can I say. Classes were boring today. I had nothing better to do than think of ways to deceive the government."

Her smile widens and my heart leaps. I'm glad to make her happy, even if only for a brief moment. Her smile is better than tears and panic. But the smile slips from her face a second later.

She hesitantly asks, "And if I tell them that you trust me...would I be telling a truth or a lie?"

I consider it a second. My answer may very well determine the rest of our lives, where we go from here. I need to tread carefully, think through what to say. But I don't. I know what I want to convey, but I can't get the words out. So I go a different route, probably making a huge mistake in the process, but whatever.

We can't keep skirting around each other.

I don't answer her, but instead say, "You have a free period next, right?"

"Uh, yeah. Why?"

I gather the remains of my lunch and stand from the table. "Come on."

She rises, too. "Where are we going?"

"There's something I want to show you."

Will I regret this later? Probably.

Do I care in this moment? Not at all.

We walk through the halls in silence and out into the crowded picnic area in the back of the school.

"What're we doing out here?" she wonders. "This isn't any less private than the cafeteria."

Some people look up as we come into sight. They give her smiles, but when their eyes skip to me, their expressions crumple as if they're confused on why Emma is hanging out with the weirdo foster kid who barely talks.

"We're just cutting through," I assure her, ignoring the stares. Emma doesn't seem aware of the attention at all. Maybe she's just used to it back at the Academy. "I don't want to risk walking out the front doors."

"I don't understand," she says as I lead her around to the front of the building.

"What I need to show you is at my house and since we both have a free period, now is the best time to go. You won't even have to lie to Cameron. He'll just think you're still at school."

I expect her to be happy, but she tenses and stops walking. "You mean we're leaving the school's campus?"

"Well, I don't live here," I joke.

She shifts on her feet. "But…but leaving during the day is against the rules!"

Chapter 28: Jesse

I laugh. "Really, Emma? You're completely fine with coming here to murder me, but the thought of breaking a few school rules is just out of the question?"

She bites her lip. "What if we get caught?"

"We won't," I promise. "Come on, Em. I'm trying to prove that you can trust me."

Her lips part and eyes widen a fraction of an inch at the slip up in her name. I didn't mean to use a nickname version. It just came out.

She blinks, shakes her head as if clearing it, and continues on as if I hadn't just called her something that usually only happens between friends. "By encouraging me to break the rules?"

"By telling you everything I know."

Her eyes dart around, like she's trying to find her next retort.

Her hand flies to her shirt sleeve and presses over where the arm band is hidden. "What about my tracker?"

I hold out my hand. "Give it to me. And your phone too in case they're also tracking that."

She slides it off and lays the teal braided bracelet in my palm, followed by her phone. I survey the area to make sure no one else is around, and then hide them in the shrubbery against the building.

"There. You can get it when we come back. No one will know you left the school."

She's finally out of excuses. "Fine. Let's go. But we better be back in time for next period."

. . .

It doesn't take long to reach my house. Thankfully, Greg's truck is missing from the driveway. Had he been home, we would have turned around and gone straight back to school. No way am I bringing someone else into that mess.

Beyond the Gates

I lead her to the bedroom. Once we're inside, I have to force down the uncomfortable feelings that threaten to escape. She already saw my house when she broke in, but it's different now that I'm with her. She's so observant, always taking in every detail. I don't want her to judge too harshly based on the terrible conditions I'm forced to live in.

The bedroom is a mess as always. I didn't exactly plan on having company today. Emma stands by the end of the bed as I remove the false paneling and take the corkboard down. I move around her and sit it on the bed.

We carefully settle beside it, each on one side of the board. The air between us is tense and awkward. Where do we go from here? This is what she's been waiting for and here I am, willingly giving it to her.

But isn't that what you do for the people you sort of trust? You help them in any way you can.

"The red tacks represent possible locations for the Academy," I begin. "The strings connect to the pieces of paper that give my reasoning and evidence for why it's a possibility. The blue tacks are places I've already investigated and came up empty."

I warily study her as she absorbs this new information. She examines the board, follows the strings and clues, reads the evidence, and asks questions about the shorthand notes she doesn't understand. Her face clears into a look of awe, a reaction I didn't quite expect.

"What?"

She shakes her head and peers at me with bright eyes. "This is just so incredible. There's so much information here about the Academy and the government, a lot of it is stuff *I* don't even know. And just...everything. You put all this together yourself?"

Chapter 28: Jesse

Her words render me speechless for a moment. She's amazed by *me*. The government's enemy. *Her* enemy.

No, I stop myself. I'm not her enemy anymore, am I? Is there even a word for what we are? I don't know, but it's not that.

She's still waiting for an answer, so I nod. "I've been working on it since I was about twelve."

Her eyes widen. "You were that young?"

I explain how I installed the corkboard right before Charlotte moved in.

She gazes at me before asking, "How did you find out about the Academy in the first place? How do you know about all of this? About us?"

Not enemy.

The words ping in my mind. She's not my enemy. I trust her, to an extent, and I want that trust to be reciprocated. But I can't give her the answers she wants. Not because I don't want her to know, but because I'm not sure I can handle rehashing the past. I'm not ready to talk about it yet, about what really happened all those years ago.

"Jesse?" she says tentatively after the silence drags on for some time.

"I'm sorry, Emma. I can't tell you."

The softness in her face, the ease that settled upon her, vanishes. She stiffens and becomes cold.

"You said you'd tell me everything," she accuses. "You told me to trust you."

"I know," I plead and reach for her like I'm afraid she's going to leave. What am I doing? She leans away and I drop my hand. "You *can* trust me, Emma. I want to tell you, I do. But I *can't*. It's too personal. Even thinking about it hurts. It's a mess and I know none of this is making sense right now, but I can't tell you. Not yet."

She sits perfectly still as my words sink in. She swallows, blinks a few times, and points to a note card pinned to the top corner of the board. "What's this one about?"

I relax with the subject change and the fact that she didn't walk out on me.

"That's all the information I gathered on you before the kidnapping. I haven't updated it since."

She reads the list, one of the few notes not written in my shorthand, since I was rushing when I wrote it. "Hmm, killing you from the inside out? Interesting."

"Hey, I didn't have much to go on other than your eyes glazed over every time we touched. How was I supposed to know you were reading and analyzing my future?"

She just shrugs and points to one of the newspaper clippings. "What are all of these for?"

"Incidents around the country where I suspect Academy kids on Missions were involved. I don't know if it'll actually help me locate the Academy, but I still like to keep up to date on the government's activity."

"Where did you even find all this stuff?"

"The Internet mostly," I reply. "I use the tablets at the library a lot to do research. I don't trust the government to not be tapped into my school tablet." That's all she needs to know for now. I'm not ready to tell her where the rest of my information came from. Not yet.

We spend some more time combing over the board. It's fine until the easy flow of conversation morphs into someone more, something I can't allow.

"So, what's it like living in foster care?" she asks nonchalantly.

Chapter 28: Jesse

I know she doesn't mean anything by it, but I shake my head. Her eyebrows furrow in confusion. Refusing to answer this time is different than before.

"Are you willing to work with me and help me find the Academy?" I ask in return. She stays silent, fiddling with her hands. "It's not a trick question. Do you want the full truth or not?"

"Yes," she agrees.

"Okay, but we need to make something clear." I keep my voice firm, definite. She needs to understand the ground rules for this situation. "This is strictly a business relationship. We have to trust each other to a certain extent for this to work, but total trust is not required or expected."

She nods. "Alright. I get it."

"But we are not friends," I continue. "We do not talk about anything outside of business and we do not engage in activities that are not related to the Academy. We do not pry into each other's personal lives. If either of us does something that makes the other question their motives or trust, the deal is off and our alliance is void. Do you understand?"

"Yes."

We stare at each other for a moment. I nod. "Okay, then."

After that matter is taken care of, we return to the board for a little while longer until I notice the time. "Free period is almost over. We should probably head back if you don't want to be late."

Her head snaps to the clock on the dresser. "Have we been here that long? It feels like we just got here."

"Yeah, well time flies when you're plotting the downfall of an entire government system."

She winces and my stomach drops.

"Sorry," I say hastily. "I shouldn't have—"

"No, no. It's fine," she interrupts. "It's just difficult sometimes to remember that I don't trust them anymore, that's all. I was there for seventeen years and it all changed in a matter of days."

"Yeah." I move to get off the bed.

"Wait," she stops me. "There's only two periods left in the day. We could just...stay."

I blink, taken aback. "Who's breaking the rules now?" I tease.

She lightly shoves me. "Shut up. Do you want to find the Academy or not?"

And that's how we end up spending an entire afternoon together, completely cutting school and ignoring all the problems around us.

. . .

"I really hope we're going to the park today, because I—"

Charlotte bursts into the room and stops cold. Emma and I look up at her, both wide-eyed. I completely lost track of time. Charlotte glances between me and Emma, her face eventually clearing. "Oh, you must be the girl my brother wrongfully kidnapped."

Emma shoots me a sideways look, her expression filled to the brim with anxiety. To Charlotte, she says, "Um yeah. We've sort of moved past that, though."

Charlotte looks at me and I give her a slight nod, confirmation that things are okay now. I already explained to her what went down in the warehouse and how messed up things had gotten, but I'm sure the fact that Emma is now in our house is a shock to her.

"That's good," my sister says and sits on the bed next to Emma. "I'm Charlotte, by the way. You can call me Char if you want. Jesse does sometimes."

Emma visibility relaxes as the tension ceases. She smiles. "We met in the grocery store that one time, remember?"

Chapter 28: Jesse

Charlotte grins and nods excitedly. She turns her attention to the bed. "You showed her the secret board?"

"Yeah, she's on our side now. I'll explain later."

Charlotte seems over the moon about that. It hadn't occurred to me until now, but she's lived with two boys and Greg for years. Maybe what she really needs is a sister. Someone she can relate to and who will understand her.

But I'm not ready for that yet. Besides, it would break the contract Emma and I just agreed on.

"We can be done for today," I say to Emma.

"Can't she come to the park with us when Oli gets home?" Charlotte protests.

"Sorry, Char. Emma has to get home. She has things to do." Even though I speak to my sister, I look at Emma. She picks up on my underlying message. It's time for her to go.

Emma slides off the bed.

"Don't forget your tracker," I remind her.

"I know." She says goodbye and walks out the door, leaving Charlotte crestfallen. That's how it has to be, though. I don't want her around the kids. I don't trust her enough for that.

CHAPTER TWENTY-NINE
Emma

Over the next week, we fall into a sort of routine. Jesse and I see each other during first period and sometimes we sit together at lunch, though Aria makes sure I sit with her most of the time. Even though I want to discuss things with Jesse, I go along with her. She *is* my only real friend here. I don't want to mess that up by ditching her. So I found a nice balance between them.

The Ambassador also backed off after I explained how Jesse is beginning to trust me more and share information with me. She seems more comfortable with letting me take my time now. And as far as I know, she has no idea of my sudden shift in loyalty or my new emotions that I'm still having difficulty controlling. I put everything I have into appearing normal every time we talk on the phone. It's exhausting, but she's never called me out for seeming different.

Every day after school, I go to Jesse's house so we can work together. Cameron thinks we're working on our school project and that I'm covertly gathering information in the process. Which isn't entirely a lie. Jesse and I mostly work on the Academy, but we do also have regular schoolwork to deal with.

Chapter 29: Emma

Right now, I'm on my stomach across his bed with my math homework that's ridiculously easy. Jesse's on the floor with his back against the closet door. The tablet he checked out from the library is balanced on his lap. His fingers skitter across the keys as he types up notes that we'll print out and add to a file later.

He's extremely focused on the task at hand. His narrowed eyes dart back and forth and his forehead creases from his furrowed eyebrows. He's only ever this concentrated when working on his Academy notes. It's an expression I've become familiar with over the past few days.

He glances up and I quickly refocus my gaze to the paper in front of me.

"Hey, I know you didn't want to tell me before, but I'm hoping you trust me a little more now." If he caught me staring, he doesn't let on. "I was wondering how the Academy chooses who gets to go on Missions and how they decide who does what. Why did they pick you for this particular task?"

Aren't we supposed to avoid personal questions? This seems personal to me. But the way he looks at me makes me think he doesn't mean it like that. It's like he needs to know solely for our search and nothing more.

So I tell him.

I explain how our training started when we were just five years old. How the government monitors our progress until we graduate at eighteen. How we're compared and ranked against each other and the very top are selected to go on Missions.

"But you're only seventeen," he says. "Unless you lied about that, too."

"I'm seventeen," I assure him. "The Ambassador thought I was good enough to be sent out a year early. Plus, you and I are the same age, so I'd blend into a high school setting better. She was wrong, though. I totally failed. Doesn't matter now, though. She was lying to us all along."

He gives me a strange look. "Were you close with her?"

I shrug. "Not really. It's more like I admired her and looked up to her like a parent. I trusted her. I wanted to *be* like her. She told us once how she used to have an ability, but some humans found out and experimented on her. This was before the Academy was created as a safe place for people like us. Or at least that's what she's always said. It could have all been a lie. I don't even know what to think anymore. Did she really do all that stuff to me? The trackers and the emotions? And why? What's the point?"

"I wish I knew. How does Cameron fit into this? Was he sent out early, too?"

I should probably stop revealing all this information, but what do I have to lose at this point? "No, he really is nineteen. He's in the program and he came with me to help out. He's not my brother, but he is my best friend. Oh, and Clarke is his last name, not mine. My name is actually Emma Grant."

That's kind of a lie, too, but I'm not about to tell him my full name.

Silence stretches between us, becoming uncomfortable.

"Sorry," Jesse says. "Probably shouldn't have asked you about all that stuff. It *was* helpful in understanding the Academy more, but it kind of ended up being a little less on the business side of things."

"It's fine," I say with what is hopefully a tone of nonchalance. What he doesn't know is how good it feels to finally talk to someone about the raging thoughts in my head. It's torture, constantly going back and forth between hating the government and trying to find a way to prove this is all some huge mistake. I would have continued talking if it wasn't a violation of our agreement.

Chapter 29: Emma

The beep of the oven timer splits the air. Jesse pops up and runs to the kitchen to turn it off. The timer signals that it's time for me to go. He wants me out of the house before his sister gets home from school. And I need to get home before Cameron starts to worry.

I pack up my backpack and sling it over my shoulder. Jesse waits by the door.

"See you tomorrow," I say. "Have a good night."

"You, too," he replies. He opens his mouth like he's going to say more, but then shakes his head. "See you tomorrow."

We are completely back to a professional tone. Like our personal conversation never happened.

And that's how it's gone on for an entire week. We go to school, sometimes meet up throughout the day, like lunch or free period, and then get together after school. We'll work on homework, the search for the Academy, or our class project until the timer goes off.

Then I leave.

The routine itself has been easy to adjust to. Life at the Academy was always routine and scheduled. On the outside, our agreement isn't difficult at all. On the inside, however, I'm still a mess. There's no schedule or predictability with my new emotions.

The worst part is the emotions that have started surfacing when I'm alone with Jesse. I really, *really* don't want to, but I can't help but start to trust him.

And I want to know more. I want him to tell me about his life outside of the search for the Academy. I want to know his siblings and his past and his plans for the future. That'll never be possible, though. Asking about his life is too personal. Having the contract is a good thing. If I know him past the business relationship we've created, I might trust him more than I already do. And I already trust him way too much.

The Ambassador still thinks I'm working against him. What's going to happen when it comes down to it and it's time for me to kill him? Will I be able to do it? Is that even still an option?

If the government finds out about my change in allegiance, it might be the only way to get back on their good side.

I also can't take everything Jesse says as the complete truth. He's not lying, but what if there's another side to the story? One that he doesn't know about.

Discreetly questioning the Ambassador might help, but what if I find out there isn't another side? That Jesse is one hundred percent right? What if I find out there is more to this?

Do I want there to be?

. . .

"I'm home!" I shout as I walk into the apartment.

There's a scraping of chairs from the kitchen.

"It's about time," a female voice says, one I certainly didn't expect. Aria appears around the corner, a grin on her face. Cameron is right behind her. "Did you forget we have a biology test to study for?"

I mentally face palm. I did forget actually. I have bigger things to worry about than some stupid biology test I know I'll get an A on whether I study or not.

"Sorry, I was at the library with Jesse. We're still working on our school project."

She follows me to my bedroom. "It's fine."

We sit on my bed and get our tablets out.

"You know, you could have messaged me," I point out. "You have my number."

She just shrugs, though a hint of a smile appears on her face. "Yeah, well. Cameron was keeping me company while I waited."

Chapter 29: Emma

"Oh, I see. So you're really here to hang out with my brother," I tease. She pushes me and I laugh. "Don't worry. I won't tell him about your crush."

"How about we just focus on studying for this test, okay?" she says, though her small grin never truly goes away. "Unless you just really want to talk about boys. How's Jesse?"

"You know, studying for this test sounds perfect."

She shoves me and I shove her back with a laugh.

It's nice to spend time with someone normal. And maybe with Aria in the picture, Cameron will get over me, if what Lacy said about his crush on me is really true. Maybe then, when Cameron finds out the truth—because he *will* find out, it's only a matter of time—he'll be more inclined to accept it rather than to immediately turn us in to the government.

The only problem, of course, is keeping Aria out of this whole mess the rest of us are in. She can hang out with me and Cameron and be our friend, but she never needs to discover who we really are. It'll just make things so much more complicated than they already are. I really don't want to lose the one friend I have here.

It's different with her. She doesn't know who I am like Jesse does, and she doesn't expect me to be the way I've always been, like Cameron. She's just Aria, my friend.

Maybe it's bad for me to get attached to a human who doesn't know the truth, but given how my whole life has been turned upside down within the past week, something as simple and stable as my growing friendship with Aria is something I need.

And I'm grateful for it.

CHAPTER THIRTY
Jesse

The agreement between Emma and I is essential to our working together. It's a necessary barrier between us that makes it less likely that she'll stab me in the back. This is how it has to be. Our relationship is built on a sprinkle of trust and a mutual desire to find the Academy and discover more about the government. I don't ask about her personal life unless it's related to our research, and she doesn't ask about mine.

I hate it and kind of regret making the contract in the first place. While it was objectively a good idea, I've realized there's more to it than I thought. And since then, I've been searching for a loophole, some way around the terms I stupidly set in place. I keep coming back to *what really constitutes a personal conversation?* but if she determines it to be too personal—if *I'm* the one to break the contract—she'll have every right to come after me again.

But I can't help it. I'm inexplicably fascinated by her. What was her life truly like at the Academy? Not just the way the program operates, but life for her specifically. How is she doing emotionally? I've almost asked her about it every day, but always stop myself before the words leave my mouth.

Chapter 30: Jesse

She's not okay. As hard as she tries to hide it, her eyes always speak the truth. She's a wreck on the inside and there's nothing I can do about it.

A little after a week of having our agreement in place, I sit alone at my table in the cafeteria. Emma's with her other friends. Not that we are friends, so it doesn't really matter if she eats lunch with me or not. Spending time together after school is more than enough.

She's across the room. The others at her table laugh at something she said without noticing the fake smile plastered to her face. She doesn't belong with them.

Enemy. She's your enemy and you hate her. Yes, you're working with her and you kinda trust her, but that doesn't change the big picture situation here.

But she never asked to be raised that way, to be controlled and taught to believe that humans are inferior to her.

She was sent here to kill *you. What if this is all part of her plan?*

What if she needs me to trust her as much as I want her to trust me?

The battle clamors in my mind. I'm not brought out of it until her head turns in my direction. From across the room, she catches me staring at her. The corner of her mouth flicks up. I quickly look down at my food.

Enemy, I remind myself. It doesn't help.

...

We go to my house after school like all the other days. Emma lays on my bed and works on our project. I lean against the closet door and type up my English paper on my school tablet.

Or at least I try. Emma shifts every few seconds, taps her pencil against her notebook, sighs and shuffles through papers. Can't she be still for like two seconds?

I have two options: ignore her or risk breaking the agreement.

The decision is easier than it should be.

"I know it's against the rules, but can I ask you a personal question?"

She peers at me with hesitation. "Depends on the question."

I shift uncomfortably. "How are you doing? You know, with the emotions and everything."

The crease in her forehead vanishes. Her body loosens, almost like she's relieved. "Definitely not as bad as the first day, but...I'm still a mess. I don't...I can't always tell what I'm feeling. But I think I'm getting better at outwardly controlling it. Internally, though, I have absolutely no idea what's going on."

"I'm here if you need me." The words tumble out before I can stop them. I rush on. "I can't begin to imagine what you're going through, but if you need to talk about it, regardless of our agreement, I'm here."

She blinks, swallows, and then says, "Thanks. This past week has just been really confusing. Sometimes I wish I could go back to when I didn't have emotions, but then I feel bad for wanting that. I should be grateful I know the truth and that I'm not still blindly believing their lies. It's just...difficult, trying to pretend that everything is okay when it's not."

Not enemy, I finally decide.

"You shouldn't feel bad," I say to her surprise. "Everything you thought you knew about your life was ripped to shreds not even two weeks ago. Your conflicted reaction seems fairly normal."

She smiles. "Thank you, Jesse. I just...thank you."

Before I can say anything else, the bedroom door opens and my siblings walk in. *Both* of them.

Panic jolts through me. In my eagerness to finish my English paper so we could resume work on the corkboard, I forgot to set the timer.

Chapter 30: Jesse

Charlotte's calm stance indicates she's not at all surprised to see Emma sprawled across the bed. Oliver is quiet as usual and sticks close to Charlotte's side. Emma is frozen.

"When did you get home?" I ask Charlotte.

With a sheepish grin, she says, "The usual time. I hung out in the living room until Oli came in since you two were working in here."

Oliver's attention locks in on Emma. She glances at me and I nod.

"Hi," she says with a tiny smile. "I'm Emma."

Oliver meets my eyes with a questioning gaze. *Isn't this the girl who was trying to kill you?*

"She's on our side now," I assure him. To Emma, I say, "This is Oliver."

If she's at all curious about his behavior, she doesn't say anything.

Oliver seeks my eyes again, a familiar expression on his face. He wants to go to the park.

"Maybe," I reply and gather my school supplies. Emma thaws from her frozen state and packs her things away, too.

Oli tugs on the hem of my shirt.

"Okay," I cave, though it didn't take much. "We can go to the park."

"Yay!" Charlotte cheers and bounds out of the room. Oli grabs my hand and races after her.

Emma laughs. An actual, genuine laugh. I glance over my shoulder as Oliver attempts to drag me through the doorway. Later, I'll probably regret what I say next. But I don't care.

"Do you want to come?"

CHAPTER THIRTY-ONE
Emma

It's difficult to resist the urge to stare at Jesse as we walk to the park. His face is unreadable every time I steal a glance. Why is he suddenly okay with my presence? Why didn't he make me leave when his siblings got home?

And most importantly, what about our agreement?

On our way, Charlotte chatters non-stop about all sorts of things, most of which I'm too wound up to focus on.

The park is a mulch-enclosed playground in a wide, grassy field. There's a swing set in the grass right outside the mulched area. Charlotte and Oliver bolt toward the playground. Jesse hangs back and sits on one of the swings. I join him.

The two kids chase each other, Charlotte shrieking with laughter and Oliver with a huge smile on his face. I smile, too, at how carefree and light they seem in this moment. There's only a trace of the gloom that weighed them down back at the house.

I turn to Jesse and familiarity washes over me. This is what I saw in his head. It hadn't made sense then, that I would smile at him like this, but we're different now.

Chapter 31: Emma

"They're not usually this happy," Jesse mutters, almost to himself. He looks at me. "So, what do you think?"

"About what?"

He shifts, loses his composure for a split second. "About them."

I look out to the playground where Charlotte hangs from the monkey bars and Oliver slides down the slide.

"I like them," I say honestly. "They're complete opposites, though. Charlotte's so outgoing, and Oliver's kind of quiet. But they both seem sweet. I understand why you want to protect them."

This conversation is so far from business, but he doesn't seem to mind, so I'm not complaining. The whole contract thing was his idea to begin with.

"Yeah," Jesse says so low I barely hear. "He doesn't talk at all."

My eyes snap to his. Incoherent fragments of questions I want to ask bounce in my mind, but I can't put them together. It doesn't matter, though, because Jesse keeps talking.

"In the entire two years he's lived with me, he hasn't spoken a single word. It might have to do with how he ended up in foster care in the first place. I don't know what happened to his family, but I've always wondered if maybe he witnessed something terrible and won't talk because of it."

I process the information. "So…so you think he *saw* his parents die?"

Jesse shrugs. "I don't know, but usually when someone stops talking, it's because they experienced something horrible."

His voice is raw with pain as he speaks. The love he has for his siblings that aren't even biologically related to him shines across his face. But his eyes hold something else, some emotion I have yet to identify.

What am I supposed to say? What do I do? My mind whirls, but I come up blank.

"You don't have to say anything," Jesse says, apparently picking up on my struggle to find the right words.

I sigh. "How do you do it?"

"Do what?"

I throw my hands up. "Live with emotions! It's so—ugh! I don't even know what to call what I feel. I never know how I'm supposed to react or what the right thing to say is. Half the time I don't even know what it is I'm feeling. I know the words for emotions and what they used to feel like, but it's different now and I can't connect them. I hate it. Why can't I just be normal?"

The wisp of control I've maintained the past week slips through my fingers at my outburst. My chest is on fire. My hands shake.

"You'll learn," he says gently. Why is he so good at this? "It hasn't even been two weeks. I told you I'd help you, remember? I don't completely understand what you're going through, but you don't have to pretend around me, okay? You don't have to act like you're normal because honestly, normal doesn't exist. Everyone is different and has their own problems and their own lives. If you were whatever you consider to be normal, you wouldn't be *you*."

I shake my head. "How…how are you so okay with all of this? With me? Just a week ago, you wouldn't let me anywhere near them and a few days before that, I was out to kill you. You don't know me and the things you do know are…bad."

He disagrees. "I don't think you're a bad person, at least not anymore. Not after this week we've spent together. Yes, bad things have happened *to* you, but that doesn't make it your fault. They were controlling you. You just have to learn to adjust to not being under that control."

Silence settles as I collect my thoughts and try to put my feelings into words. "I think it's…amazing that you take such good care of Charlotte and Oliver, even though you don't have to."

Chapter 31: Emma

He winces. "I do have to. I try to be their brother, but sometimes I have to step in and be their parent. They wouldn't have anyone if I didn't."

"But what about your foster dad?"

He visibly flinches this time, and a thought occurs to me. "Is he…is he the reason for the bruises?"

His throat bobs as he swallows, then nods. "Greg is hardly ever home, which is good because he can be…abusive. Mostly towards me, but sometimes I'm not there and they get hurt instead."

My heart drops out of my chest and into the pit of my stomach. "Jesse, that's…that's…well, I don't know the name for what I feel, but it's not good."

"Terrible, horrible, awful, etcetera."

I nod. "Yes, all of those things." It's going to take a while, but hopefully I'll get the hang of this whole emotion thing. Then I ask, "Have you ever told anyone?"

"No, I can't," he says with a forceful shake of his head. "CPS would remove us from his care for sure, but the three of us would probably get split up and there's no way I'm ever letting that happen."

"But if they would be better off somewhere safer—"

"No," he cuts me off. "You don't understand the system, okay? Despite everything the government's done, you've always had a home. You've always had food and a bed to sleep in. Trust me, all of us have had worse situations than this. If it means we get to stay together, I'm willing to put up with him."

I swallow the rising lump in my throat. The more we talk, the further away he gets from the image of a psychotic teenage boy the government planted in my head.

"So, what about Charlotte?" I ask, genuinely curious.

"She's been living with me for five years. She doesn't really talk about her situation much, but her parents basically abandoned her. They took off, left her behind, and never came back. If there was a specific reason why, she's never told me. Just that CPS picked her up when she ended up on her own. She's been in foster care ever since."

"Wow, that's terrible," I say, using one of the words from earlier.

"Yeah, she's always making me promise that I'll never leave her. I think she's scared that one day, she's going to be left alone again."

I dig my feet into the grass. "I can kind of relate because of my whole parent situation, but I never actually knew them. It must be a whole lot worse to have your parents abandon you after seven years."

"It doesn't really matter how it happens. It hurts whether they leave you on purpose or are taken from you, whether you're seven or seventeen. Losing the people you love will always hurt."

"Your family died in some kind of accident, right?"

Jesse flinches like I've slapped him across the face. That probably wasn't the best thing to say in this particular moment. My filter is something else I need to work on.

His eyes glaze over with a far-away look.

"I'm s-sorry," I stutter. "You're...upset?"

He closes his eyes, presses his lips into a tight line, then shakes his head. "I just wasn't aware you knew about that."

I'm terrible at reading and understanding emotions, but even I can tell he *is* upset. "See? This is what I mean. I don't know how to think before I speak."

He shrugs and glances at me with those haunted eyes that reveal the true weight of his struggles. "It's fine. And yeah, it was an accident. A house fire. How did you know?"

Chapter 31: Emma

I bite my lip. No more secrets. "Um, it was in a file the government gave me before I came here."

He raises an eyebrow. "I have a file?"

I nod. "It's not much. Just basic information, but it did say your family died in an accident and you've been in foster care ever since."

"Okay," he says, tone suddenly changing into one of amusement instead of anger. "You have a file about me, you broke into my house, you've read my future multiple times without permission. It's time I learn a little more about you, don't you think?"

A smile spreads across my face. For once, I don't want to deflect the attention from myself. Telling him anything else is definitely further betrayal of the government, but I don't feel bad about it anymore. Especially with all he's shared with me. The government crossed me first. They don't deserve my loyalty.

"What do you want to know?"

"Anything." His eyes hold mine. He looks at me like I'm some puzzle he's trying to solve but is missing most of the pieces. "What was it like growing up there?"

Images of random moments flash through my mind and send a pang through my chest.

"It's somewhat similar to life out here. We still have to take core content classes in school like English and math. Our progress is ranked, like I told you before. We also have...special classes that I'm positive you don't take outside the Academy."

"Like learning how to kill people?"

A laugh bubbles out of me. How is it that we're already able to joke about that now?

"Yeah, something like that. In elementary and middle school, we mostly worked on perfecting our abilities. It's high school where things get really fun. We learn self-defense and how to use weapons.

And yes, I did take a beginner class on how to stealthily extract information from people and how to kill without getting caught."

"Stealthy?" he snorts. "I knew exactly what you were doing."

I roll my eyes. "If I had graduated and gone through advanced training, I would have been better at it, trust me. Besides, you're a unique case. Most people don't know about us, remember?"

After that, I tell him about the graduation process and more about the ranking system, including my status as number one in my class.

"So you're the best in everything?" he says in awe. "That's amazing."

My face warms at his compliment. "Almost everything," I correct and then admit one of my greatest weaknesses. "I can't shoot a gun."

He blinks. "Wait, really?"

I nod and avert my eyes from him. "My aim is terrible when it comes to guns. I can throw a knife perfectly, shoot an arrow, throw a punch, but I can't aim a gun and hit even a stationary target to save my life."

"Then how exactly were you planning to kill me?"

I shrug and look back at him. "I hadn't thought that far ahead but trust me. I don't need a gun to kill you. I'm expertly trained in operating a variety of weapons, but I can also knock you unconscious with my bare hands."

"Really?" he grins. "You think so? I'd like to see you try."

It takes me a second to respond. What is this new, playful tone between us?

"Sure, maybe I can teach you a thing or two after you regain consciousness."

"You seem pretty confident," he comments.

"Well I *have* been involved in this since birth."

Chapter 31: Emma

"You do remember *I'm* the one who knocked *you* out and kidnapped you, right?"

I throw my hands up. "You slipped a pill in my drink to make me fall asleep. That's cheating."

"Point taken," he laughs.

Why are we so comfortable speaking to each other like this? When did our relationship change from professional to something more? Why does he feel more and more like a friend, and less like a business partner?

"So," he continues. "Now that you've told me about school, what do you like to do for fun?"

"What do you mean?"

"Like, when you aren't in class or on a dangerous secret mission, what do you do?"

I give him a blank stare. "Well I have to eat and sleep."

He shakes his head. "Do you not understand the definition of fun? I can assure you it doesn't involve school, eating, or sleeping."

I look at the ground. "That's all I do with my life, so you're going to have to be more specific."

Oblivious to my discomfort, he says, "What are your hobbies? What do you love? Do you like to read? What TV shows do you enjoy? What about movies or music or sports?"

His face is expectant, curious. He doesn't get it. He doesn't understand what life at the Academy is truly like. Not that I blame him. No one could ever understand what it's like unless they've lived there and experienced it firsthand. We don't do stuff 'just for fun.'

Well, okay, maybe that's not entirely true. I guess you could consider hanging out with friends and wandering the City on weekends as 'fun.' But as far as what he's asking about specifically…

I try to explain. "The only books they have are nonfiction, they don't have access to much television, and sports were never offered. We don't have time for entertainment. We're supposed to focus solely on our training."

He runs a hand through his hair. "That's crazy, Emma. Maybe you can teach me self-defense and I'll teach you how to have fun."

"Maybe," I smile, though I'm unsure if he's serious or not. "What do you like to do?"

He grins. "You mean when I'm not obsessing over my need for revenge, taking care of the kids, or abducting teenagers? I like to drive."

"Your car?"

He just smirks and says, "I'll show you what I mean tomorrow after school. If you're up for it, of course."

His eyes hold a mischievous glint, a nice contrast from the usual emptiness. It's refreshing to see him so full of life.

I agree to meet him. Getting close to each other is such a bad, destructive idea, but I don't care anymore. I want to know what fun feels like. I'll deal with the consequences later.

"So is the contract thing over?" I ask. I have to know for sure where we stand.

"Definitely."

CHAPTER THIRTY-TWO
Jesse

"Hey, Jesse!"

A girl I don't know, but have seen with Emma's lunch group, stands in front of me. We're in the cafeteria and it's Emma's day to sit with me.

"Yeah?" I reply.

Her smile brightens. "You should come sit with us. It makes more sense for all of us to sit together instead of Em going back and forth. The group would love to meet you."

So now they want to be friends? Where was that invitation nine years ago? They only notice me now because of Emma. Which is why I politely respond with, "No, thanks."

Her face falls. "Oh, okay. Em, you coming?"

Emma shakes her head. I bite my lip to keep from smiling.

"Well, see you around, I guess."

She walks off to join the group.

"I can't believe that just happened. Your friends really seem to have taken an interest in me since you showed up."

"They're not my friends," Emma says firmly. "Not really. I just hang out with them so I'll blend in like I'm supposed to. Aria's the only one I consider a friend."

"Aria? How is she any different from the others?"

"I don't know," she shrugs. "She was nice to me when I first moved here. I mean, she's not Cameron or my friends back at the Academy, but it's nice to have a normal conversation with someone once in a while. Even if it's just talking about school. In a way, it's helped me deal with everything that's happened."

I nod. That seems reasonable.

"The others, I try to limit the time I spend with them. It's too much work, pretending to be something I'm not. One wrong move and they'll know something is wrong with me." She looks away and picks at her food with a plastic fork. "I don't have to worry about that when I'm with you, now that we know the truth about each other."

"Good point. And just so you know, there's nothing wrong with you." But she's undeniably right about it being easier. I don't have to pretend around her either. And it's certainly an improvement to being completely ignored. "So we're still on for this afternoon, right?"

"Absolutely. I'll meet you outside at the usual spot."

. . .

My hands shake as I gather my backpack from my locker at the end of the day. Why am I so nervous? We're just going to drive my car. She's already seen it and ridden in it, so this isn't a big deal.

Except that it is. I'm not just taking her to the car. I'm taking her to the place where I *store* the car.

The location is just as important as the car itself. It's where I go when the overwhelming stress of life gets to be too much, when I hit yet another dead end with the corkboard, when the devastating

Chapter 32: Jesse

loss of my family strikes me as it occasionally does. No one else has ever been there. Not even Charlotte and Oliver know of its existence or the meaning it holds in my life.

Emma's at the bottom of the steps when I make it out of the building. Her last class must be closer to the exit than mine, because she always beats me to our meeting spot.

We weave in and out of the crowd of teenagers and set off down the sidewalk.

"Where exactly are we going?" she asks.

"It's a secret," I say with a grin. I clench my fists to stop my hands from shaking. It doesn't matter if my heart is rapidly pulsing. She can't see that. Although, would she even understand what my body language meant if she did see?

"Of course you won't tell me," she grumbles. "You're probably luring me somewhere so you can brutally murder me."

I fake a scoff. "Am I really that sketchy? I think we're to the point now where we can trust each other a little more than that."

She gives a short laugh, but says, "Can we though? You said yesterday that our agreement is over. But what does that mean? Where does that leave us?"

I mull it over. "It means that we don't have to be strictly impersonal all the time. We can still work together on finding the Academy, but we can also talk about other things. We can ask each other personal questions. We don't have to answer if we don't want to, of course. But that option is there if we want something more than just allies against the government."

She grows quiet for a few minutes. We're almost there when she says, "Like friends?"

"Yes," I grin. "Kinda like friends."

We round a corner and come upon the forest. I lead her to the edge, and she turns to me. "You brought me to a secluded forest? Tell me, how is that not suspicious?"

"I promise this isn't going to turn into a horror movie. Not that you've ever seen one to know what I'm talking about. We'll fix that another time. Come on."

We cross the threshold and the trees envelop us. The leaves rustle with the cool breeze. The car is parked a few feet from the entrance. Out of sight, but easy to drive in and out.

"Oh, yeah. You wanted to show me your car."

I nod. "But there's something else I want you to see first. We'll come back to the car."

A dirt path winds through the forest. It's so familiar to me I could walk it in my sleep. After a few minutes of stumbling through the overgrown brush, the trees thin and open into a clearing. A waterfall spills over a mound of rocks and drops into a gurgling stream. A walking bridge connects one side of the embankment to the other.

Emma's eyes go wide and her lips part in awe. "It's beautiful," she breathes and steps onto the bridge. We stop in the middle. She leans against the railing and stares up at the waterfall. "This is so amazing!"

She takes everything in. The blue of the stream below us, the vibrant green of the trees around us. The forest is alive with the sounds of wildlife. She's right. Everything about this place is beautiful. The way she examines the world fascinates me. It's like she's never seen trees or water before. If I brought her here a few weeks ago, the magnificence of this place would have meant nothing to her. It's spectacular how much a little emotion can change a person.

Chapter 32: Jesse

Sunlight streams through the gaps in the trees. Her blonde hair shimmers as the light catches it. Her green eyes sparkle. Something stirs inside me when I see her like this, so full of life and emotion.

"Thank you, Jesse. For bringing me here. It…it really means a lot to me. There was so much I never got to do when the government had control over me. I've missed out on so much. I never even knew there was stuff like this out here."

"You're welcome," I say softly. "We can come back here whenever you want. I come here a lot anyways."

We stay a big longer, then hike back to the car.

"So now what?" she asks.

I pat the car's hood. "Whenever I'm stressed or worried or just want something fun, I drive on all the back roads that no one uses anymore. It clears my mind and, in a way, it's my own personal way of defying the government since my car is kind of illegal."

She nods.

Please don't freak out over what I'm about to say.

"You want to learn to have fun and live life, right?"

She eyes me warily. "Right," she says slowly with caution in her tone.

I take a deep breath. "Great, because I have the perfect way to start. You're going to learn how to drive."

CHAPTER THIRTY-THREE
Emma

"Are you out of your mind?" *Drive?* He wants to teach me how to drive. I step back and vigorously shake my head. "No, absolutely not."

"Come on," he persuades. "Who knows, maybe you'll need to know how to do this one day."

You did say you wanted to have fun.

With a deep breath to calm my racing heart, I say, "Okay."

"Wait here." He gets into the car and eases it out of the forest and onto the dirt road. He waves me over once he gets it positioned. I reluctantly approach him and the death machine, though my mind screams in protest.

Jesse jumps out, holds the door open, and gestures for me to get in. He shuts it behind me. I run my sweaty palms along my jeans and try to cease their shaking.

"Don't forget your seat belt," he says after settling into the passenger seat.

"My what?"

He frowns. "Don't tell me you don't know what a seat belt is."

Chapter 33: Emma

When I continue to stare blankly at him, he leans over. My breath sharpens as he reaches across me and pulls a strap over my body. He snaps it into place and leans back.

"I guess you wouldn't know since the driver-less cars don't have them. I forget sometimes how isolated you were at the Academy. Basically, manual cars have these straps called seat belts that hold a person in place if there's a crash. Driver-less cars don't have them since crashes are rare."

I think back to the last time I was in his car. "We didn't wear seat belts before."

"Well, yeah, because I was driving and I know what I'm doing. You've never been behind the wheel before, so we're wearing seat belts."

I nod and fidget in the seat. The seat belt strap rests uncomfortably against my shoulder and waist, making it difficult to concentrate. A thin smile plays across his face, but my stomach is too squeamish for me to return it.

"We're going to go over some basic stuff first, okay?"

"Sure, but before we do that, what am I feeling?"

It's similar to the first emotion I ever truly felt. Fear. But this isn't entirely the same. A definite word to put with the physical sensation will be beneficial later on.

"How should I know?"

"Seriously?" I splutter. "You have way more experience with this than me!"

"Okay, calm down." He looks me over. "I'd say given the way you're stalling right now and the situation of driving for the first time, you're probably nervous."

I let that sink in. "So nervous means accelerated heartbeat, shortness of breath, and shakiness. Good to know."

"Sure," he shrugs. "If you want to be technical about it, I guess." He turns the topic back to driving. "So, there are two pedals on the floorboard. The right is your gas and the left is the brake. You're only going to use your right foot to press them."

He puts his hand on the control thing between the seats. "This is the gear shift. It's pretty self-explanatory. D for drive. R for reverse. P for park. You can also adjust the mirrors if you need to."

My pulse lurches when he finishes speaking. We're almost to the actual driving part. What if I mess up? What if I crash and wreck one of the few things that makes him happy? What if we get hurt?

"Hands on the steering wheel," he instructs. I slide my sweaty hands up and down the wheel, unsure of how to place them in a way that's both safe and comfortable. My heart threatens to escape right out of my chest, and I can't breathe. Nervous is not an emotion I like experiencing.

"Here," Jesse says softly. Before I can protest, his hands cover my own, his skin warm on mine. I wince at the pull in my mind as he moves my clammy hands to the correct position and pulls away. "Just relax. I'll be right beside you the whole time. Nothing bad will happen, I promise."

His words do little to calm me. To waste more time, I say, "You're brave, you know that?"

He raises his brows like I'm crazy. "What?"

"To touch my hands, knowing I can see pieces of your future through hand-to-hand contact."

His face instantly pales. "D-Did you just…"

"No, lucky for you, I blocked it out. After being in someone's head a few times, I'm able to get tuned to them, to their mind. When you touched me, I felt my mind wanting to connect with yours, but I was able to break it this time. I should be able to keep you out from now on, but you didn't know that, hence the bravery."

Chapter 33: Emma

Jesse shrugs indifferently, but I can tell he's a little freaked out by the reminder of what I can do. "I actually forgot about it in the moment. I wasn't thinking. Anyway, stop stalling and let's get started."

He's right. I can't keep putting this off.

I take deep, steadying breaths and hone all my attention into the stretch of empty road before us.

"Okay, put your foot on the brake pedal and press all the way down." He moves the gear shift from park to drive. "Now slowly release the brake."

I ease some of the pressure off the pedal. The car starts forward. *We're moving!*

I slam down on the brake and we jerk forward. The seat belt digs into my shoulder, but luckily keeps me strapped to the seat.

"Sorry," I squeak out.

"It's fine. That's why we're wearing the seat belts. Besides, we weren't even going that fast."

"Going that fast?" I'm close to hysterics. "We were practically flying down the road."

He chuckles. "See the speedometer? We barely went over the zero miles per hour mark."

I huff but try again. We move forward as I slowly raise off the brake. My knuckles turn white with how tight my fingers are curled around the wheel. The car coasts along at an unpleasantly fast pace.

When I say as much, Jesse responds with, "Turtles would be passing us up right now."

"Shut up," I say, and he laughs.

"You're actually doing pretty well. Now give it some gas."

The car bolts forward, leaving my heart behind. I was wrong before. *This* is dangerously fast. But I don't want a repeat of earlier, so I let it happen. I make it all the way to the end of the road, right before the turn. I'm definitely not ready for that yet.

"Come to a complete stop."

I try to gently press the brake, but we jerk forward again. Silence settles over us, my heavy breathing the only sound. Jesse puts the car in park.

"Do you want to go again or be done for today?"

The knots in my stomach unfurl. "Let's be done."

Jesse and I switch seats, an act I'm grateful for. The passenger seat provides comfort and safety. He drives around the curve and loops back around to where we started.

He slows the car to a flawless stop and trains his eyes on me. "So, I was thinking we could go to the warehouse next. If you're still interested in teaching me all you know about knocking someone out cold, of course."

"Yeah, sure."

He grins and drives off.

We arrive at the warehouse in no time. The decrepit building looks so different now than the last time I was here. It's not threatening anymore. It's just a building and we're just two teenagers who need a secluded location.

Jesse slides the door back and flips on the lights. The chair and rope are still in the center of the room.

"Sorry," he mumbles and hauls the stuff off to the side. "I haven't been back here since...you know."

"It's fine. You maybe didn't go about it in the best way, but if you hadn't done what you did, we'd still be against each other. We've made a lot of progress since you kidnapped me and got me out from under the government's control."

And it's true. I'd still be the government's emotionless robot and he'd still be the boy obsessed with revenge. Not that he doesn't

Chapter 33: Emma

want payback anymore, but at least he's considering his options more rationally than before.

"Okay, stand across from me and position your legs shoulder width apart. You'll also want to stay on the balls of your feet, but you don't have to do that until we're ready to actually start practicing. For now, make a fist."

He curls his fingers. I'm pleasantly…surprised? by the outcome.

"Look at you, knowing the thumb goes on the outside instead of between the fingers."

He rolls his eyes. "Well yeah. I'm not stupid."

"That's debatable."

He blinks and his eyebrows dip. An offended expression flashes across his face.

"Lighten up. It's sarcasm, a joke."

He relaxes. "Oh, yeah. Right."

I shake my head with a smile. "Honestly. I'm the one who lacked emotions for seventeen years."

"Yeah, yeah." He waves dismissively, but that grin reappears.

I shake out my shoulders to loosen up and say, "Okay, now punch me."

The smile melts off his face. "I'm sorry, what?"

"Punch me."

"Are you crazy? I'm not gonna punch you."

"Come on, Jesse. I can't teach you anything if I don't first see where you're starting at. Throw a punch. You won't hurt me, I promise."

He shakes his head, uncurling his fists.

"Fine," I huff. "You don't want to punch me? Then I guess you'll have to be on defense."

"Wha—"

Beyond the Gates

I lunge. His eyes fly wide and he jumps out of my reach. He has surprisingly fast reflexes. I swing at him a few times, in enough control that it's impossible for my fist to ever come in contact with him. But he doesn't know that. I need him to raise his arms and fight back. Jumping out of the way can only get a person so far.

He refuses to strike at me. I soon grow tired of the game he's playing and strategically back him into a corner. His back hits the wall and I dive forward. I press my arm against his chest, pinning him to the wall. Our chests move in sync with our heavy breathing.

We stand face to face, closer than we've ever been. "Why won't you fight back?"

His gaze fills with pain. "Because I know what it's like to get hit. I don't want to ever inflict that on anyone else."

My irritation dwindles. I didn't consider his past experiences with violence.

"You can't hurt me," I whisper. "You won't learn how to defend yourself if you don't try. And it starts with throwing a punch. Trust me, you won't make contact with me. I drove a car for you even though I was scared. It's time for you to face your own fears."

He stares at me, blinks a few times. His throat bobs when he nods. "That. That was the right thing to say."

I wasn't even focused on trying to make words fit together. I just told him exactly what I was thinking. How interesting that when I'm not stressed over saying or doing the right thing, the right thing happens.

I release him and return to the center of the room.

"Okay," I say after repositioning him. "You're far enough away that you can't touch me. Now punch."

He thankfully listens this time and punches...it's just not very good. It's more of a pathetic toss of his fist in my general direction.

Chapter 33: Emma

"Wow," I blow out a breath and take a step toward him. He instinctively backs up. "Really? You're not going to hurt me. I need to get closer to help you. Even if you do manage to land a hit, it won't be any worse than what I experienced at the Academy. I've been taking self-defense classes for years and received my fair share of bruises as a result."

"Fine." He steps forward. "What do you want me to do?"

"You need to punch with your whole body. Your dominant arm should be pulled slightly closer to your body than your other arm. Keep your elbows tucked in, but not so close that they're touching your sides. When you extend your arm, twist your body and shoulders into it to maximize the force behind it. Try again."

He squares his shoulders, brings his arms up, and punches.

"Better," I comment. It's much like me with driving. I'm not perfect, but even over the course of one session, I improved. Jesse is the same.

We work on his punches for a while. When we're done for the day, I ask, "Do you know where I can buy a safety mat?"

He shrugs. "Probably the store. Why?"

"Because eventually I'll need to teach you how to bring people to the ground."

"Of course you will," he sighs.

We walk outside to the car. "You did good today."

The corner of his mouth pulls up. "Thanks. You, too. We should probably head back now, though. I have to be home by the time Charlotte gets there."

We drive back to the forest. He parks the car and we begin the walk back, stopping at the point where we have to go our separate ways.

"You can come over if you want." He shoots me a sideways glance as if I'm afraid I'll laugh at him.

My stomach twists and heart jolts from the unexpected offer. "I uh…I'd love to, but I have to get back before Cameron gets suspicious. Plus, the government will be calling soon."

He nods with understanding. "So I'll see you tomorrow?" His tone is questioning. Does he really think after everything we've been through, I suddenly wouldn't want to see him?

I offer up a genuine smile. "Yeah, I'll see you tomorrow."

CHAPTER THIRTY-FOUR
Jesse

"What's got you so happy?" Charlotte asks the following morning. She and Oliver are eating breakfast while I clean up the kitchen. My hands are submerged in scalding water as I wash the dishes Greg left behind last night. We used to have a dishwasher, but it broke a while back and Greg refuses to fix or replace it.

"What are you talking about?"

I have my back to her, but I can pretty much hear the impatient eye roll. "You're doing chores and don't seem all that upset about it. I got home right before you did yesterday, which never happens. This doesn't have anything to do with Emma, does it?"

I freeze, the sponge mid swipe across the plate. "Why would you think that?"

She scoffs. "I don't know, maybe because you wouldn't let her anywhere near us, then all of a sudden she's going to the park with us and you're spending time with her doing friend-like things which you said you were going to avoid."

I swing around, spraying soap suds in my haste. Charlotte and Oliver snicker. "Just because we're working together and have become more relaxed around each other doesn't mean we're friends."

Even though our conversation from yesterday basically confirmed that we are. It still feels weird to call us that though.

"Pretty sure you are."

I shoot her a look and turn away. "Eat your cereal."

"Aww does Jesse have a crush?" Charlotte giggles.

"Char," I say sternly.

"Fine, fine. I'm eating. Jeez."

The relationship between Emma and I isn't mentioned aloud again.

I drop Charlotte and Oliver off at the library and continue on to the high school. Emma is already in first period when I arrive. She looks up from her tablet when I enter. Her eyes light up and she smiles kindly. Some of my tension eases. This is the same girl from yesterday.

Neither of us speak as I slide into the chair beside her. She turns her attention back to the tablet. I can't see what she's doing, but her expression shines with concentration. Her forehead is creased, and her teeth are sunk into her bottom lip, something she only does when she's either determined or nervous.

Her blonde hair cascades in waves over her shoulders and down her back. Her eyes possess a focused glint I usually see when she's trying to figure something out.

Her eyes meet mine. "What?"

My mind clears. "What?"

"You were staring at me. It's distracting."

This is the second time she's caught me staring at her. She's not upset, though. Her words are laced with amusement and teasing.

"So, what're we doing after school?" I ask.

Her eyes flick down to the tablet, then back to me. "I want to try driving again."

"Would your tablet have anything to do with that?"

Chapter 34: Jesse

Pink creeps into her cheeks as she bites back a smile. "I was sort of researching how to drive. I found a lot of old documents from before cars were driver-less that are pretty interesting."

I grin. "No wonder you were so focused when I came in. You know, I wouldn't mind another round of self-defense either."

Her face lights up again. "Awesome."

...

"Are you ready?" I ask that afternoon from the passenger seat. Emma stares straight ahead, hands gripping the steering wheel just as tight as yesterday. She gives a curt nod. "Don't worry. You've got this. It can't be worse than yesterday."

She eases her foot off the brake, and we move forward. Without prompting from me, she presses the gas and we gain speed. It's still jerky and uneven but a definite improvement from the day before.

"Slowly come to a stop," I say when we reach the end of the road before the curve. She presses down almost too slowly, but we do roll to a smooth stop, so that's something.

"How was that?"

"Better," I compliment. "Much better. Are you ready for turning?"

She blanches. "What? No."

"It's not that hard," I reassure her. "Just turn the wheel in the direction you want to go and try not to get your arms all tangled up."

"Easy for you to say. This isn't your first time. I didn't get to this part in the manual."

"I don't think you're going to learn how to drive by reading a manual," I laugh. "Put the car in drive and make the turn. We won't crash. Promise. Your reflexes are too good. You'll slam on the brakes if you even *think* something might happen."

She rubs her palms along her jeans and shifts from park to drive. The car rolls forward, toward the curve in the dirt road.

"Okay, now turn the wheel," I instruct. She does, but it's hesitant. "Sharper. You don't want to go in the grass."

She cranes her neck to see over the dashboard and turns the wheel faster.

"There you go. Keep going. We're almost done."

Emma audibly sighs in relief as we round the bend. The car slows to a stop.

"See? That wasn't so bad. Ready to loop back around?"

She looks at me like I've grown a second head. "Are you kidding me? Do you know how many turns it takes to get back to where we started?"

"Yeah, four. It makes an easy loop."

"Easy is a relative word."

"So you're saying you want to switch seats and be done for today?" I challenge.

She narrows her eyes. "No. No, I don't want to be done."

Her determination returns and she drives the car through the other three turns. It's not perfect, but it's pretty good for only her second day of driving.

I don't know what she's so afraid of. Maybe it's because she's grown up with the idea of driver-less cars? It's understandable to be frightened by something you have to control yourself, when you're so used to it doing everything for you.

We practice the loop a few more times until Emma can get through the whole thing without panicking. Her braking has improved tremendously, too. After she's had enough, we switch seats and head to the warehouse.

"What're you teaching me today?" I ask once we're situated inside.

Chapter 34: Jesse

Emma takes a hair tie from her backpack and pulls her hair into a ponytail. "We'll do a quick review on punching, then move on to blocking punches."

We quickly go through yesterday's lesson. I'm surprised to discover I retained most of it.

"Okay, so yesterday, I said at some point, you'd need to stay on the balls of your feet. Here's where that comes in," Emma explains. "When you're in an actual fight, staying on the balls of your feet and bouncing around creates movement. This has several advantages, some being that it quickens your reflexes and can distract your opponent. It also makes it harder for them to predict your next strike. Try it out."

It's my turn to feel uncomfortable. Payback for all my previous teasing about her driving.

I bounce around a bit. "I feel ridiculous," I mutter.

"You just need to get used to it. Bend your knees a little and raise your arms into a fighting stance like yesterday, but keep them stiff."

I do so.

"Good," she says and moves closer to make minor adjustments. "Make sure you move around randomly, too. If you fall into a rhythm, the other person might figure it out and time their attacks accordingly."

"You're really good at this whole teaching thing, you know that?"

She goes still, her face falling. "You know, before all of this happened, I thought that if I didn't get picked to be a Level One, I'd teach self-defense to the younger kids. Or even if I did go out on Missions, it would be something I could do in between assignments. I guess that won't be happening anymore."

Because of me. Because I messed everything up for her.

"I'm sorry."

She shrugs. "It's okay. I'm teaching you now."

She moves on to the actual concept of blocking.

"I'm going to punch my arm out. You need to knock it out of the way. We'll go slow the first couple of times, so you understand what I'm talking about."

She flings her arm at me as if in slow motion. Though maybe fling is the wrong word. Even slowed, the movement is crisp and precise.

I throw my arm up and push hers out of the way. She corrects, adjusts, and gives me tips. We go a little faster. She punches. I block.

I thought I was doing well, until she exclaims, "No, stop. You're doing it wrong. You're not swatting my arm away like a fly. I'm attacking you and you are defending yourself, possibly fighting for your life. Block like you mean it. Like you want to live."

"Well sorry," I huff. "I'm not a natural born fighter who has been training to fight my whole life."

"Calm down," she scolds. "You're actually doing fairly well. Let's go a few more times and then we can be done."

Her arm shoots out faster than the times before. I throw my arm up on instinct and knock hers out of the way before I realize what's happened.

"Yes!" she cheers. "That's what it should be like every time."

A radiant smile bursts across her face at my accomplishment. It makes me feel good, knowing that I did something right and she approved of it. I return her smile with equal enthusiasm.

When it gets close to the time Charlotte gets out of school, I drive the car back to the forest and we walk back.

"We probably won't see each other until Monday," Emma says when we have to part ways. "I really need to stay with Cameron this

Chapter 34: Jesse

weekend and pretend to help with the Mission. The last thing we need is him getting suspicious."

I nod. "That would be bad. We should also probably work on the Academy next week. I don't want to get behind or neglect it."

"Of course," she smiles. "See you Monday."

CHAPTER THIRTY-FIVE
Emma

"Okay. Okay, you can do this," I mutter to myself. I'm standing in front of the apartment door, pumping myself up to enter. Every time I go home now, I have to become the person Cameron expects me to be, instead of who I've been while hanging out with Jesse.

I take a final breath and open the door. Cameron is at the kitchen table on his tablet. "Hey, how was your day?" he asks without looking up.

"Fine." I keep my voice as even as possible. "Nothing really important happened at school, but my target definitely trusts me now. He told me about the Academy today."

Cameron finally looks up. "Seriously? Oh my god, that's incredible!"

"Yeah, he showed me the corkboard and explained some of it to me. He believes I want to help and has no idea who I actually am."

"Wow, Emma. That's awesome. I knew you could do this. I'm proud of you."

"Thanks," I say and try to ignore the crushing guilt in my gut. Everything I tell him these days is a lie.

Chapter 35: Emma

Cameron and I spend the afternoon working on the Mission. We have our own map now and I've tacked off places to correspond with Jesse's. I have an idea, but I'll have to wait for the Ambassador to call.

When she does, I rattle off what I told Cameron earlier. "A lot has changed in the past couple of days. My target trusts me so much more now. He lets me into his house and even around his siblings. He actually said he considers us friends, and he's told me about the Academy."

"That's excellent, Emma." The delight in her tone is soothing. She believes me.

"He told me about the corkboard and what a lot of the stuff means. He has a region map for North America on it and he's been ruling out possible locations for the Academy. Right now, he's really focused on the Mountain region as a serious possibility."

"That's great," the Ambassador says. "I want you to really encourage him to look more into that. It'll buy us some time."

Bingo. She just inadvertently admitted that the Academy isn't in the Mountain region. That's a whole section of the map Jesse can check off.

"I was also thinking I might be able to get one of the kids to reveal some information," I add. "They could know something, but not realize or understand that it's something he doesn't want to share with me yet."

"Great idea. Nice job, Emma. You've done exceptionally well this week. We are finally making some real progress on this Mission. I'm proud of you."

My face crumples at her kind, sweet tone. It's surely fake, but it's also a reminder that she used to be my role model, and now I'm flat out lying to her on a daily basis.

"Thank you," I force out. "I really feel like I have a handle on this now. Hopefully I'll get some more concrete information soon."

"You're doing great. Take your time and make sure you maintain his trust. I'll talk to you tomorrow."

After the call, I retreat to my room. I can only handle being around Cameron so much anymore, and I hate that. I miss the days when we could sit and talk for hours about everything and nothing. When we didn't keep secrets or lie.

That's why I can't sit out in the living room with him. It hurts to interact with him in this new, closed off way. And he doesn't know the difference because anything he feels isn't real.

I shift around on my bed, trying to get comfortable. I wish I was with Jesse, Charlotte, and Oliver right now instead of trapped in an apartment with someone who barely knows me anymore.

...

The tension between Cameron and I only increases by the next day, though he's oblivious to it. We've always had a fairly easy relationship. Sometimes we fought or argued, but what friends don't? I've never felt at a loss for words around him, though. I can't think of anything to say. Not even topics of small talk rise to the front of my mind as we eat breakfast together. Is this how it's going to be from now on? Now that I have emotions and know the truth and he doesn't?

I need to get out of here, just for a little while.

"So, um...there's this group of people from school who want to get together today and they invited me. I don't know if I should go or not, you know, for the purpose of blending in."

He buys right into it.

"You should. It might help for you to take a break from the Mission. How long do you think it'll be?"

I pretend to think about it. "Probably an hour or two."

Chapter 35: Emma

"Is Aria going to be there?"

I bite back a smile. "Not this time. Why?"

He shrugs. "No reason. You should go, though. I'll be fine here on my own for a while."

"Okay, cool."

I wait around a little longer and then leave. It takes a lot of energy to restrain myself from sprinting down the sidewalk. Even the dreary sky can't dampen my mood. I planned on staying in the apartment all weekend, but there's only so much I can handle before needing a break.

I arrive at Jesse's house in no time.

It hadn't occurred to me until I knock on the door that maybe he won't want to see me. I've never shown up unannounced before.

He opens the door, a look of surprise on his face. "What are you doing here? I thought we weren't going to see each other until Monday. Are you all right? Did something happen?"

He *is* upset that I'm here, but not angry. Concerned.

"Yeah, I'm fine. I just needed a break from Cameron. I can't stand lying to him and pretending everything is the same as it's always been."

His gaze flicks behind me. Then he opens the door wider and ushers me in.

"Are *you* all right? Is it okay that I just showed up here like this? I wasn't really thinking."

He shifts uncomfortably, stuffing his hands in the pockets of his jeans. "Yeah, it's just...I don't want you here when Greg is home. We have a routine for whenever he's in the house. I don't want you caught up in that mess."

"Oh."

He adds, "You can come over whenever you need to, but if his truck is ever in the driveway, promise me you'll turn back around and go home."

"I'm sure I can handle your foster father. I'm trained, remember?"

"That's not the point," he counters. "I don't know how he'll react to you. I can't put you or the kids at risk. So please, if he's ever here, go home. Go to the park or the library or the waterfall. Anywhere but here."

"But—"

"Emma." His voice is stern, unwavering. It doesn't matter that I can take on his foster father as easily as anyone else. This is clearly not up for discussion.

"Okay, I promise."

"Thank you," he says and finally relaxes. "Come on. Charlotte and Oliver are in the living room."

Both kids are at the coffee table, Oli with a snack.

"Emma!" Charlotte squeals when I enter the room.

"Hey," I greet with a smile. "Hi, Oli."

He waves and goes back to his crackers, silent as ever.

Charlotte jumps to regain our attention. "What are we doing? The park?"

Jesse checks out the window. "I don't know, Char. It looks like it's going to rain soon. Maybe we can go to the library instead?"

"Sure, as long as Emma can come."

Jesse shakes his head with a laugh. To me, he says, "It's only been a few days and she's already gotten attached."

"Is that a bad thing?"

"No, not a bad thing. More of a surprising thing." He lowers his voice. "After what happened with her parents, she doesn't trust

Chapter 35: Emma

people easily. She doesn't have many friends at school either, so I didn't expect her to latch onto you so quickly."

"Are you coming?" Charlotte calls. Oli has cleaned up his snack and is now standing beside her.

Jesse smiles, the type of smile I now recognize as the one he saves for his siblings. The smile of a protective brother who will do anything to give his kids the best life possible.

"All right, then. Let's go."

It's a different feeling walking into the library this time. I'm not here to meet with my target and gain information. I'm here to hang out with my friends. That realization casts the room in a different light.

The first time Jesse brought me here, curiosity swelled in me for a split second before the chemicals in the tracker snuffed it out. That feeling doesn't go away this time.

Charlotte skips off to the junior fiction section, Oli trailing behind her.

"I want to get some books," I say. Jesse glances at me. "I want to read things that were always forbidden by the government."

"Well, I don't know how much help I can be as far as suggestions. I'm not much of a reader."

"Really? But you spend so much time here."

"Yeah, doing research on the government," he explains. "I've always had trouble staying focused long enough to actually make it through a book. My obsession with the Academy used to occupy the majority of my mind."

"Used to?"

He grins. "My mind's been kind of occupied by other things recently. Driving, self-defense, etcetera."

"Sorry about that," I say with a small grin of my own.

He shrugs. "It happens. Come on, I still know a little about books. We'll find something you can check out."

We wander up the aisles of the young adult section until I find a couple possibilities. I'll probably have to read a wide range of things to figure out what I like best, though.

We return to Jesse's house after that.

"Okay, we've taken care of books, now you need to experience the wonders of television."

"We had TV at the Academy," I point out.

He sinks onto the couch and pats the spot beside him. "Yeah, but never TV that's unrestricted. *Real* TV."

I give in and settle beside him. He flips through channels, shows me various things. The kids join us after a while. We laugh and talk and joke around.

This. *This* is the kind of life the government took from me. I've missed seventeen years of this. I won't give up any more.

But eventually I do have to leave. I've already been out longer than I told Cameron.

"Can't you stay?" Charlotte protests as I walk to the door.

"I wish I could. I'll come over again soon, though." To Jesse, I say, "Bring my books to school on Monday. I'll put them in my backpack and sneak them past Cameron that way."

"You got it."

"Oh, and also. The Academy isn't located in the Mountain region. The Ambassador told me last night."

His eyes bug. "Way to bury the lead. Jeez, why didn't you say something when you first got here."

I shrug. "I was just happy to see you that I kind of forgot. But that helps, right? Now you've got it narrowed down to two places?"

"Definitely."

Chapter 35: Emma

I leave after that, aware that there's nowhere else I want to be than with them.

CHAPTER THIRTY-SIX
Jesse

I was wrong when I said people are stupid. I should have said *most* people are stupid. But not all of them. Not Emma Grant.

As the next few weeks pass, we spend even more time together. This secret friendship of ours is dangerous. We both know that, but neither of us cares. It's too late and we're in too deep.

So much has changed. Emma and I are barely the same people we were before I kidnapped her. She's getting so much better at identifying her own emotions and her driving skills have improved quite a lot. We've gone driving almost every day after school. Our self-defense lessons have come far, too, though she still manages to beat me every time. I'm only able to pin her to the floor when she lets me for demonstration purposes.

She spends a lot of time with Charlotte and Oliver, too. Of course, we occasionally visit the corkboard and work on our search, but it's taken a back seat lately. I'm not as concerned about it as I used to be. It's been so long since I've felt like this. Happy, excited, not dreading each day of my existence. And the corkboard will still be there tomorrow. Right now, I want to have fun.

Chapter 36: Jesse

We're at my house now, a board game strewn across the coffee table in the living room. Charlotte sits right next to Emma, while Oli sits in her lap. They completely adore her.

"Yes! I win," Charlotte cheers. She springs up from the floor, pumping her fist in the air.

Emma laughs at her enthusiasm. She's surprisingly good with children, a quality I never saw coming.

Charlotte begins resetting the board so we can play again.

"So," Emma says to me. "When can we continue my driving lessons?"

Here we go again. "I don't know."

"Come on," she presses. "You said I was ready for the big road."

I did tell her that. A few days ago actually. She's been impatient ever since. She is ready skill wise, but I'm not sure if it's safe.

But I know she won't relent. So, with a sigh, I say, "We can go tonight if you want, but we'll have to wait until dark. You know, with it being an illegal car and all."

She bites her lip and casts her eyes downward. "If we go at night, I'll have to sneak out of the apartment."

Warning bells go off in my mind.

"Maybe it's not a good idea then. I don't want you getting in trouble." If Cameron finds out, he'll surely report us to the government. Emma wants to tell him the truth, hoping he'll side with her, but nothing is guaranteed.

"No, I want to do this," she protests and stands up. "I have to go. Cameron is expecting me home soon, but I'll meet you down the street from my apartment at midnight. I'll leave the tracker at home. No one will know I'm gone."

I agree despite the danger it puts us both in.

Hopefully I won't regret it later.

. . .

Several hours later, I stand at the predetermined meeting spot with doubts she'll actually show. There's a possibility she won't be able to get away undetected. I have no way of knowing what is going on since we don't have a way to contact each other.

But then her blonde hair breaks through the darkness. A smile tugs at my lips as she approaches.

"How did you get away?" I ask when she reaches me.

"Easy. Cameron's a pretty heavy sleeper. Once he was out, I walked straight out the front door."

"That's my little rebel. Skipping school and sneaking out of the house."

She rolls her eyes and shoves me.

We walk to the car in comfortable silence, the night air cool and breezy. When we arrive, she immediately gets into the driver seat. No fear. No hesitation.

I hand over the keys and she starts it up. Despite how comfortable she is now, I remain alert in the passenger seat, ready to help if needed. She maneuvers the car out of the forest and onto the dirt road.

She drives the back roads smoothly.

"Instead of turning right up ahead and looping back around, we're going to turn left. That'll take us straight to the main road."

She does as I say, her expression tight with determination. It masks the nerves that are also there. I know her well enough by this point to know that. Though there's excitement there, too. She's worked hard to get this far.

"You're okay. You've got this," I encourage.

With a deep breath, she pushes the car forward and we're off. Given that it's the middle of the night, we don't encounter any cars. It's not as realistic as if there were other cars in play, but this is the best we can do for now. It's an accomplishment nonetheless.

Chapter 36: Jesse

She rolls our windows down and cold air blasts in. Her hair whips with the rush of it as we race down the highway.

"This is amazing!" she exclaims. "This is the fastest I've ever gone. I get it now, why you like to do this. It's freeing."

My heart leaps. We understand each other. It's just a car, just driving down the road in the middle of the night. But to us, it holds a deeper meaning. A meaning we now share.

It was worth it, bringing her to the car all that time ago. Her eyes are bright, her mouth stretched into a wide smile. She looks so alive and free. I'll do anything to give that feeling to her.

A thought prickles the back of my mind as it often has these past couple of weeks whenever I'm with her. It attacks suddenly with a glance in her direction or the sound of her laugh. I force it away like always and scold myself. It's all part of training my mind not to go there. No point in contemplating things that will never happen.

"How do you ever go a day without doing this?" she asks. "Even if you can only go at night, I'd just stop sleeping."

I chuckle. "Yeah, I don't think never sleeping would go over too well."

She just shrugs and speeds up.

We stay out for over an hour, but eventually have to go back. Her face falls with disappointment, but we can't stay out here forever. Emma parks the car in its spot and we walk home.

The whole way back, she goes on and on about how great driving is. Her excitement warms me despite the chilly air.

"Once you get comfortable enough on the main road, you might be able to go out during the day."

"Really?"

I nod. "We have to make sure your driving is perfectly smooth and as close to the driver-less cars as possible, but yeah."

We stop at the spot we met at earlier. She turns to face me. The light from the lamp post allows me to see the tense, conflicted expression on her face. Why is she nervous?

It's been happening recently. Everything will be fine and then she'll act weird. Her face clouds over or she'll take longer than normal to respond. I've never asked her about it, about where her mind goes during those times. Maybe she's just taking a moment to sort out and identify her emotions.

"Goodnight," she whispers. It looks like she wants to say more but can't get the words out.

"Goodnight," I echo.

But neither of us move. She stares at me, eyebrows pulled together and teeth dented in her bottom lip. A storm brews in her eyes and a war rages in her mind. She's trying to make a decision, that much I know. Her eyes glitter in the lamp's flickering light. Those same eyes then clear as a decision is made.

A split second later, her arms are around my neck as she hugs me tight, her face against my shoulder. I stiffen in surprise. She squeezes me, a silent command to relax. I do, and wrap my arms around her to bring her closer. My face rests in her hair.

"Thank you," she whispers. "For everything."

I pull away just far enough to look at her. Our eyes meet and I know we're on the same page.

Fear and anxiety of the unknown fills our lives, not knowing what tomorrow will bring. Though we haven't spoken of it since becoming friends, we're different people, worlds apart. And we both know it's not a matter of *if* we get caught, but *when*. For this, what we have, can only last so long before crumbling.

But right here, in this single moment, none of it matters. It doesn't matter that she's from a government agency that brainwashes children into obedience and makes them destroy innocent

Chapter 36: Jesse

people. Or that my entire life is built on revenge and heartache. It doesn't matter that we're living in a bubble and pretending it won't ever pop. It doesn't matter in this moment, because for the first time in years, I'm home.

CHAPTER THIRTY-SEVEN
Emma

Jesse agreed that we could go driving at night as much as I want…as long as there's not school the next day. So really, I can only drive on the real road during the weekends. Tonight will be it until next weekend.

I wait for Cameron to fall asleep and then slip out of the apartment. Jesse isn't at our spot from yesterday. I wait there a few minutes, under the orange glow of the streetlamp, but he never shows. Somehow, I suspect he's not coming.

I set off toward his house. He's okay, right? Surely nothing's happened since I saw him last night. Since I *hugged* him goodnight, something I really shouldn't have done.

I stop in my tracks as a thought crosses my mind. Maybe nothing is physically wrong. Maybe he's just upset about something. In which case, he won't be at home. He'll be at the waterfall. Without a second thought, I change course.

I've been to the waterfall enough times now to know my way there on my own, even in the dark. After pushing through the tree branches and underbrush, I find him standing on the bridge,

Chapter 37: Emma

leaning against the railing. His head whips around as I approach, but he relaxes upon seeing it's just me.

"Hey," he smiles. Then his face drops. "Oh no. What time is it?"

"Almost twelve thirty."

He sighs heavily and roughly drags a hand through his hair. "I'm so sorry, Emma. I came here to think and must've lost track of time. I meant to be there by midnight. I really did."

"It's okay. Are you all right, though?"

He turns away and looks back out over the water. "I'm fine."

Wrong thing to say. I still have trouble with emotions and reading other people, but even I know he's lying.

I take a tentative step towards him. "Jesse, what's going on?"

"Nothing," he mumbles. How did we go from being so open with each other to so closed off so quickly?

"Jesse," I repeat and lightly touch his shoulder. He shrugs me off.

"It's just…everything is a mess now. How am I supposed to get anywhere or do anything when I'm so distracted?"

"Distracted?"

He drags a hand down his face. "Self-defense. Driving. The park and library and everything I've been doing instead of searching for the Academy. I was supposed to find balance. Maybe we should just stop altogether. We went too far."

His words don't fully sink in, but each one strikes me down. "What are you talking about? Where is this coming from? You said you were fine spending time doing other things. You…you said—"

He spins around to face me, his eyes wild. "How am I supposed to get revenge against them now?"

My stomach drops at his words laced in ice.

Revenge. He still wants to destroy the Academy.

"Are you serious?" I exclaim. "*That's* what you're thinking about? Revenge? I thought we were past that?"

"What? You think just because we're friends now I suddenly don't hate the government? Just because you aren't working for them now doesn't erase what they've done."

"Why not?" I retaliate. "I'm not trying to kill you anymore and we both know the truth now. Why can't that be enough? Why can't you just let it go and move on?

"They kill people!"

I roll my eyes in annoyance. "Well yeah, we go after people who are a threat to us, but we don't intentionally kill innocent people."

He scoffs, malice in his tone that I haven't heard since I was tied up in the warehouse. "Listen to you, using 'we' and 'us.' I wasn't aware you were still part of them. And for the record, they're after me and I'm innocent."

"You were planning on blowing up the Academy!" I yell back. "That doesn't exactly scream innocent."

"How else was I supposed to get revenge? They deserve it."

"Why do you even need revenge in the first place?" I clench my hands into fists to cease their shaking from my anger. "I know they've done some pretty messed up stuff with the trackers and the emotions, but what can they have possibly done to you that was so horrible?"

"They *murdered* my entire family!"

My mouth falls open. I stare at him, at his scrunched-up face and the tears that prickle his eyes. I try to say something, anything, but the words die in my throat.

"But you don't care about that, do you? No matter what happens between us, how much time we spend together or how that makes me feel, how much you say you hate them for what they did

Chapter 37: Emma

to you, they will always be your family. You will always choose them."

His words are daggers to my heart. My chest tightens painfully at the blow. So far, I hate this emotion more than anything else. This feeling of horror, guilt, regret all rolled into one. It's in that split-second moment I find myself wishing I could go back to how things used to be.

I miss home. I miss my dorm and Lacy. I miss knowing exactly how each and every day is going to go. I miss my lack of emotion. Things were simpler back then. Surely feeling nothing is better than feeling like *this*, like I let him down.

I stay silent for too long. Jesse huffs and turns away from me. His shoulders still move up and down from his heavy, outraged breathing.

I stare at him and let the familiar roar of the waterfall soothe me. I chew the inside of my cheek as I try to think of what to say. Because I need to say *something*. He deserves that much. The split-second moment passes and I know my life is better now with the truth than it was when I lacked emotions.

This boy in front of me has changed my whole life. That doesn't necessarily mean his need for revenge is okay, but there's so much more to him that that. There has to be.

"You're wrong," I finally say and step forward to lean against the bridge beside him. "They haven't been my family since you ripped the tracker from my arm and gave me the truth. But that doesn't mean I won't miss the life I used to have, before I knew how corrupt everything was. And I know there is still so much I don't know about them. I know they've done terrible, unforgivable things. But you have to understand that I lived there for seventeen years. Sometimes I'm going to slip up and say stupid things. But you are so wrong if you think I'm still one of them, that I still *want* to be one of them."

I breathe deeply and let him process. He continues to stare straight ahead, as if he didn't even hear me.

"I didn't know," I continue in a whisper. "I didn't know they killed your family. They told me it was an accident and you never corrected me. I'm sorry. I should've realized you had a larger reason for going against them."

He still ignores me.

Look at me, I plead. *Say something. Say anything.*

Then he sighs and scrubs a hand over his face. Even just from seeing his profile in the dark, I can tell he's exhausted. He sits down on the bridge, his back to the railing. He refuses to meet my eyes, but I move to sit beside him. I wait him out a few more minutes before he speaks.

"I was eight when they died. It was so long ago, but…I remember so many little details about that day. It was a Saturday and I wanted to play with my friend who lived down the street. I left the house at 3:08pm. I'll never forget that, because I looked at the clock right before I left. My mom told me to be home by five. Two people, early twenties maybe, stood across the street. I noticed them, but didn't pay them any attention at the time."

He pauses, squeezes his eyes shut, and takes a breath. "When I came home, there were police and ambulances and firetrucks everywhere. By then, the fire had been put out, but the house was nothing but rubble. My parents and older brother were trapped inside. They didn't make it out."

My stomach churns. "Jesse…" I whisper as I bring a shaky hand to my mouth.

"I thought it was an accident at first." His voice cracks and tears finally break free and spill down his face. "That's what the police

Chapter 37: Emma

said. But it wasn't. I figured out much later that the two people I saw when I left were from the Academy. They used their abilities to set the house on fire and trap everyone inside, intentionally killing my parents."

"*Why?*" I exclaim. How can I come from a place that does that to people? How did I not know about it?

"Almost everything was destroyed by the fire, except a stack of files that were locked away in a fire-proof safe. I stole the files before the police got a hold of them. My parents…they told me and my brother that if anything ever happened to them, we had to keep the files safe and away from anyone else. The papers didn't make sense at the time, but even then I could tell they were important, that they meant something. So I hid them away and didn't revisit them until I was twelve…and then my obsession started."

"I don't understand," I admit. The stress of the situation is making my mind slower than usual. "What's so special about the files?"

"Both of my parents were scientists. Work was a big thing for both of them, so they had us later in life. Years before my brother and I were born, they were recruited to work for a special, top-secret government program. They tested and analyzed DNA sequences, searching for a particular coding that was compatible with the formula the government created. From what I read in their notes, they didn't realize what the formula was actually for. They did everything the government asked of them, without knowing what was really going on. By the time they found out what all their experiments and research had been used for, the Academy was already underway. They spent many more years trying to put a stop to it. But once the government found out, they sent two Academy kids out on an assignment…to murder my parents."

Beyond the Gates

A heavy weight presses on my chest. A billion questions race through my head. "All of that was in your parents' notes?" I manage to get out.

He shrugs. "Most of it. Some of it's my own conclusions. Some from government files I've gotten a hold of over the years."

"And this…formula. That's what controls our emotions?"

He finally looks at me. There's pain in his sad, tired eyes. I look away. "That's not all of it. I've never completely understood all the technical science stuff, but basically the formula reacts with a special, evolved kind of DNA sequence. That reaction allows them to control you, but it is also what created the abilities each of you have."

My eyes snap back to his as everything I thought I knew shatters once again.

"But…but I thought we were born with abilities. That's why my biological parents abandoned me. They didn't want me because I'm different. The government took me in. They took care of me when no one else would."

Jesse shakes his head. "They lied to you. My parents documented everything they were able to discover before the government caught on to them. The Academy has people working inside the hospitals that run DNA tests on all newborns. Anyone matching the correct sequence is taken from the hospital and sent to the Academy. I tried to tell you before, in the warehouse, but you were so overwhelmed by all the emotions. Emma, your parents didn't abandon you. You were taken from them. The parents think it's some tragic accident. No one has ever put two and two together. The government has been so careful."

My chest tightens. A gasp of pain tears out of me. "I can't believe this. All my life…I've never met my parents, but I've always

Chapter 37: Emma

hated them on principle. I thought they gave me up. I thought they hated me."

"I'm so sorry, Emma. I should have told you sooner. I just didn't know how. You've been through so much and we were having a lot of fun these past few weeks. And then I go and screw it all up anyway by bringing up my revenge like it wouldn't upset you."

"It's okay." I wipe my face with the back of my hand. "I mean, it's not. But I know you've been through a lot, too. What's the point of all of it, though? Why do they want kids with special abilities? Why control our emotions and train us the way they do? What do they want? What are they working towards?"

So many questions.

"I wish I knew," he says. "But at least now you understand how I knew about the Academy and why I want revenge. They took *everything* from me. You have no idea what it's like to have a home, a life, a family, and then in a blink every bit of it is gone. My family was ripped away from me and I got stuck in foster care. I moved from place to place without anyone to tell me it was all gonna be okay. I've been beaten and starved and abused." He shakes his head. "You think Greg is bad, but it's nothing compared to what I've dealt with in the past. I know I don't talk about it much, because…I get uncomfortable and I hate thinking about those years before the kids when I was all alone, but I need you to understand. They broke me."

Tears flow freely down my face now. "I'm sorry. God, Jesse. I'm so sorry. We'll figure it out, okay? We'll make them pay for what they did. We just have to be strategic about it. We have to go after the government, not the kids who are being controlled by them."

He nods.

We fall into silence. I continue to process all the information he dumped on me, but it's a lot. I doubt the full weight of it will hit me until tomorrow morning.

Beyond the Gates

A breeze whispers through the trees. I run my hands up and down my bare arms. I didn't bring a jacket since I expected to spend the whole time in the toasty car.

"Are you cold?"

"No." If I tell him I'm actually freezing, he might decide it's time to leave. I'm not ready to go home just yet. I'm not ready to leave him after what we've just been through.

"Liar," he chuckles anyway. "Here."

He removes his hoodie and ignores my protests. "Arms up." He slips it on over his head. Warmth instantly engulfs me. It's too big on me—the sleeves extend a bit past my hands—but I don't mind.

"Thanks," I mumble sleepily and lean my head against his shoulder. Is this considered stepping too far out of bounds? We've gotten a little too close recently. We haven't mentioned it, but it's still there and we both know it. He wraps his arm around me, hugging me to his side. So I give up thinking about it for now and just enjoy the moment.

"No problem," he replies. "That's what friends are for."

Guilt flashes through me again. We *are* friends, but I didn't exactly act like one tonight.

"I'm sorry for all the things I said earlier. I just didn't understand."

"I know. It's okay," he says, and pauses for a long moment. "I'm sorry, too. Spending time with you…it's not a mistake. I shouldn't have said that it was. Truth is, you make it easier. I can't begin to describe how messed up my life was before I met you." He laughs dryly. "I mean, it's still messy, but you've made it easier to deal with."

That's surprising. "Are you sure? I feel like I've only made it thousands of times worse."

Chapter 37: Emma

He thinks over my words and slowly says, "Knowing you has definitely created some…complications. But you've made other things better."

That warms my heart and I smile. "You've made my life better, too."

CHAPTER THIRTY-EIGHT
Jesse

All has returned to normal with Emma and I by the next day. It's almost like our argument never happened. It still lingers between us, but neither feels the need to mention it.

After school, I took Emma out driving on the back roads. Now we're at the warehouse. Today, she's teaching me one of her favorite moves: knocking people to the ground by hooking a foot behind their knee.

Emma stands a few feet from me. She finishes tying her hair up and raises her fists. A few stray hairs escape and hang down to frame her face.

"Okay, let's go," she says.

I bring my hands up to match her and stalk forward. We dance around each other, light on our feet. I swing, no longer afraid of hurting her. Honestly, there's a greater chance *she'll* hurt *me*.

She blocks my punch, but it allows me to get in close. Now it's time to take her down. She'll let me win this time for demonstration purposes. Under normal circumstances, beating her is completely impossible.

Chapter 38: Jesse

I raise my leg up and swing around, replicating the movements she showed me. I don't make it that far.

A pressure hits the back of my knee, forcing my leg to bend. I tumble and slam into the safety mat. Emma's hands curl around my wrists in a vice-like grip. She hovers over me, her breath heavy.

I guess she isn't going to let me win after all.

"What did you do wrong?" she asks, though she obviously knows the answer. This is her favorite way to teach. Make me correct my own mistakes. Apparently I learn better that way.

But I can't think straight. Not with how close she is to me. She gazes down at me intently, waiting for an answer. Her fingers dig into my skin, her eyes ablaze with life. I keep my eyes locked on hers, afraid that if I look anywhere else, I won't be able to restrain myself any longer.

I have to tell her something, anything, to cover up the blankness in my mind. I need to reverse this situation.

"Nothing," I breathe and bring my leg up. I push against her side and we roll over. Now she's beneath me.

If I thought we were close before, it's nothing compared to now. Her eyes are still trained on me, a fraction of an inch wider than before.

This girl is going to be the death of me, I swear.

We're way too close. I see it on her face. The frantic glint to her eyes as she assesses the situation, the way her lips part as a strangled breath escapes, the heavy rise and fall of her chest. Our close proximity affects her, too. It's still there, no matter how much we've both tried to ignore it.

Dangerous. This is so, so dangerous.

But I can't move. I can't stop looking at her. Beads of sweat dot her hairline. Her cheeks are flushed, and I have a feeling it's not from the exercise. And her lips…

"Jesse," she whispers, a warning in her tone.

My eyes snap back to hers. There's a warning there, too.

Not happening. Not possible. Not safe.

I roll to the side and lay on the safety mat beside her. We stay silent for a while, our heavy breathing the only sound in the room, though that eventually regulates.

"We should probably be done for the day," she suggests, a slight tremor in her voice.

"Yeah," I agree, even though we haven't been here very long. "We should head home."

But neither of us moves from the floor. It's then I realize that maybe what we *should* do and what we *want* to do are two completely separate things.

"You can…you can come over to the apartment if you want. Cameron is out at the grocery store and running other errands. He shouldn't be back for a while."

Again, death of me. Maybe she *is* still trying to kill me.

I should say no. Every part of my mind screams at me to say no. But logic doesn't win this round. I find myself saying, "Okay."

And that's how I end up standing in the living room of her apartment. She leads me down the hall and into her bedroom. The room has a queen-sized bed, dresser, and nightstand, but it's vacant of anything that actually makes it seem lived in. There are no pictures on the walls or a mess on the floor. Not that my bedroom has pictures or anything like that, but it's definitely a mess with the three of us sharing it. Her backpack sits in the corner, the only indication she actually uses this room at all. The bed is perfectly made, until she flops down on it with a sigh of relief.

"I'm exhausted," she says.

Chapter 38: Jesse

I laugh and lay on my back next to her. "Yeah, well maybe you wouldn't be if you hadn't stayed out past midnight for two nights in a row. Just a thought."

"Yeah, yeah." She waves it off. Things have calmed between us. This is how we usually interact with each other. This I can handle.

She closes her eyes, though it doesn't erase the lines of stress in her forehead and the way her eyebrows crease together just slightly. I want to smooth those lines away. I reach out towards her and almost touch her face before I come to my senses.

What am I doing? I can't just touch her face! I thought I had myself back under control. I retract my hand before she can open her eyes and see me.

She doesn't open her eyes, though. I start to think she's going to fall asleep, when her phone rings.

She groans in annoyance, but sits up anyway and grabs her phone from the nightstand. "It's the Ambassador. Time for my update call."

She answers it. "Hello?"

Although I try to appear stoic, my insides squirm. She's talking to the leader of the people who want me dead. And here I am, sitting next to the girl who's supposed to carry it out. How messed up is that?

Emma's eyes flick to mine as she speaks. "I went back to the warehouse today. There's more stuff he left behind. Maps and diagrams and stuff. None of it makes much sense yet, but I'm planning to discuss it with Cameron tonight. Hopefully together we can get a better understanding."

The lies roll right off her tongue.

There's a long pause as the Ambassador responds.

"Okay, thank you. Yes, I'll talk to you tomorrow. Have a good evening."

She hangs up and falls back against the bed, releasing a long breath. "I'm glad that's taken care of for the day. At least she's backed off recently now that I've given her more to work with."

My stomach clenches. "Yeah, you sure know how to lie, don't you."

She looks up at me with big, innocent eyes. "I would never lie to you. Not anymore. Not after everything."

The sincerity in her voice settles my uncertainties. I even feel a little guilty for doubting her, but it's difficult to ignore how easily she can invent a complex lie off the top of her head. But I believe her, so I let it go.

I lower myself back to the bed and turn on my side to face her. "Speaking of the Academy, can you tell me more about it?"

Her eyebrows scrunch together in a way that makes me want to smile, though I refrain from doing so. "Like what? I've already told you a lot about it."

"Yeah, the big stuff. Tell me about the things that were only special to you. I know you didn't have emotions and you basically did everything you were told, but like…what was your favorite place?"

She closes her eyes and her lips turn up in a smile. "Definitely the quad. It's this area where all sides of the campus meet. There's a bunch of trees and a fountain in the middle. In the spring, all the trees bloom and it's so beautiful." She lazily peels her eyes open. "I wish I would have appreciated it more when I actually lived there. I was so indifferent to it then."

"Do you wish you could see it again? Having a different perspective?"

She shakes her head without a single thought. "I hope I never see it again. If I do, it probably means I got caught."

True, very true.

Chapter 38: Jesse

"Besides, the waterfall is a billion times better than the quad."

I do smile that time.

"I'm so tired," she whispers through a yawn. My own eyelids grow heavy, too. "Cameron shouldn't be back for a while. We probably have time for a short nap."

I don't have the energy to tell her that it's probably a bad idea. I shut my eyes and we both drift to sleep.

. . .

I groggily wake some unknown amount of time later. Emma's still asleep next to me. Much of her hair has fallen out of the ponytail and is now splayed out in several directions. Her face is so innocent and peaceful, the stress cleared. If only she could be like this all the time. It seems no matter what, there's always something new to worry about. Some new danger to stress over.

Her fingers twitch against mine. That's when I realize the tips of my fingers are resting against hers, as if we reached for each other while unconscious.

I can't stop looking at her. And she's asleep, so it's not like she'll ever know. We've been so careful these past weeks, but nothing can go wrong with her if she's not awake.

She's still learning about emotions, though. Maybe she doesn't even know or understand what's going on between us. Though the incident at the warehouse suggests otherwise.

She's beautiful, even with her hair all messed up and tangled. Thinking that is dangerous, but I can't help it. She—

The front door opens. My heart lurches to my throat.

Cameron is home.

I spring up from the bed, suddenly wide awake and alert. "Emma, wake up," I whisper urgently. I shake her, but she shifts and curls into the bedspread.

"What?" she yawns.

"Cameron's home."

Her eyes pop open. That got her attention. "*What?* No, we couldn't have been asleep that long. Were we?"

"I don't know. Does it really matter? He's about to come in here and that'll be it. The end to all of this."

I don't mean to scare her with the intensity of my words and harsh tone, but it's the truth. Now is not the time to be sugarcoating situations.

"No," she says with defiance. "This is *not* the end." Her eyes dart around the room. "The closet. Get in the closet."

I bolt across the room and slip inside, knocking over her stack of library books in the process. I pull the door closed and darkness engulfs me, though I can still see through the thin slats in the door.

Cameron enters the room mere seconds after I disappear into my hiding spot.

"Hey," Emma says cheerily as if everything is normal and she's not harboring a government enemy in her closet. "I just got off the phone with the Ambassador. She's pleased with the new information I gave her."

Confusion sweeps over his face. "New information?"

She starts talking really fast, a sign that she's nervous. "Um, yeah. I found some more stuff that Je—the target left behind at the warehouse."

So they refer to me as 'the target.' Interesting.

"Warehouse? I thought you were at the library doing schoolwork, or something?"

The slip up only makes Emma more anxious. She blinks a few times, clearly on the verge of tears. Everything is exploding around us. This is not how today was supposed to go.

Don't cry, Em. Hang in there. Don't tip him off.

"Y-yeah. I had some extra time, so I did both."

Chapter 38: Jesse

"Huh," Cameron grunts. My heart sinks. He's not done. He knows something, something he can hold over her. "And where were you last night? I know you left and didn't come back until almost two."

Yep, we're doomed.

"Oh, I was just…I—"

Cameron paces the room, eyes sweeping everything.

"What're you doing?" Emma inquires.

"You're acting weird. And it's not just today. Something has been off for a while now."

He walks dangerously close to the closet door, but thankfully passes it. I stay perfectly still, barely daring to breathe.

I try to reassure myself.

Just give him time. Once they finish talking, he'll leave the room. Then I can sneak out of here. Everything is going to be okay.

It doesn't matter though, because when Cameron comes back around, he flings the door open.

Emma's eyes fly wide, as do Cameron's. I'm not sure what he expected, but it definitely isn't me. He stares at me and I stare back. Everyone is frozen.

And then he slowly turns around. "Emmalyn," he sighs heavily in disappointment.

Emma steps forward. "Just hear me out. I can explain everything."

CHAPTER THIRTY-NINE
Emma

Cameron is livid. Or as livid as one can be when their emotions are chemically suppressed. But I guess in a way, the chemicals are designed to allow us *some* emotion, as long as it benefits the government. Get angry when the government is threatened. Stay determined and focused on training. Never feel curious about anything, that way you don't start thinking for yourself.

"Explain what?" Cameron snaps. "That this isn't what it looks like? Do you think I'm stupid?"

Everything is spiraling out of control so fast.

"Cameron," I say with feigned calmness. "This is Jesse. We have a class together and we're studying."

Yeah, he doesn't buy it. Not that I blame him. What kind of pathetic excuse even is that?

"That's crap and you know it," he retorts, eyes blazing. "If this was you playing your part for the Mission and getting information from him, you wouldn't have hidden him in the closet or spoken about the Academy to me in front of him. Don't try to tell me that you didn't betray the government, because that's exactly what this is."

Chapter 39: Emma

He grabs the front of Jesse's shirt and yanks him out of the closet. Jesse stumbles forward, off balance.

"Cameron!"

"Oh, what? You're even defending him now? How long has this been going on? Being on the same side as him? Not seeing him as the enemy anymore?"

My voice breaks. "I'm not—"

"Don't deny it," Cameron yells. "It makes sense. It *all* makes sense now. The way you've been acting. Spending more and more time out of the apartment. Rarely having concrete information. You turned on us. On me."

He flinches at that last bit, as if realizing how true it really is.

Jesse glances at me with wide, frightened eyes. He's just as scared as I am. We both knew this day would come. We knew we'd eventually get caught.

I just didn't expect it to be today.

"Jesse, you should go," I whisper.

"No," he protests firmly and takes a step toward me. "Absolutely not. I'm not leaving you alone with him."

Cameron moves between us. "*You're* the one she shouldn't be left alone with. Who knows what you've done to her mind if she believes you're a good person now."

"He hasn't done anything to me!" I yell. "Look, Cameron. There is information you don't know, things you don't understand. If you just give me a chance to explain everything once Jesse leaves—"

"I am *not* leaving!" Jesse exclaims.

I push past Cameron to get to Jesse. I grip his arms and look him straight in the eyes. Under my breath, I beg, "Please go. I need you somewhere safe while I handle this, while I try to make him understand. He won't hurt me, but he might hurt you. Let me deal with this and I'll meet you at the park as soon as I can."

"Emma…"

His eyes beg me to let him stay.

"Please," I whisper.

I see the pain in his eyes, how much it hurts him as he sighs in defeat. "Okay, just be careful."

Before I can stop him, he wraps his arms tight around me.

Cameron explodes. "What do you think you're doing? Get your hands off her!"

Cameron grabs me by the shoulders and pries me away from Jesse.

"It'll be okay," I say as Cameron hauls me back.

"Just…just don't let them take you away."

"If you're leaving, you've got about two seconds to get out of here," Cameron hisses.

Jesse looks at me with panic-stricken eyes.

"Go," I order and he finally leaves.

Cameron lets go of me and I exhale once Jesse's out of the apartment. He's safe, for now anyway.

I turn to Cameron, ready to talk, only to find him with his cell phone out. I lunge and swipe it from his hands.

"What are you doing?" I demand.

"Calling the Ambassador. I have to turn you in, Emma. You need help. He completely ruined your mind."

"No, he didn't. He fixed my mind. He *saved* me. Jesse was never the bad guy. The government only wanted us to think that he was. Yeah, he's after the government, but only because they killed his family when he was a kid. He just wants revenge."

"And how do you know he wasn't lying to you, huh? How do you know he didn't just say all that to get you to trust him?"

Chapter 39: Emma

"Because he kidnapped me!" I blurt out before I can stop myself. This isn't exactly how I wanted this conversation to go, but at least it renders him speechless. "That's where I really was when I went missing for three days. I wasn't following a lead."

Cameron shakes his head. "He *kidnapped* you and *that's* what made you trust him? Do you even hear yourself?"

Random bits of information pour out of me. But it's all happening too fast. I'm losing control.

"The government implanted trackers in us when we were born. Jesse cut my tracker out, but it wasn't just a tracker. It's also a mechanism that changes the chemicals in our bodies to control and suppress our emotions. It took three days for my body to get back on track, and then everything changed."

Cameron glares, his whole body trembling. "You're wrong. God, Emma. You think you're the first one to fall to the enemy's side and rebel against the Academy? These humans can be so deceptive and manipulative. You aren't the first one to spew off random accusations against the government. But if you'd just let me call the Ambassador, I promise we can fix you."

Fix me? Really?

And I'm not the first one? That means there are others out there who know the truth! Or used to, anyway. They've probably all been brainwashed and never allowed to leave the Academy again.

I can't let that happen to me.

"I can prove it," I say. "Just give me three days. Three days and if you still don't believe me…then you can call the Ambassador. You can turn us in. But there's something you should know." I swallow back tears. "If you make that call, you'll be putting innocent lives in danger, possibly getting them killed."

Cameron scoffs. "He's hardly innocent."

"Not him," I growl. "His siblings. Without Jesse, they have no one and no chance at making it on their own. They're just kids. Don't do this to them. Don't do this to *me*. I'm your best friend, Cameron. If our twelve years of friendship mean anything to you, at least give me a chance. Trust me enough for that. If you turn me in, they'll either kill me or brainwash me. Let me prove it."

He groans in frustration and paces the room. I let him. Let him work out all I've said and what I offer.

He stops, studies me carefully, and releases a heavy sigh. "Fine. Three days. But I swear Emma if you're wrong, if you're lying, it won't matter who's innocent or not. I have to do the right thing and that's reporting back to the government."

I force his threat away and focus on the positive. It's not much, but I bought us a few more days of safety. It'll have to do. "Thank you, Cameron. Thank you so much."

He just looks at me, *really* looks at me, like he's seeing me for the first time in his life. "You really believe him, don't you."

I give him a half smile. "He's a good person. He just has a lot of issues. But that doesn't make him the enemy. In a way, it kind of makes him a lot like me. Speaking of which, I know this is all really confusing and you don't believe or trust me, but I need to leave for a little while. I need to go talk to him and explain what's going on."

Cameron instantly moves to block the doorway. "No. You aren't going anywhere alone with him. He's too dangerous."

"I've spent most of my time here with him. He'd never hurt me. In fact, all those times you thought I was doing school stuff or following a lead, I was with him. He's helped me experience what it's like to live."

But Cameron stands his ground.

"Get out of my way," I demand.

He sneers. "What're you gonna do? Punch me?"

Chapter 39: Emma

That's the last straw.

I lunge at him. He dodges, but not quick enough. Our tussle doesn't last long. We're a blur of flailing limbs and then I have his arms behind his back and his face pressed into the bed.

I reach around his neck, toward his throat. He thrashes against me when he realizes what I'm doing.

"No, wait. Emma—"

I press my fingers into the pressure point of his throat until he blacks out. Then I gently ease him onto the bed. I take both of our phones and tablets so he can't contact anyone in case he wakes up before I return.

Then I walk out the front door.

...

I find Jesse at the park as expected. He's on his usual swing, frowning at the ground in anguish. Charlotte and Oliver aren't there, obviously. It's unsettling to see the playground so eerily vacant.

I sit beside him. He doesn't look up or question me on what happened. Surely part of him is dying to know, but the other probably hopes he'll never have to find out.

"He's not going to turn us in," I say, finally breaking the tense silence. "At least not yet. He's giving us three days to prove that the government is corrupt and you're not evil like he thinks you are."

His brown eyes meet mine. "Why three days?"

"Because that's how long it'll take for his body to reset after you cut the tracker out of his arm."

Comprehension dawns on his face. "That's actually not a bad idea. Do you think it'll convince him?"

"I hope so," I reply with a shrug. "By the way, where are the kids?"

"Oh." He glances out at the empty playground. "They're at the library. I thought about picking them up, but I decided I'm not really comfortable bringing them here in the midst of mass destruction."

I crack a smile at that.

He peers at me again, this time with a mischievous glint in his eyes. "So, Emmalyn, huh?"

"Unfortunately," I sigh and then fix him with a firm stare. "And you'll never call me that again if you know what's good for you."

He smirks. "Duly noted…Emmalyn."

My blood boils, but not from anger or irritation like usual. It's something else, something I'm not sure I have an exact word for.

I kick his foot. "Jerk. What did I just say?"

He kicks me back.

But then the smile fades from his lips.

He stands and begins pacing around. "What are we going to do if it doesn't work? If he turns us in after we run out of time? This is bigger than just us. We put Charlotte and Oliver in danger. God, I'm so stupid."

He tugs at his hair. "I shouldn't have gone back to the apartment. It was reckless and stupid and I wasn't thinking straight. Or I should have climbed out the window instead of hiding in the closet."

I stand, too. "Oh, so you could fall and break your neck? I don't think so. It'll be okay, Jesse. It has to be."

"You don't know that." His voice breaks as he steps forward and envelops me in a crushing hug. I press my face against his shoulder and swallow hard to prevent the tears that want to burst free. He mumbles into my hair, "Everything was perfect an hour ago."

Chapter 39: Emma

"It's not over yet," I point out. "Maybe one day, we can look back at this and laugh at how we thought our world was about to end."

He chuckles. "Yeah, maybe."

He holds me a minute longer until we're both back under control, his pulse steady against mine. When he pulls away and our eyes meet, something flashes across his. It's that same look from earlier during our self-defense lesson. It's a dangerous look. One that holds whispers of a line that can never be crossed. We're standing so, so close. Too close.

He leans his head down slightly and rests his forehead against mine. My eyes slide closed at the flutter in the pit of my stomach. My chest tightens, lungs burning with lack of oxygen.

"What's happening," I mutter.

"I think you already know the answer to that."

I do know. I've suspected for a while. That doesn't make this any easier.

Because it's wrong. So wrong. It can't ever happen. Things between us have already gone too far, but this is definitely out-of-bounds. I've been so careful with my outward display of emotions lately and then he had to go and mess it all up by looking at me the way he did in the warehouse. He didn't use words, but he didn't have to. His eyes while I laid on the mat beneath him said it all.

He sighs heavily. I open my eyes to see him again. There's a sadness to him now, a desperation.

"It'll never work," he whispers, and my lungs collapse. How can three words be so simple, yet so crushing?

"I know," is all I manage. Because how can it? We aren't and never will be normal teenagers. There's too much baggage between us, including but not limited to his family issues and my connection to the government.

Step away, I tell myself sternly. *Step away from him, Emma. Staying there any longer will only cause you more pain in the end. You need to get out of his arms, no matter how badly you want to stay there. No matter how safe he makes you feel. Just because you feel safe right now doesn't mean danger isn't lurking right around the corner.*

Jesse must be thinking along the same lines because he drops his arms and steps back as if I burned him. "It's getting late. We should probably head back if you want me to remove his tracker."

I only nod.

Air still refuses to properly enter my lungs. My heart pounds and my hands shake. I try to act as normal as possible on the walk back, but it's a walk filled to the brim with awkward silence.

When we reach the apartment, I cautiously open the front door, suspecting that Cameron is awake by now. Sure enough, he's sitting on the couch with his head in his hands. He immediately springs up upon our arrival.

"Really, Emma?! The pressure point trick? Really?"

"I'm sorry, Cameron, but you weren't going to let me leave and I didn't want you following me."

Cameron huffs and looks past me, where Jesse is standing by the door. "What is he doing here?"

I take a deep breath. "He's here to remove the tracker from your arm. Once we do that, we'll wait the three days and then you'll feel real, undiluted emotions for the first time."

Cameron steps back, eyes wide and hands raised. "No. No way I'm letting that psycho dig around under my skin for a tracker that's probably not even there."

"You said you'd let me prove it to you," I protest. "This is me proving it. I can knock you unconscious if you'd like. Then you won't feel a thing."

Chapter 39: Emma

Apparently he's not in a joking mood because he takes me literally.

"No, I do not want to be unconscious. How stupid do you think I am? Who knows what he'd do to me then."

I roll my eyes. "Relax, Cam. I wasn't serious."

"Fine," he huffs. "Let's do this."

We relocate to the kitchen. I have Cameron sit in one of the chairs while Jesse disinfects a knife.

Jesse positions the knife on Cameron's upper arm. "This is obviously going to hurt, but it's important that you stay still so I can get this done as quickly as possible. The tracker is a tiny chip right below the skin, so it shouldn't be too difficult to extract. At least Emma's wasn't."

Cameron grits his teeth and braces himself as the knife pierces his skin. I'll hand it to him, he stays statue still and doesn't so much as whimper from the pain.

Jesse has the bead-sized tracker out in seconds, probably a much faster procedure than mine considering the amount of blood left behind from my wound. I immediately take to cleaning the sore once Jesse is done. I bandage it up and Jesse cleans the knife.

Cameron looks up at me with hard, stubborn eyes. "This doesn't prove anything."

I don't fight him on it, since I believed the same thing when Jesse first told me about the trackers.

I walk Jesse to the door.

"I'll get Charlotte to make another arm band so he can carry his, too. Assuming the government doesn't come to get us in a few days."

"Yeah. So, I'll see you at school?"

"Unfortunately. Even with the looming threat of the government, we still have to get a proper education."

I grin. "Goodnight, Jesse."

"Goodnight, Emmalyn."

For the first time in my life, I don't cringe at the sound of my full name.

CHAPTER FORTY
Jesse

My foot taps against the classroom floor the next morning. I drum my fingers on the desk and fidget in my seat. The bell's going to ring in three minutes and Emma still isn't here.

I'm not sure how removing Cameron's tracker will affect him since I doubt everyone has the same reaction. I just hope he didn't do something last night that would have caused her harm or put her in danger. She's usually here by now.

Just as I'm about to completely lose it, Emma walks through the door. My shoulders relax as I sigh. My foot ceases tapping, and my fingers stop their dance across my desk. I want to interrogate her right now, but Mr. Jones starts class. Luckily, today is a project day.

"Remember," he announces. "The final products are due by the end of the week. You can use the entire period today to work on them, but this is the last in-class opportunity. As usual, you can leave the room, but stay on campus and don't disturb the other classes. You are dismissed."

Emma and I stand up rather abruptly.

"Library?" she suggests and I nod.

We end up sitting on the floor of the school's library behind some bookcases so we won't be overheard. We aren't exactly working on our project, but that's because we finished it over a week ago. Instead, we discuss far more important matters.

"How were things after I left last night?"

Her eyebrows furrow as she thinks long and hard before answering. "Okay, I guess. He still refuses to believe a word I say, but hopefully that'll change once his brain catches up to being disconnected from the tracker formula. I mean, I wasn't exactly receptive to you until then."

She has a point.

"And what about this morning? You were almost late."

She winces. "Yeah, sorry about that. Cameron and I had a…disagreement on if he could be trusted with his phone."

"And?"

She reaches into her backpack and pulls out a phone identical to hers. "I couldn't risk it. This is our *future* we're talking about. I'm not letting the fate of mine rest on whether or not Cameron breaks our deal. I turned it off so the government can't track it."

"Smart move," I compliment. But once that's out of the way, an uncomfortable silence descends upon us. I glance at her from the corner of my eye and know we're thinking the same thing. We're just too embarrassed to say anything. This conversation is inevitable though. Might as well get it over with. "So, are we going to talk about yesterday? About what happened?"

So much happened, but she knows exactly which part I'm referring to. She tenses and at first, I think she's going to pretend she didn't hear me, but then—

"What's there to talk about?" she exclaims and throws her hands up. "You said it yourself that it won't work, and you're absolutely right. It *won't* work. It's too dangerous."

Chapter 40: Jesse

My words have come back to haunt me. "I know I said that, but you don't think it's possible at all?"

She closes her eyes and leans back against the shelf. "Jesse, I can't talk about this. Okay? I can't."

I should have backed off. I shouldn't have pushed her. But once I get started, it becomes difficult to stop.

"Look, I'm sorry I brought this up. But this…this thing between us, it's not just gonna go away. You know that, don't you? I know you don't fully understand emotions and all that, but—"

"I do understand," she retorts. "You think I didn't notice how you looked at me yesterday? I knew exactly what it was and what it meant. I know what you feel, what *I* feel, but it doesn't change anything."

"Emmalyn…"

She opens her eyes. "You really like using my full name, don't you?"

Does she always have to stall and change the subject? I sigh but play along anyway. "I like your name. Why do you hate it so much?"

She slowly releases a breath and runs a hand through her hair. "It's kind of stupid given everything I've discovered recently, but old habits die hard as they say, and this is one I've harbored for seventeen years." She pauses with a breath to collect herself. "My birth parents gave me that name. The Academy tends to keep the names we were given at the hospital. I always hated my parents because I thought they abandoned me. Therefore, I hated the name by association."

Heat sears through me. Words tumble out of me. "Wow, Emma. I'm sorry. I had no idea that's why it bothers you so much. I'm such an idiot. Here I was, constantly saying your full name. I can't believe—"

"Jesse," she interrupts. Probably for the best considering I'm rambling on like a complete moron. "It's fine. You only found out my full name yesterday. I didn't expect you to magically put two and two together and figure out how my brain works. And now that I know the truth, I don't think I hate my parents as much as I used to. It's still there, of course. It's not something I can just turn on and off, but I'm working on it. And for the record, hearing my name from you doesn't bother me as much as when other people say it."

We fall into silence again, but it's brief this time. Emma reverts back to our previous topic.

"It's not that I don't want to," she says slowly. "But it's too much of a risk. It's already going to be bad enough when they find out we're friends. Imagine what they'll do if we take it any further. They'll use it against us. They'll use it to *control* us, and I'm done being under their control."

"I understand that. It's just..." I trail off, unable to find the right words.

"Yeah, I know." Her shoulders droop as if the weight of everything has finally crashed into her. She swallows and blinks, just like I taught her. It's not enough to prevent a tear from sliding down her face. Not this time.

"What's wrong?" I ask softly, though it's a stupid question. What *isn't* wrong?

Her voice trembles. "I can't handle this, Jesse. I can't lose—" She breaks off and sinks her teeth into her bottom lip. She pauses a second before continuing. "What if this thing with Cameron doesn't work out? You could be *dead* in three days. We both could."

"Hey." I open my arm and she slides in against my side, leaning her head on my shoulder. I wrap my arm around her. "Everything's going to be okay."

"You don't know that," she sniffles.

Chapter 40: Jesse

"I don't," I agree. "But I feel it, you know. I feel like we're going to be just fine in the end."

"I hope so," she sighs.

"You can read my future," I offer. "Would that help?"

She shakes her head. "It'll just show the current path we're on. If our plan works, then the future will change. But because Cameron believes he'll be calling the government in a few days, that's what the future will currently reflect. That's the downside of my ability. It isn't always accurate because things shift, which affects the future."

I nod, but I hate feeling so helpless, like there's nothing we can do but sit back and hope things turn out in our favor. It makes me restless, anxious.

"Let's leave during study hall again," I suggest.

"Really?"

"Yeah, we can go to the waterfall if you want. Get away from here. Besides, you're on a secret mission, which you miserably failed, I might add. Is school really that important?"

I mean it jokingly, but she frowns. "Not to me, but it should to you! I thought you wanted to go to college and the only way it's going to happen is through scholarships."

"Missing half a day won't kill me. It might even help. I just need to get out of here for a while and get my mind off all the things that might happen. This is as much for me as it is for you, Emma."

"Lyn," she replies to my bewilderment.

"What?"

She tilts her head to look at me. "I'm giving you permission to call me Emmalyn. And yes, we can go to the waterfall. I'll meet you between lunch and fourth period."

. . .

As always, Emma beats me to our meeting spot.

"You ready?" I ask when I reach her.

Her eyes light up. "Yeah, let's go."

The tension drains out of me the farther from school we get. I feel her relax a little, too. We're both in a better mood by the time we get there. For a few hours, we can forget the train wreck our lives have become.

"I love this place," Emma whispers. She leans against the bridge's railing, gazing out across the glittering lake.

"Me, too."

Is this the last time I'll ever get to come here? Emma wasn't wrong earlier when she said we could be dead in a few days. That outcome is entirely possible.

This place means so much to me. I discovered it after the first time Greg hit me. I was just barely twelve years old and had only lived with him for a couple months. I ran out of the house after it happened and wandered around until I found the forest. Looking back, entering a strange wooded area by myself at such a young age maybe wasn't the smartest decision, but I don't regret it. This place is my sanctuary, my peace of mind. It'll always have a special spot in my heart.

I take a deep breath that fills my lungs with fresh, clean air. Now is not the time to get all emotional and nostalgic. If I really do only have two and a half days left, I need to make them count.

I focus on the scene before us, watch as the water falls and splashes against the rocks.

"Let's go swimming," I randomly blurt out, because what else are you supposed to do when everything around you is falling apart?

A smile tugs at the corner of my lips when Emma turns to me with a baffled expression. "Excuse me?"

"I *said*—"

Chapter 40: Jesse

"Yeah, I heard what you said. Are you *insane?* It's November, Jesse. I'm sure the water's freezing."

I slip off my shoes and socks. Her eyes widen even further. Maybe she thought I was kidding, but I'm completely serious.

"And *I'm* sure we agreed you'd let me teach you how to have fun."

"Yes, because freezing to death in a lake sounds like *so* much fun." Her eyes travel down my torso. "Besides, we don't have anything to swim in."

I roll my eyes. "Nice try. We can swim in our clothes. It's not like we're going back to school after this. Come on. Live a little before we can't anymore."

She chews her lip for a moment longer, then slowly nods.

Not wasting any time, I climb up onto the railing. I steady myself and then drop. The air abandons my lungs the moment I split the water. I expected it to be cold, but not like this. The water pricks my skin like icy needles as I go under completely. I sink until I hit the bottom and then kick up.

I gasp for air when I resurface. Emma laughs from the bridge. "How's the water? You look at little cold."

I wipe the water from my face and shake my wet hair out of my eyes. "It's perfect. Jump in."

"You're shivering."

"Come on, Emmalyn." I shout over the roaring waterfall. "Don't make me pull you in myself."

She huffs, though I know she's not actually mad. She pulls her shoes and socks off and leaves them next to mine. She climbs onto the rail and dangles her legs over the side.

I wade closer, pushing through the water plants at the bottom. She studies the water below and hesitates. She pulls back but I lunge before she has the chance to escape.

I jump up, wrap my arms around the bend of her knees, and sweep her off the bridge. Her shrill scream pierces the air for a split second before we both go under.

She struggles and kicks out of my grasp and pushes to the top. When I break the surface, my face is met with a ton of water.

"I hate you," she exclaims and splashes me again, less vicious this time.

"I know," I grin. "But hey, I had to get you in the water somehow and I *did* warn you about what would happen if you didn't get in on your own."

She responds by hurling more water at my face.

"Can you stop?"

"Make me," she smirks, a glint in her eyes. She's teasing me, provoking me.

"Sounds like an invitation to me," I mutter and throw water back at her. She laughs, the sound pealing across the open space, and swims away to the other end, right under the waterfall.

We continue our splash fight for a while, the frigid temperatures and our impending doom long forgotten. Yeah, we're being childish, but I got her to laugh. We're ignoring our problems, sure, but for a little bit, we aren't scared.

Eventually, when the shivering gets to be too much and our lips turn blue, we get out.

I lay beside her on the bridge. The sun filters through the trees and warms the exact spot where we rest. Hopefully it'll dry us enough to at least stop the dripping. We didn't think about not having towels. Or that we could have taken our shirts off so we'd have something to dry off with. Oh well, I guess.

It's nice at first, lying there with nothing but silence between us and the sounds of wildlife and the rustle of leaves. But then the thoughts creep back in, no matter how hard I try to keep them out.

Chapter 40: Jesse

"Do you think we should come up with a plan or something?" I ask. "In case all of this goes sideways, should we have some sort of strategy to fight back or escape or something?"

She doesn't look at me as she says, "I don't think it would matter. We're just two people. There's no way we can fight back on our own and win. They'll overpower us like it's nothing. As for escaping…I can't leave Cameron behind."

Her words knock the breath from my lungs. Not even Emma, number one in her class, thinks we have a chance against the Academy.

"Even though he'll be the one to turn us in?"

Emma shrugs. "It's not his fault. The government is controlling him just as much as they were me. We don't know how much taking out the tracker will affect him. He might not change much at all, but it doesn't matter. I'm the one who messed up. I'm not leaving him behind to deal with the government on his own. He's my best friend."

"But you're not the person he grew up with," I say gently. "To him, you changed so suddenly and switched sides and he probably doesn't know what to do with all that. He thinks you betrayed him. Friendship might not matter to him anymore."

"I don't care." There's a bite to her tone. I'm on the brink of pushing too far. "I don't care what he thinks of me. I can't just take off and leave him. I can't give up on him. We've been through too much together. If it comes down to it, I'll do whatever it takes to fight my way out. But I'm not abandoning my best friend."

"Okay, I'm sorry."

She takes a few deep breaths, which seems to calm her down. "Speaking of which, I need to get home soon. Got to make sure Cameron's okay."

Officially back to reality.

Reluctantly, I hoist myself up and offer her my hand. She takes it and I pull her up, too. We begin the journey back.

"Thanks for today," she says as she pulls her wet, stringy hair into a ponytail. "I did have fun."

"No problem," I reply. I give her a quick hug despite our damp clothes, and we part ways.

One day down. Only two more to go.

CHAPTER FORTY-ONE
Emma

Anxiety pumps through my veins on the morning of the third day. The past two were calm for the most part, but today will be chaos regardless of how things go. Either Cameron will feel real emotions, or the government will come busting down the door to take me in.

A clatter of dishes sounds from the kitchen. After getting ready, I hesitantly enter to find Cameron at the table with a bowl of cereal.

"Hey," I say cautiously.

He fixes me with a cold stare. "It's been three days. I don't feel any different. Your time is up, Emmalyn."

I blanch. "No, the day isn't over yet. You promised me a whole three days."

He fights back. "And when did things supposedly change for *you* on day three?"

"It's different for everyone. You have to give it until the end of the day, at least." I keep my voice steady, but he caught me on that. I woke up on the third morning completely different.

"Fine," he grumbles and turns back to his breakfast. "I'll give you until the end of the day, but then I'm calling the Ambassador and you better not fight me on it. I gave you what you asked for. I gave you extra time. It's not my fault you broke the rules."

I wince, my conversation with Jesse at the waterfall surfacing to mind.

"This isn't you," I whisper.

"Yeah, well this isn't *you*," he retorts, gesturing to me. "What happened to you? We were supposed to always look out for each other, to tell each other everything. And instead, you've been lying to me for weeks, maybe months."

Needless to say, I leave the apartment without breakfast. I can't deal with him and his smug attitude. Maybe he thinks he'll get some kind of reward for being the one to turn us in. I don't know, but I hate him for it.

Jesse waits by my locker when I arrive, his face tight and his eyes filled with fear of the unknown. I don't hesitate before crashing into him. His arms slide around me, holding me against him. I press my face into his chest and listen to the rapid beat of his heart.

We don't speak at first. We hold each other, lost in our own little world while everyone else moves through the halls that are filled with chatter and laughter. No one pays any attention to us and for that, I'm grateful.

"Whatever happens today, Emma, remember that…that I'm with you. We're in this together. You and me. Whether we fight or leave. Until the end."

I swallow the sob that threatens to tear from my throat. I was barely stable before, but hearing his words completely breaks me. This is it. The day we've been dreading since the beginning of our unexpected friendship, but knew would eventually come.

"Until the end." My voice cracks. He grips my hands tight in his and presses a soft kiss to my forehead. Then we walk to class as if everything is normal.

Chapter 41: Emma

I keep my hand in his all through first period and lunch, unwilling to break the connection, though we have to when it's time to go home.

We had a good run, but now we're out of time.

...

I slowly type in the apartment's four-digit code and scan my finger. I prolonged the walk home as much as possible, but there's only so much one can do to drag out the inevitable.

I push the door open and find an empty living room. Where is he? Why isn't he waiting by the door, ready to destroy me?

He's not in the kitchen either.

"Cameron?" I call.

Maybe he found a way to contact the Ambassador without his phone. Maybe they're already here. Maybe they're ambushing Jesse right now.

Jesse.

My heart constricts. I'm going to lose him. This is really happening.

Just as I'm about to sprint out of the apartment and straight to Jesse's house, a gasp and a whimper comes from down the hall.

I find him in the bathroom, gripping the edge of the sink, knuckles white, face ashen, and eyes wide. His chest convulses as he tries to draw breath.

"Cameron!" I rush in and grab him, pull him to me. "It's okay. You're okay."

His whole body trembles in my arms. He tries to speak but can't get the words out. Is this how I acted and looked to Jesse that morning so long ago?

"I – I…Emma, I can't bre-breathe."

"It's okay. You don't have to talk. Just breathe with me, okay? In and out."

It takes a few minutes, but I get him to calm down enough to speak coherently. "You were right, Emma," he chokes out. "I'm so sorry. You were right. I can't believe I almost turned you in and got you killed. You should hate me. Oh my god, you were right."

"Shh, it's okay. It's not your fault."

Never in my life have I heard him ramble on like that. And then, as if things aren't already weird enough, tears leak from his eyes and streak down his face.

He's crying. An Academy kid other than me is actually crying.

It's then that the relief finally crashes through me. We're safe. Everything is going to be okay. We aren't going to die. At least not yet. Not today.

He clings to me, relying on my strength to hold him steady while he falls apart. Without letting go, I lead him to the living room and ease us onto the couch.

We stay silent for a while, his sobs the only sound that fills the room. I wait patiently. My life isn't on a countdown anymore. He can have all the time he needs.

Eventually, his tears subside and he gets enough of a grip on himself.

"How do you deal with it?" he asks.

I dry his face with my shirt sleeve and smile gently. "I've had a lot of practice. Jesse's the one who helped me through it, and now I can help you."

I take his trembling hands in mine. He looks at me with wild, frantic eyes. "I don't even know what I'm feeling. I know all the words to describe emotions, but I've never felt anything like this before. It's so strong and—and..."

"Overwhelming?" I supply. "I know. It's hard to put words to feelings when the feelings have been wrong your entire life. I *know*, Cameron. I went through this, too, but now I'm out on the other

Chapter 41: Emma

side. I survived. I know you're scared and filled with guilt, and pain, and anxiety, and you're going to spend the next couple days questioning everything you thought you knew. But you will be okay. Just breathe."

His head drops against the back of the couch. He inhales and exhales several times to calm down even more. "I'm sorry, Em," he says again. "Sorry for not believing you. For scaring you and him. For not trusting you enough to actually listen." He pauses and his face crumples. "I guess it was true, all those times an Academy kid on the outside rebelled and then tried to explain why. I just never believed any of it."

"It's okay, Cameron. Everything you've said, everything you've done…it wasn't your fault. The government has been manipulating us our whole lives."

"Why, though? Why control a bunch of kids? It doesn't make any sense. What do they *want*?"

"I don't know," I say honestly. "That's what we're trying to figure out."

He goes quiet again before hesitantly asking, "Can you tell me about it?"

"About what?"

His deep blue eyes hold mine with genuine curiosity. "The whole story. You and the tar—I mean Jesse. How the whole kidnapping thing went down and how that led to where you are now. What else have you found out about the government? What else have they done to us? I want to know everything. I want the truth about who we really are. I want to help."

So I tell him.

. . .

I stay with Cameron until he falls asleep on the couch. It's dark by then and I still haven't updated Jesse. Surely, he isn't panicking out of his mind. After all, he has to know that no news is good news, right?

Regardless, I scribble a quick note to Cameron in case he wakes up, then slip out of the apartment. It's late, but Jesse's driveway is vacant of Greg's truck as usual.

I knock on the door and Charlotte opens it.

"Emma!" she exclaims, face lighting up. Jesse clearly hasn't told her about our situation. She steps aside to let me in.

Just as the door closes, Jesse emerges from the bedroom. He stops in his tracks and our eyes lock. His expression asks the question I know he won't be able to voice.

My lip quivers and I nod. He doesn't need more explanation than that. His face breaks out in relief and I charge. He catches me in his arms and holds me close. I press my face into his neck as he wraps his arms around me.

We really are safe.

We stand there for a moment, his breath ragged against my ear, heart rapid against mine.

He pushes me away enough to look into my eyes. "It worked? He's really on our side?"

I smile through my blurry vision. "He really is. I explained everything to him. He wants in on what we're doing."

Jesse pulls me back in and hugs me tight.

"What's going on?" Charlotte wonders from behind us. We turn to face her.

"Nothing," Jesse says. "It's over now."

"But—"

"Trust me, Char. You don't want to know. It doesn't matter now. Everything's okay."

She frowns, but doesn't push it, and leaves to join Oli on the couch.

Chapter 41: Emma

"So," Jesse says, voice low so only I can hear. "What do you want to do now that our lives aren't about to end?"

"Well, I probably need to get home, just in case Cameron wakes up and needs me. I just wanted to let you know that everything worked out."

"Or you could stay. Just for a little while. Besides, Cameron's asleep and probably will be until morning. I'm sure experiencing emotions for the first time takes a toll on a person."

"Fine," I sigh dramatically. There's no point in trying to convince him otherwise. "What do you suggest we do?"

He mulls it over. "We could watch a movie. You still have a lot of catching up to do since you missed out on seventeen years' worth."

I agree and the four of us end up piled on the couch. Jesse sits in the middle with Charlotte and I on either side. Oliver sits on the floor in front of me with his head leaned back in my lap. Jesse puts on a movie and I'm instantly immersed. I really have been missing out.

But as it gets later into the night, my eyelids take on more and more weight. I curl up against Jesse's side, lean into his warmth. I never make it to the end of the movie.

. . .

I'm jostled awake when I'm lifted into the air. One of his arms goes under my neck while the other goes behind my knees.

I blearily peel my eyes open. "What're y'doing?" I slur, mind too foggy from sleep to form complete words.

"Shh, go back to sleep," Jesse whispers.

I squirm in his arms. "Put me down. I can walk just fine."

"Well you weren't awake when I picked you up. But now that I already have you, there's no sense in putting you down. Deal with it."

"You're going to drop me," I say through a yawn.

He laughs. "You're not that heavy."

"Yeah, but maybe you're just weak."

"Wow, half asleep and you still manage to insult me."

I force my eyes all the way open despite how exhausted I am. "I need to go back to the apartment, Jesse."

He sighs and gently lowers me to the floor. "Do you have to?"

I shove him. "Stop complaining. I already stayed and watched a movie with you. But I really need to be there when Cameron wakes up. I promise you can see me tomorrow."

"Fine, but I'm going to hold you to that."

I just smile.

Cameron is still asleep on the couch when I get home. I creep past him to my room so I don't wake him. I quickly change into pajamas and crawl under the covers.

I'm not asleep very long before my bedroom door opens.

"Emma?" Cameron's voice is soft. I sit up. The room is dark and he is nothing but a silhouette in the doorway.

"What's wrong? Are you okay?"

He doesn't move. "I—I woke up and I can't fall back asleep…I'm sorry. I shouldn't have just come in here. You were sleeping."

"No, no. It's fine," I assure him. "Come here."

I move to one side of the bed to make room. He slides in beside me and I roll on my side to face him.

"You need to relax. I know it's difficult with everything hitting you all at once, but if you want to sleep, you have to calm down."

"How did you even keep all this from me? It's so intense all the time." He pauses and glances at me through the dark. "Is this what you felt like that night when you came home and I yelled at you for disappearing?"

Chapter 41: Emma

I chuckle at the memory of how a mess I was back then. "Pretty much. That was…not a good night. I basically cried in the shower and then went to my room and cried some more until I passed out."

"Wow," he sighs. "I wish you would have told me sooner."

"Yeah, well, I didn't know if you'd believe me. And I was kind of right considering what happened when you *did* find out."

He winces. "I really am sorry."

"Stop saying that. I reacted the same way when Jesse first told me about the trackers. I didn't believe him and I tried to make excuses for the government. But that doesn't matter anymore. We're all here on the same side again."

"I'm glad," Cameron whispers. "Everything's a mess, but I'm glad I know the truth now. I'm glad to have you back."

I smile. "Me, too."

...

A bang jolts me from sleep. I shoot up in bed. Soft light filters in through the window. Cameron's asleep beside me, mouth hanging open and arm pushed under the pillow.

Another knock sounds at the front door, more urgent this time. My mind first jumps to the government, but that's stupid. If it was the government outside my apartment, they wouldn't be so polite as to ask permission before bursting in.

My next thought is confirmed when I open the door to find Jesse on the other side.

A grin splits over his face when he sees me. "Good morning."

"Hey." I step aside and let him in. "What are you doing here?"

His grin turns sheepish. "You said I could see you tomorrow. It's tomorrow."

I laugh. "You are such a dork. I didn't mean this early in the morning."

He looks at me strangely. "It's a little after ten. I've already taken Charlotte and Oliver to school."

"*Ten!* We should be in third period right now. Especially since we've already missed a lot lately."

He shrugs. "We've been super stressed the past few days. I think we deserve another day off from school. And even if the school happens to call home to report all of my unexcused absences, it's not like Greg will be the one to answer. He's hardly ever there."

"Okay," I give in. A day without school after the week we've had sounds amazing.

"How's Cameron?" Jesse asks.

"He's fine for now," I reply. "We had a bit of a rough night, but he's sleeping now."

"And you just got up?"

I glare at him. "Yeah, because someone so rudely disturbed me from my sleep."

He leans closer. "How about I make breakfast to apologize for waking you up."

"I'm not hungry."

And then my stomach growls right on cue.

He smirks. "Your stomach says otherwise." He pauses, realizing what he said. "Hey, it's like old times."

I can't help the laugh that escapes. "Oh, you mean that time when you kidnapped me?"

"You're never gonna let that go, are you?"

"You're the one who brought it up," I point out.

"I'm just going to go make you breakfast now." Ha. I win. He slips past me and wanders into the kitchen. "Any requests for food?"

He opens a cabinet and of all things, pulls out the pancake mix I idiotically used for the first and last time on my second day here, and still haven't thrown out.

Chapter 41: Emma

My lightness from our banter fades. "Anything but pancakes."

If he's thrown off by my strange request, he doesn't show it. He shoos me out of the kitchen and says he'll let me know when it's done.

I go into the bathroom, brush my teeth, and brush through my tangled mess of bed head. I check on Cameron again, but he's still asleep.

"Okay!" Jesse calls after I throw on a tee shirt and sweatpants. I return to the kitchen where the sizzle of bacon fills the air. "I hope bacon and toast is all right. I didn't want to take too much time. Plus, you know, there's only so much I actually know how to make. I usually have to force Charlotte out of bed, so it's almost always cereal for us in the morning."

"It's perfect. Thanks."

He separates it onto two plates, leaving some behind for Cameron when he wakes. He hands me mine and we sit at the table.

"You making breakfast for me wouldn't happen to be another ploy to drug me, would it?"

He laughs. "No, I think you've gotten enough sleep for a while."

I kick him under the table.

We talk and laugh and eat. It's such a normal morning for normal people that it almost doesn't feel real.

After we're done, we move to the couch in the living room. I'm still tired from how emotionally draining the last few days have been, so I rest my head on his shoulder and close my eyes.

The silence is peaceful, relaxing. Until he says, "Hey, can I ask you something?"

"Mhmm."

"Why no pancakes?"

My heart squeezes at the horrid thoughts that pass through my mind. I sigh. "Any question but that."

"What?"

I squeeze my eyes shut, as if that will somehow block out the pain. "Sorry. It's just…it still hurts every time I think about it."

"Oh, okay." He slides an arm around my shoulders. "Well, you don't have to tell me anything you're not ready for."

"No, I want to. You've told me a lot of things that were difficult for you. It's my turn. It's just hard to talk about. Back at the Academy, everyone knew about it. But I've never actually talked to anyone about it before."

You can do this, Emma. Just remember to breathe.

"When we enter our freshman year, each student is assigned a mentor that graduated a few years previously. They help us out and are there to guide us if we need it. Each mentor only has a few students, so it can be more individualized and personal. My mentor…his name was Ian."

Recognition sparks in Jesse's eyes.

"What?"

"Nothing," he says. "It's just…you mentioned him once, when you had the meltdown in the bathroom at school."

"Oh, yeah. I forgot about that."

"It's okay. Keep going, if you want. You had a mentor."

"Yeah, and most people aren't all that close with theirs. They're usually just like teachers. But Ian was my whole world. He trained me, gave me advice, looked out for me. He was there whenever I needed someone to talk to and didn't feel like going to one of my friends. He was the big brother I never had, and I admired him."

"What happened?" Jesse's voice is barely audible.

I swallow back tears. "He wasn't just a mentor. He was also in the Missions program. When I was a sophomore, he was offered a

Chapter 41: Emma

Mission. It was his first since he'd been assigned to me. He was torn between going and staying because he didn't want to leave me behind. I told him…I told him I'd be okay and that he should take the job. It wasn't even a long assignment. He would probably only be gone a month at most."

I can't prevent the tears any longer. Jesse's arm tightens around me.

"That conversation I had with him was what convinced him to go. So he went, but he never came back. I still remember the day an Academy official sat down with me and told me he'd been k-killed while on the Mission."

Breathe, Emma! You're supposed to breathe!

I try to listen to myself and draw breath, but the air refuses to enter my lungs.

"It's my fault he's dead. I'm the one who told him to go. He'd still be alive if it weren't for me."

"Hey," Jesse says firmly and runs his hand up and down my arm. "It was not your fault. He's the one who decided to be in the program to begin with. Maybe you told him to take the job, but every decision he made was his own. You weren't the one who killed him."

He holds me tighter and the pressure, his words, his warmth, calm me down.

"How?" I whisper. "How do you always say just the right thing?"

His laugh is soft in my ear. "I'm just awesome like that."

Despite everything, I smile.

"If you don't mind me asking," Jesse says. "How exactly does your aversion to pancakes fit in."

My chest loosens just a bit and I finally breathe.

"It's kind of stupid, but I used to really love blueberry pancakes. I still do, I guess, but I haven't had any in the two years since…anyway, Ian and I met for breakfast a lot to go over my progress and stuff or to talk about strategies for improving so I could get into the Missions program. We almost always ate blueberry pancakes. When he figured out how much I loved them, he started bribing me. Like promising me pancakes if I improved in a certain skill by the end of the week. It became our thing. Our tradition. So now every time I think of pancakes, I think of him."

"I'm so sorry, Emma."

"I've never told anyone," I sniffle. "It destroyed me when I found out two years ago and that was even without proper emotions. When I felt real emotions for the first time, it felt like he died yesterday. I can't imagine what it must feel like to lose someone when you do have emotions that work the way they should."

"Trust me, it's not fun."

Right. He would know.

Jesse lets out a long sigh. "Can I ask you something else?"

"Man, you're full of questions today."

He gives me a small smile. "I just want to know how you're doing with everything. A lot changed in just a few days."

I shrug. "I'm fine, I guess. I'm mostly just focusing on Cameron right now and trying not to think about, you know, how my parents apparently have no idea what happened to me, how the government is out to get me, and how messed up everything has gotten."

"Yeah, well if you ever want to talk about it, when you're ready, I'm here."

"Thank you."

Cameron emerges shortly after. He trudges into the living room, scrubbing a hand down his face. He freezes when he sees

Chapter 41: Emma

Jesse. Then his eyes widen just slightly when he sees me curled up next to him.

Cameron and Jesse just stare at each other for a moment. And then Cameron simply says, "I'm sorry."

Jesse shrugs. "Don't worry about it. It's all okay now. There's breakfast in the kitchen if you want it."

"Thanks," Cameron says and walks off.

And that's that.

CHAPTER FORTY-TWO
Jesse

Emma skips again on Friday to take care of Cameron. I wanted to help, but she insisted I go to school.

School is over now, though. I took Charlotte and Oliver to the park like usual and now we're on our way home. I haven't seen or heard from Emma all day, but we're safe now, so surely she's okay.

Today was actually a good day compared to the stress-filled days we've experienced recently. But that all ends when we get close to the house.

Ice floods my body at the sight of Greg's truck in the driveway. He hasn't been home in a few days—an absolute miracle—but he apparently returned in the hour we were gone.

I pause outside the door and turn to the kids. "Here's the plan. I'm going to open this door. We are going to enter as quietly as possible and go straight to the bedroom. I'll lock the door once we're inside, and we're going to continue to be quiet until he's gone again. Let's not give him a reason to come after us."

They nod and I ease the door open. The front room is empty. We creep inside and down the hall. I usher Charlotte and Oliver into our tiny bedroom and start to follow them.

Chapter 42: Jesse

I never make it.

A hand fists in my hair and yanks me backwards so hard I fall, knocking my head against the corner of the wall on my way down. My forehead by my eyebrow stings from the impact, but that's the least of my problems right now.

I've already lost this fight. Being on the ground makes me weaker, more vulnerable than usual. There's no way I can pick myself up, get around him, and safely inside the room until he finishes taking his anger and frustrations out on me.

I've learned over the years that the most important thing to remember in this situation is to protect my face, head, and ribs. I raise my arms to shield those areas just as he lands the first blow. His foot connects with my stomach, a sharp kick that knocks the wind out of me. I curl inward at the impact, but that doesn't stop him.

He starts screaming at me, too, but I only catch a little of what he's saying.

"—all your fault…said I'm supposed to have better control over you…not paying enough attention…took everything from me!"

He kicks again and again, until I can't feel it anymore. I can't feel anything.

Blood pounds in my ears. I try to draw breath, but to no avail. He leaves me like that, coughing and wheezing on the floor, wishing I was strong enough to fight back. Even after all my training with Emma, I'm still not good enough to stand up to him.

The sound of Greg's bedroom door slamming shut rattles my brain. I inhale again, but still nothing. That's when the panic sets in. I know he knocked the wind out of me, but that doesn't diminish how scary it is to breathe in and not have air actually enter your lungs.

I squirm on the ground, trying to get into a more comfortable position. My chest aches with the inability to find relief. I squeeze my eyes shut and wonder. Is this what it will feel like to die? Massive amounts of pain and agony until you just can't hold on any longer?

A hand suddenly brushes the hair away from my face. I open my eyes and Charlotte's face swims into view as she kneels beside me.

"It's okay," she whispers. "Calm down. Just keep breathing. It'll come back faster if you relax."

I do as she says, continuing to inhale and exhale, even though it's not working. I force my muscles to relax. She combs her hand through my hair until I finally gasp as air enters my lungs. My vision clears.

"Thank you," I whisper.

"Thank *you*," she replies. "You always put mine and Oli's safety above your own, even when it leaves you unprotected. You take care of me in a way no one ever has."

I force myself into a sitting position and pull her into my arms. "What have I always told you? I'm here to protect you, no matter what. I'll always be here, Charlotte. I'm not your parents or any of the foster homes you've been in. I won't leave you."

"I know." She hugs me tighter. "What was he going on about anyway?"

I answer her honestly. "I don't know."

...

Greg is gone again by the following morning. Emma and Cameron are coming over today so we can get Cameron up to speed on what we know about the government. According to Emma, Cameron is doing a lot better now that a few days have passed. She thinks he's finally ready to be let in on our little operation.

While we wait, Oliver watches TV, Charlotte works on her homework, and I fidget on the couch. A knock sounds at the door.

Chapter 42: Jesse

I stand and flinch as pain shoots through my abdomen. Thanks to Greg, I have yet another collection of bruises.

Emma stands on the other side, a huge grin on her face. She's alone.

"Where's Cameron?"

She waves it off. "Oh, he's coming later."

"Emma!" Charlotte exclaims and runs over, Oliver right on her heels. They tackle her in greeting. It's fascinating how good she is with them. Once things settle, Charlotte returns to her homework and Oliver to his show. Emma and I go to the bedroom, where I already have the corkboard set up on the bed.

We sit down, and I wince as pain spirals through me. And of course, Emma just happens to be looking in my direction when I do.

"What's wrong?" she asks, concerned.

"Nothing," I lie, though attempting to deflect her is pointless.

"That wasn't nothing. What's going on? You look like you're in pain."

I grimace at her comment. I *am* in pain, but she doesn't need to know that.

Her eyes narrow. "Jesse." Her tone is firm and dripping with warning. She's not playing around.

I sigh. "Look, it's not a big deal. It happens all the time."

Her face darkens. "You mean *Greg*? He hurt you again?"

"Emma—"

"Don't," she cuts me off. Fire sparks in her eyes, a cue that she's close to exploding. "Where, Jesse? Where did he hit you?"

"He didn't hit me," I mumble. She casts me a pointed look and I sigh again. "He *didn't* hit me…but he grabbed me and threw me on the ground. My mind blanked and I couldn't remember any of the tips you gave me about blocking. He kicked me until I couldn't breathe."

"Where?" she whispers.

There's no getting around her, so I give in. "My stomach."

Before I can utter another word, her fingers find the hem of my shirt. She pushes it up just enough to reveal the bruise on my lower torso. She's silent with wide-eyed horror at the nasty blue-purple blob smeared across my stomach.

"Jesse…" she breathes.

I stay perfectly still, despite how much I want to yank my shirt back down. I know she won't let me though. Not until she's satisfied with her inspection.

"It looks a whole lot worse than it actually is," I supply. She ignores me.

Her hands flit over my stomach, light and warm against my bare skin. She places her palm against the bruise, probably in an attempt to figure out the severity of it.

I hiss as my stomach explodes.

"Sorry, sorry."

I grit my teeth. "It's not that. Your hands are cold."

She rolls her eyes, then lifts them to meet mine. "Do not lie to me, Jesse Reynolds."

I grin through the pain. "I would never lie to you, Emmalyn Grant." Besides just then, of course. She knows what I mean.

"Why does he hate you so much?"

I shrug, just slightly, still very aware that the tips of her fingers rest on me. "I don't know if it's necessarily me. He's just…always been like that. I mean, last night he was yelling about something being my fault. But I'm pretty sure he was drunk, so it's not like he was in his right mind. Not that he ever is."

Emma bites her lip. "Maybe it's time you told someone."

Chapter 42: Jesse

I immediately shake my head. "I can't. We've already talked about this. Charlotte and Oliver could end up in an even worse situation than this and then I won't be there to protect them. I'm willing to take whatever Greg throws at me if it means the kids won't get hurt anymore."

"I'm sorry," she whispers. "That you have to live like this and you can't do anything about it. It's not fair."

"It's not that bad," I say honestly. Especially lately. Greg has been home less and less it seems. "Like I said, we've all had worse situations than this one."

"Okay, sorry for bringing it up again."

"It's all right. You're just concerned for us, I get it."

A hush falls over us as we stare at each other with locked eyes. Her hands burn me where they continue to lay on my stomach. It's happening again. We're losing ourselves in a trance.

She opens her mouth to speak…and then the doorbell rings. The spell between us shatters to pieces. She springs away. I fix my shirt.

"That's probably Cameron," she says hastily. I don't point out that she just stated the obvious.

"Yeah, we should go let him in."

We leave the room as if nothing happened. Always pretending like we aren't inches away from crossing a line and breaking the rules. Or rather, her rules that I'm willing to respect. I understand where she's coming from, but it doesn't make this any easier.

Charlotte is already at the door, standing in front of an uncomfortable looking Cameron.

"And what exactly do you plan to do with the information they show you?"

"Uh—"

I walk up behind her. "Char, what are you doing?"

She spins around, hands on her hips. "Interrogating him, obviously. I have to make sure he's actually on our side. We have to be suspicious of everyone. It keeps the balance, too. You protect me from psychotic foster fathers and I'll protect you from potentially dangerous Academy kids."

"I appreciate that Char, but I took his tracker out. There's no need for an interrogation. He's on our side, so please let him come in."

However, part of me does agree with her. Although I'll never admit it to Emma, I don't trust Cameron the way I trust her. Sure, we've reached a sort of unspoken agreement, but something is different about him. I keep it to myself, though. Emma clearly trusts him, and I trust her.

"Whoa," Cameron whistles when we walk into the bedroom and he lays eyes on the corkboard. I move the board to the floor so we can all sit around it. Then I give him the run-down of what it all means, though definitely not as in-depth as the explanation I gave Emma.

After I finish, Cameron points to three of the red tacks in the Southwestern Central region. "The Academy isn't located at any of these. Or anywhere in that region."

I look up, as does Emma.

"How do you know that?" she demands. He shrugs in reply. Her eyes narrow. "Cameron, if you know something…if you know where the Academy is, tell us right now."

Huh. Maybe I'm not the only one with suspicions.

"No, no." Cameron says hastily. "I don't know where it is, but those places are too far from here to be the Academy."

"And how do you know how far away it is?"

Chapter 42: Jesse

He huffs, clearly aggravated. "Because unlike you, I actually paid attention during our car trip here. We left at 10pm and arrived by eight the next morning."

My heart stops as I do the math. "Ten hours?"

He nods. "We're looking at a ten-hour radius between here and the Academy."

"How much does that help?" Emma wonders. "Will you be able to find it?"

"Maybe," I respond. "I mean, that narrows it down to one region: Northwestern Central. I can cross-reference it with my other notes and see if I can find anything else to help us narrow things down even more."

"So, is that all or is there something else I should know?" Cameron asks. I get the feeling I'm not the only one who is uncomfortable by this situation.

I glance at Emma and she gives a subtle shake of her head. I turn to Cameron. "No, that's all. Thanks so much for your help."

We walk him out and then it's just me and Emma again.

"I'm sorry," she says once we're back in my room. "That was really awkward. He's still getting used to everything and it's all happening a lot faster for him than it did for me. We didn't exactly put trust in each other right away."

"It's fine," I assure her. "He needed to know the basics and his information *was* seriously helpful."

She sits on the edge of the bed. "So, now what?"

I contemplate my next move. I know what I have to do, but it's a big step for me. I've told her about it, but I've never shown anyone, not even Charlotte. But Emma deserves the full truth, and I need a fresh set of eyes.

"There's something I need to show you."

Beyond the Gates

I gingerly walk to the closet and feel around on the floor until my fingers hit the bump in the wood. I lift the floorboard and extract the stack of files and reports.

"What is it with you and hiding stuff?"

It's her attempt to lighten the mood, but I can't find it in me to laugh. Instead, I hand it to her.

"That's everything I know about the Academy. Some of it is from my parents, like I told you. Some of it is other stuff I've figured out over the years."

I show her the formulas that failed for years. The real one isn't in there, but there are notes on my parents' suspicions for what their work had actually been used for. I show her the proof that the government steals children from hospitals. I show her everything. It's freeing in a way, finally sharing all this knowledge with someone else.

Everything changes when she notices something I haven't.

"Database," she mumbles. I put down the file I was looking over.

"What?"

She looks up. "The government has a database specifically for the Academy. Information, records, everything."

I sit up straighter and snatch the file from her hands. "Are you serious?"

She points to a paragraph on the page. It's not explicit, but after reading it a few times, I realize she's right. It refers to the storage of Academy records.

"How did I miss this? I've been over these files hundreds of times."

She moves closer to peer at the file gripped tight in my shaking hands. "Does it say how it can be accessed?"

Chapter 42: Jesse

"We'll need some kind of clearance code." I grab a stack of folders and hand them to her. "Let's start looking. See if you can find anything that may resemble a passcode, like random strings of letters and numbers."

We pour over the papers forever with no such luck.

And then Emma gasps.

I look at her. "What? Did you find something?"

She doesn't answer, just stares at the page with wide eyes. When she finally looks up, she only says one word. "Tablet."

I must look confused, because she snaps her fingers. "Tablet, now. Get your tablet."

I scramble off the bed and pull the tablet out of my backpack and hand it to her. Her fingers fly across the screen. I don't dare ask any more questions while she's as focused as she is.

Then she stops and stares at the screen. Her mouth falls open with a small gasp of disbelief. I move closer to see what she's doing. She's on the Internet, using an interactive map. The box on the left doesn't have an address typed in, but coordinates.

The coordinates don't show anything in particular, just miles and miles of forest. I pick up the paper she dropped and scan it. There, buried in the middle of the page, is the same coordinates she typed in.

I look back at her. Her eyes hold the answer I'm looking for, but she says it in words, too.

"We found it."

The Academy. Right there, all this time.

"What do we do?" I ask. Because I feel so lost now. I've spent so much time trying to find the Academy that I never thought much about what the next step would be if I ever actually found it.

"I have an idea," she says slowly. "But we're going to need Aria…and possibly your car."

CHAPTER FORTY-THREE
Emma

"Where have you been?"

I sigh, shut my locker, and turn to face an irritated Aria. It's Monday, my first day back to school since Cameron got emotions. I haven't seen or talked to Aria since then.

"I'm sorry. There were some...family issues I had to deal with," I say.

She brushes her dark hair over her shoulder and pushes her glasses up her nose, her ice blue eyes trained on me. "But you're okay now, right? I was worried about you."

A pang of guilt flashes through me. I've been dealing with so much lately that I didn't think about how my absence would affect her. I ignored all her calls and texts and disappeared from school. But I'm not about to drag her into my messed up life.

We do need her though. I want to stall, but Jesse said I have to ask her today. We can't afford to waste any time.

"I'm fine. But actually, I was wondering if you could help me with something?" I say casually as we head down the hall.

"Like what? Catching up on the work you missed?"

Chapter 43: Emma

"Not exactly." I lower my voice. "I need your skills like what you used for Jesse when I first moved here."

She stops abruptly and grabs my arm to stop me, too. Her eyes are wide. "What? You want me to…"

The look on her face says we're on the same page. I nod.

"For what?" she exclaims, her voice barely audible above the chatter and bustle of students in the hall around us.

"I can't tell you," I say slowly, fully knowing she won't like that answer. "I just need you to hack something for me, but you can't ask questions about it. It's too dangerous."

Her face pales. "Too dangerous? What are you trying to do?"

"That's a question," I sigh. "Look, I hate keeping you in the dark. You've been such an amazing friend to me, so the last thing I want is to put you at risk. But you're the only one I know who can do this. Please."

"I don't know…"

"What if I said that the information I need can stop something bad from happening?"

She stares at me and her face softens just a little. "Fine. But you owe me. And I mean big time. This is the second time I've hacked for you."

"Yeah, okay. Whatever you want, you've got it. Can you come over today after school?"

"Sure," she says as the warning bell rings. "I've got to get to class and think about what just happened. My friend disappears off the face of the earth for a week and returns demanding I do illegal things for her and bad things will happen if I don't."

Her sarcastic tone brings a smile to my lips. "Thank you, Aria."

She backs away toward the stairs with a tiny smile. "Anytime."

Jesse is waiting for me when I arrive to the only class we share.

He speaks as soon as I sit down, the words rushing from his mouth before the teacher starts class. "How did it go? Did you talk to her?"

"Yeah, she's confused on what we've gotten ourselves into, but she's on board. She's coming over after school."

Jesse visibly relaxes. "Great. That's great." He shakes his head. "I can't believe this is really happening. We're going to find out…I don't know what, but something important or they wouldn't keep it so hidden."

"Yeah," I agree. "We're almost there."

. . .

First period passes quickly and then Jesse and I go our separate ways until lunch. I don't want to sit through five more classes. I want to get home so we can get into the database. But we've missed way too many days of school recently and I'm already asking a lot of Aria.

So I go to my next class. However, as soon as I walk through the door, the teacher stops me. "You're wanted in the office, Emma."

My blood freezes. "What for?"

My mind immediately jumps to the government. Does that make me paranoid or realistic?

"I'm not sure. Something about a new student."

I turn and walk back out of the room, hoping I kept my face neutral. Now that class has started, the halls are deserted. I cautiously enter the front office.

The principal is waiting for me in the lobby. A girl stands beside him.

"Hello, Emma. Thanks for coming." He gestures to the girl. "This is April Evans. She just moved here to Willow Creek. I

Chapter 43: Emma

thought since you're also relatively new, you could show her around the school, make her feel welcome, all of that."

I survey the girl. She has long black hair that curls at the ends and vibrant green eyes. She looks eerily familiar, but that's not possible. I've never been anywhere but here and the Academy. I brush off the gnawing sensation in the pit of my stomach and lead April from the office.

"Okay, um, well. This is the main hallway," I say awkwardly. Of all the people in this school, the principal had to choose me to show this girl around. Me, who barely knows how to communicate with humans.

I point out the different doors. "Through there is the library…the gym…the cafeteria. The hallways with the classrooms branch off from this one."

As I show her around, I attempt to ask questions to fill the silence in between the information.

"So what grade are you in?"

"I'm a freshman," she says. "Just turned fifteen."

"Nice. Why did you move here?"

Wow, I sound just like every curious human on *my* first day here. She probably doesn't want to be bombarded with a ton of questions.

Nonetheless, she answers. "For my dad's job. We used to live in the Pacific region until he got a really great offer a few weeks ago. Now here we are."

"You don't sound very happy about it."

She shrugs. "It's fine. It's just hard moving to a new place."

"Tell me about it."

She smiles. I show her all of her classes and the quickest routes to each. I continue asking questions and she answers and asks questions of her own.

Beyond the Gates

Surprisingly, I find that I'm genuinely curious and want to get to know her. Aria's the only other person here that I've felt like that with. Besides Jesse, of course. Talking to her feels completely natural.

"Do you have any siblings?" I ask. "I have an older brother."

Her face darkens. "Um, I have a younger brother. Somewhere."

"Somewhere?" I say before I can stop myself. Then, "Sorry. It's none of my business."

"No, it's okay. It's just…I kind of have a complicated family life. Our parents died a couple years ago. Total accident. But we didn't have any family to take us in. My brother and I got separated when we went into foster care. My foster parents adopted me a year ago, but I don't know what happened to him. I don't even know where he is or how to contact him." She pauses. "Sorry, I don't know why I'm telling you all this like you want to hear my sad life story. I get kind of talkative and rambly when I'm nervous."

I say something to her, but I'm not really paying attention anymore. My mind whirls as I put the pieces together.

Her parents died two years ago. She has a brother who is younger than her. She has black hair and emerald green eyes.

I understand now why she seems so familiar. It's because of her eyes. I've seen them before, in the eyes of a seven-year-old boy.

CHAPTER FORTY-FOUR
Jesse

I beat Emma to the cafeteria today. I sit at our usual table, feeling oddly energized. I'm going to make some kind of huge discovery about the Academy today. I know it. Finally, after years of searching and research, I'm going to get somewhere.

But then Emma slides into the seat across from me. My excitement melts away the second I see her face.

"What's wrong?"

With zero context, she asks, "What's Oliver's last name?"

I blink, thrown off by the random question. "What? Why?"

"Just answer me."

"Evans. His name is Oliver Evans. What's going on?"

She releases a breath and looks up at me with wide eyes. "I think I just met his sister."

"His *what*?" I blurt out. I can't possibly have heard her right.

"I got called down to the office and the principal introduced me to this girl who just moved here named April," she explains. "April Evans."

Beyond the Gates

She tells me everything: April's story about being separated from her brother, being placed in foster care, the color of her hair and the green of her eyes.

"Are you sure?" I wonder. "No one ever said he had any living family when they placed him with us, and Oliver obviously hasn't said anything. It could just be a coincidence."

But Emma shakes her head. "You have to see her, Jesse. You'll understand once you see her." Emma sits up straighter. "Look, there she is."

I turn in my seat. As if on cue, a girl with long dark hair walks into the cafeteria. She scans the room until her eyes fall upon Emma. Her green eyes. Oliver's eyes.

It knocks the breath from my lungs.

Emma waves her over.

"Hi," the girl says shyly when she reaches us. To me, she says, "I'm April."

I force a smile and try to calm down. "I'm Jesse."

I feel like I should say something more, but what are you supposed to say to the sister of the mute kid you've taken care of for the past two years?

"You should probably sit down," Emma says, taking over. "There's something you need to know."

April glances back and forth between us, her forehead creased with confused. "Um, okay."

Emma shifts in her seat, apparently unsure of what to say. I'm not sure either.

"What's going on?" April asks, concern in her tone.

With a deep breath, Emma says, "You mentioned your brother earlier. Is his name Oliver?"

April winces. "H-How do you know that?"

Chapter 44: Jesse

Emma glances at me and tilts her head, prompting me to step in.

There's no way to ease into the information, so I blurt it out like ripping off a band-aid. "He's my foster brother."

April's mouth falls open. "I…what? Are you serious?"

I nod. "He's been living with me for two years."

She opens her mouth like she's going to say something, but no words come out, just a jagged sob. Tears well in her eyes. She looks so hopeful and scared all at once.

Emma leans forward. "The thing with Aria. I can move it to tomorrow and tell her something came up."

I nod. As much as I want information on the Academy, Oliver is more important. I've waited years. I can wait one more day.

"Do you want to see him?" I say to April. "You can come over after school if you want and wait for him to get home."

"Really?" April's face lights up. She wipes the tears from her cheeks. "You don't even know me."

I give her a genuine smile this time. "Of course. He's your brother. I might not know you, but I know him. I'd never keep him from you, especially after being apart for so long."

Her lip quivers. "Thank you, Jesse. Thank you so much."

...

When the final bell rings, I immediately go to our usual meeting spot at the bottom of the steps. But Emma isn't there this time.

Hoards of students spill out of the building and push their way around me. People head off to the busses or the parking lot or stand around and chat with friends. None of them are Emma. She's not here and she always gets here first.

What if something happened? Surely, I'd know if the government stormed the place and took her. They would have come for me, too, right?

My heart hammers against my chest. I step towards the building, fully prepared to reenter and tear the place apart to find her, when she emerges with April.

The tension, the anxiety, the unexpected panic ebb upon seeing that she's safe.

"What took you so long? I never get here before you," I demand, possibly a little harsher than necessary. She raises an eyebrow at my tone. "Sorry, I was just worried."

Her face softens. "I'm fine, Jesse. I found April first before coming out, so she'd know where to go."

April glances between us, obviously confused by the exchange. Hopefully she'll never find out why we act like this. We don't need to bring another person into this.

"Okay, let's go."

We head off towards the house. When we get there, I let them in, and we all sit on the couch in the living room. April is restless. Her leg bounces up and down in anticipation.

"Hey, it'll be okay," I assure her. "I'm sure he'll be super happy to see you."

She nods. "Can you tell me about him? What's he like now? I'm sure a lot's changed since I last saw him."

Emma shoots me a knowing look. Apparently, she deems now to be the moment to let April in on her brother's situation.

"He's smart and kind and loving," I begin. "He loves going to the park and he's, uh, very good at…communicating without words."

April smiles, a far-away look in her eyes. "Yeah, before we got separated, I could always tell what was on his mind, even if he didn't say it out loud."

"So he did use to talk, then?"

Her eyebrows pull together. "What do you mean?"

Chapter 44: Jesse

I swallow. "He hasn't spoken at all in the entire time I've known him. Not a single word."

April stills as the information sinks in.

"I'm sorry," I say gently, but she shakes her head.

"No, it's okay. I mean it's not, but I should've known he wouldn't be the same after what happened. Of course he doesn't talk. I probably wouldn't either if I'd seen what he had at that age."

"Wait, what did he see?" Emma chimes in rather abruptly. When she catches April's pained expression, she backtracks. "Sorry, I tend to say things without thinking."

April takes a deep breath. "It was an accident. Oli was at his friend's house and my parents went to go pick him up. I stayed home because I was working on my homework. After they picked him up…I don't really know the details, but the car malfunctioned."

She pauses and squeezes her eyes shut for a moment before continuing. "Apparently our dad lost control of the car because it locked up or something and they crashed. Our parents died on impact, but somehow Oli survived. He witnessed the whole thing. He had to watch his parents die, while being so scared and confused as to what was happening. The days between the accident and when we got separated in the system, he kept asking when mommy and daddy were coming home. I had to keep explaining to him that they weren't."

Fresh tears stream down her face. My stomach churns sickeningly after hearing the story. Oliver was only five at the time. He lost his parents and then was separated from his only other family member shortly after. No wonder he doesn't speak.

The front door suddenly opens. April stiffens beside me. "It's just Charlotte," I tell her. Char comes into the room, stopping when she sees the newcomer.

Beyond the Gates

We explain everything to her. She's just as baffled as Emma and I were.

Not too long after that, the door opens again. We all stand from the couch as Oliver enters the room.

He stops dead. His eyes silently pass over each of us and finally rests on his sister. His eyes widen in shock. His backpack drops to the floor.

"Hi, Oli," April says softly, delicately, as if afraid she's dreaming.

And then the unbelievable happens.

"April?" he whispers. His voice is so small, so shaky. Like it physically hurts to speak. His lip trembles and he bolts towards her. She catches him in her arms and holds him tight.

The rest of us stand there, stunned. He just said his first word in two years. This girl—his *sister*—gave him his voice back.

"It's okay. It's okay. I'm here." April murmurs over and over into his hair, rubbing his back as tears slip down his pale face.

"I missed you," he says. His voice is a little clearer and less scratchy, but still so small and innocent sounding.

"I missed you, too. You have no idea how much." She wipes the tears from his face.

He buries his head against her. His voice becomes muffled. "How are you here? How did you find me?"

"My foster parents. They adopted me. We happened to move here for my dad's job. What a coincidence, right? Then Emma and Jesse figured out who I am when we met at school."

He pulls away. "You got adopted?"

She nods. "But I guess you didn't yet. You're okay, though, right?"

Oliver's eyes flick in my direction for a split second before returning to his sister. "Yeah, I'm okay."

Chapter 44: Jesse

He doesn't mention the Greg situation or all the other terrible foster homes he's been in. I'm not sure if that's a good idea or a bad one.

April and Oliver sit on the floor for a long time, holding each other, filling each other in on what they've been up to during their separation.

"I was in a couple other homes before my current one. They weren't too bad, it just wasn't forever, you know. Then I got placed where I am now. I was with them for about six months when they decided to adopt me. I've been with them ever since."

"This is the only one I've been in," Oli says. "It's okay, I guess. I like being with them." He gestures to us and I smile.

"I'm sorry I didn't try harder to find you, or even try harder to keep us together. I wish we hadn't been split up and I'm sorry I haven't been there for you these last two years."

He hugs her and they cry some more.

After their reunion, Oliver sits beside his sister and faces the rest of us. His eyes sweep over us again, moving to each person.

"Charlotte," he says and she beams, looking like she's on the verge of tears. His eyes shift. "Emma…lyn." A mischievous grin appears on his face.

Emma shoots me a look and I shrug in response. It's not my fault he picked up on my use of her full name.

Finally, his eyes land on me. "Jesse."

If not for the situation, Oliver speaking our names would've been such a small thing. But to me, to *us*, it's the most incredible thing in the world.

Oliver and April go back to talking to each other, swapping stories and information from the past two years. The more he speaks, the stronger his voice gets.

Eventually, April and Emma have to leave.

"You can come over whenever you want," I promise April on her way out. It's a dangerous thing, getting involved with her, but I'm not going to deny Oliver his one real family member. If she finds out about the other part of our lives, then we'll deal with it when the time comes.

Oliver and April have one last, long, parting hug. Once April and Emma are gone, Charlotte leaves to take a shower, leaving Oliver and I alone. He sits beside me on the couch.

"Thank you, Jesse," he says softly. "For taking care of me. I know I had a lot of problems. You could've made me get sent somewhere else, but you kept me."

"Hey," I say firmly and make him look at me. "Don't ever think that. You're not some *thing* to be kept or gotten rid of. You're my family. Yes, it was difficult sometimes, but we learned how to handle it. You never had to speak for me to understand you. It never affected anything. And you talking now doesn't change anything either. You are still my brother, Oli. You always will be. So don't think for a second that I wish I could have made you someone else's problem."

He throws his arms around me.

This. This is what's important in life. I often get caught up in my need for revenge and finding the Academy that I forget that. But at the end of the day, I'll give anything and everything to make Charlotte and Oliver happy.

CHAPTER FORTY-FIVE
Emma

We're able to put our plan into action the next day. Right after school, April goes to the library to wait for her brother. Jesse told Oli to meet her there so they can spend time together. He doesn't want them alone in the house without him in case Greg comes home. Jesse came home with me, and Aria promised she'd be over within half an hour.

Now, Jesse and Cameron are sitting at the small kitchen table with a tablet in front of them. Jesse checked it out from the library yesterday. If the government ever does some digging, it won't be hard to guess that Jesse's the one who used a tablet illegally, but at least this buys us some time since they're surely monitoring the activity on his personal tablet.

I stand behind the two of them and watch as they fiddle around, as if they're actually skilled enough to hack into a secure government database.

The room is silent except for Jesse's keystrokes and occasional sighs of frustration. He leans forward, brows furrowed, eyes narrowed. He chews his lower lip and his eyes dart back and forth across the screen.

After a while, he groans and falls back against the seat.

Cameron shifts toward the tablet and hits a few buttons.

Jesse swats his hand away. "No, stop. I know what I'm doing."

Cameron snorts. "Yeah, it sure looks like it."

"Hey," Jesse snaps. "You wouldn't even be here if it wasn't for me. I'm the one who took your tracker out so you wouldn't be under the government's control. Back off."

The tension in the air is palpable, enough so that I debate stepping in.

Until someone knocks on the door.

I open in to find Aria on the other side.

"Finally, someone with knowledge. The boys have been at it for twenty minutes and haven't gotten anywhere. They're completely clueless."

"Yeah, I bet." Aria laughs. I lead her into the kitchen. She drops her bag to the floor. "All right. Move aside losers and let me do my job."

They thankfully move to give her space. We quickly explain what we need her to do, without giving away any harmful details. She sits in front of the tablet, rolls her shoulders, and begins.

She sticks a flash drive into the tablet's port and downloads some kind of software. Her fingers dance across the keys on the screen. I try to keep up, but none of what she's doing makes any sense to me. I continue to watch her work, though, completely in awe at how easy she makes it seem.

Every now and then, she mutters to herself. "Come on, come on. Almost there."

The three of us crowd around her, waiting. And waiting. And waiting.

Then—

"Yes!" she exclaims and looks up at me. "I did it. I'm in."

Chapter 45: Emma

I exchange a quick glance with Jesse. This is it.

"Okay, let me just pull this up and…" She deflates. "No."

I move forward. "What? What's wrong?"

She shows the screen. "I got into…whatever this is, but it's encrypted. I can hack into stuff, but I'm not that good. I can't decrypt it without a code. I'm sorry."

So close. We were so unbelievably close.

The light dies in Jesse's eyes. We both know what this means. We have to move on to plan B.

"It's okay," I reassure her, even though it's not. This was our easy shot at information. Now we'll have to take the much more dangerous route. "Thanks for trying. It wasn't that important anyway."

I try to play it off, but she doesn't look convinced. "And you still can't tell me what all of this is about?"

"I'm sorry," I say. "It's really better if you don't know. I'm sorry I brought you into this at all."

"It's fine," she says and stands up. "It's getting late and I need to get home. Sorry I couldn't be more help."

"Don't worry about it," Cameron says with a forced smile.

I walk her out. As soon as she's gone, Jesse rounds on me. "What are we going to do now?"

"You know what we have to do now," I say. "We break into the Academy and get the information from there. Maybe we'll be able to find the encryption code and bring it back. That way we won't be in there as long."

"Shouldn't we have some sort of plan before we sneak into the place that will probably want to kill us if they catch us in the act of betraying them?" Cameron asks.

I shrug. "We can plan on the way there. It's going to take at least ten hours, probably longer since we can only travel at night."

Beyond the Gates

"What about the kids?" Jesse mentions. "I can't leave them alone but there's no way they're coming with us. Do you think April's family will let them stay with her for a couple days?"

"I don't know, maybe?" I reply. He *is* her brother, after all, but it's not like her parents know him. "You can ask at the very least. If it's a no, they can stay here. It won't be as safe, but at least you won't have to worry about Greg. There's plenty of food and stuff to last until we get back."

He nods. "Okay, so how about we pack tonight, plan tomorrow, and leave as soon as it gets dark."

"Works for me."

We look at Cameron. "You all are crazy," he says. "But if you're really going to do this, you're probably going to need someone with a more physical ability, so I guess I'm in."

"Great," Jesse says. He moves towards the door to leave. I hug him without thinking, forgetting that Cameron is in the room and that I'm supposed to be pretending this part of our relationship doesn't exist.

Oh well.

Once Cameron and I are alone, we plop down on the couch.

"How are you doing?" I ask. This has become a usual thing for us, checking in with each other every so often.

"I'm okay, I guess. It's almost been a week, so it *has* gotten easier," he explains. "And I think I'm starting to really understand basic emotions and how to control them, like you said I would. It can just be…frustrating sometimes."

I chuckle. "Yeah, it definitely can. But it's worth it in the end. Living with emotions. I mean, without them, are you really even living at all?"

Chapter 45: Emma

He cocks his head to the side, surveying me like he's trying to figure something out. He eventually comes to some sort of conclusion, it just isn't what I expected.

"You really like him, don't you?"

I don't need clarification. My heart stutters and I choke out, "*What?*"

"Don't deny it," Cameron says with surprising vigor. "I may be emotionally impaired, but I'm not blind. I see the way you look at him."

"I-I don't—"

"And I see the way he looks at you. Why do you think he hates me so much?"

"He doesn't look at me in any way and he doesn't hate you," I say hastily. "He just gets…irritated sometimes." I won't deny the animosity that's risen between them several times but hate seems pretty strong.

"Fine, then why do you think he gets irritated with me so easily?"

I shrug. "Because you're annoying."

Cameron ignores my attempt at playful banter and sighs, "He likes you, Emma. He'd do anything for you. I can see that now that I know the truth about what's really going on. You're not an Academy kid anymore. You're one of them now. Maybe you aren't human. Maybe you grew up differently. But it doesn't take a genius to see how well the two of you work together."

I lean my head against the back of the couch as my mind swirls with a billion conflicting thoughts, but I don't try to argue with him. Deep down I know it's the truth. All of it.

"What does any of that have to do with you?"

My face is on fire.

"He thinks *I* like you, and he feels threatened by that."

I shake my head. "That's insane. Why would he think that?"

Cameron rubs the back of his neck. "Well, uh…" He awkwardly clears his throat. "I sort of used to."

"Used to what?" I ask stupidly. He gives me a pointed look. "Used to *like me?*"

The second the words slip from my mouth, a memory surfaces to the front of my mind. The conversation I had with Lacy before I left for the Mission.

"Lacy was right," I realize. "She knew you liked me, but I didn't believe her. You…you don't anymore?"

"Honestly? I don't think I ever did."

I stare at him, bewildered. "Make up your mind, Cam. You're making my head spin."

"What I'm saying is that we never had emotions while we were at the Academy. Not real ones anyway But I liked you for as long as I can remember. And then when Jesse took the tracker out and I felt real emotions, I stopped feeling that way about you."

I catch on. "So, you think the government controls who we fall in love with by manipulating the fake emotions they allow us to have?"

"Why not? They've apparently been controlling every other aspect of our lives. It makes sense that they would…pair us up. Probably has something to do with our DNA. Maybe they paired us up because ours is more compatible or something and would create kids with the kind of DNA they need. The kind they look for when they take babies from the hospital."

I consider his theory. It makes sense. Once people graduate and move to the City, they have kids who always end up like them with abilities and whatnot. I haven't heard of any instance of a child who wasn't like us.

Chapter 45: Emma

"It's possible," I agree. "I definitely wouldn't put it past them. It's so weird, though."

"What is?"

"You and me," I reply. As an afterthought, I add, "No offense or anything."

He laughs. "No, it's fine. Now that I feel actual emotions, it's definitely weird. It's strange just knowing that I used to think of you like that."

"I'm glad you know the truth now," I say softly. "I really missed you."

"Yeah, me too. I noticed you were distant, almost like you were pulling away. I told myself you were just stressed over the Mission, but I think part of me worried our friendship was falling apart. I'm glad to know it wasn't either of those, but something else entirely."

I lean my head against his shoulder. "You'll always be my best friend, Cameron. Nothing and no one will ever change that."

"Good," he smiles and tilts his head on top of mine. "Because you'll always be my best friend, too."

We sit in silence for a while until I lift my head from his shoulder. "Hey, now that you don't have feelings for me, maybe Aria will have a chance."

He looks at me strangely. "Aria?"

"Yeah, don't you like her now? I thought that's why she was always here when I wasn't."

"Oh." He shrugs. "I don't know. She's cool and all, but I never really thought about her like that. I don't think I'm ready for anything yet, anyway. I'm still trying to sort through all my emotions."

"Fair enough."

I lean back against him.

Beyond the Gates

Life isn't perfect, but it's pretty good for now. After all this time, Jesse is finally going to make progress. I have my best friend back. Tomorrow, we'll be on the road to the Academy.

If all goes well, we'll have the information we need. Maybe enough to take them down.

CHAPTER FORTY-SIX
Jesse

Charlotte is very vocal about how much she disapproves of me ditching her and Oliver to *go on an adventure* as she puts it. Oliver just shrugs when I tell him. Even now, he's not a big talker. They are, however, happy about missing a day of school while we're gone.

The next morning, we stand outside Emma's apartment, each with a bag. Emma opens the door with a tired smile. She's still in her pajamas, hair thrown up into a messy bun, and dark circles rimming her eyes.

"You okay?" I ask once we're inside.

"I'm fine," she yawns. "Just didn't get much sleep last night. Cameron and I were up discussing potential options for our plan."

"Plan?" I echo and sit my bag down by the couch. "We have a plan?"

Cameron walks out of the kitchen. "We do now. Maybe. It's not the most solid thing. It could fall apart as soon as we get there. But it's something."

Charlotte and Oliver stay in the living room, happy to entertain themselves while the three of us sit at the kitchen table.

"Are you sure you're okay with them staying here?" Emma asks.

I shake my head. "I thought about it a lot last night and I think it's too dangerous. What if someone from the government comes by while we're away? I can't leave them here defenseless. So, they're going to stay at the warehouse. I found some air mattresses and blankets in one of the back storage rooms. They've got food and water packed to last them a few days. I'll feel so much better if they're out of the way."

Emma smiles. "I agree. I was going to say I wasn't sure how safe the apartment will be anymore after what we're about to do."

"And what exactly are we about to do? What is this plan you two came up with?"

Cameron claps his hands together and leans forward. "So basically, I'm going to use my telekinetic ability to get you two over the wall. Our abilities don't work on each other, so Emma will have to hold onto you. While you're on the inside, I'll circle back around to the front gates and cause a distraction to draw away the guards in the City. Once I get away from that, I'll meet you back in the same spot and get you back over the wall. Hopefully we'll be in and out within an hour."

It sounds simple enough, but I can already see the holes. "What kind of distraction? And how will you get away after?"

Emma bites her lip, trying to stop her mischievous smile from growing. "He's going to run up to the gate yelling about how I'm dead. We're going to kill my tracker first, of course, to make it more believable. I'm hoping it'll send up a real panic when they find out their perfect little robot was killed by her own target."

I blanch. "You're going to tell them *I* killed you?"

"Well, yeah. Who else would? Hopefully it'll cause the other guards to come running and give us a clear shot to the archives building. Cameron will drop us off in the City, as far away from the gate as possible. Our cover might be blown at any minute, so we'll

Chapter 46: Jesse

have to hurry. But if we go in at night, there's less of a chance we'll be seen or recognized."

We spend hours talking it over, working out the details. Even after everything, I still feel uneasy. I've waited years for this, but the way we discuss it, it all seems too easy. Can we really just break into the Academy without anyone noticing? Will Cameron really be able to get away? Won't they wonder how he found his way back to the Academy in the first place? What'll happen if we do make it out and the government really believes Emma to be dead? What then?

But Emma and Cameron glow with confidence. They insist it'll work. It has to. I want to believe them, but I've been disappointed too many times in my life to fully give in.

As night approaches, I take Charlotte and Oliver to the warehouse. We get everything all set up, and then it's time for me to leave.

"Listen," I say firmly. "We shouldn't be gone more than two days. You've got plenty of food, the air mattresses to sleep on, and the stuff you brought from home to keep you busy. I know it's going to be a rough couple of days, but no matter what, I need you to promise to not leave the building, okay? I don't want you out and about when I'm so far away and can't get back here quickly."

"What if someone from the Academy shows up?" Charlotte whispers, voice wavering just slightly.

"They won't," I assure her. "We're going to break Emma's tracker right before we leave. Cameron is taking his with him, so the government will have no reason to even go to the apartment, let alone here, if they know Cameron's not there. But if at any time you do feel like you're in danger, there are doors in the back you can leave through and get somewhere safe and preferably public. But I'm serious, guys. Only if it's an emergency. If someone's trying to get in here or something. Please don't make me regret leaving you alone."

Charlotte looks offended by that last statement. "Come on, Jesse. Really? What do you think we're gonna do? Throw a party and run wild? I'm more responsible than that and in case you haven't realized, we don't exactly have friends or anywhere else to go."

"I know, I know. Just stay safe, okay?"

Charlotte's face darkens. "We will, as long as you do, too. Come back in one piece, okay? Don't break your promise."

I pull them both into a fierce hug. "I promise. Everything will be fine."

We stay like that for a few minutes. Negative thoughts batter my brain, but I force them out. This won't be the last time I see my siblings. We'll break into the Academy, steal the information, and be back in time to enjoy the weekend before returning to school on Monday. Everything is going to work out.

I release them and move to leave when Oliver grabs my hand, his eyes wide. He could have easily used words, but in this moment, he chooses to tell me with the intensity of his stare.

"I love you, too." I whisper. "It's okay, Oli. I'll be okay. I *promise.*"

When I return to the apartment, Emma and Cameron are in the kitchen. Emma has pried her tracker from the arm band Charlotte made her. Now it sits in the center of the table. Cameron hands me a hammer.

I take it. "Where did you even get this?"

"I bought it last night," Cameron explains. "Now hurry up. We don't have time to waste."

I resist the urge to pick an argument over his tone. I position the hammer above the device that signals Emma's life. With a glance in her direction, I say, "Ready to die?"

Chapter 46: Jesse

She fights to suppress a smile. "Shut up and smash it already."

"Fine. Jeez. So demanding."

She laughs a little that time. Then I bring the hammer down and crush the tracker beneath it.

We rush out the door not a minute later. Cameron was right about that. We only have so much time. We burst into the pitch black and run to my car. My backpack bounces between my shoulders. I scramble into the driver seat, Emma in the seat beside me, and Cameron in the back.

I start it up and pull out of the parking lot.

"Wait, hold up." Cameron's voice is frantic. "You didn't tell me we'd be driving a *manual car*."

Emma turns around and glares. "Why did you think we wanted to get most of the driving done at night? Even though we probably would blend in during the day, it's safer in the dark. Plus, driver-less cars can be tracked, dummy, and we don't have one anyway. So unless you want to steal someone else's car, this is all we've got."

"Yeah, but…what if we crash?"

I practically hear Emma roll her eyes. "Relax. Jesse drives all the time. It'll be fine."

"But has he ever driven this far without knowing exactly where he's going?" Cameron shoots back.

"I've been driving for three years and we still have the tablet I got from the library to help get us there," I retaliate. "So shut up and let me do my job."

We bicker back and forth until Emma shoots me a look that clearly says *knock it off*. We fall silent. Message received.

I drive onto the expressway and we leave our small town behind.

. . .

"Come on, Jesse." Emma whines. "You've been driving for almost four hours. It's not healthy. You need to take a break and rest."

"I'm fine, really." I grumble. But I *am* exhausted, straining to keep my eyes open, struggling to stay alert.

"There's no one out here. I can do it."

I glance over at her and see the shine of determination on her face. With a sigh, I pull the car into the emergency lane so we can switch seats. Cameron is asleep in the back, oblivious to the change.

Emma gets comfortable and drives back onto the road, as smooth as my own driving had been. I hold the tablet in my lap, watching as we inch closer to the coordinates we entered. We're making good time, but there's still a long way to go.

We continue on in silence, though it's not uncomfortable. Emma is focused on the road and I'm too tired to form words. I doze in and out of sleep until Cameron shoots up behind me.

"Oh my god! Since when do you know how to drive?"

I turn around to see his frantic expression.

"You're driving. You're actually driving. Are you crazy? Or I guess next you're going to tell me you have three years of experience, too."

"No, I only learned a couple months ago. But Jesse and I practiced almost every day and I've driven on a road like this before, so it's fine."

"That's supposed to make me feel better?" he splutters.

"Will you just calm down," I snap. "We've got everything under control."

The tension between us rises once again.

"What's your problem?" Cameron retorts.

"You," I hiss. "You're always complaining or questioning me or causing problems. We know what we're doing, so stop messing it up."

Chapter 46: Jesse

Cameron is about to retaliate when the car suddenly lurches as Emma pulls over. She turns and gives us both stern looks. "That's enough. We still have several hours to go until we get there and I'm tired of listening to you two act like this. So here's what we're gonna do. Since Cameron seems deathly afraid of cars and the two of you can't seem to get along with each other, why don't you teach him how to drive."

We both stare at her and then—

"You've officially lost your mind."

"We're on our way to break into the Academy. I'm not wasting time teaching him how to drive."

She narrows her eyes further and our protests ebb away.

"Look, you said it yourself when you started teaching me. There might come a day when we need a third driver. You never know. We're out on the road in the middle of nowhere with no one around. It's the perfect opportunity."

I hate how she's kind of right. I glance back at Cameron. He just shrugs his shoulders.

"Maybe it wouldn't hurt to try it out," he says. "But if I crash, it's not my fault."

"Deal," Emma says and hops out to switch places with him. This road trip is becoming a nightmare.

But if I'm being honest, despite Cameron's earlier fears, he's not as timid as Emma was her first lesson. I show him the gear shift and how to drive and brake. He seems eager to prove something, so we move along faster than I expected.

"Ease up a bit," Emma says from the back. "It's a little jerky."

I turn to look at her. "Hush up back there. You were scared to even let go of the brake."

Cameron snorts and Emma childishly sticks her tongue out at me. I grin in response. Maybe this wasn't such a bad idea. At least

Beyond the Gates

Cameron and I aren't at each other's throats at the moment. Eventually, I decide Cameron's had enough. I get back into the driver seat to get us through the rest of the night.

When the sky turns gray and the sun peeks over the horizon, I decide to stop. I pull off the expressway and onto the first back road I find.

"We can sleep for a while," I suggest. "Even though it's probably fine to drive during the day, I'd feel better if we kept going at night. We're only a couple hours away, so once we get there, we'll have the whole night to put our plan into action."

We eat some of the food we packed and then settle in.

Cameron, who's in the middle row, quickly falls asleep. I relocate to the back row with Emma, since there's much more room back there than up front. I get comfortable, my eyes drooping. The last thing I feel before falling asleep is the weight of Emma's head against my shoulder.

CHAPTER FORTY-SEVEN
Emma

I wake to the rocking of the car. I wipe the sleep from my eyes and sit up. Cameron is driving and Jesse is in the passenger seat guiding him.

Jesse turns to see me. "Morning, sleepyhead. It's about time you woke up."

"You know, it's technically night," Cameron chimes in. Jesse gives him a look.

"What time is it?" I ask through a yawn. The last time I was awake before falling asleep again was around 8:00pm. I dozed in and out all day. Even after not getting any sleep for almost twenty-four hours, I slept fitfully.

"Almost midnight. We'll be arriving at the Academy soon. We're running a little behind schedule since I've been teaching Cameron to drive, but we're still making good time."

I nod and the car fills with silence again. It's amazing how quickly the two most important people in my life are getting along. My whole plan with the driving really paid off.

A while later, Jesse says, "Turn left up here."

Cameron does so, turning a little too sharply, and we drive onto what feels like a gravel path. The forest envelops us. It's pitch black outside and the farther in we go, the denser the trees get. We have to be getting close.

The path winds around for a few minutes until I recognize where we are.

"Stop!" I say. "This is near where we got into the car that took us to Willow Creek. We'll be out of the forest soon."

"This is it," Jesse breathes. "We're really here."

Cameron turns the key and the car shudders into silence. The air tightens, growing colder. We've been in the car forever with hardly any stops, but now none of us are clambering to get out.

Both boys turn to look at me. I look from Cameron's deep blue eyes to Jesse's warm brown ones. There's determination there, but also fear.

We have our plan, and we made it here. It's the middle of the night and the Academy has no idea of our presence. But despite all of that, there's a chance the three of us will go in and not all will come back out.

"Ready?" Cameron says. All the pieces of the plan fly through my mind. Just one thing has to go wrong for everything to blow up in our faces. And those pieces aren't exactly stable.

What were we thinking?

But we're already here. It's now or never. Besides, with destroying my tracker, the government probably already knows something is up.

I open the door. "Let's go."

It's even colder outside the car. Goosebumps work their way up my arms. I pull my jacket tighter around me.

Chapter 47: Emma

I lead the way off the path and through the trees until we're far enough away from the main gate. The last thing we need is to get caught before we even get started.

When we walk out of the forest, the large steel reinforced concrete wall emerges. Jesse's jaw falls open and his eyes widen in a mix of awe and disbelief.

"This is really it," he whispers and glances at me. Just from that one quick look, I know what he's thinking. Ten long years he's waited to be standing exactly where he is right now. We made it.

No one moves for a second, so I take the lead and approach the wall. Jesse follows behind. I watch him as he steps closer. He hesitantly brushes his fingers against the wall, like he's afraid it isn't real.

Cameron steps up. "Okay, you guys ready?"

"Should you maybe practice on an object first? Just to make sure you can get it over the wall and everything?" I suggest. "Better to mess up on something else before trying it with us. I don't want you to like, drop us or something."

"Wait, what? No one said anything about getting dropped."

"He's going to be lifting us like twenty feet in the air with his mind, Jesse. You didn't think that could potentially be dangerous?"

"Okay, I get it. No need to get sassy."

I grin. Now's not exactly the time to be teasing each other like this, but at least it alleviates the nervous tension.

Cameron finds a heavy rock and lifts it up and over the wall. It's still not the same as us, but it's something.

"All right, I guess we're ready to do this. You can like…get together or whatever," Cameron says.

Jesse and I peer at each other. I take a step towards him, then another. This is going to be uncomfortable, but it's the only way Cameron can get both of us in. I walk up to him until we're face to face. I wrap my arms around his shoulders. He snakes his arms around my waist and pulls me close to him so there's no space left between us.

"This is awkward," I whisper against his ear. His uneasy laugh rumbles through me.

"Okay, brace yourselves. I've still never done anything like this before, but I'll try to make the landing as gentle as possible."

Cameron closes his eyes. His brows furrow and forehead creases in concentration.

"What if it doesn't work?" Jesse murmurs. "We've never discussed a back-up if he can't get us over the wall. Or if it only works on me."

"It'll work," I whisper. "It has to."

"Will you two zip it?" Cameron mutters. "No one's getting over the wall if I can't focus."

We go quiet. Cameron strains himself so much it looks like he's in pain. Just when I'm about to call it off and suggest we find an alternative, a jolt runs through my body and my feet lift off the ground. Jesse gasps and tightens his grip on me.

Cameron opens his eyes. He's visibly shaking with the effort of keeping us airborne. Jesse's hands fidget on my back.

"Wrap your legs around me," he says, his voice strained.

"What?!"

"I feel like I don't have a good enough grip on you. I don't want you to slip. Please. We don't have to like, make it weird or anything."

It's already weird. The fact that we're already clinging to each other is pretty weird. I do it, though, because he has a point. And once I wrap my legs around his waist, I feel a lot more stable. We rise to the top of the wall. It's mostly steady, but there are a couple times when we waver, and my stomach drops out from under me.

Chapter 47: Emma

"You're doing great, Cam," I force out. "Halfway there. Remember, as soon as you get us over, don't waste any time worrying about us. Get out of here and cause the distraction."

"I know. Good luck. Be back here in an hour."

With that, he guides us over the wall and disappears from sight. We waver again on the way down and hit the ground hard, but we're safe. He didn't drop us. Nothing is sprained or broken. Jesse lowers me to the ground.

We did it.

Getting back out will likely be more difficult, but Cameron thinks that since he's tuned into Jesse now, that he'll be able to feel us and guide us back over the wall even without being able to see us at first. At least that's what we're hoping for.

"Keep your head down and stay quiet," I whisper. "We're going to walk through the City to the archive building. Hopefully the distraction will call the guards away and what we need is actually in there."

"Yeah," he agrees. "It'd be bad if we went through all this trouble and what we need isn't even here."

"Now who's being sassy?" I joke.

He smiles for a second and then reality descends on us. It's time to put the more dangerous part of this plan into action. I move to start walking, but he grabs my hand and pulls me around to face him. His eyes search mine.

"Emma…if we don't…" he pauses and swallows. "If we don't both make it out, I just—"

I squeeze his hand. "I know. I know." I'm not exactly sure what I know, but it's more a feeling than something concrete. We're on the same page, whatever that is.

We creep into the City. Buildings line the streets, all dark and empty. It's been months since the last time I've been here. Even before I got a Mission, I hadn't left campus since the week we had off school back in May. I had spent most of my free time doing additional training. It's strange being back.

The shops eventually give way to the residential side of the City. Apartments and houses fill the space.

"You know, I always thought I'd eventually live here," I say under my breath. "An apartment and then maybe a house later on. I'd get married and have kids. And I'd help them through the Academy. Maybe they would've wanted to do the Missions program like me, or maybe they would've been perfectly content with a normal job in the City. But I would have been there for them no matter what. I'd have a family that I loved while helping the government and changing the world. I was so stupid back then."

"Hey," Jesse whispers. "You weren't stupid. You just didn't know any better. And even though things are different now after everything that's happened, it doesn't mean you can't still have a family, that you can't still change the world."

I want to hug him. "Why are you so amazing?"

He just chuckles softly.

I sigh and resist the urge to look up at him. There are cameras everywhere and I don't exactly need my face caught on tape. Hopefully if anyone is watching, they'll assume we're two adults who live in the City and are out for a midnight stroll. Does anyone even do that, though?

When we make it to the archives building, I'm pleased to see it vacant of any guards. I'm not entirely sure there's ever guards for the building, but if there are, Cameron's distraction successfully drew them away.

I push the door open and duck inside, Jesse close behind. I flip on the light and almost gasp at what we're met with. I haven't given much thought to what I expected, but it certainly isn't this.

Chapter 47: Emma

A single computer sits on a table in the back, but it's not like any device I've seen in person. Only in history books. A desktop, it's called. Similar to the thin glass ones we have now, but way outdated. This computer is a boxy block on the table. The rest of the walls are occupied by large floor to ceiling filing cabinets.

"How long do we have?" Jesse asks, his eyes wide at the endless amounts of information in front of us.

"We need to be back at the wall in about forty-five minutes."

"Let's get to it, then. You start working on the computer. I'll try to find something useful in the files," Jesse says.

He immediately starts pulling drawers open and thumbing through folders. I sit down in front of the computer and switch it on. That's as far as I get. The screen illuminates to life and prompts for a ten-digit passcode.

I groan and lean back in the chair. "It's locked. And we don't have Aria to hack into it for us this time."

"The passcode might be somewhere in here. Help me look for it. Anything with ten digits is a possibility."

I get up and start searching alongside him. Every time one of us stumbles across a potential match, we hurry to the computer and try it out. We're rejected again and again. Honestly, it's a miracle we haven't been locked out yet.

"Hold up, I found something," Jesse says after many more anxiety-filled minutes of combing through file after file. He shoves a folder in front of my eyes. I open it and see random strings of symbols stretching across the page.

"I don't understand." I look up at him. "What is this?"

"Look at the next page."

I do so and find that it consists of the standard alphabet and numeric system.

"I think it might be the encryption key," he says softly. "I mean, they've got one sketchy database. What else could they possibly need a key for?"

I don't want to think about the possibilities.

"Well if we ever get into this stupid computer, we can try it out and see if it works. But we need to hurry. We're almost out of time. Cameron's gonna freak out if we're not at the wall when he gets there."

We continue searching, but still no luck. I put yet another string of digits into the login bar and this time something does happen. Just not what we want.

A message pops up, asking for ID. It prompts me to slide a card through the device lying next to the computer and to scan my thumb print.

"We have a problem," I say over my shoulder. "I think we locked the computer up. I don't know how to get back to the other screen."

Jesse comes over to see for himself. He lets out a frustrated sigh and runs a hand through his hair. "Why can't anything ever be easy?"

"Maybe it'll pop back up eventually if we leave it alone? I don't know, let's just keep looking with the little bit of time we have left. Worse case we get out of here with the encryption key and pray it's the one we need."

We spend the next couple of minutes gathering everything we want to take with us and cleaning up the rest. It'll be like no one was ever here. No one will know.

And then the alarms go off.

CHAPTER FORTY-EIGHT
Cameron

After Cameron uses his telekinetic ability to lift Emma and Jesse over the Academy wall, he runs. He's not even sure if they're okay, if his ability got them over safely, but he doesn't have time to wait around and worry. They're counting on him to cause a distraction, so that's what he's going to do.

He races along the wall, knowing it will eventually take him to the main gate. The cold wind whips against his face with the promise of rain.

He desperately hopes this plan will work, but there are so many things that could go wrong. What if there are too many guards? What if they don't believe him?

But when the wall gives way to the Academy's entrance, Cameron stops. There's only one guard, an anomaly. Throughout all his time at the Academy, there's always been at least four. Have Emma and Jesse already been discovered? Is that why there's minimal security? Because they know the threat is already inside?

He continues with the plan anyway.

He runs up to the gate, curls his fingers around the bars, and musters up the act of a distressed Academy kid whose best friend and partner has just been murdered.

"Help! Let me in," he screams. "She's dead. Emma's dead."

Even though it's not true, just saying those words hurts. He can't imagine ever losing her for real.

The guard turns around and Cameron steps back, stunned.

"*Aiden?*"

He knew Aiden was training to be a guard, but Cameron wouldn't have guessed that in just three short months, he'd be guarding the gates by himself. But if Aiden is here alone, maybe he'll help in causing the distraction. Maybe the other guards will be more apt to believe the lies of one of their own than of someone who suddenly turned up.

"What are you doing here?" Aiden hisses through the bars. "What do you mean Emma is dead? How did you get here? What the heck is going on?"

"I'll tell you everything, just let me in."

Aiden stares at him a moment longer and then goes over to the control panel to enter a code. The gate shudders, then slides open with ease.

Once Cameron is through, Aiden says, "Are you serious? Is she really dead?"

His eyes are wide, fearing the answer.

Cameron steps toward him. "If I tell you this, you have to promise not to freak out or call for the other guards or anything. I mean it."

"Okay, okay. What is it?"

"She's not really dead," Cameron says. "It's a really long story that I don't have time to explain. Can you call Lacy down here? Once I tell you, you're probably going to want her to know, too."

Chapter 48: Cameron

"You know there's a curfew, right?"

"Aiden, this is serious. There's a lot of stuff you don't know about. Trust me, I wouldn't risk getting her in trouble if it wasn't important."

Aiden sighs and pulls out his phone. Hopefully Lacy will get his text. Hopefully she'll come. Cameron doesn't know how long they have before the other guards return from wherever they are.

But he believes that if Emma knew of the situation, she'd want him to try to save Lacy and Aiden.

Lacy appears, stomping across the lawn in her pajamas. "What do you want? I had to sneak past the supervisor in the lobby and...Cameron?"

"Hey, Lace."

Lacy looks at him. "Where's Emma?"

"Not here, apparently. But also not dead."

"Shut up, Aiden," Cameron says, irritated. "Look, the government is not what we think. Everything they've led us to believe is a lie. I know you're probably not going to believe me, but it's true. We've learned a lot these last few months on the outside. The government is corrupt and they're using us. The humans are not that bad and not that different."

"What are you talking about? The government raised us," Aiden exclaims. "How are they possibly using us if they took care of us and trained us?"

"They implanted us with trackers," Cameron blurts out. "They're controlling our emotions for their own benefits and agenda. I know it sounds completely insane, but after Emma found out, she took my tracker out and I felt real emotions for the first time. Just let me prove it to you."

"Prove it how?" Lacy asks, stepping forward. Between the two of them, Lacy was always the more gullible one.

"The trackers are right below the skin," Cameron explains. "All I have to do is take my knife, make a tiny incision, and get it out. It'll hurt, but I'll try to make it as easy as possible. I watched when Jesse did it for me. I should be able to replicate the process."

"Who's Jesse?" Aiden demands.

Cameron pales. How could he be so careless?

"No one. Just a human on the outside who knows a little about the government's true nature."

He's sure they won't be so calm about the situation if they knew the person who set all of this in motion also just happened to be Emma's target.

"I'm in," Lacy says. "Maybe you're right. Maybe you're wrong. But it can't hurt to find out, right?"

"I don't know, Lacy," Aiden says. "This might be a bad idea."

Lacy shrugs. "You don't have to do it if you don't want to, but I do. And I trust Cameron and Emma."

That was easier than Cameron expected. He thought there'd be more push back against his plan considering the government basically controlled their minds. But thinking back, he didn't exactly fight against Emma when she suggested it for him. It's harder to say no to someone you know and trust.

Cameron pulls out his pocketknife. Lacy steps closer. Her eyes glow under the blue tinted lights that line the gate. He pushes up the sleeve of her tee shirt and places the edge of the knife against her skin. He presses down and she lets out a yelp.

"Hold still," he says through clenched teeth. He must have gone too deep, because blood leaks from the wound.

He feels the knife graze something solid and digs it out. The blood-soaked bead falls out into his palm.

Lacy's eyes widen at the device in his hand. "You weren't kidding."

Chapter 48: Cameron

"No," Cameron says. "It's going to take two to three days for the chemicals to leave your system, but then you'll know for sure that I'm telling the truth. When that happens, though, you have to act like everything is fine. You can't let the government find out what happened."

He rolls the tracker against the rim of his shirt to dry the blood away, then hands it back to her. "Keep this on you at all times so they don't get suspicious."

Lacy nods.

"Take mine out, too," Aiden says. Cameron was right. If he could prove it to Lacy, Aiden would soon follow.

He gets Aiden's out a little easier, but there's still a lot of blood. Aiden, being a guard, digs out bandages from his medical pack for both of them.

"Okay, Lacy. You need to go back inside now."

"What? Why?" she exclaims. "What about you? What about Emma?"

"Look," Cameron says firmly. "I'm here for a reason and I need to get on with our plan. You can't be here for the rest of it. You're not supposed to be out of the dorm."

She doesn't look too happy about it, but eventually Cameron convinces her to go back.

"Now what?" Aiden asks.

"Now I need you to radio the other guards and play along with the whole Emma being dead thing."

"Where is she really?"

"I can't tell you that. Just trust me."

Aiden pulls out his tablet and taps away at it. The guards come a few minutes later and Cameron puts his distressed act back on. The guards seem taken aback by his behavior, but try to calm him down, nonetheless.

Beyond the Gates

"What happened?" one of them asks.

"Emma's target...he killed her," Cameron chokes out. "I didn't know what to do. He almost killed me."

Maybe that'll take care of the blood that's starting to dry on his hands and the flecks on his arms.

"How did you get here?" another guard asks.

Cameron's heart stutters. Why didn't they consider the fact that Academy kids don't know the location of the Academy?

"I uh...I drove around a lot. I knew it's surrounded by a ton of forest. And the ride to our Mission station was about ten hours. So that helped me narrow it down."

They don't seem too convinced.

"And when I couldn't find it on my own, I called the Ambassador and she gave me coordinates. She said it was okay because it was an emergency. Maybe you could um...call her down here. She needs to know what happened."

"Where did you get the car?"

"What?" Cameron asks as he squeezes more tears out of his eyes.

"You said you drove around a lot. We didn't leave a car with you, so where'd you get it?"

Cameron tries to think of an answer, but he's shaking so bad and he's wondering how long it's been and what Emma and Jesse are doing.

Before he can say anything, a third guard suddenly steps forward at the chime of her tablet.

"We have a problem," she says. "There's been a breach in the archives building."

Aiden's eyes meet Cameron's. His lips part as comprehension dawns on his face. Now he knows where Emma is.

"Sound the alarm and lock this place down. I'll send an alert out to everyone and get people stationed at all exits."

Chapter 48: Cameron

A shrill sound splits the air, reverberating throughout the entire Academy. The next moments are a blur. More guards swarm the area. Confused, half asleep students pour out of the dorms, rubbing their eyes and complaining about the noise.

Cameron can only hope Emma and Jesse make it out before they get caught. He needs to find a way out, too. This was such a stupid, reckless idea.

The guards speak in a cluster, voices inaudible amid the blaring alarm and chatter of students. And then in one collective movement, they turn to face him.

They know.

They close in around him. One asks, "Where is she?" and another grumbles, "Traitor."

Everything from the past couple days is falling apart. In just a few minutes, they figured out everything. Emma is still alive. Cameron is just a distraction. A traitor. They'll soon piece it together and figure out why Emma broke into the archives building, that they're working with Jesse instead of against him, that they can't be controlled anymore.

Cameron knows the guards surrounding him are either going to kill him on the spot or take him to the Ambassador, who would then decide what to do with him herself. Either way is not an option.

But maybe using his ability is.

He can use the growing wind around them like a physical object. His telekinetic energy swells up in him. He'll release it on the guards, just enough so he can get away.

But of course it doesn't work out that way. His ability comes out too strong, blasting everyone within a ten-foot radius into the air and tumbling back to the ground away from him. One of the guards falls close to him, hitting the ground hard with a wet crunch.

Beyond the Gates

The world sways around Cameron as he backs away. The limbs of the body before him are bent at awkward angles. The grass is stained red in a pool beneath the guard's head.

No one else seems permanently injured, but they're all definitely disoriented. Cameron breathes deep but can't manage to pull air into his lungs.

He can't stay here any longer though, so he runs.

He doesn't think about what just happened, what he did. He has to get out of here and find Emma and Jesse. With blood-soaked hands, red spots dotting his shirt, and the scream of the sirens, Cameron races through the gates as the first drops of rain fall.

CHAPTER FORTY-NINE
Jesse

It explodes through the room, through the Academy. The sound of the alarm is everywhere, resonating through my very bones.

Emma's head snaps up and our mirrored wide eyes meet. Without any verbal communication, we both leap into action. I scramble to pick up all the files and shove them back into their respective cabinets. Emma tries to shut the computer down, but it's still locked up.

The sirens blare even louder and I cover my ears. "What *is* that? Is it because of us or Cameron?"

Emma clicks random buttons on the computer. "I don't know. I don't know. Maybe us because we didn't identify ourselves fast enough after getting the passcode wrong so many times and it triggered something. Maybe Cameron because they realized he was lying. Maybe both. I don't know but we have to get out of here *now*."

The computer's screen finally goes black.

My heart thumps in my throat. My hands shake as I gather everything we want to take with us.

I knew it. I knew it from the start that something would go wrong, and our plan would fail. We made it out to be such a simple thing. Break in, steal the information we need, break out.

Nothing in our lives is ever easy. Why would it start now?

"Let's go!" Emma hisses, her hand on the door handle. "Leave the rest. You don't have time to put it back. They know something is up anyway."

I abandon the remaining mess on the floor and scramble over to her as she pulls the door open. Two guards are waiting for us on the other side. I freeze immediately, completely useless despite all the training I've gone through.

Emma, however, doesn't even hesitate. She leaps into action, kicking and twisting her opponents' limbs until she has them both on the ground.

I don't move, unsure if what I just witnessed actually happened.

"Don't just stand there," she snaps. "Cameron's waiting."

As if I'm not supposed to be shocked that she just threw two fully grown men to the ground like it was nothing.

I take off after her and we race through the City. The alarms pierce my ears and rock me to my core, but I don't have time to focus on that now. This time, the streets are populated. Doors open and people step out, wondering what's going on to cause such a disturbance in the middle of the night.

As we barrel past, I catch fragments of confused conversations. Most of it sounds like complaints and questions. But there's one word that stands out and turns my blood cold.

Emma. Emma. Emma.

Her name whispers through the streets. They saw her. They know she's still alive despite our lie. Which means the government probably isn't going to leave us alone even if we do somehow manage to escape.

Chapter 49: Jesse

It's a struggle keeping up with Emma, what with her added endurance from not being fully human. But we make it to the wall in time, just as raindrops begin drizzling from the sky.

"Cameron!" Emma whisper-shouts, panic in her voice. "Cameron, we're here."

Nothing.

"Cameron," she says again, louder this time. "Cameron!"

She screams it that time, and it's definitely audible above the sirens. She looks at me, rain trailing down her cheeks, and I know. He's not there.

"What do we do?" I ask. We can't just stand here forever, waiting for someone who might never come. There are surely guards looking for us, people in the City pointing the way we went.

We have to get out of here.

"Follow me," she says and bolts across the grassy field. She stays along the edge of the wall. "We'll reach the gate eventually. Maybe there will be enough commotion that we can slip by."

That sounds like a wonderful idea. One in which we both end up captured and killed by the government.

I don't voice this opinion, though. Emma knows this place a thousand times better than I do. She knows what she's doing. I hope.

The rain picks up as we run. It drips into my eyes, glues my hair to my forehead. The ground turns from innocent grass to a muddy death trap. I stumble several times in my attempts to keep up with Emma.

Finally, we reach the gate Emma was talking about. *The* gate. The entrance to the Academy that had been such a big deal to both of us. It was her ticket out and I always thought it'd be my way in. It's standing wide open.

Beyond the Gates

I have to hand it to her. She was right when she said there would be a commotion. The courtyard in front of the gate is filled with guards, teenagers, and younger kids. They have to be students who left the dorms because of the noise.

Cameron is nowhere to be seen.

Emma slows down and tries to move stealthily toward the gate, so we don't attract attention to ourselves. But of course that doesn't work. We make it to the mouth of the gate when people start shouting and running toward us.

Emma grabs my hand, pulls me to face her, and looks me dead in the eyes. "Whatever you do, whatever happens, *do not let go of my hand*. Got it? I need you in this with me. We can't get separated, okay? Are you ready?"

I nod, unable to form words.

And we're off.

Emma drags me along through the gate, and then through the trees and scratchy undergrowth of the forest. The branches claw at my skin. It would probably sting if not for the insane amount of adrenaline pumping through me.

The trees do nothing to shield us from what is now a downpour. Thunder claps and lightning forks across the sky. I can barely see, but Emma seems to know where she's going. Or maybe she's just getting us away from the mob, which could mean we're getting even more lost.

After a while, when my legs scream in agony and my lungs ache, I gasp, "Stop. I need to stop for a second."

She slows but keeps walking. "We can't stop. They might still be onto us. We have to keep going. We have to find Cameron."

Her voice breaks on his name and she finally stands still.

"He wasn't at the wall," she whispers. Her voice trembles. Her whole body shakes, actually. "He was supposed to be there and he

Chapter 49: Jesse

wasn't. What if they took him? What if something happened to him? What if he's de—"

She can't spit the rest of the word out.

"Nothing bad happened," I say in a fruitless attempt to soothe her. The alarms are evidence enough that things went wrong. "Let's just backtrack and try to find the car. Maybe he's waiting there for us. Maybe he couldn't get to the meet up spot because of all the guards."

"But what *if*," she cries, tears mingling with the rainwater on her face. "He's my best friend. I can't lose him."

"I know."

"I *need* him."

"Emma, I *know*." I grab her by the upper arms and face her. "Look at me. Look at me." She finally does, her eyes a darker green than usual. Stormy. "It is going to be okay. You will be okay. I need you to believe that Cameron is okay. We can get through this, but you have to focus. You have to breathe. I need you like you need Cameron, okay? I can't lose you either. So please help me through this. We'll find him."

I almost add an *I promise* to the end of it but hold back. There's a good chance I'd end up breaking that promise.

We start back up again, though slower than before. Just when real fear starts to kick in that we'll never find Cameron or our way back to the car, we burst into the clearing.

The car is right where we left it, untouched. Cameron is there, too, but definitely not in the same condition we last saw him.

He's on the ground by the front tires, hunched over, body shaking. He scrubs furiously at his hands. His head snaps up upon our arrival and his face breaks out in a mix of relief and fear. The latter isn't an emotion I expected.

Emma runs to him. "What happened? Are you okay? I was so scared."

He holds his hands up to stop her from getting any closer. It's then that I see his blood-coated hands. The red flecks on his shirt.

Emma stares in wide-eyed horror. But before she can utter another question, Cameron says, "Don't worry. It's not mine."

"Then whose is it?" Emma demands.

"On my hands, I'll explain that part later. On my clothes…Emma…I think I killed someone."

"*What?*"

He goes back to rubbing and scratching at his hands. "It won't come off. It's even raining and I can't make it go away."

Emma takes a hesitant step forward. "It's okay, Cameron. Just tell us what happened."

He's crying now, and he curls his fingers into the wet grass. "You were right. My distraction did cause commotion, but it didn't last long enough. One of the guards got an alert that their security system was breached and they sounded the alarms. I think they realized then, what happened. They came after me and I just…I just panicked. I didn't mean to hurt anyone. I just wanted to get away." He explains how he used his ability to blast the guards away from him. "But the ones standing closest got the worst of it. There was one…I heard something crack when he landed and there was so much blood. But I just ran."

Emma moves closer and slowly places her hand on his back. She whispers soothing words, so soft I can't hear from where I'm standing.

He nods and she brushes his tears away. She helps him up, steadies him, and guides him to the car. I jump into action, pulling the keys from my pocket and climbing into the driver seat. It's time to get out of here.

Chapter 49: Jesse

I drive as quickly as I can through the forest. Once we're out, I know we're in the clear. At least for now.

I grip the steering wheel tight with my sweaty hands. Emma's in the back next to Cameron, stroking his hair and whispering to him. He seems a little better. I can't imagine what he must have gone through, wondering if he really did accidentally kill someone, especially with how easily his emotions can be thrown off balance.

My heart slows and I loosen my grip on the wheel the farther away we get. The act of driving soothes me into a more focused mindset.

I drive for hours until Cameron falls asleep and Emma demands she drives for a while so I can rest.

"Did he say anything more?" I ask.

She shakes her head. "I tried, but I didn't want to push him. I feel bad that he took most of the hits. Aside from running through the forest, we didn't have to deal with much. He had swarms of guards and Academy kids on him."

"He'll be okay," I say in an attempt to be reassuring. "Just give him time. Maybe he'll feel better after a good sleep."

"Yeah, maybe."

We don't speak after that, but it's not a comfortable silence like it was on the way here. I can't help but wonder if everything we've gone through in the last twenty-four hours has somehow shifted the dynamic between all of us.

We stop when the sun emerges. Cameron is awake again by that point. He's also finally ready to talk about the rest of what happened.

He tells us about a kid named Aiden being the only guard at the gate and how he got Aiden to call down a girl named Lacy. He then cut out both of their trackers before having Aiden alert the other guards of his arrival.

"That's where the majority of the blood came from," Cameron explains. "I didn't know what I was doing, but I got their trackers out."

"And they just *let* you cut their arms open?" Emma exclaims.

Cameron shrugs. "I mean, it took some convincing. I gave them a quick talk about the government using us and all that. But you know how gullible Lacy can be. Once I proved there really was something in them, Aiden wanted his out, too."

Emma isn't giving in though. "What about in a few days when they have emotional meltdowns while surrounded by people who don't have emotions?"

"I don't know!" Cameron throws his hands up in exasperation. "I didn't give it much thought in the moment. I explained to them what will happen, and they seemed to understand. I just…when I saw Aiden by himself, I knew it was our chance. They're our friends and it's not fair they're being controlled like that without even knowing it. I couldn't just stand by and do nothing about it."

Emma stares at him for a moment, then sighs. "I know. I know. I would've tried to save them, too. What's done is done. Hopefully they'll be able to get through it on their own. And the important thing is we got the key and hopefully it works when we put it in. Maybe we'll even find something that can help everyone else."

"What if it doesn't?" Cameron says, voicing the question in my own head. What if we went through all of this, only to get home and realize it won't work?

"It will," Emma declares. "It has to."

We rest for a little while after that, but not for long. The government is surely looking for us and even though we're far from the Academy now, we aren't entirely safe. I'm not sure if we'll ever be.

Chapter 49: Jesse

So after talking it over, it's decided that we'll risk driving during the day, rotating between the three of us. It's not as safe as the darkness that night provides, but we have to keep moving.

The sooner we get home, the sooner we can find out what is in the database, and hopefully, the sooner we can put an end to all of this.

CHAPTER FIFTY
Emma

It's almost night again when we pull up outside the warehouse. A few hours into our trip home, we had to stop at a charging station to repower the car. Jesse's car is old, but thankfully it's not so old that it still runs on gasoline. Gas stations are practically nonexistent these days. But the re-charge ended up setting us back about an hour.

I half expect the warehouse to be surrounded by government vehicles when we arrive, but the lot remains vacant. If they're really still after us though, hopefully they'll go to the apartment instead of a random place I mentioned to the Ambassador months ago. Even so, we probably won't be able to stay here for long.

Jesse stops the car and we all get our stuff and head inside. The main room is empty except for the two air mattresses that are against the wall, blankets tossed around haphazardly.

"Charlotte? Oliver? It's me."

There's a pause and then Charlotte peeks her head out of the other room. Upon seeing it's really us, her face splits into a wide grin and they both burst into the main room.

"You're back!" Charlotte exclaims, hugging Jesse.

Chapter 50: Emma

"I promised I would be."

"We heard the car," Charlotte explains. "We thought it might be the government. That's why we hid."

"It's okay," Jesse assures her. "It's just us. We're safe now."

I doubt he truly believes that.

Cameron walks over to one of the mattresses and sits down. He pulls the tablet out of his bag. "Are you ready for this?"

Jesse and I join him. I pull out the encryption key and take the tablet. I bring up the database, or as far as Aria was able to get into it, and enter the key. It starts translating. We wait in tense silence. Either this will work, or everything was for nothing.

"What do you think we'll find?" Cameron asks.

"Hopefully something actually helpful," I say. I'm going to lose it if we went through all this trouble and don't find any new information.

Jesse shifts nervously beside me. "You know whatever we find, once we see it, there's no going back. We can't unknow it."

"I know," I say softly. "But we have to keep going. I have to know the truth, however much of it I can get."

The tablet bings and I jump, startled. We all look down at the screen filled with folders upon folders. We're in.

I scan the list. Each folder is labeled with a year. I click on one at random and it brings up a list of names. After looking through a few, I come to a conclusion.

"I think these are sorted by graduation year."

Sure enough, I find the one for 2123, my graduation year. Although I guess I won't be graduating anymore. I find my file immediately.

Name: Emmalyn Grant
DOB: January 23, 2105

Age: 17
Sex: Female
Hair, eyes: blonde, green
Rank: 1
Ability: read future of others through physical contact
Parents: Brandon and Elizabeth Grant

I stop when I reach that line. There's more below it, but I can't focus on anything else.

Brandon and Elizabeth Grant. My parents. *My parents!*

"Emma?"

I shake my head. "Sorry, I just…"

Cameron squeezes my hand. "I know. Let's see if we can find something else, because I seriously hope we did not go through all of that just for a list of every Academy kid that's ever existed. Surely there's more to this secret database than that."

"You don't want to see your own page?"

He considers for a second, but says, "I don't want to know."

With that, I navigate back to the main screen and sift through the list of folders. All have graduation years. Until I get to the bottom.

The very last folder is labeled 'X.' I click on it and a list of documents appears. I open one at random.

It's a letter addressed to President Richmond.

"Who's that?" Cameron asks. We both glance at Jesse.

"Don't look at me. He's not the president for North America. Maybe he's like the president of a company or something? But it sounds like he's working with the Academy in some way."

"Let's just read it," I suggest.

And we do.

Chapter 50: Emma

5/18/2082
President Richmond,

The formulas have been working wonderfully. As previously discussed, our experimental group had a 98% success rate. I am happy to report that these additional rounds have expressed a 99% success rate. Subjects who did not develop abilities or who could not be kept under control were taken care of accordingly. As we continue to add new groups, the Academy program will monitor the progress of each subject throughout their lives to ensure they remain useful and under our complete control.

The process of building a new society entirely of submissive Academy children will likely take decades to achieve, but once our numbers are significant, I have faith we will be able to proceed with Operation X at the previously discussed locations.

Furthermore, the issue regarding the scientists is under control as of now. If they become uncooperative later, you can rest assured it will be taken care of swiftly and with discretion.

Please let me know if you have any input or would like any additional information or data on the program.

I hope you are well,
Ambassador Jayne Ward

"Oh god," Jesse whispers from beside me. I feel too sick to even speak. I can't fully comprehend what I just read, but my subconscious seems to pick it up before my conscious mind does.

Cameron eases the tablet out of my hands and searches around for more. I can't even look. Jesse stares ahead, gripped by shock.

"There's more," Cameron says after a few minutes.

I blanch. "How could it possibly get worse?"

Cameron shows me another document. "The formula the letter referred to is the tracker code that links to our brains and blocks emotions. Apparently, the formulas don't work in every case, despite the subject having the correct DNA for the process. If a kid doesn't exhibit signs of an ability and are unable to be controlled within the first few years, then the government...gets rid of them."

I let that sink in. "Gets rid of them as in...*kills* them!"

It's not a question. The tone in his voice already confirmed it. Before I say anything else, Jesse unfreezes and shoots off the mattress.

"We have to do something," he exclaims, his eyes wild and frantic. "We need to end this. The government wants to wipe us out and make room for their controlled society? Well we need to attack them first. End the program."

I jump up, too. "Jesse calm down. Yes, we need to figure out how we're going to take down the Academy and the Ambassador, but there's no need to rush into it. We already tried that once and nearly got caught. And what do you mean the government is going to wipe us out?"

He shakes his head, eyes hardening to amber stone. "Not us. *Me*. You don't have to worry about anything happening to you. The letter said they're building a new society. *You're* that new society. The Academy kids. Sounds to me like humans don't have a place in it."

"How can you possibly get all that from one sentence in a letter that was written forever ago?"

"Because it all makes sense!" he explodes. "The Academy has always seen humans as inferior to them. We don't have abilities like you, strength like you, submissive minds like you. They can't control us, can't use us. Not like they can with people like you."

Chapter 50: Emma

"People like me?" I echo. My voice cracks, betraying how much his comment hurts me. Haven't we been through this before? Doesn't he know I'm on his side, not the government's?

His eyes soften just a little. "You know what I mean."

That only makes me angrier. "Do I? Because it sounds like you want to do to the Academy exactly what you think they're planning to do to the rest of the world."

"Would that be so bad?" he counters. "You could help me. We can still use my original ideas to take them down. We know where it is now. We can end this, end them."

My heart constricts as it finally clicks that this boy standing in front of me isn't the Jesse I've come to know over the past few months. This is the Jesse who is driven by his overwhelming need for revenge.

"Are you insane? Even if I was okay with your messed up plans, you can't just storm the Academy. Sneaking in is one thing, but actually attacking them? There's no way. And there's bound to be extra security after our first break in. Plus, what about all the innocent kids in there? They can't help they're being controlled."

He scoffs. "Of course you'd run to their defense again, even after everything. Even after swearing you hated them. When are you going to get it, Emma? The Academy is bad. It's evil."

"I know, but my *friends* are in there, Jesse. I'm not just going to abandon them or turn on them." My hands curl into fists at my side. Something dark bubbles up from deep within me. "And what about you, huh? I thought you were supposed to be on my side. I thought we agreed we'd find a way to fight back that doesn't put the other Academy kids in danger."

"They're a danger to *us!* Just because they don't realize they're being controlled doesn't make them any less dangerous."

Beyond the Gates

Cameron forces himself between us. In the heat of the moment, I actually forgot he was there. "Both of you need to take it down a notch. Or twenty. Twenty's good."

"Stay out of it, Cameron," I growl and push past him.

"Oh, so you'll be mean to him? I thought you wanted to defend all the Academy kids."

"Shut up! Stop taunting me!" I shout. Traitorous tears spring up in my eyes. What is happening to us?

"I'm not taunting you. I just think it's pathetic and cowardice that you continuously revert back to the Academy way of thinking, instead of facing the truth."

"Hey!" Cameron shouts. "Don't talk to her like that. You need to calm down before you say something stupid. Both of you. But Jesse, Emma has a point. Our friends are in there and they didn't do anything wrong. Just like we didn't. You can't just eliminate all the Academy kids. It's not any different than the government wanting to eliminate all humans."

Jesse doesn't even acknowledge Cameron's words. He continues speaking directly to me. "Don't you realize that's exactly what they want you to do? Revert back to protecting them and thinking like them? You're not one of them. Or at least you aren't supposed to be. But maybe you still are. I guess you'll always be one of them at heart. Once a monster, always a monster, right?"

I don't think, I just act. Fury explodes out of me. I have no idea what's even happening until my hand cracks against skin as I slap him across the face.

He staggers back, hand raised to his cheek. My heart plummets and the anger drains right out of me. My own hand rises to cover my open mouth. Did I really just do that?

His eyes well. The expression on his face is one of utter hurt and betrayal.

Chapter 50: Emma

"Jesse," I whisper pleadingly, taking a step forward. "Jesse, I'm sorry. I—"

He backs up towards the door, shaking his head. "No, Emma. I'm done."

He calls out for his siblings and they appear from the other room. Their faces make it clear they were listening in on everything. Jesse storms out of the warehouse, the kids trailing behind him. He leaves me standing there in a swirl of frustration, hurt, and confusing emotions.

CHAPTER FIFTY-ONE
Jesse

How dare she! How dare she accuse me of plotting behind her back. How can she jump back to their side so easily after everything we discovered about the government? How can she still support them after everything we've been through?

Fire pumps through my veins as I stomp home, Charlotte and Oliver hurrying to keep up. I'm not accustomed to having my deepest thoughts explode out of me the way they had like that. I'm used to bottling them up, locking them tight inside me. But I couldn't help it once we started yelling at each other.

Does our friendship that developed these past couple months mean nothing to her? Does the *truth* mean nothing to her? But as angry as I am, the longer I walk, the more the rational part of my brain kicks in.

I stop in the middle of the sidewalk and sigh heavily as familiarity washes over me. This isn't the first time we've gotten into a fight. Of course, I didn't storm out the first time, but is it really that different? Both times, we accused each other of practically the same thing, of returning to who we were before any of this happened between us. Regret floods through me.

Chapter 51: Jesse

Emma's only been out of the Academy a few months. She's been tracker-free for less than that. How do I keep forgetting that? She lived there her whole life. She only recently became part of my world. Those kids *are* still her friends, even if she's not like them anymore. It makes sense she'd want to protect them. It's not any different from the way I'd protect Charlotte and Oliver from any threat against them.

I squeeze my eyes shut. How did things get so messed up between us so quickly? One moment we were trying to get into the database and the next, we were in a screaming match that somehow ended with me getting slapped.

Not that I didn't deserve, because I definitely did.

The things I said to her…

I didn't mean any of it. Maybe it's the way I feel about the government in general, but not her. Never her. Not after everything. Not after seeing her so alive and full of emotion. Not after being her friend and watching Charlotte and Oliver get so attached to her.

It's in this moment I realize how much I need her. My life got so much more complicated the second she walked in, but I've also never been happier.

I open my eyes at the touch of Charlotte's hand on mine.

"Are you okay?" she asks. Her face is tight, concerned.

"No…I don't know."

Oliver looks at me too, a serious expression passing over his face. I've always been good at reading him, but the words that leave his mouth are utterly unexpected.

"Do you love her?"

"*What?*"

Charlotte's face lights up. "Yes! I need a high five for that."

Oliver grins and slaps his hand against hers.

"Why do you two find so much amusement in this?" I force out.

"Jesse, come on." Charlotte says gently. "We might be younger than you, but don't think we don't notice the way you are with each other. Why do you think you get so angry with each other sometimes? You're both so stubborn, but you also care about each other. So it hurts when you throw blame and insults at each other, but you can't let it go because it's not in your nature to give up a fight so easily without defending yourself."

I stare at her for a moment, the glow of a nearby lamp post the only source of light. "How did you get so wise?"

She shrugs. "Like I said, I don't really have friends. Blending into the background makes it easier to observe other people. I've picked up some things along the way."

"Clearly."

"So are we gonna go back?" Charlotte asks, hopeful.

"Not yet," I say. "We only packed enough stuff to last you a few days. Let's go get whatever else we need and then we'll go back."

We start walking again and I feel a little lighter. Things aren't fixed between us yet, but maybe I can fix them when we get back.

I freeze at the sight of Greg's truck in the driveway. I didn't anticipate him being home. I cautiously enter the house. Maybe he came home and went straight to bed without realizing we weren't there. Or maybe he came home days ago and is waiting for our return.

But the house is quiet, dark. Maybe we got lucky.

We creep through the house to our room.

"Okay, grab some clothes, anything you might want or need. Try to take as much as you can. I doubt we'll be back."

I grab clothes and stuff them into a backpack. I add my documents and research on the Academy, and the file for Charlotte that I'll soon have to figure out what to do with. I can't take the

Chapter 51: Jesse

corkboard for obvious reasons, but that's fine. We found the Academy and anything I need now will be in my notes somewhere.

Charlotte and Oliver are both ready to go a few minutes later. We leave the room to head back out the front door, which is a mistake. We should have gone out the window.

I lead the way but stop when the lights flip on and Charlotte yelps behind me. I spin around to see Greg, his hand gripping Charlotte's wrist. Her gray eyes meet mine. The pure fear in them is more than enough to force me into action.

"Let her go, now!"

He releases her and swings at me instead. But I've lived here for years. I know what to expect, and for once, I'm finally prepared.

Emma's lessons don't abandon me this time. Everything she taught me clicks into place as I dodge his punch and throw one of my own. His cold eyes widen as I shoot my arm up and push his out of the way. I've never fought back like this before.

My fist connects with skin. It's the first time I've ever truly punched someone. When I practiced with Emma, we rarely made contact and when we did it was controlled and not enough to hurt.

But now I'm unleashed. There's a force behind every punch, every kick. Adrenaline thrums in my veins and it feels good.

I duck his next blow, circle around and lift my leg. My foot catches behind his knee. I twist to apply greater pressure and he falls to the ground.

Emma would be proud.

"Get out," I say to the kids. They do so without protest. I turn back to Greg, a heap on the floor after what I put him through. "Come after us again, and I will end you."

And if I don't, Emma will.

I turn and leave the house, and Greg, behind for good.

Beyond the Gates

This isn't home anymore. Maybe home isn't even a place at all, but a person. A group of people. My home is my family. No matter how much we fight or yell at each other, family has a bond that can't break.

We will fix things. *I* will fix things. Everything will be okay.

It has to be.

CHAPTER FIFTY-TWO
Emma

The worst is over. My tears have slowed. But my heart is still heavy, still aches with what happened. I lay across one of the air mattresses, my head in Cameron's lap as he runs his fingers through my hair.

"I'm so stupid," I mumble, the first words either of us have spoken since Jesse left.

"No, you're not. You got angry and yelled at each other. It happens. Especially when you've barely slept in days."

"I can't believe I said all those things to him. I can't believe I *slapped* him. He probably hates me now and he'd have every right to."

"You're so dramatic."

I sit up, blood rushing to my head. "What?"

"You are being dramatic," he repeats. "So what if you yelled at him? He doesn't hate you and he said some pretty awful things to you, too. Honestly, he deserved to be slapped with the way he was talking to you."

I wipe the dried tears from my face, but I only start crying again. As if I'm not already congested enough.

"You don't understand, Cameron. His foster dad physically abuses him on a regular basis and I just hit him. How does that make me any better?"

Cameron grips me by the shoulders and forces me to look at him. "You are *nothing* like that, Emmalyn Grant. Understand? You are *not* going to lose him, and he doesn't hate you. He could never hate you. Just like I could never hate you. Even after all *we've* been through, we're still best friends. We made it out the other side."

"Doesn't mean I'm not a terrible person," I mutter and lean against him. "He's done so much for me and this is how I repay him."

"He just got mad and scared. You both did. He'll come around, I promise. And if he doesn't...well, then that's his loss, not yours."

I shift. "But...but what if I still stand by some of what I said? I hate that I yelled at him, but I don't think it's right to attack the Academy the way he's wanting to. I don't want our friends getting caught in the crossfire. I hate the government and what they did to us, but we shouldn't punish the Academy kids along with them."

"I know," he agrees. "Just let him cool down. Maybe we can work something out, a plan we can all agree on. Just give it time."

I don't press the matter any further. Instead, I lay back down and close my eyes as exhaustion takes over. I just want to sleep, to forget our fight, to stop thinking.

It's not long before I get my wish.

...

I'm dazed and disoriented when I wake some unknown time later. What I do know is that Cameron is no longer there beside me.

I rub my eyes and the warehouse comes into focus. That's when I notice the other air mattress that's about a foot away. It's no longer vacant.

Chapter 52: Emma

Jesse is asleep, looking so calm and peaceful that it splits my already fractured heart. What is he doing here? Where are Cameron and the kids? How did they come in without waking me up?

I push those thoughts out of my mind for now. It doesn't matter, because he's here.

I reach over and skim my fingertips across his cheek, the one I slapped. His breathing shifts and his eyes flutter open. I freeze, hand still resting against his face.

He stares at me. I stare at him.

There's no more anger in his eyes.

"You came back," I whisper, breaking the deafening silence.

He swallows. I retract my hand.

"I did," he says. Just hearing his voice, so soft and gentle now, is enough to ease that ache in my chest. Though it doesn't prevent the guilt from rushing in to fill the gap. "I realized something during my outraged walk back to Greg's house."

I wince at the mention of Greg, but say, "And what's that?"

"We're both stubborn idiots who had a similar fight not too long ago. Of course, no one got slapped the first go around, but you get the point."

I flinch. "I'm sorry."

He shakes his head. "You didn't hurt me, Emma. You didn't even leave a mark. I'm fine. It was more the shock than anything. And trust me, I deserved it. I'm the one who should be apologizing. I shouldn't have spoken to you like that. All those things I said, I didn't mean it."

I feel like crying all over again. "It's okay, Jesse. I—"

"No, it's not okay," he protests.

"Stop cutting me off."

"I'm trying to apologize."

"So am I."

We both stop talking and just stare at each other. A grin finds its way to my face. I can't stay mad at him and I suspect he can't either.

He smiles too, and then becomes serious again. "What I was *trying* to say is that you aren't pathetic, Emma, or a coward. I get that you still have friends at the Academy that you want to protect, and I get that that doesn't mean you support the government. Reading that letter just really freaked me out. It's like I shut down and all I could think about was taking them down, no matter the means. I screwed up this whole thing with us because of it. I am so, so sorry I hurt you."

I draw myself closer, hanging off the edge of the mattress. "So you don't hate me?"

He releases a shaky breath. "God, no. You're one of the best things that've ever happened to me. As cheesy as that sounds, it's true."

"Really?" I mumble. "Even if I still don't agree that we should blow up the Academy?"

"Even then," he laughs softly. "You were right. It's not fair to blame the Academy kids for any of this. It's out of their control. That was you just a few months ago and look how far you've come. But that doesn't mean I'm going to stop trying to get my revenge. I'll just have to find a way around all the other kids."

"I know. I'm sorry, too. For everything I said. For slapping you."

He chuckles. "It's not your fault. It was mine. We're just a lot alike, you and me. We're both stubborn people who tend to jump to conclusions and don't always know how to properly communicate with each other. But you know what?"

"What?"

Chapter 52: Emma

"At the end of the day, we're still us. No matter how angry or frustrated we get with each other, we'll always work it out."

I smile and sit up. "Come here."

He moves off his mattress and onto mine. We sit with our backs against the wall and I rest my head on his shoulder.

"Where is everyone else?" I ask.

"In the other room," Jesse replies. "After I left, we went back to Greg's house and got what we needed. Greg freaked out on us, of course. But I finally took him down. By the way, you never said that real punching actually hurts once the adrenaline wears off."

She laughs. "Yeah. You get used to it."

"Anyway, I have no intention of ever going back. You were asleep when we got back here, but Cameron insisted I stay out here with you. He found a couple more mattresses and set them up in the other room."

We fall into silence until I ask, "Where do we go from here? What do we do with all the information we've discovered?"

He pushes me off his shoulder enough to make eye contact. He sticks out his hand. "You tell me."

It takes me a second to realize what he means. My eyes widen when I do. Is he serious? He voluntarily wants me to read his future?

I readjust myself so I face him. "Are you sure?"

In answer, he shifts too, and gathers my hand in his own. I let down my guard, the block that keeps him out, and am instantly pulled into his mind.

The first thing I see is myself.

He looks at me, his chest tight with worry. We stand before a brown wooden door. He squeezes my hand. "Ready?"

"Not really," I reply. I look about as anxious as he feels. With his free hand, he reaches out and rings the doorbell. The scene shifts. He's driving the car. He glances over and there I am in the passenger seat.

Beyond the Gates

The scene shifts again. It's mostly small snippets without any context. Bright colors, a rough grainy texture between his toes, the kids, me and Cameron. We're all there. One thing I do gather is that not a single piece of his future as it is now involves major movements against the government. He's not planning to act on anything soon.

I'm about to let go of his hand when I'm jerked into another scene. But it's different this time. I don't just see myself through his eyes, I *feel* what he feels every time he looks at me. It's not his future. It's his *thoughts*. His thoughts during scenes of the past.

He watches me with awe as I stare out at the glittering lake and waterfall for the first time. His heart slams against his chest as he looks down at me, pinned to the training mat. He watches me sleep in the few moments before Cameron comes home. Even with my hair sprawled across the bed and my mouth hanging open, he thinks I'm beautiful. I also feel how scared he is. How terrifying it is to feel the way he does, and know that the second the government finds out, it'll be used against us.

The reading abruptly shifts back into the future and I see something I most definitely did not expect to see.

With a gasp, I rip my hand out of his. My wide, shocked eyes mirror his own.

"What did you see?" he asks, breathless.

How can I ever answer that? My heart thrashes against my ribcage. I swallow to clear the dust from my dry throat. He raises a brow when I don't say anything.

I shrug and try to play it off. "Nothing really. Just the usual vague stuff I've seen before."

"Like a brown door." Jesse says. It's not a question.

My heart skips a beat. Or maybe three. "Excuse me?"

"I saw it," he says. "In my mind."

I shake my head. "That's not possible."

Chapter 52: Emma

It can't be. There's no way he could've seen what I saw. It's a coincidence. That's all.

"Maybe it is," he counters. "Maybe you can project what you see into the other person. I saw what you did, Emma. I know I did."

I've heard of people projecting their abilities before, but it's not the case for every Academy kid, and it's never happened to me until now.

Fearing the answer but needing to know, I ask, "Was that all you saw? Or did you see…more?"

"I saw enough." He doesn't just hold eye contact with me, he looks directly into my soul. "The door, the car, how I feel about you…what's about to happen."

I jerk back. "The future isn't set in stone. Things change. The future can change."

"Do you want it to change?"

No.

"It *needs* to change. I'm sorry, Jesse, but we can't. We just can't."

Someone please come in here and interrupt us before we do something that messes everything up.

"I don't *care*," he exclaims, fire in his voice, "what we can or cannot do, what we should or shouldn't do. I don't care about the rules anymore. I'm done with following them. I don't care about the government right now. They already know way too much, so why not go all in? We'll find a way to deal with them. So don't tell me what we *need* to do, Emma. Tell me what you *want*."

What do I want?

His brown eyes hold mine. They're molten now, a stark contrast from the hard stone of earlier. His chest heaves from his outburst, but I can barely draw air into my lungs.

I want—

No.

But I'm so sick and tired of listening to the stupid, rational voice in the back of my mind. So, I ignore it. For once in my life, I listen to my heart instead of my head, instead of the rules. I do what we both want.

I don't cross that final line between us. I obliterate it. And then I kiss him.

It doesn't last long. The moment my mouth brushes his, I pull back. I catch a glimpse of confusion in his eyes before I cast my own downward.

"Sorry," I mumble. "That was awkward."

Especially when there was so much build up to it in my mind.

I feel the rumble of his silent laughter. "You know, saying it was awkward makes it even more awkward."

Pink creeps into my cheeks. "I just…I don't—"

He lifts my face to meet his. "It's okay. You don't have to understand or analyze every little thing. You don't always have to have a plan. Sometimes it's better to just live in the moment."

He leans in, searching my eyes and expression. His eyes are steady, firm, looking for an answer. He hesitates, giving me the chance to pull back. When I don't, he leans in further and presses his lips to mine.

We both tense again, but then ease into it. His hands slide into my messy hair and I bring mine around his neck, pulling him closer. Something warm and fuzzy seeps into me and spreads throughout my entire body. I feel more alive, more filled with emotion, in this moment than I've ever felt in my whole life.

All thoughts about the government, the danger, the questions of what will happen after this, flee my mind. Nothing matters but this. Him. Right here. Right now.

Chapter 52: Emma

I pull away and open my eyes. I stare at him, and he stares back. I feel like I'm seeing him in a way I never have before. He looks at me that way, too.

He whispers my name and I kiss him again. It's a short kiss, barely anything. But it's different this time. Something sparks between us and suddenly that little peck just isn't going to cut it.

He grabs the back of my head, fingers fisting into my hair, and pulls my face to meet his.

This. This is a kiss.

Everything intensifies. I can't get close enough to him.

The next thing I know, he's readjusting us, pulling me against him. I kiss him with everything I have, one hand pressed to the dingy brick of the building and the other tangled in his hair.

All the pent-up fear and anger and all the times we've held back. It all comes rushing out.

Why? Why didn't we give into this sooner?

Suddenly the door to the other room opens and we break apart.

Cameron stands there, mouth hanging open and eyes wide. "Oh god. Oh my god. Sorry, I was just…never mind. I'm just gonna, yeah. Okay."

He spins around and retreats into the room. I look at Jesse and we erupt into a fit of giggles.

"Poor Cameron. I don't think he was expecting that." I say.

"*I* wasn't expecting that," Jesse exclaims. "Jeez, Emma. Kiss many boys at the Academy?"

"What?"

"There's no way that was your first kiss. Not with the way you just kissed me."

I shrug. "Well, it was."

He hugs me, presses his face into my shoulder. "I really, really like you."

"I know. You weren't exactly subtle," I grin. He laughs and shoves me.

"Why did we wait so long?"

Hearing it out loud crashes me back into reality.

His eyebrows crease together. "What's wrong?"

"This doesn't change anything," I say. "We're still in danger. The government knows we betrayed them. Sooner or later they're going to find us."

He considers this for a moment and then says, "Then let's get out of here. We already ditched the trackers and phones. We have the essentials and my car that we know for sure is safe during the day." He looks at me with urgent, pleading eyes. "Emma, we can go somewhere they'll never find us. We've come this far. There's no way I'm letting them take you away now."

I let his proposition sink in.

"Okay," I nod. The more thought I give it, the clearer the plan forms in my mind. "We can leave tomorrow morning after we get a lot of much needed rest. But it isn't going to be easy. The Ambassador is going to send people out to look for us. They might not be able to track us, but I doubt she's just going to let me and Cameron disappear that easily, or you for that matter. My Mission was supposed to end with you dead. The Academy won't just let that go. So, we're going to have to be prepared to lay low for a while, possibly a long while."

"It's okay," he assures me. "We'll find a way to make it work."

I give him a small smile and a soft kiss and lay back down, turn so that my back is against his chest. He curls an arm over me to hold me closer.

After everything we've been through, we're only a few hours away from freedom. Freedom from the government, the rules, the sneaking around, praying they don't find out about me.

Chapter 52: Emma

It's been a long couple of days and an even longer night. But we survived.

And we're stronger because of it.

CHAPTER FIFTY-THREE
Jesse

    I lazily trace my finger up and down her arm as she dozes in and out, swirling the path into random shapes. For the first time in a long time, I feel at peace.

    This girl before me is mine and I'm hers. No matter what, we'll be there to protect and defend each other. The rest of my family sleeps soundly in the neighboring room. After coming up with our plan, Emma and I decided we'd give them a couple more hours of peace. Then we'll wake them up and leave this place behind forever.

    For just a moment, it feels like everything will work out. We will truly be okay. Nothing can hurt us.

    And then the main door bursts open.

CHAPTER FIFTY-FOUR
Emma

I shoot into a sitting position, dizzy and disoriented, as the front door slides open with a screech. Jesse's arms protectively tighten around me on instinct.

A man and woman barrel through, dressed in black, full body protective gear. The same gear used by the guards at the Academy, which only means one thing.

They found us.

I knew this would happen eventually, especially after the break in, but the thought of running away gave me hope.

I untangle myself from Jesse and spring off the mattress. I'll fight my way out of here if I have to. Given that there are two of them, one is meant for me and the other for Jesse.

"Emmalyn Grant and Jesse Reynolds," the woman says. "We are from the Academy. We're here to take you in and would appreciate it if you'd cooperate."

Jesse glances at me and I shake my head.

"Not a chance."

Beyond the Gates

The man lunges for me. I duck beneath the punch he slings at me. I have to get to Jesse. He's only been fighting a couple months. There's no way he'll be able to walk away from this on his own.

But it's already too late. The other guard has Jesse pressed up against the wall, his arms pulled behind his back.

I swivel to face the guard after me, but his fist connects with the side of my head, knocking me to the floor. I slam into the concrete with nothing to break my fall. It's then that I know for sure that they aren't human guards. They're former Academy students with abilities of heightened strength. Of course they are.

He digs his foot into my back, preventing me from getting up. I struggle against him, but it's useless. It doesn't matter how good I am. I'm pinned down and they're stronger. The Ambassador knows that. She specifically sent guards who I wouldn't be able to take down on my own.

The guard twists my arms behind me and hauls me up. This can't be happening. After everything I've struggled through, this is how we go down, with hardly any fight at all?

Movement catches the corner of my eye. I look and see the slightest sliver of Cameron's face as he peeks out of the other room. Charlotte stands beside him, eyes wide and face pale. Oliver clings to Cameron, tears running down his cheeks.

I shake my head a fraction of an inch. He gets the message, because they disappear back into the room a second later. The last thing we need is the kids getting mixed up in this, too. Cameron will take care of them while I figure out what to do.

The guard drags me toward the door. I flail around in a fruitless attempt to escape.

"Jesse!" I scream. I can't see him anymore. I twist and kick and struggle against the inevitable. The guard doesn't ease up.

"I'm okay, Emma. I'm right here."

Chapter 54: Emma

I finally see him when the other guard shoves him through the door. His eye is bruised and will no doubt swell soon. He also staggers forward with a bit of a limp. Not a good sign.

But it's the expression on his face that's the most concerning. The frown, the despair in his eyes, the exhaustion. It pierces my heart. He knows, too. Knows how bad this really is.

They yank us out of the warehouse. I stop struggling once we pass through the door. What's the point? If I keep at it, they'll just drug me. I'd rather be conscious during these next few hours. I need to devise a plan so we can escape once we arrive at the Academy.

I have no idea what time it is or how long we were asleep, but it's still dark outside. My mind goes numb with shock. The only thing that penetrates my brain as they shove Jesse and I into the back of the car is: at least we aren't handcuffed.

Jesse sits on the right. They place me on the other side, but I move to the middle seat to be closer to him. He wraps an arm around my shoulders and draws me against his side.

The guards get into the front seats and then we're off. I'm grateful for the barrier between the front and back that the Academy cars have. Our voices will be muted to them, and if we whisper, they likely won't hear us at all.

"We'll be okay," I murmur, though the second the words leave my mouth, my lips quiver and a few tears skid down my face, hot and fast. "I'm sorry. I'm so sorry, Jesse."

He leans his head against mine. "It's not your fault. There's nothing to be sorry for. We knew this was bound to happen at some point."

"But you're in this situation because of me," I protest. "It *is* my fault. I shouldn't have gotten you involved. I should have left after realizing what the government was really doing. I shouldn't have taken things as far as I did."

He runs his fingers up and down my arm soothingly, sending tingles down my spine. "There you go again with the shoulds. You didn't force me to do any of this, Emma. We make our own choices. I chose this. I chose *you*. And believe me, I don't regret a single thing. No matter what happens to me, to us, it is not your fault."

I shift and rest my head in the space between his shoulder and neck. We should probably be discussing an escape plan, but there's several hours to go until we reach the Academy, and I just want to sit with him for a while.

Eventually, he mumbles, "We're going to die, aren't we? They're going to kill us."

"Do you really want to know?"

He shrugs. "It would be nice to know what we're walking into, but I won't make you do it if you don't want to."

I sigh. I don't want to see, but he's right. "Give me your hand."

He slips his hand into mine. Images burst across my mind. I concentrate on the near future and anything to do with the Academy to filter out the random scenes, most of which might not even be in our future anymore.

The Ambassador's office comes into focus. He watches me as I scream at her.

Leaves fall from trees and blow across the empty quad.

I can't see the next clip, but I feel it. *His face is raw, his lips sticky with blood. His stomach aches where he's been kicked again and again.*

And then comes the most horrifying thing I've ever seen in someone's future.

He kneels in the grass, head bent. His hands shake, but his heart beats steady and calm. He's not afraid. He doesn't want to leave me or the kids behind, but he knows it's for the best. The best for him, the best for everyone. He won't have to hurt anymore. This is nine years overdue. It's time.

Chapter 54: Emma

He peers up and meets the eyes of a guard. A guard who aims a gun at him.

Bang!

I rip my hand from his. His wide-eyed expression says he saw it, too.

"Oh my god," I choke out. I gasp for air with no such luck. It's not true. It can't possibly be true. Even though survival is near impossible, I still clung to that shred of hope.

But that's gone now.

"It's okay." Jesse pulls me to his chest. His hands thread through my hair and tighten. "It's okay." He murmurs those words over and over until I catch my breath. My stomach roils and my head pounds. How is he so stable right now when I'm losing my mind?

The details of the reading surface. What he thought, what he felt. It all clears in my mind. My eyes narrow with confusion and I look at him. "You were calm."

"What?" he blinks.

"I could tell what you were thinking, how you felt in that moment." I stare at him through blurry eyes. "And you were calm. You weren't scared at all. It's like you were…you were *okay* with them killing you."

"Emma—"

He doesn't say my name like he's about to provide a reasonable explanation, like I misunderstood. He says it like I'm right, and he doesn't know how to explain himself.

So I cut him off and keep talking

"You were thinking about how it was time and that it was overdue. What does that even mean? Why would you just give up like that? Why wouldn't you fight back?"

Getting mad at him is wrong. He can't be held responsible for the thoughts and actions of his future self, but I just witnessed his death...his *murder*. I have a right to be upset.

"I should have died nine years ago, Emma." He swallows and closes his eyes. "I'm not supposed to be alive."

"What are you talking about?"

He shifts away from me. "Nothing. It doesn't matter."

I take his chin and turn him back to face me. "No, you don't get to shut me out. Not now. Not after what we just saw."

"You wouldn't understand. And it's not your problem to deal with anyway. Let it go. I'm sure we can find a way to get you out alive."

"Us. We'll find a way to get *us* out alive."

His eyes meet mine and I know. He has no intention of walking away from the Academy. "From what we just saw, it doesn't look like there's going to be a way around that."

His blatant disregard for his own life sets me off. "There won't be if you just give up, if you don't even try to fight back. Why are you so okay with this?"

He explodes. "Because I should have died in that fire! Sometimes I wish I had. It would've made things a whole lot easier for everyone."

"Jesse," I gasp. "Don't say that!"

"What? That I sometimes wish I was dead?" He stares me down, face contorted with pain. "Do you think I want this? Do you think I wanted any of this? I hate that I'm the only one left in my family. I hate that I've spent over half my life seeking revenge. I hate having to hide everything I do and be so cautious so I don't attract too much attention. I'm just so tired of it all, Emma."

I flinch.

Chapter 54: Emma

He sighs and softens his tone. "I'm so *tired*. And I hurt. I hurt *all the time*. I know I don't act like it. I try to lock the pain away. I try to put on a smile for Charlotte and Oliver. And I love them, I do. But I miss my family. I miss my parents and my brother. I miss the life I used to have, the life I could have had. It's like this constant burning weight on my chest." A tear escapes his eye. "I can't do it anymore. I don't *want* to do this anymore."

I open and close my mouth, trying to find the right words. What am I supposed to say? He just told me he doesn't want to live anymore. There are no words for that.

So I wrap my arms around him and pull him close. I hold him in complete silence for a while, until he speaks again.

"I should have waited a little longer before leaving the house. Then I would've been there with them. I could've died with them. I wouldn't have had to deal with all the pain and guilt from the past decade." He squeezes his eyes shut. "I used to think it would get better, that the pain would eventually go away, or at least ease up. But it just gets worse. It builds and builds and strikes harder at the most random times. Occasionally it lifts just a bit and I start to hope I might finally be getting somewhere, but then it always punches back twice as hard. I just can't do it anymore. I'm sorry."

I brush his tears away and focus on what I want to convey. It's difficult, but I manage to put the words together and get them out.

"I can't even begin to understand what that kind of loss must feel like. I never knew my parents, so I *can't* miss them. But you are so wrong if you think you don't have a family. They will always be your family, and no one will ever replace them, but that doesn't mean Charlotte and Oliver aren't your family, too. They love you. They need you. *I* need you. And we're here when you need us. That's how family works."

He looks at me, unshed tears clinging to his eyelashes. "It's just so unfair. Why should I get to live when they don't? Why do I have to live with this pain and they don't? I don't want to hurt anymore. But I don't know how not to."

"It's not fair," I agree. "But it's how it is. You are so strong, Jesse. You can keep pushing through. I know you can. Don't die with them. *Live* for them. Your life is so much more than revenge against the government. If you had died all those years ago, who would've been there to take care of Charlotte and Oliver? Who would have been there to show me the truth about the government? No one. You're a good person, Jesse Reynolds. You are important and needed and loved. You've changed lives. One day you're going to change the whole world. And if you really want it, then eventually you will get your revenge."

He sniffles and slowly shakes his head. "There's no point to revenge. I see that now. Revenge will only help in the moment. It won't heal the ache in my soul or stop the pain. It won't bring them back. That's why it doesn't matter if they kill me. Without my revenge, what do I even have to live for? Who am I? That's all I've ever worked towards. It's not like I'll actually go to college or do anything useful with my life. Once I turn eighteen and age out of the foster system, I'll be tossed out with nowhere to go. At least this will be quicker than living homeless and slowly starving to death."

"What happened to running away?" I remind him. "You were fully prepared to leave everything behind a few hours ago. If we can get away from the Academy, we can still do that. And what about Charlotte and Oliver? You're just going to leave them to fend for themselves?"

That last comment is a low blow, but at this point, I'm desperate enough to say anything if it means he'll fight back.

Chapter 54: Emma

"It's not like I want to abandon them, but you saw it yourself. They beat me up, then shoot me point blank."

"That doesn't mean that's how it'll actually play out. The future can always change. Don't give up. Not yet. No one can ever replace your parents and brother, but you still have a family and we still need you."

He looks at me through tired eyes and sighs. "When did you get so good at words?"

I give him a small smile. "I learned it from you."

The corner of his mouth flicks up just slightly. He draws me in and presses a kiss to my temple.

"We're going to survive, Jesse," I say with more confidence than I actually have. "We're going to live."

CHAPTER FIFTY-FIVE
Jesse

The ride to the Academy is both exhaustingly long and not long enough. We only stop a few times so they can let us go to the bathroom. Once, they even let us split a bag of chips. But that was hours ago and I'm starving again. Not that it matters anymore. I only have a few hours left at most.

I can tell when we arrive, even though the windows are blacked out. The ground beneath the car changes from smooth pavement to the crunch of gravel. I imagine us weaving through the forest, back again just a day later. Not too long after, the car rolls to a stop.

Emma's cheek is pressed into my shoulder. Her eyes are closed, but the circles her thumb draws on the back of my hand as she holds it tells me she's awake. After my meltdown, we switched the subject to discussing a plan. Emma still wants to believe the plan is for both of us, and after a while I stopped trying to convince her otherwise.

We didn't speak much after that.

There's so much I want to say to her, but I can't get the words out. Sitting there in silence though, we reach an unspoken understanding of all the things we wish we had time to say and do.

Chapter 55: Jesse

Sunlight floods the car as the back doors swing open. The guard from before grabs my arm in a crushing grip and yanks me out. The other does the same with Emma. Why should they care about jostling us? We're their prisoners in this situation, after all.

Our captors lead us down the remainder of the gravel path. I grab Emma's hand in my own and squeeze. I watch her from the corner of my eye. She swallows nervously and bites her lip as we approach the gate.

Four guards are positioned on the outside, and two more on the inside. I wonder if her friend Aiden is among them.

The grounds are strangely deserted. It has to be Saturday by now, since it's daylight. Surely students would be out and about in the middle of the day on a weekend.

Neither of us dares to speak as we trek to wherever we're going. But I don't take my hand out of hers. It's our only connection. It lets the other person know that we're both here and we're not alone. At least not yet.

Eventually, we enter a circular area divided by walkways. A fountain gurgles in the center and benches line the paths. The whole area is surrounded by trees that are splashed with the colors of fall.

I glance at Emma. Her expression is stoic, but her eyes reveal how much pain she's in being back here. We didn't come over here when we broke in, but from that look, I know this place has to be the quad. Her favorite place. The place she said she never wanted to see again.

We arrive at a building that I assume is the Ambassador's. Who else would they be taking us to but the leader of the program?

The guards lead us into the building and my nerves finally take hold. I'm not prepared for this. What if Emma's plan doesn't work? What if I can't get her out in time before they kill me?

Beyond the Gates

We ascend a flight of stairs and stop at a door down the hall. One of the guards raps on the door and then pushes us inside.

An older woman sits behind a desk covered with computers, tablets, and paper files. She looks up upon our entrance. Her dull blonde hair hangs to her shoulders and her cold eyes fixate on us.

Her gaze lands on me first and contracts with recognition before flicking to the girl who stands beside me.

The Ambassador stands up. "Welcome back, Ms. Grant."

Emma visibly flinches at her menacing tone. I grip her hand tighter, reminding her of my presence.

Her gaze turns back to me. "And Jesse Reynolds. You've caused quite a bit of trouble for us."

"Good," I sneer, despite how timid I feel inside. "But trust me, whatever problems I've caused for you, it wasn't enough."

Her eyes narrow. "You relentlessly searched for my program for years. I sent someone out to take care of you and you mess that up as well. You turned one of my best and highest ranked students against me and used her and her partner to break into this facility."

Emma drops my hand and steps forward. I resist the urge to pull her back, to wrap her in my arms and never let go, to protect her from all of this. She needs to stand her ground and push forward with her part of the plan.

"He didn't turn me against you. I've been playing him this whole time, going along with everything he says, and pretending he swayed me to his side. I know his plans now. All of them."

My turn.

"Is that true?" I exclaim. "You've been lying to me this whole time? How could you? I trusted you! You made me think we were friends and partners!"

Chapter 55: Jesse

Emma turns to me. She looks at my nose, unable to meet my eyes. "You were trying to destroy my home and my family. Why would I ever be on your side?"

The Ambassador watches us go back and forth. "Well this is interesting. Smart move, Emma. You even had me fooled. Now that that's figured out, I guess there's really only one thing left to do."

She opens a desk drawer, pulls out a gun, and hands it to Emma.

"Kill him, and you will have successfully completed your first Mission."

This time, our eyes do lock. She keeps her face blank, but I can see the fear in her eyes. She's terrified.

"Go on," the Ambassador encourages. I want to scream at Emma to turn and shoot the Ambassador instead, but I have a feeling that won't actually work. Emma walks up to me, gun held limply in her hand.

"It's okay," I whisper low enough so the Ambassador can't hear. "If you don't do it, she will. I'm dead either way. At least this way, you'll be safe."

"I can't, Jesse," she mumbles. Then louder, she says, "But I can do this."

She spins around and points the gun at the Ambassador.

"Oh, I'm so surprised," the Ambassador says sarcastically. "I knew you were faking it. You're a terrible liar, Emma. Do you really think I'd be naïve enough to hand you a loaded gun?"

All color drains from Emma's face. She pulls the trigger to confirm it. Nothing happens. I'm not shocked. I had a feeling the Ambassador wouldn't just give Emma a weapon without being perfectly certain it was safe.

"You betrayed us!" the Ambassador yells at her. "Your own family. After everything we've done for you, trained you, housed you, fed you. You believed the lies of a psychopath, the *enemy*."

"Don't you *dare* turn this around on me," Emma seethes. "*I'm* the traitor? I'm not the one keeping secrets from generations of students. I'm not the one brainwashing them into obedience by controlling their emotions. I'm not the one stealing babies from hospitals and later telling them their parents didn't want them. I'm not trying to create a society that's completely submissive to the government. We're not the enemy. You are."

So much for our plan.

Anger rolls off Emma in waves as the animosity escalates.

The Ambassador emits a dry laugh. "You think you are so smart, like you understand everything. But you're wrong. You may have once been the best in your year, but you've let the outside world cloud your judgement. You are weak and pathetic and out of control."

Her words jar me, not because of the harsh tone, but because she obviously knows something we don't.

But Emma keeps going. "Well despite that control you have over everyone and everything, I still managed to evade you for over two months. Every time you called me, you thought I was perfectly fine. You had absolutely no idea I turned to the very side of the target you assigned to me until we got past your security and broke into the Academy."

The Ambassador smiles, wide and unnerving. "Wrong again." I internally shudder at the words as chills course down my spine. "I knew exactly what you were up to."

For the first time, Emma seems off balance. She doesn't have a snarky comeback. So the Ambassador continues.

Chapter 55: Jesse

"I first realized something was wrong when you didn't answer your phone. When I called Mr. Clarke, he said you were out following a lead. Your tracking device showed your location, but I couldn't imagine why you wouldn't have taken your phone with you. You returned a few days later and the tracker moved consistently after that, although sometimes it stayed in the same location for hours at a time. Even then, I couldn't be sure."

Emma is shaking. In anger or terror, I'm not sure.

"It was our later calls that confirmed it for me. The flicker of emotion in your voice, even though you tried to hide it. The way you stalled giving me new information, because you weren't actually trying to gain anything new anymore. That's how I knew for sure that you were no longer on our side."

"Fine, so you knew. Why didn't you pull the plug on the Mission when you realized? Why wait until *after* we broke into the Academy and hacked the database?"

"Because it wasn't about the Mission," she says. Emma tenses. "Did you really think we would send out an underage student who hasn't even graduated the program yet with someone who's only been in the Mission's program a year?"

Emma stumbles back a step, realigning herself with me. Her body deflates and my heart drops from my chest as we both realize what this means.

We weren't the ones who'd been fooling the Academy.

"Did you never stop to think why we didn't just assign the Mission to someone who was already in the field? Someone who actually went through the proper training. Someone who would certainly be more experienced and better at their job than you, even before your tracker came out."

"Because you didn't have enough people and I'm the right age," Emma says. She looks like she's going to be sick. Everything she believed is crashing down around her. Again.

"Of course we have enough. Just because only two students made the cut this year and some retired doesn't mean we're low on our higher ups. And many of our participants look young enough to pass for seventeen."

"Then why?" Emma demands. "Why would you send *me* out if you knew I wasn't ready? If you had other people available?"

A new voice chimes in from behind us. "She already said it was never about the Mission, you stupid girl."

"Ariana!" the Ambassador snaps.

I whip around to see the girl with the black hair and ice blue eyes that are no longer hidden behind thick glasses. My insides twist at the sight of her. Emma gasps.

"Aria…"

Emma's face crumples. Seeing her supposed friend in the doorway of the Ambassador's office and realizing she's been used is the last straw for her.

"What?" Aria says to the Ambassador, who does not look pleased to see her.

"What are you doing here? I never said you could leave your post."

"What was I supposed to do? My Mission got picked up and brought here."

"If I recall correctly, Cameron Clarke was also part of your mission and he was left behind. You could have kept an eye on him, watched the situation while I dealt with these two."

"Hey," Aria says defensively. "I'm the one who told you to keep an eye on the database after they asked me to hack into it. And I told

Chapter 55: Jesse

you about her emotions, what he was up to, how much Cameron knew about the two of them."

"So none of it was real?" Emma whispers. She looks so lost. "Our friendship, hanging out with me and Cameron, helping us out. You were just spying on us? *Using* us?"

"Oh, please," Aria spits. "Like you weren't using me, too. No, Emma. We were never friends and to be quite honest, I don't know if you ever really considered me your friend either. You used me for information, too. I gave you stuff about Jesse, though that was actually to help your Mission. I pretended to hack into the Academy's database for you. You asked, I answered without explanation."

"You *were* my friend," Emma says. "I trusted you."

"Yeah, well I never trusted you. I'm actually surprised you didn't figure it out, but I guess you were always so caught up in your boyfriend over here to pay that much attention to me."

"But...but if you're from the Academy, why don't I know you? Or why doesn't Cameron know you?"

"You don't know me because I'm not from your little Academy," Aria retorts. "I work for the Ambassador, but not from within the walls. No one here knows me."

"That's enough from you," the Ambassador snaps before Aria says anything more.

Emma looks like she's about to cry, so I interrupt. "What was your goal then if her Mission wasn't real?" I ask the Ambassador.

"Oh, the Mission was real," she says. "If things had gone smoothly and ended with your death, then it would've taken care of two problems at once. But that, of course, is obviously not what happened. But no matter. We have you now *and* collected all the information we need."

"Which is what?" Emma demands. "What was the real reason for sending me out?"

"And why do you think I'll tell you that? Why would I disclose any of my plans or knowledge with you? You don't need to know anything, Emmalyn, except that we got what we needed, and you played your role beautifully. Take comfort in the fact that you are part of something so much bigger than you thought. You'll see one day. Maybe even soon."

Frustration bubbles inside me. She's being so vague and dismissive.

Emma's hands curl into fists by her side. I try to reach for her, but she shakes me off. "So now what? Now that you've used me for whatever you needed, you're just going to kill us?"

The Ambassador has the gall to look offended. "Now why would you think that? You are much too valuable to us. Your mind, your ability. With proper training, you would be even more useful than before. It would be a waste to destroy that. So, you will be re-installed with a tracker and kept in isolation until the formulas properly take effect over your mind and body again. Then, you will be placed back into the Academy with an updated schedule for the remainder of your senior year."

"No," Emma growls. "I'm not going to be your puppet again. I'm done being a pawn in your quest for world domination or whatever the hell it is you're working towards."

"Like you have a choice in the matter," the Ambassador scoffs. She nods to me. "You on the other hand. You are expendable. I don't need you anymore. You would've been eliminated months ago had I sent out a proper student to complete the Mission. No worries though." She motions to one of the guards by the door. "Take him down to the field and prepare him for execution, but do not act until I am present. I will be down shortly. Try to gather a crowd so we can make an example."

Chapter 55: Jesse

It's almost time. Emma's vision is about to come true. I guess the future doesn't always change.

"NO!" Emma screams and lunges for me just as the guard jerks me backwards. The next few moments all happen in a blur of movement and confusion.

I throw my arm out to her as they drag me to the door. The other guard holds her by the waist to prevent her from coming after me.

My fingers graze hers for a split second, but that's enough. It fills me with the comfort and courage I need as I'm led away to die.

Just last night, we laid on the beat-up air mattress together and spoke of running away, escaping and leaving it all behind. But it wasn't real. It was just the fantasy of a couple of naïve teenagers who thought everything would work itself out because they had each other and that's what mattered.

And now it's over. The fantasy has come to an end. *This* is real.

Everything will be okay as long as Emma makes it out alive. She can escape while everyone's distracted. She can find her way back to Cameron, Charlotte, and Oliver. They'll take care of my siblings for me. I want to raise them myself, watch them grow up, but there's nothing more I can do. If they have Emma and Cameron to watch out for them, they'll be okay.

And I'll get to see my family again soon. I'm almost there. I won't hurt anymore. I won't be tired anymore. It's almost over.

I glance over my shoulder as I pass through the office door.

Her pale green eyes burst with fear and loss and grief.

Goodbye, Emma.

CHAPTER FIFTY-SIX
Emma

It's torture watching Jesse walk out that door. I can't breathe. I can't move. I can't think about anything but the fact that he's gone.

Aria, my friend, the girl I spent so much time hanging out with, shoots me a glare and stalks out of the room. The door slams behind her. Now it's just me, the Ambassador, and the remaining guard who has released me and now lurks in the corner. How fun.

I find my voice and turn to the Ambassador. "Whatever it is you're planning, it won't work." I pack as much bite into the words as I can, hoping to stall. The longer I keep her in here, the longer I keep Jesse alive.

"That sounds much like an empty threat to me, Ms. Grant. You have no idea what is happening or what is going to happen. You can try as hard as you want, but you will never win. It will be easier on everyone if you just let him go and rejoin us."

I shake my head. "You don't get it. You think all you have to do is pump some chemicals into me and everything will magically go back to the way it was. It doesn't work like that. It doesn't erase what happened. And what will you tell everyone else? The contents

Chapter 56: Emma

of my Mission were secret, but the fact that I was on one has surely spread by now, especially with the leak before I left."

"Yes, they all know about your Mission. But no one knows you went rogue. They think you did the best you could, but then your target found out and attacked you, forced you to help him break into the Academy. That's when we stepped in and saved you, thus his execution. Everyone will be told not to speak to you about it, that it took a great toll on you and you need time to recover. By the time we release you, the chemicals will prevent you from saying anything. Not that you would want to once your emotions are gone, of course."

Something inside me shatters. "You know, I used to admire you. I thought it was incredible you took all of us into the program and accepted us for who we really are, despite our parents abandoning us. You helped *raise* us. But none of it was real, was it? You just want to control us."

She stares at me for a moment, looks like she's going to say something, but then sweeps out of the room before I can stop her. She calls for the guard to watch me until her return. Then she's gone.

The little air I managed to pull together is knocked from my lungs. Our original plan fell apart, but Jesse had a backup that he made me agree to. If they took him, I was supposed to get out while everyone was distracted.

But I'm not leaving here without him.

He's about to die.

I'm about to be put back on the wretched formulas that ruined lives. *I'd* rather die than be subjected to that again.

I'm being held prisoner in this office. I need to escape.

So that's what I do.

Beyond the Gates

I lunge for the guard, using the element of surprise to my advantage. I get a couple of punches in before he retaliates. Luckily this guard doesn't have super strength. That one went with Jesse. I stay light on my feet, making sure he doesn't have the opportunity to grab me. If he gets a hold of me, it's over. Adrenaline floods my veins as we fight. The only thought in my mind is *save Jesse*.

The guard catches my arm, twists it, and slams me into the wall. I kick my legs and knock against him. He throws me to the floor, letting go of me in the process. I jump, grab him by the neck, and jam into the pressure point. In a few seconds, I have him unconscious.

Now I just have to get out undetected. The building is no doubt swarming with guards and supervisors. Before all of this, I'd have thought sneaking out would be super easy. Now I'm not so sure. Everyone was right. I'm not the same girl who left the Academy to go on a Mission. But I don't have time to stand around and contemplate. The longer it takes me to get out to the field, the more time the Ambassador has to kill him.

I pry open the office door. A quick survey of the hall tells me it's empty. I dart out of the room and to the stairs. My heart pounds furiously against my rib cage, so hard it's painful.

Yes, I'm nervous. But it's kind of comforting in a way. Being nervous means I have emotions and emotions mean I still belong to myself.

I make it to the first floor and take a deep breath. I can do this.

"Hey!" a voice yells behind me. I whip around and see a supervisor standing there. Her eyes bug at seeing me. Did these people really think I wouldn't try to escape? How stupid are they?

Unfortunately, her shout draws attention, because others come running. Time to go. I leap toward the door and barrel out across

Chapter 56: Emma

the quad, ignoring the pain that punches through my chest at seeing this place again.

I've walked across this lawn so many times on the way to classes, meals, the dorms. Never did I think I'd run across this place like my life depended on it, heart frozen with fear. Not fear for myself, but rather fear for a boy. A boy I'm not supposed to fear for. I do anyway. I let the fear course through my veins, turning the ice into a furious, raging fire.

The guards chase me, as if they can actually catch me. I'm too fast for them with the adrenaline on my side. They can't stop me.

I spot Jesse as I crest the hill. He's down in the valley below, on the field where I've participated in so many training activities and social gatherings over the years. The Ambassador stands there, surrounded by a variety of guards, supervisors, and instructors. Two of them train their guns on Jesse as he kneels in the grass.

Several Academy kids, and even adults who have long since graduated the program, stand around and watch as the events unfold. There's an excited energy in the air. The Ambassador must have already spread the lies about Jesse, because the crowd seems pleased and eager to watch him die.

It makes my stomach churn.

I tear down the grassy slope towards Jesse. Towards danger and possible death.

I don't care.

Saying that everyone is surprised to see me would be the biggest understatement ever. I don't know what stories the Ambassador has told about me or how I fit into the puzzle of this elaborate fabrication, but this isn't exactly what they expected.

They believe this boy has hurt me, attacked me. What do they think of the situation now that they can see I'm perfectly fine?

What they think of me doesn't really matter in the moment, though. I slam into Jesse, nearly knocking him backwards. But he steadies me like always.

I feel the stares of all the people. Stares of shock and horror. I hug Jesse tight against me, and the people I can see behind him freeze with wide eyes and gaping mouths. Gasps ring out.

I guess their reactions are called for. After all, the girl who always had it together, who was one of the highest ranked Academy kids of all time, who always did as she was told without question and without emotion, is now in the arms of a boy who isn't even one of them.

But I drown out everyone around us. None of them matter. I refuse to let them ruin these last few moments. It's just me and him.

"Emmalyn," he breaths into my hair like he can't believe it's really me. "Emmalyn."

My whole life, I've hated my full name. I never allowed anyone to say it. It symbolized the life I never had because of the parents who hated me. Cameron was the exception to the rule, but even he was limited.

But I love my name when Jesse says it.

"Emmalyn, what are you doing here?" He pulls away enough to look into my eyes. His voice is strained and the pain in it breaks me even more. "You aren't supposed to be here."

Being this close to him, I notice his face. I gently skim my fingers over the bruises that pepper his skin and run my thumb across his busted bottom lip.

"What happened?"

"What do you think? They beat me up, just like we saw it." He draws a shaky breath. "Emma, why are you here?"

"Because," I say. "The future can't change if someone doesn't do something to change it. Well, I changed it."

Chapter 56: Emma

He touches his forehead to mine. "I appreciate that, Emma. I really do. But you have to go."

"What? No!" I exclaim urgently. I pull away to look into his brown eyes. The bad one is swollen shut now. "Jesse, they're going to kill you."

"Yeah, and if you stay, they'll kill you, too," he protests. "Emma, it's okay. Just go."

"No!"

"God, you're so stubborn. You have to get out of here. I need you to take care of Char and Oli for me."

"I can't, Jesse." A sob tears from my throat. "I don't know the first thing about raising kids. I can't do it without you. *I need you*."

"They love you, Emma. You'll be okay. Now get out of here."

"And what if I don't manage to make it out?" I challenge as a tear slips down my face. "I won't be their mindless robot again who can't feel a thing. We're in this together, remember? Until the end."

His face scrunches, like my words broke him.

"Emma," he whispers pleadingly.

He leans close like he's going to kiss me one last time, but hands grab me from behind, yanking me up off the ground and out of his reach.

I come back to my senses, our bubble having popped. Guards are yelling at each other, the Ambassador is barking orders, the students seem confused. How much time has passed? I felt like I was there with Jesse for hours, but it couldn't have been more than a minute.

"No!" I screech. Several guards cling to me, ensuring I won't escape this time. I kick and scream and try to break free. "No! Jesse!"

Tears pour from my face, clouding my vision.

It can't end. Not like this.

Beyond the Gates

The guards drag me away. My feet scrape the ground, catching on rocks and uneven patches. The crowd is in utter chaos. People are upset and confused. Supervisors try to calm them down. The Ambassador wanted an audience. She got one.

I lock eyes with her. Hers are filled with a triumphant gleam.

"I hope you're happy," I shout, venom in my tone. "You're murdering an innocent kid. Who knows how many more lives of children you've taken." I look out to the crowd and raise my voice. "She's controlling all of you. She doesn't love you. She doesn't care about you. They stole us away from our parents. They turned us against the humans who are not that different from us. He didn't do anything wrong. Please…please don't let her hurt him."

The Ambassador calmly turns to the crowd and says, "The Academy is the future."

"The Academy is the future!" the crowd shouts back like the brainwashed husks they are. Then they go silent and do nothing but watch. They won't help me. They don't feel compassion or understand the bond I feel for the boy whose life the government is going to take. And it's not their fault, but I still hoped maybe, just maybe…

The Ambassador nods to the guards with the guns. "Finish it."

There's nothing more I can do. I squeeze my eyes shut, not wanting to see it happen. I wish I could block my ears, too. I brace myself for the gunfire that'll signal the end of Jesse's life.

But it never comes.

Instead, a low rumble makes everyone pause. I open my eyes as the sound grows. And then I see it. It comes into view at the top of the hill.

An old, red van with tinted windows and my best friend hanging his head out the window.

CHAPTER FIFTY-SEVEN
Jesse

The seconds stretch out. Why are they hesitating? Why don't they just get it over with?

Instead of gunshots, the air rings with shouts from the crowd. I open my eyes and see my car just as Cameron bursts out of the driver side and races down the hill.

Everyone stares, like the whole world is frozen except for him.

How is he even here? And if he's here, then where are the kids? Surely he didn't bring them here, right?

Cameron waves his hands and the field is instantly set in motion again. The guns fly out of the guards' hands and launch across the clearing, far out of anyone's reach. Then two Academy kids, a boy and a girl, force their way out of the crowd and into the center.

Fire explodes from the boy's palms and the way the girl moves suggests her ability is speed. I flinch against the heat of the flames as dreadful images invade my mind. But it seems they're here to help us, not hurt us. They must be Emma's friends who got their trackers removed.

Emma twists out of the guards' grips while they're distracted by the commotion. Once she's free, she turns and attacks them.

Complete chaos ensues after that.

I stand up from the ground, but that's it. I stand there. My mind feels blank and like it's going a hundred miles all at the same time.

What am I supposed to do? Even after all my training with Emma, I'm not ready for *this*. There's no way I'll be able to hold my own in any kind of fight like this. I didn't spend the majority of my life learning how to fight. I don't have an ability. I don't know how to actually be helpful.

A guard comes at me, swinging his arm out. Emma's lessons flood my mind and I raise my dominant arm to block.

I'm just not fast enough.

His fist hits me square in the face. I stagger back as blood pours from my nose and drips down onto my lips. I try to remember all she taught me. Stay on the balls of my feet. Keep my elbows tucked in. Always move around. Keep tension in my stomach.

It doesn't help.

I'm punched, kicked, knocked down. It's a wonder I'm still conscious considering I also took a beating right before all this happened. I can't see out of my left eye. My stomach and face ache with all the blows they've received.

I'm not sure how much longer I'll last.

And then something strange happens. Something changes as I pick myself up off the ground *again*.

I let go of everything. I let Emma's lessons drain from my mind. I stop worrying about Charlotte and Oliver and if they're safe. I focus on my breathing and the rhythm of my heartbeat.

Adrenaline sears my veins, floods my body.

I catapult forward and punch a nearby guard in the side of the head, followed by a kick to the stomach. My limbs take over, acting of their own accord. My body works with a mind of its own.

Is this what Emma feels whenever she fights?

Chapter 57: Jesse

I punch and kick and block. Over and over and over. I hold my own now. But I'm not invincible. With all of my attention focused on each new fight in front of me, I lose regard for my surroundings.

My head explodes in pain as something cracks against the back of my skull. My vision blurs and I crumple to the ground. My eyes water at the ringing in my ears.

And then the oxygen abandons my lungs.

Pressure engulfs my neck and I force my eyes open. A guy from earlier is on top of me, hands curled around my neck. His gaze pierces me, eyes filled with hate.

Having him this close allows me to see how young he is. He looks as if he just graduated not too long ago. My heart aches with the realization that this used to be Emma. What would this kid be like if his tracker was removed? Who would he be without it? If he wasn't under the government's control?

But I don't have the luxury of contemplating that now. This is a fight for life and I'm losing. I push my hand against his face and try to throw him off. I claw at his arms, knee his stomach, struggle against him.

Air. I need air.

I grow weaker by the second.

No. No. I did not *come this far to be choked to death.*

Then the crushing weight suddenly vanishes. I greedily gulp down a lungful of air. Oxygen has never been so beautiful. My vision clears in time to see my attacker hit the ground several feet away.

I jerk around. Cameron stands on the opposite side of the clearing, eyes concentrated in my direction. Our eyes meet and I know.

Cameron Clarke just saved my life. I nod a thanks and heave myself up.

Despite one enemy off my back, there are plenty more to go around. Another swipes at me, bringing me into another fight.

But when will it end? What are we hoping to accomplish by this? Escape? It doesn't seem possible, not with how many people surround us. And much to my dismay, the adrenaline is starting to wear off. Every part of my body aches with exhaustion as I continue to fight back. Sweat slides down my face. The pain in my head grows enormously. Pressure increases behind my eyes.

But I can't give up. Not anymore. I have to keep fighting.

I knock more people to the ground. I'm not sure how I'm doing it, why I'm holding up so well against those who have been trained for this, but I'm grateful, nonetheless.

A new emotion surges through me. Hope. We can do this. *I* can do this. And maybe, just maybe, we have a shot at survival if we can just get to the car.

I allow that possibility to sink in. I could see Charlotte and Oliver again. I could actually experience this new phase Emma and I have entered. I could live.

We're going to live.

As I search for a new fight, I survey the clearing. Cameron and the boy with the fire actively use their abilities. Objects and people fly through the air. Flames burst in every direction. Scorching, engulfing, devouring.

For once, I don't mind the fire.

The girl on our side uses her ability of speed as much as possible. However, I can tell within a few seconds of observation that she's not much of a fighter. But she's trying her best and is clearly willing to put her life on the line for us. Or at least for Emma.

Emma. Where is Emma?

I turn in a circle, stopping once I spot her. My heart steadies at the sight of her, though I have no reason to be worried. She's without a doubt capable of taking care of herself.

Chapter 57: Jesse

I find the Ambassador next. She's on the sidelines barking orders to the guards and supervisors. I thought she would have been more involved in the fight, but maybe she's not a fighter either. Just the one who pulls the strings.

I'm soon roped into another fight with someone who looks about my age. She's a strong fighter like the others, but it's different this time. She doesn't use the usual maneuvers.

Instead, she relentlessly tries to make contact with any of my exposed skin. I'm not stupid. Her ability must involve physical contact. I dodge her for as long as I can.

But when her fingers graze my arm, that's it.

I drop to my knees as a shrill sound cascades across the field. That horrific scream comes from me. And her skin only touched mine for a split second.

The *pain* it caused.

She gets down and curls her hand around my wrist. My mind blanks and then fills with the dazzling colors of fire. Red, orange, yellow, hints of blue. White light eventually drowns out the rest.

I know I'm screaming, but it sounds distant, like I'm underwater.

I am burning. I am melting. I am dying.

And I was wrong.

I will not survive this. I will not see Charlotte and Oliver again. I will not experience any more life with Emma. I will not get to live.

Emma's words pierce my mind. *"Why would you just give up like that? Why wouldn't you fight back?"*

Fight. I need to fight back.

"What'll happen to me and Oli when you're gone? When you leave us behind?"

I made a promise to my sister to always come back.

"Thank you, Jesse. For taking care of me."

Beyond the Gates

There's a little boy out there who needs me to take care of him, to love him.
My family needs me.
So I fight back.

CHAPTER FIFTY-EIGHT
Emma

We are going to win. We have to. It doesn't matter that we're outnumbered. We'll keep pushing back until we're free or can no longer fight. We can do this.

And then I hear his screams.

My heart stops. I jerk around on instinct. Jesse kneels in the grass across the field, eyes closed, and mouth open as a blood curdling screech erupts from him. A girl has him by the wrist. I narrow my eyes to see through the smoky haze caused by Aiden's flames. It's not just any girl. It's Laurel.

Of course she's mixed up in the battle. Anything to gain her notice by the officials. She has her sights set on being granted a Mission upon graduation. She wants it as badly as I did, if the confrontation in the bathroom before I left the Academy says anything about it. Her ability causes pain to the point of death.

And she has Jesse.

I move toward them, fully prepared to take her down. Our abilities don't work on each other, after all. She won't be able to harm me.

But before I can take more than two steps, someone jumps on my back. I crash to the ground and roll as heat splices through my arm.

One second. I turned my back for one second and it cost me everything.

A boy hovers over me, presses me into the cool grass. His eyes flicker with fire. Hate and disgust pours off him. It's strange seeing that much emotion in an Academy kid, but I guess we were never truly emotionless. The little bit we did feel just happened to be fake and beneficial to the government.

I look up into his dark eyes and a jolt passes through my body. It's the same boy from the last Academy self-defense class I had. Jamie. He's so different that I almost don't recognize him. Before, he seemed like any other person, but I didn't know yet what an actual, uncontrolled person looked like. Now, despite the rage brewing inside him, I can see how empty he is. How empty all the Academy kids are.

My heart aches for all of them. This isn't their fault. They'll never get to experience real life like I did.

It's even scarier to remember that I used to be one of them. I was once exactly where this boy is now, fighting against the supposed enemy, drinking in every word that fell from the Ambassador's lips, and following every rule down to the last detail.

How far I've come since then.

I struggle beneath the boy as Jesse's screams continue to rattle my bones. It's a miracle I can even concentrate on the danger in front of me while Jesse is audibly in peril. All I want to do is save him and then get us out of here along with Cameron, Lacy, and Aiden. As worried as I was about Cameron cutting out their trackers, they pulled through after all.

Chapter 58: Emma

Just as I'm about to jab my knee into the boy's stomach, something cold and metallic presses into the center of my forehead. My heart drops to the pit of my clenched stomach.

I freeze.

A gun. He has a gun.

My mind reels with ways out of this situation, but I come up empty. I'm too aware of the weapon that's pressed against the thin barrier of skin that protects my skull and brain.

Honestly, it's ironic that something as simple as a handgun will be my downfall. Such an ordinary weapon compared to the government's chemicals and Academy kid abilities. And the gun is my one weakness. It always has been.

I stare into the boy's eyes with defiance, daring him to end me. He's close enough that he'll have to watch the life leave me. If this is really it, then I'm not going to give him or anyone else the satisfaction of my fear or defeat.

His eyes cloud over, seemingly confused as to why I have yet to fight back. The barrel of the gun quivers against my skin.

He's hesitating. He's never killed anyone before, meaning that shred of innocence is still there. Despite everything the government has done to us, we all still have to have pieces of humanity deep down, right? For some, *way* deep down, but I'm sure it's still there. It has to be.

Jesse's screams suddenly cut off. Wary of the gun, I tilt my head to the side enough to see what's happening. What I see is impossible. Jesse has opened his good eye. His face glistens with sweat and he shakes terribly, but he's alive.

And Laurel is still touching him.

It's not possible. No one should be able to resist her ability. But Jesse somehow has. Even from across the clearing, I notice when his gaze meets mine. Our eyes lock. A thousand words are exchanged in that one look.

That split-second moment between us is every time I drove the car while he rode in the passenger seat. It's every punch thrown during self-defense lessons. It's every stolen glance and heightened feelings we tried so hard to suppress. It's board games and color-coded tacks, park swings and the waterfall. It's stories and smiles and hugs and our first kiss. That split-second moment is everything.

I would have lived in that beautiful moment forever if I could have. Lacy is the one who finally breaks our connection. She barrels across the field with her super speed and rams into Laurel, sending them both crashing away from Jesse.

I make to get up until Jamie shoves me back down. I zing with surprise. I completely forgot about him despite the weapon still on my face. He presses it harder against my skin.

Where is Cameron? Earlier, he used his ability to send weapons, as well as people, hurtling across the field. Now I'm about to die and he's nowhere to be found.

Fear shoots through me. He's okay, right?

But I have bigger issues at the moment.

The boy won't hesitate this time. I can see it in his eyes.

I don't think. I just grab for the gun and push the barrel up. It fires toward the sky. The earsplitting noise leaves my ears ringing, but I'm alive. I rip the gun from his hands and throw it aside.

Then I grab his hands to push him off of me, but instead, I'm thrown into his mind.

He punches and kicks and uses all the tactics he learned in his theory classes. It's never enough when it comes to actual fighting. He falls back against the safety mats as he's defeated by his opponent yet again. At this rate, he'll never qualify for the Missions or the Elite. He'll probably be stuck with something awful that he won't be able to mess up.

Chapter 58: Emma

I pull my hand from his. His dazed expression tells me he saw it, too. But that can't be right. Neither of us should have seen anything. Our abilities aren't supposed to work on other Academy kids.

Unless that was somehow connected to the trackers, too. Another way for them to manipulate us. Another lie.

I don't give it much thought though, because my whole perspective changes within seconds. I roll out from under the boy, who is still out of it from witnessing a small snippet of his own future.

All this time, I thought of my ability as tame, something that couldn't be used in a life or death situation, unlike those who possess the elements or super strength.

But it can. My ability can be used as a distraction.

I resume fighting and embrace this new tactic. When someone comes up to me, I latch onto their hand and images burst across our minds. It's always unexpected for them, but completely natural for me.

I see several different scenes: a supervisor watching over a class of students as they practice their abilities. A guard manning the front gates of the Academy. A kid eating dinner in the dining hall after a day of self-defense.

Every reading is pretty much what I expected from people caught up in the government's mess. Their futures consist of mundane, everyday things. Class, work, believing the lies of the government. There's nothing exciting or interesting. Nothing that resembles true life as I've come to understand and experience it.

In between my own fighting, I keep a lookout for Jesse, who is somehow back in the thick of it. I surge with pride every time I catch a glimpse of him as he takes someone down with the lessons I taught him. It's unbelievable how far he's come in such a short amount of time.

My heart swells with hope again. Maybe we do still have a chance.

Of course, all of this would be a whole lot easier if the Academy kids would just stay out of the way. Guards and supervisors are manageable, even after the second wave of them showed up.

But a bunch of middle and high schoolers who have absolutely no idea what's actually going on? They only make the situation worse. All they do is get in the way and honestly, I won't be surprised if at least a few of them end up dead or at least seriously injured by the time this is all said and done. Their brains are wired to defend the government, not to think of their own wellbeing. I fear for the younger ones, though. The ones who haven't had much training.

But we have to get out of here. There's no way we'll be able to incapacitate every single person here. We need to escape and soon. I can tell Jesse is wearing down, especially after the Laurel incident. Even I'm closing in on the amount I can handle as fatigue sweeps over me.

My breath comes out ragged and my head spins. I hit my breaking point just as the familiar grumbling sound splits the air as Jesse's car starts up. Even down in the valley, I can see Cameron behind the wheel through the open window.

That's our escape.

So instead of fighting at random, I urge my way through the crowd and toward the car. I slide my hands into others' whenever the opportunity presents itself. The car coming back into play causes quite an uproar because the crowd seems to thicken.

People push and shove in every direction. I'm jostled around, but I use it to my advantage. There are so many people everywhere I turn that less of them notice me as I squeeze by. I can only hope Jesse is having the same luck as me.

Chapter 58: Emma

When I reach the edge, I shoot out of the blob of people and sprint up the hill. Somehow, Jesse managed to get out before me. He throws a relieved glance over his shoulder. Lacy and Aiden are not too far behind me.

Our enemies chase us up the hill, but we have a head start thanks to the confusion of the crowd below. My legs scream in agony, but I will them to push faster for just a little longer.

Almost there.

As soon as Jesse reaches the car, Cameron hops out to let the more experienced driver take control. Cameron relocates to the middle of the van. I reach the car next and jump into the passenger seat, slamming the door shut.

My breath comes out so fast and sharp that I'm practically hyperventilating. We're so close to getting out of here alive. So close.

Aiden and Lacy climb into the back row of the car. Jesse floors the gas pedal the second the last door bangs shut. Now that we're in a moving vehicle as opposed to on foot, I know we'll make it. They don't stand a chance at catching us now. Even once the guards make it to the Academy's cars, we'll be long gone.

The car is dead silent as Jesse drives us through the Academy's gates. He follows the winding gravel path through the forest and doesn't slow until we emerge and turn onto the main road.

We're safe.

Jesse slowly releases a long breath of relief and slows the car to a normal pace to blend in with the other vehicles on the road.

"Is it safe now?" a small voice asks. I whip around. I know that voice.

"Charlotte?"

The auburn-haired girl pokes her head up. She's curled up on the floor next to Cameron's feet.

"Yeah, it's safe," Cameron says. She readjusts herself to sit in the actual seat next to Cameron. She buckles herself in and sighs heavily.

If Jesse is upset about Cameron bringing the kids along, he doesn't say anything or show it. I think he's just glad we all made it out alive.

He glances in the rearview mirror. "Is everyone okay? Anyone severely hurt?" They all shake their heads and he peers at me. "What about you? Are you okay?"

I nod weakly. "I'm fine. Are you all right?"

He shrugs. "For the most part. I can only see out of my right eye, my face feels like it was repeatedly hit by a bus, and my arms still ache from…you know. My mind is still a little fuzzy too, but other than that I'm okay. I'll live."

"How did you do it?" I wonder. "How did you resist her? What you did was impossible, Jesse."

He shakes his head. "I don't know. My mind went blank and I was in excruciating pain. I was ready to let go. But then I remembered the words someone yelled at me not too long before that. Something about how I had given up and why didn't I fight back." His eyes dart to the mirror. "I recalled the promise I made, about how no matter what, I'd always come back for you, Char. And Oliver, I—"

His eyes widen and he actually turns around in his seat to scan the entire car. "Where's Oliver?" he demands frantically.

"Watch the road!" I yell as the car swerves. I did not come all this way and survived the government only to be killed in a car accident.

Jesse turns back around but doesn't calm down. I turn to the back and realize he's right. I'd gotten so used to Oliver's silence that I didn't notice he wasn't here.

Chapter 58: Emma

"Charlotte, where's Oliver?" Jesse repeats.

Charlotte's face scrunches up and her eyes well with tears, though she fights hard against them. "He wanted to come, Jesse. He really did. But April couldn't come. He didn't want to be separated from her again after just getting her back, so he decided to stay, and her parents agreed to take him in."

Jesse's face slackens, like he's unsure of what to say or how to even process the information.

"He told me to tell you how much he loves you and he says thank you so much for everything. For taking care of him."

I take one of his hands in mine. He leaves the other on the steering wheel. "It's okay. He's safe. Way safer than we are right now. We'll see him again one day, but at least he's out of danger."

"I know."

Silence falls across the car once again. I stare out the window and watch the scenery breeze by. It's unbelievable how messed up my life has become in just a few months, but also how wonderful in a way.

We're on the run now, as we definitely can't go back to the warehouse. But I'm finally living life on my own terms. I no longer have a physical home, but these people *are* my home. I'm here for them and they're here for me.

We're a family.

END OF BOOK 1

ACKNOWLEDGEMENTS

There are so many people who helped make this book happen. First and foremost, to my family. Thank you for always being supportive and encouraging. Even back in middle school when my books weren't very good lol. I couldn't be where I am today without you. I love you!

A special thanks to my best friend Natalie Shain for always being there for me no matter what, and for designing the incredible cover art for this book.

Thank you to Brittany Lowe, my best friend and go-to person to bounce ideas off of. Thanks for loving Emma and Jesse as much as I do!

Thanks to my amazing editors, Christy Howell and Kelly Hartwick, for polishing this story and helping it shine.

Special thanks to my wonderful critique partner, Rachel Walker, whose kind yet constructive feedback allowed me to shape this hot mess of a book into the story it is today.

Thank you to my awesome beta readers who read a much rougher version of this book: Anna Bowman, Jeanette Diaz, Paul Engles, Liam Hall, and Emmy Tomforde. And a special thank you to beta reader Jeffrey Thomas for providing extensive feedback and continuous support.

To my booktube friends, thank you for all the love and support over the years. Love you guys!

And finally, to everyone reading this, thank you for taking a chance on this book. I hope you enjoyed it and I'm excited to see where this journey leads us next!

ABOUT THE AUTHOR

Kayla Davenport has been an avid reader and writer her whole life. She'll consume almost any type of story, but her favorite to write are YA dystopians that delve into compelling characters and their struggles. When she's not reading, writing, or working as a freelance editor, she can likely be found binge-watching a Netflix show, spending time with friends and family, or playing with her guinea pigs. *Beyond the Gates* is her debut novel.

Connect Online

Website | kayladavenportbooks.com
Instagram | @thebooktubeturtle
Twitter | @booktubeturtle
TikTok | @thebooktubeturtle
Email | kayladavenportbooks@gmail.com

Made in the USA
Columbia, SC
19 May 2024

35478445R00264